REDEMPTION

SPIRITS OF THE BELLEVIEW BILTMORE

REDEMPTION

SPIRITS OF THE BELLEVIEW BILTMORE

BONSUE BRANDVIK

"Redemption" Spirits of the Belleview Biltmore, Book Three
Copyright © 2018 by Bonnie-Sue/BonSue Brandvik

Published by: Bonnie-Sue Brandvik

Cover Design by: Cathy Casteleiro
Interior Layout by: Maureen Cutajar
Edited by: Chrissy Jameson and Cara Lockwood

All rights reserved. No part of this book may be reproduced, scanned or distributed in any printed or electronic form—except in the case of brief quotations embodied in critical articles or reviews—without permission in writing from the author. Please do not participate in or encourage piracy of copyrighted materials in violation of the author's rights. Purchase only authorized editions with book covers.

The characters and events in this book are fictitious or are used fictitiously. Although actual persons, places and historic events are cited on occasion, all details about these persons, places and historic events are a product of the author's imagination. Any similarity to real persons, living or dead, places and/or historic events is purely coincidental and not intended by the author.

First edition: May, 2018

Library of Congress Control Number: TXu 2-071-351

ISBN Print: 978-0-9896462-7-7
ISBN Electronic/Digital: 978-0-9896462-8-4)

Belleview Biltmore 1940s

Belleview Biltmore 2009

DEDICATION: This book is dedicated to my husband, John, the center of my universe. His unfailing support and calm disposition makes it possible for me to write these books, and his steadfast love allows us to share wonderful adventures together.

ACKNOWLEDGEMENTS: As a writer who makes an effort to merge factual historic information with fiction, it seems I am always searching the internet for odd bits of information and personal accounts of events that transpired. During such quests, the generosity and helpfulness of friends, acquaintances, and total strangers never ceases to amaze me. A few of these individuals and groups are listed below:

The Clearwater Writers Meet-up – Thank you for your critiques, encouragement and support throughout the development of this novel. It's a better story because of your efforts on my behalf.

The Facebook group "You Know You Grew Up in Old Florida..." – I can't say enough about the helpfulness of this group's members, many of whom lived in the area during WWII, or had relatives who did. No matter how many questions I ask about local history, they supply accurate answers – often supplemented with photographs. Special thanks to Stella Laursen, for her wonderful stories about families that lived in the area before and during the WWII, and for sharing her knowledge about flower farms like the Constantine Gladiolus Farm, which once played an important role in the local economy. And to author Thomas Pavluvcik, for generously sharing memories and photos about local railroads and the Japanese Gardens. And to Gary Winter, for his efforts to preserve local history and his willingness to network and share his amazing treasure trove of historic photos.

Thank you to Clint Daniel for answering a bevy of questions about the training of Army Air Corps pilots during WWII, airfields, flight crews, airplanes, procedures, and uniform details. If you want to learn more about this subject, I highly recommend his fascinating website: www.DanielsWW2.com.

THANKS ALSO TO: Sharon Delahanty, resident historian and docent at the Belleview Biltmore Hotel, who not only taught me a tremendous amount about the hotel over the years, and once gave me a private tour, but also agreed to become a part of my fictional storyline.

Deirdre L. Schuster, whose thesis, "The Lady Leaves a Legacy: The Belleview Biltmore and Her Place in Pinellas" offered great insight and was the inspiration for the fictional elevator scene in this book.

Ed Thompson for his helpful knowledge of the sprinkler system installed by the Army during WWI and for the following quote from a fire marshall whose name has been lost to time: "The sprinkler system at the Belleview Biltmore is so overbuilt, that folks staying there are more likely to drown than to die in a fire."

The Belleair Bluffs Fire Department – thanks for believing I wasn't planning an attack when I asked all those questions about bombs and fires, and for understanding the difference between "a plausible outcome" in fiction and "a probable outcome" in reality.

Finally, thank you to everyone who supports my efforts to capture and preserve the history of the exquisite Belleview Biltmore Hotel and for sharing your personal stories with me.

Please note: We'll probably never know what really happened to the artifacts that went missing from the hotel following its occupation by the military. The hypothesis I suggest in this story is total fiction.

Chapter One

"Yes, I'm at the departure gate," Summer Tyme said, hoping her voice sounded more confident than she felt. "But I won't get on the plane unless you let me talk to Justin."

"Miss that flight and he's a dead man."

She closed her eyes and concentrated, but the mechanically-altered voice provided no clues to the caller's identity.

"*Please* let me talk to my brother."

There was no reply. No background noises. Nothing. She was about to give up when she heard her twin's voice on the line.

"Hey, there. How's my number one sis?"

Her knees went weak with relief. But despite Justin's attempt at bravado, she could tell he was terrified. "One more week, bro. Maybe only six days."

"Feels like forty-four all ready," Justin said. "I've already told you this sixty-seven times, but I'm sorry I got you into this. I'll make it up to you if it takes two hundred years."

"No, Justin..."

"That's enough," the robotic voice ordered. "I'll call you again at ten tomorrow night. Now, go do your job."

The line went dead, but Summer kept the burner phone pressed to her ear as she played Justin's words over in her head. The person holding her brother prisoner didn't know the twin's conversation contained a secret code that they'd created as children – soon after they'd realized they were different from all the other foster kids.

1

Justin possessed a nearly eidetic memory, and hers was better. Each number, from one to one-hundred, represented a specific question or response, allowing them to communicate privately, even in a crowd.

1: I love you; 6: Are you okay?; 44: Don't worry, I'm all right; 67: No time to argue

They added the number two-hundred to the code after they learned that their special gift made them valuable to all the wrong people.

200: Forget about me – save yourself.

Summer would rather die than abide by number two-hundred. She turned off the cell and boarded the plane, her mind racing. She had always tried to live in the shadows, concealing her unique ability. Justin, on the other hand, could never resist showing off for the ladies. He had gotten into scrapes before, but nothing like this. This time, intervening on his behalf was going to cost Summer dearly, but the alternative was unthinkable. She focused her thoughts on the job ahead.

"Thank God for open-seating and my mark's habit of sitting in the last row," she thought, waiting for the sweaty-faced man in front of her to muscle his huge suitcase into the overhead compartment. She tried to peer around him to the back of the plane, but the seat backs were too high to allow her a glimpse of her objective.

"Jamming yourself into the back row of a plane for safety's sake is stupid," she mused, focusing on the black fabric of the man's suitcase. *"First of all, the odds of dying in a plane crash are one in fourteen-million. And even if a plane crashes, most of those are controlled crashes, in which ninety-five percent of passengers usually survive. And if you're super unlucky and the plane crashes into a mountain or a bomb goes off, well... no one walks away. With odds like that and millions in the bank, why not sit in first class?"*

Summer shook her head with distain, just as the suitcase gave up its protest and slid into the overhead compartment. She ignored the sweaty-faced man, refusing to acknowledge his smug look of satisfaction as he heaved himself into his seat, which was an equally tight fit.

Thinking of Robert McNeal in derogatory terms helped ease Summer's conscience. He was a cheapskate and an idiot – an easy mark, not a victim. She tugged down the hem of her tight, pink knit top as she made her way down the aisle, pretending not to notice as several men cast eyes at her large breasts and slender hips, hoping she would sit next to them. Unfortunately, even a glimpse made them a permanent part of her memory. She searched for more pleasant sights – a little girl clutching a pink bunny – an old woman playing peek-a-boo with a wide-eyed baby – a teenager playing Candy Crush on her iPad…

The last row had only two seats on either side of the aisle. She smiled at her target and pointed to the seat next to him. Then she stretched on her tip-toes to slide her slim carry-on bag into the overhead compartment, taking longer than necessary, in order to give him a good look at her long, tanned legs, and short black skirt. As Robert McNeal stood to let her pass, Summer gave him her best smile – the one that showed off the dimple on her right cheek, her full, pink lips and perfect teeth. When she bent to scoot into the seat next to his, her tortoise-shell glasses slid down her nose. She pushed them back into place, hoping they enhanced her honey-brown doe eyes, and then checked to make sure her shoulder-length blonde hair was still wrapped in a loose bun, with only a few wisps intentionally escaping. In her experience, rich, dumb guys always loved the slutty-librarian look.

Summer studied the man as he settled back into his aisle seat. He was taller than she had anticipated – six feet or more – and better looking than his photograph, too, in a nerdy sort of way. He wore his short, dark brown hair combed back in a wave, and she was certain his black-rimmed glasses were the real deal, unlike the non-prescription pair she was wearing. After fastening his seat belt, he opened a thick book.

Summer's smile drooped. *"What the hell? He barely even looked at me!"* She frowned. *"Maybe he's just tragically shy."* Turning toward him, she arched her back and let out a breathy sigh. "I wish I felt as calm as you look. Do you fly a lot?" She blinked her long lashes and rested the French-manicured fingernail of her forefinger against her bottom lip.

Robert glanced up, the sky-blue color of his eyes catching her by surprise. The photograph had most definitely *not* done justice to those eyes.

"Don't worry. This airline has an excellent safety record," he said. Then he returned his attention to his book, thwarting further chit chat.

She slid her finger from her mouth and narrowed her eyes imperceptibly. This assignment might be more difficult than she anticipated, but failure was not an option – not if she wanted Justin to keep breathing.

Summer closed her eyes, considering her options, until the plane began taxiing to the runway. Then she gazed out of the window and watched as the pilot adjusted a flap on the white topside of the wing. The wingtip was painted the same blue and orange color scheme as the rest of the plane, including the Boeing 737 jet engine.

A white stripe marked the concrete runway at five-hundred-foot intervals. As they passed the fourth white stripe, Summer noticed a gray, corrugated metal Quonset hut in the distance. Nearby, a man, wearing a white jumpsuit and an orange, high-visibility vest, was bent over the engine of a white, Ford pick-up. Just after they passed the tenth white stripe, the wheels lifted off the ground and they flew into a cloudless, powder-blue sky – with every detail of the experience locked into her memory forever.

She closed her eyes again and gulped, remembering her recent conversations with the man known only as The Broker. No one knew his true identity, and Summer knew better than to try to uncover his secret. He was an independent contractor in the underworld, able to negotiate and enforce illegal bargains between those with power, and those who were willing to do whatever it took to keep themselves or someone they loved from going to jail or being killed. Once a deal was struck with The Broker, there was no turning back. His reputation was iron-clad. Anyone arrogant enough to attempt to violate the terms of a deal, faced retribution far worse than anything they might have suffered, had they upheld the terms of the agreement. His reputation was the reason Summer had hired The Broker three years earlier, to negotiate her own release from the mob's control.

It's also the reason she felt faint when he phoned two days ago and said, "You have one hour to decide if you want to save your brother's life. Call me back."

She hadn't been lying when she told her boss, Denise Matthews, that she suddenly felt sick and needed to go home. Terrified, she had raced to the small cottage she rented near Lake Union in Seattle, trying to imagine what price she would have to pay for her brother's freedom. She couldn't allow herself to be pulled back under the mob's control, but neither could she leave Justin in the clutches of Gordo Adolphus. She knew *exactly* what horrors he was capable of inflicting.

Summer shuddered, thinking about what happened to Dave and Edward, her former partners. The team had no idea they were stealing mob money when they fleeced five-hundred-thousand dollars from a Las Vegas woman during one of their *Camp Sucker* scams. But instead of offering them a chance to set things right, Gordo had unleashed his pet monster, Marty Russo, with instructions to make an example of the trio.

When Summer came up missing and Edward's mutilated body was found in his van, missing several appendages, Dave had turned himself in to the police, hoping to confess in exchange for protection. Unfortunately, he was *accidentally* put into the general prison population. The next morning, he was discovered hanged in his cell, after having been beaten, tortured and raped.

Gordo had a use for Summer's phenomenal computer hacking skills, so instead of having her killed, he made her his slave. On his orders, she hacked into financial networks and took part in cons, always aware that one false move would mean her death. When she wasn't engaged in a con, she was imprisoned in a shabby house with no internet access, along with a few high-end prostitutes. This small group of women were under Gordo's protection, but they lived in fear, knowing that if they ever disappointed him, they'd be turned over to Marty – to do with as he pleased. There were days when she actually envied Dave and Edward.

Summer had managed to save herself by concealing her eidetic memory until after she had stashed overwhelming amounts of evidence about Gordo's illegal activities in the bowels of random computer systems throughout the city. Then she escaped and contacted The Broker to negotiate for her freedom in exchange for her silence. According to their agreement, if Summer ever came up missing or dead, The Broker would release the irrefutable evidence about the crime syndicate's activities to the local police, the FBI, and international media outlets. For her part, Summer agreed to disappear, "go straight," and never disclose anything about Gordo's business practices to anyone. If she reneged on the agreement, The Broker would assassinate her, along with the only person alive who mattered to her – Justin.

For the last three years, Summer honored the deal by working as a researcher in the criminal investigation department of a law firm in Seattle. The pay was good by legitimate job standards, and she respected the manager of the department, Denise Matthews. The two had bonded over their ability to uncover evidence of criminal behavior by tying seemingly unrelated or minute pieces of research data together. The staff often referred to Denise and Summer as the *Blonde Dynamic Duo*, because their combined skills helped bring so many criminals to justice. Denise traveled extensively for the firm, and over time, she had come to rely on Summer to run the department in her absence.

But that had all changed two days ago.

Curled into the fetal position on her bed, Summer had returned The Broker's call, pressing the numbers with trembling fingers. He wasn't one to mince words. He informed her that Justin stole from a casino owned by the syndicate, which gave them leverage to negotiate a deal with her.

The Broker had quickly spelled out the terms of the new deal. The mob would assert absolute control over Summer, but not on a permanent basis. They were planning a high-stakes robbery. If she played her role in the scam to perfection, Justin would be set free, his debt erased, and she could resume her life as a legal researcher. If she failed or got caught, Justin's life would be forfeit and she would go to prison, where the mob could make her life miserable – and short.

With a sinking heart, she had agreed to the deal and then called her boss to request a leave of absence from work. Even though Denise approved the leave request, Summer was certain she didn't believe the story about needing to care for her ill brother in Florida.

The next day, Summer was horrified to learn that she would once again be at the mercy of none other than Gordo Adolphus. He gloated as he explained the elements of the con – his masterpiece, while Marty sat hunched in a corner, lapping up her fear like warm, sweet milk.

Summer was to pose as a graduate from the School of the Art Institute, Chicago, referred to as *SAIC* by most people. She would pretend to be vacationing in Florida before starting her job search. Her mark was Robert McNeal, Chairman of the McNeal Foundation – a rich, eccentric art dealer, who preferred hosting high-end art exhibits and antiquity sales at historic locations rather than in sterile galleries. After explaining her role, Gordo loaded Summer down with books and an airline reservation, reminded her of what was at stake, and then dismissed her.

The plan had been for her to meet McNeal on this flight from Chicago to Tampa, and impress him so much with her body and knowledge about rare paintings, that he would hire her to intern with him at his upcoming art show at the historic Belleview Biltmore Hotel. Her *real* job was to obtain the bank account information of every one of the wealthy art collectors who registered at the event, and to help steal a masterpiece from the exhibit.

Summer frowned at McNeal. Despite their close quarters, he was so focused on his book, they might as well be on separate airplanes. *"Well, so much for Plan A,"* she thought, already beginning to plot her next move.

Chapter Two

Summer's next chance to get McNeal's attention occurred when the flight attendants came down the aisle offering drinks. *"If I spill water or soda on him, he might just wipe it off or ignore it. But..."*

After Robert politely declined anything to drink, Summer smiled and ordered a cup of coffee. For her, tipping the hot liquid onto his lap without it looking intentional was child's play.

"I'm soooo sorry," Summer said, doing her best to look aghast. "I can't believe I did that! What can I do to help?"

Other than a sound that was somewhere between a gasp and a growl, Robert didn't respond as he struggled to release his seatbelt. He leapt to his feet, dropping his wet book onto his equally wet seat. The flight attendant started to hand him some cocktail napkins, but noting the distress etched on his face, she instead pushed the drink cart forward so that he could get around her and into the bathroom. She gave Summer a compassionate shake of her head. "It's all right," she comforted. "Accidents happen. Here are some cocktail napkins for his seat. Would you like another cup of coffee?"

"I'd better not," Summer said, doing her best to appear contrite. "And I'm not sure those little napkins are going to do the trick. Do you have something plastic that he can sit on when he returns?"

"I'll go check," the flight attended said, pushing her cart back up the aisle.

A moment later, Summer snatched up his book and glanced at the title: *The National Gallery – A World of Art, Second Edition.* She thumbed to the coffee-stained section and scanned a few of the preceding pages as quickly as she could, while absently swiping at the spilled coffee with the cocktail napkins.

The book contained photographs and detailed information about the paintings on display at the National Gallery of Art in Washington. The section Robert had been reading featured works by the greatest masters from the Middle Ages. She had spilled coffee on the photograph of Leonardo da Vinci's portrait of *Ginevra de' Benci*. The book said she was a sixteen-year-old Florentine noblewoman who married Luigi Niccolini in 1474. Apparently, experts still disagreed about who commissioned the portrait. Some believed it was commissioned by her parents as an engagement or wedding portrait, but others believed it was commissioned by Bernardo Bembo, the Venetian Ambassador to Florence who was rumored to be Ginevra's close friend and admirer.

"Yikes. For a woman who's about to get married, you sure look miserable, Ginevra," Summer mumbled. "I'll bet you had the hots for Bembo, but were forced to marry Luigi. If that's the case, I guess having coffee spilled on your picture probably isn't the *worst* thing that ever happened to you."

She did her best to clean up the mess and then sped through the pages describing other old masters, including Rembrandt, Rubens, Monet, van Gogh, and Cézanne. She had just closed the book on her lap when McNeal returned.

"Don't sit yet," Summer warned. "The flight attendant is getting something to cover your seat." She glanced down the aisle and watched as the woman came toward them, carrying a bright yellow object.

"This is an extra life vest," the flight attendant explained. "It's the only waterproof thing I could find."

She handed it to Robert, who thanked her before spreading it over the seat and sitting down. He looked so uncomfortable that Summer began to giggle. Robert turned to her, annoyed with her unexpected reaction.

"I'm so sorry," she said. "I get the giggles when I'm embarrassed. If this wasn't a full flight, I would have run away and hid before you got back."

"Don't worry about it," he said, his expression softening. "This is exactly why I always wear black pants when I travel."

"People spill stuff on you a lot, do they?" Summer teased, pleased that he wasn't angry.

"It's usually me doing the spilling," he replied. "That's why I don't eat or drink on flights."

Summer squeezed the book against her chest, forcing the tops of her breasts into pop into view. "Maybe I should adopt that philosophy," she continued. "I'm afraid I spoiled a page of your book, too. I'd be happy to replace it."

Robert stared at the book, as if he only just now remembered that he had been reading one. "That's all right," he said, prying his eyes from the seductive view. "I was just reviewing the work of a few of my favorite artists... I'm an art dealer."

"Bingo!" Summer thought. "No kidding? That's my field! Well, I mean, it will be... I just earned my BA in Art History. This trip to Florida is a graduation present from my aunt. I get to attend an art and antiquities exhibition at an old hotel and then..."

"What hotel?" McNeal asked, his curiosity piqued.

"It's called the Belleview Biltmore," she said. "I've never been there, but according to my aunt, it's amazing. I'm arriving a few days early, hoping to meet some of the people involved with the show and maybe volunteer. It would be a great intern experience for me." She glanced down, hoping she hadn't said too much. "Anyway, here's your book." She opened it to the stained page. "I'm afraid I ruined the photograph of the Ginevra de' Benci portrait, but otherwise, the book is alright."

Robert McNeal raised his eyebrows. "You're familiar with the piece?" he asked.

"Sure... it's the only portrait by Leonardo da Vinci currently in North America." She shifted her eyes to meet his, being careful not to regurgitate the contents of the book verbatim. "I know I'm a bit of a romantic, but I always thought she looked sad... like she might be marrying the wrong man."

"Really?" McNeal asked, studying the portrait.

"Yeah. I like to pretend that she had a secret lover and after her husband died, she cut the bottom of the portrait off so she wouldn't have to see the wrong man's wedding band on her finger anymore."

"You have quite an imagination," he said. "But I'm impressed – most people don't know this portrait has been cut down."

They discussed art for the next hour of the flight. Between the books Gordo had provided and her quick study of McNeal's art book, Summer was able to hold her own in the discussion and then some. Finally, he told her his name and confessed that he was the art dealer who was sponsoring the antiquities show at the Belleview Biltmore.

"No freaking way!" Summer said, with wide, innocent eyes. "This is kismet, don't you think? I mean, not the part about me spilling coffee on you, but the fact that you…the one person I was hoping to meet in Florida…is seated next to me on the plane." She narrowed her eyes, pretending doubt. "Wait a minute. Why would Mr. McNeal be sitting in the last row on an economy flight to Florida?"

The statement was intended to put him on the defensive – to force him to prove that he was the President of the McNeal Foundation. It worked.

"You can call me Robert. And I like sitting in the last row of a plane because I don't like the noise of the engines and usually nobody bothers me back here."

Summer didn't alter her doubtful expression.

"Listen, didn't you say you're staying at the Belleview Biltmore?" he asked. "I don't think I need any extra help organizing the exhibit, but maybe I could introduce you to a few people on the day of the show."

The smile that spread across Summer's face was genuine. Her plan was falling into place. When they disembarked in Tampa, the fact that Robert hadn't asked her to share his limo ride to the hotel was a mere technicality. She stayed glued to his side until he had no choice but to extend the invitation.

Summer's jaw dropped when the Belleview Biltmore Hotel came into view, just beyond the gated entrance. She had read a book about the sprawling white hotel with the green gabled roof – courtesy of Gordo.

He thought knowledge about the hotel's layout would help her when it came time to pull off the heist of *Bride On Stairs,* a painting by the master, James Jacques Joseph Tissot. The book claimed the hotel had expanded over the years to a whopping 820,000 square feet, not including its basement, and was arguably the largest occupied wooden structure in the world. But reading statistics in a book hadn't prepared her for the experience of seeing the magnificent structure up close, surrounded by old oak trees and manicured flower gardens.

"Wow," she said, resting her champagne glass in the holder on the limo's sideboard. She pressed the button to open the sunroof and stood up as they turned off the boulevard and onto the long drive, giving her a great view of the hotel, and giving Robert a great view of her personal assets.

"Beautiful, isn't it?" Robert asked, trying to avert his eyes from her long, bare legs.

She dropped back into her seat as they pulled beneath the covered entrance. "Can you show me around? I can't wait to see everything!"

Robert smiled at her unbridled enthusiasm. "You're a delightful woman, but I'm afraid I can't..."

Without waiting for Robert to complete his response, Summer accepted the limo driver's hand and popped out of the car. "You go on and get checked-in," she said, as though they were traveling companions. "I'll be right there. I just want to take a few pictures."

Summer ignored Robert's puzzled expression as she withdrew a small Nikon from her purse. She aimed the camera this way and that, pretending to be taking pictures, while watching from the corner of her eye as the doorman pulled the huge glass door open for Robert.

Once she was sure Robert had checked-in, Summer entered the vast, domed lobby. "Jesus Christ," she murmured under her breath. "I can't believe Gordo's going to set fire to this piece of art, just to steal a *different* piece of art."

She smiled at Robert as they crossed paths near the registration desk. "Can you believe this lobby?" she asked, making sure the young, thin desk clerk noticed them talking. "I feel like we just stepped back into the Victorian Era. Come on... let's take a walk around."

"Yes, it's amazing. They call this place *The Hotel That Time Forgot.* But, as I said...I've got a lot of work to do, so I'm afraid you're on your own from here on out. I hope you enjoy your stay – and don't forget to look me up at the show."

Summer grinned. "Come on. Our meeting was *kismet,* remember? I'm sure the fates will bring us together again real soon."

Robert shook his head and smiled, then turned away to follow the bellhop to his room. Summer watched him for a moment. *"Seriously nice butt,"* she noted. Then she approached the registration desk. "I just arrived with Robert McNeal. I believe my reservation is for the room next to his?" She smiled. "My name is Summer Tyme – with a 'y'."

"Great name," the young man said, typing it into his computer. He furrowed his brow and tried a few different keystrokes. Then he shook his head. "I'm sorry, Miss Tyme, but I can't find your reservation."

"What? I don't understand." Then her brown eyes grew wide, filled with mock alarm. "No way. What a jerk! He must have thought that since he's a rich art dealer and I'm just an intern, that of course I'd be willing to sleep with him in his suite! Well, he can forget that! I'll take the room next to his, please."

The tips of the desk clerk's ears turned pink. He scowled in the direction of the elevator, but McNeal was already gone. He tapped on his computer some more. "I'm afraid he's staying in the Presidential Suite. The closest open room is a suite down the hall, but it's expensive..."

"That's all right. He can afford it," she said, her tone dripping with indignation at Robert's imagined affront to her virtue.

"I'm not supposed to put a room on someone else's card without his permission," the clerk said.

"Please?" Summer pouted. "I'm sure he'll agree to pay for it once I threaten to expose his perverted plan to the art professor who arranged for my internship."

"All right," the clerk finally agreed. "But only the room rate... you'll have to pay for any incidentals yourself."

"Of course," Summer said, giving him a broad smile. "No problem." A few moments later, she wheeled her small bag toward the elevator; an antique key to the nearby suite clutched in her hand.

When the elevator doors closed, she pushed the fourth-floor button, still smiling to herself. Then she stiffened. Although she was alone in the cold elevator, she could hear voices.

"Granted, she has a silly name like your sister did, Andy...but that's hardly enough of a similarity to form a connection," the voice of an older woman gently chided.

"That's not the only similarity and you know it," an invisible man replied. "And if my kid sister was headed for serious trouble, I'd want someone like me to step in and help set her straight."

"Perhaps you're right," the woman said as the elevator came to a stop.

The doors opened and Summer peeked into the hallway, wondering if there was another elevator next to this one. There wasn't. A shiver ran down her spine as she stepped into the less frigid hallway.

"What the heck was that?" she mumbled, watching the elevator doors close. She tried to shake off the odd experience as she rolled her suitcase down the rich, patterned carpet of the historic hotel, but she couldn't resist glancing over her shoulder every few steps. Her hand trembled as she unlocked the suite, stepped inside, and locked the dead bolt.

Unfortunately, she couldn't rid herself of the feeling that someone was still watching her.

Chapter Three

Summer's first coherent thought was that Gordo had somehow managed to place a listening device on her, and it had malfunctioned.

"No way," she reasoned. She hefted her suitcase onto the bed and opened it. *"He's not that tech savvy. I probably overheard a conversation being carried up the elevator shaft and my mind played a trick on me, making me think the voices were coming from inside. That makes more sense. After all, I've barely slept for two days."* As if to corroborate that theory, she yawned.

While unpacking, Summer debated whether to snatch a credit card to use for the clothes shopping she needed to do, or just pay for the items herself. She paused. She hadn't stolen anything for three years, but her old lifestyle was coming back to her with alarming ease. "No stealing unless I absolutely have to," she finally decided.

She stored her empty suitcase in the closet, along with a small, black leather backpack that was filled with tools of her trade, and then sat on the edge of the king-sized four-poster bed, examining her posh surroundings. She idly traced her fingers over the magnolia flower pattern on the maroon comforter. Normally, she would have found the bedspread and drapes gaudy, but she liked the way the Victorian pattern coordinated with the mahogany furniture, wide crown molding, tiffany-style lamps, and glass doorknobs.

"The hotel that time forgot," she murmured, repeating what Robert had said about the Belleview Biltmore. She stood and walked from the bedroom, down a short hallway that contained a vintage black and white tiled bathroom, and into a parlor, furnished with a small, round mahogany table, four high-backed chairs, an over-stuffed burgundy fainting couch, and a large wardrobe that held a television, mini bar, and coffee service.

Gordo had given her a book about the hotel that included a description of the room configuration when the winter resort first opened in 1897. Summer tried to imagine the suite as two, separate guest rooms with a common bathroom.

"I suppose sharing a bathroom with Robert would be one way of getting closer to him," she mused, yawning again. She needed to gain her mark's confidence, but right now, her mind was too filled with worry and fatigue to think straight. She kicked off her high-heels, flopped onto the one-armed couch, closed her eyes, and began her version of counting sheep – reciting the list of codes she had developed over the years with Justin.

"One – I love you, Two – I hate you, Three – That was funny, Four – Mind your own business, Five..."

It was as if an anesthesiologist had placed a mask over her face. Her last conscious thought was that the temperature of the room was dropping. Then she was floating in a bank of thick clouds. The sensation was disorientating. Whether she was wide awake or sleeping, Summer's thoughts were usually sharp and her dreams conveyed clear meaning.

"What the hell?" she mumbled, reaching out to touch the mysterious mist. She sliced her hand through the clouds with ease, but at the same time, she felt no danger of falling through them. In her mind, she began quoting one of the many books she had read on the subject of interpreting dreams. Although it had been several years, she read the page of text as if she were still holding the book in her hand.

"Dreaming of clouds can have several interpretations, depending upon other aspects of the dream and the color of the clouds. Sometimes they have religious implications."

"Nope," she adlibbed.

"Other times they indicate the dreamer's life is under the influence of someone or something else."

"No shit!"

"Sometimes clouds can warn the dreamer about difficulties or dangers ahead."

"Yep – definitely."

"Silver clouds usually symbolize coming to the end of a depression."

"They're definitely not silver."

"Dark clouds predict danger and adversity."

"Hmm – they're not dark, either."

"Small white clouds can represent finding peace after troubled times."

"Not very damn likely..."

"What a bunch of poppycock," a woman remarked from somewhere beyond the clouds.

Summer glanced around, but saw no one. Then the mist began to dissipate and she felt herself sinking through the clouds, as if they had turned into quicksand. She searched her memory, but found nothing to explain this particular dream.

When the air cleared, Summer was seated at a small, round table, across from a stout, middle-aged woman, dressed in Victorian Era clothing. Her gauzy, cream-colored dress had a high-neckline, puffy long sleeves, and was trimmed with several yards of white lace and light blue ribbon. Her brown hair was piled on her head in a series of complicated twists and braids and decorated with a miniature silk rose that matched the color of the ribbon on her dress.

"Hello darlin' girl," the woman said with a warm smile. "My name is Margaret Loughman-Plant. I suppose this all seems quite strange to you. I promise you that your current set of circumstances cannot be found in any book, but I am impressed by your analytical attempts. I do so enjoy connecting with well-read women."

"I might not have read it yet, but I'm sure dreams like this one can be found in a book somewhere," Summer replied. *"Maybe in a book about mental illness,"* she thought.

"Then, perhaps you're not so learned as I first imagined," Margaret said. "A true scholar would know that it is impossible for *every* experience to have happened before and therefore, impossible for any person to have already recorded them."

"Maybe I should just play long until I figure this dream out," Summer thought. "Nice to meet you, Margaret. My name is Summer Tyme."

Margaret raised her eyebrows, but said nothing. Instead, she reached her hand out and, as if by magic, a steaming teapot appeared on the table. She picked it up and tipped it into two matching teacups, which appeared the moment she began to pour. Likewise, two teaspoons materialized, along with a sugar bowl. "Summertime is a season, not a proper name," Margaret stated. "What was your given name?"

The twins had changed their names a decade before – the moment they turned eighteen. They took their father's family name – something their angry mother thought she had prevented them from ever doing, by choosing first names that would sound ridiculous when paired with *Tyme*.

Summer squinted her eyes. *"This is my dream. Why doesn't she already know my name was Carlson?"*

"Other than marriage, changing one's name should only be done when necessary to save a life," Margaret continued.

"Maybe that's what my brother and I were doing," Summer said. "Our father died when we were kids – killed by the bitch who gave birth to us. They weren't married, so at least we made sure his name was saved."

"Oh my," Margaret said, her eyes widening.

"Yeah. After good ol' Mom went to jail, we bounced around in the foster care system. Most foster parents don't like kids with good memories, but our last ones did. They hired us out to bookies. Not that it was all bad or anything. They gave us a small cut to keep us quiet, so by the time we aged-out of the system, we had enough money and knowledge to survive on our own."

Suddenly, a young man, dressed in a military uniform materialized at the table.

Summer gasped. *"What kind of crazy dream is this?"* she wondered.

"She was put through the wringer as a kid," the soldier told Margaret. "That's another thing we have in common."

Margaret nodded and poured tea into a third cup. "Perhaps this connection is an opportunity for you both."

"Who are you guys?" Summer asked, becoming more confused by the second.

"My name is Andrew Turner – Andy to my friends," he said. "I was a lieutenant in the Army Air Corps, stationed at MacDill Field and housed at the Belleview Biltmore Hotel during the second World War."

Before Summer could reply, the room filled with clouds and she began floating once again. *"What in the hell is going on?"* She tried to wake herself up, but even a hard pinch on her arm didn't do the trick.

She heard a noise that reminded her of a loud weed-eater. It took a few seconds for her to realize that she was sinking through the clouds into a different illusion. A moment later, she was seated in the back of a small, open-cockpit airplane, being piloted by a young boy. Stunned, Summer looked around and saw one set of wings overhead and a second set beneath the plane.

Just then, the boy – who appeared to be in his early teens, dropped the nose of the plane down until Summer thought they were going to crash in a farmer's field below. At the last moment, he pulled up, reached over his head and yanked on a cord, releasing a powdery substance that rushed down a chute at the back of the plane and blossomed into a long, white trail behind them. He pulled back on the stick, taking the plane up, well above the tree line. Then he circled around and repeated the process – dropping down just above the crops and pulling a second cord to release the powdery substance from a pouch underneath the opposite wing.

Never had a dream felt so real or been so thrilling. Summer could feel the wind whipping through her hair and even smell the pungent substance billowing out behind the plane. She whooped with glee as they rose into the low-lying clouds once more. "This is wonderful!"

she yelled, hoping her voice could be heard above the sound of the plane's engine.

The instant she spoke, the plane, the boy, and the panoramic view dissolved, sending her plummeting through the bottomless mist.

Chapter Four

Summer gasped, grabbing for anything that might break her fall. Her hand smashed against something hard and she yelped. Her eyes flew open in time to watch her fist recoil in pain from hitting the floor next to the low couch where she had been napping.

"Ouch!" she cried, cradling her injured hand against her chest. Her mind instantly assessed what the dream book had to say about the vivid nightmare.

"Falling in a dream is a red flag from your subconscious. It means one or more important aspects of your life are headed in the wrong direction and you should take immediate corrective actions."

"Very helpful – thanks," she muttered sarcastically.

Fighting the urge to fall back to sleep, she stood and stumbled to the bathroom. She gave the claw-footed tub a wistful glance, wishing she could forget her mission and take a relaxing bubble bath. Instead, she stood at the pedestal sink and splashed cold water on her face. While patting herself dry with a soft, white towel, she noticed the lights on either side of the mirror were made to look like old fashioned oil lamps, with flame-shaped bulbs. Even the small, separate shower stall – an obvious addition to the original construction – had been furnished with antique-looking hardware.

"This hotel is incredible," she said. "I sure hope Gordo doesn't burn the *whole* thing down."

"Our sprinkler system will put the kibosh on such stupidity," a man's voice whispered.

Summer sucked in a breath and spun around; the hair rising on the back of her neck and a shiver racing down her spine. She was certain she heard a man's voice, but no one was there.

"Gordo, you son of a bitch," she hissed. She stripped off her clothes, jewelry, and even the bobby pins holding her hair in a bun, stuffed them into the sink and filled it with water. "I don't know how you did it, but let's see how well your bug works under water."

Now wide awake, she slipped on a pair of blue jeans, a grey tee-shirt, emblazoned with the word *GEEK*, and pair of black sneakers. Then she tossed the cell phone into her backpack and pulled out a receiver, designed to look like an iPod. She pushed earbuds for the handset into her ears and slipped into the corridor. She stopped at Robert's door and held the small receiver near the handle. She could hear Robert's deep voice as clearly as if she were standing inside his room.

"Yes, several items have been added to the catalog," Robert said, "mostly jewelry, but also a few minor works of Martin and a Land-seer." He fell silent, obviously listening to someone talking on the phone. "Oh, really? You're expanding your collection to include Victorians? Well, then, I'll have Dana send you an updated list of our new acquisitions."

Despite her determination to keep her distance, Summer couldn't help but admire Robert's professional manner and smooth temperament. A part of her wanted to continue listening, but since she was convinced he wouldn't be coming out of his room anytime soon, Summer set out to investigate the hotel. She planned to look for construction details not identified in books – such as good hiding places. As she approached the elevator, she switched the receiver function off, but left her earbuds in place and bobbed her head as if listening to music. Across from the elevator, a short, attractive brunette sat on a bench under a window, talking on her cell phone. When she finished her call, she stood and stretched, reaching one hand around to massage her lower back. Summer noticed the unmistakable bulge of pregnancy. Just as the elevator door opened, the woman's phone rang again. Summer jerked her thumb at the open elevator, silently asking if she was getting in. The woman gave Summer a polite shake of her head and took the call.

"This *is* Dana," she said, annoyance obvious in her tone. "Of course, I sound funny. I told you, I'm fighting off a cold." She rifled through her purse, pulled out a small notebook and began searching her purse again, presumably for a pen. "Pull together a list of John Martin's known works and current locations? Sure, no problem. I'm just going downstairs for a bowl of chicken noodle soup. I'll work on it when I get back to my room."

Summer stared at her as the doors closed, not believing her good fortune. *"I guess the hotel tour will have to wait... I have a sudden taste for chicken noodle soup!"*

Summer took her time, strolling down the wide corridor to the restaurant. She knew Dana's only choices would be to eat in the Terrace Café or on the Terrace Patio, just outside of the restaurant.

"She's got a cold, so I doubt she'll want to eat outside," Summer reasoned. *"The tricky part will be getting to know her without letting on that I know she works for Robert McNeal."*

Her slow pace allowed Summer the added bonus of scoping-out the hotel's main hallway, called the *Promenade Corridor*. The book that had been issued to celebrate the hotel's 100th anniversary, with its small, black and white photographs, hadn't prepared her for the dramatic reality of standing within a twelve-foot-wide and sixteen-foot-high arched corridor, lighted by a series of elaborate chandeliers, hanging from intricately carved corbels. Together with the huge photographs and paintings on the walls, the cream brocade wallpaper, and wainscoting, the corridor gave Summer the odd sensation that she could step back in time without too much effort.

"If only these walls could talk..." she thought, a half-smile flickering on her face for an instant, *"I'll bet this place has seen its share of shenanigans!"* Once again, she felt a twinge of guilt about being involved in a robbery that would probably destroy the grand hotel.

"Gordo and those other assholes don't have a shred of decency between them. There must be some way to pull off this heist without setting fire to this place. Maybe if we..." She shook her head. *"Stop it.*

If this thing goes sideways, a jury's much more likely to sympathize with me if I had nothing to do with the crime other than doing exactly what I was forced to do, to save Justin's life."

When she glanced back in the direction of the lobby, a black and white photograph of a stout woman, wearing a large, ruffled hat and floral print dress, caught her eye. Her jaw dropped. She had never seen this photograph before, but this was the woman from her dream – Margaret Plant. She hadn't paid attention to the small, blurry, full-length photo of Margaret Plant in the book about the hotel, but now she brought it to the forefront of her mind, comparing the book's image of a frail, older woman, with this robust, middle-aged version of her.

"It's her," she thought, *"but how in the world did I imagine exactly how she looked when she was younger?"*

The thought nagged at Summer as she resumed walking toward the restaurant. She had walked only a few yards, when she peeked down a side corridor and noticed three narrow phone booths. She knew from the book that the booth on the left had been installed in 1925, soon after the coin-operated phone had been invented, and that the two on the right were installed in 1942, when the Army Air Corps occupied this hotel, but again, reading about such things and seeing them were two entirely different things. She wandered over to the oldest booth, opened the door and lifted the receiver. To her surprise, there was a dial tone. She smiled, imagining long lines of soldiers waiting to call home. That thought reminded her of sandy-haired, hazel-eyed Andrew Turner and soon, the odd dream began to nag at her again.

"There's absolutely no question about it," she decided, returning the phone to its cradle. *"I never heard of him before and I've never seen his picture. So why did my subconscious invent him?"*

Her mind began to quote from the same book as before:

"Dreaming of soldiers is associated with confrontation and challenge, as well as fear. Depending on various aspects of the dream, soldiers can be connected to a fear of change. The soldier is usually a warning to pay attention to your life and apply some discipline to it."

She continued to puzzle over the strange dream as she ambled back into the Promenade Corridor, but her musings were cut short when the elevator doors opened and Dana stepped out, her gaze fixed on her phone. The idea came to Summer in a flash. She pulled a cloning phone from her backpack and slipped it into the pocket of her tee-shirt. Then she flipped a control on the receiver in her hand, switching it into a limited-range jamming device. By the time she caught up to Dana, they had reached the empty hostess station at the restaurant. A sign next to the station read: *Please Wait To Be Seated.*

Dana, whose elfin stature was more noticeable up close, thumped the cell phone against the palm of her hand, frustrated that it had suddenly lost all functionality. "No... don't do this to me, you stupid piece of junk!"

"Yeah, smart phones aren't always that smart, are they?" Summer said, with a sympathetic smile on her face.

"It's a conspiracy," Dana wailed. "I'm sure of it! They get you hooked on technology and then, once you can't live without it, the stuff breaks at the worst possible moment and you have to spend hundreds of dollars to replace the darn things."

"I can take a peek at it, if you want," Summer suggested, pointing a thumb at her tee-shirt. "Being a geek is a good thing sometimes. I'm pretty handy with cell phones."

"Really?" Dana asked, handing Summer the phone. "That would be great... I was sending a text and it suddenly just went blank. I charged the battery before I left my room, so I know that's not the problem."

Scamming someone so trusting was a piece of cake. Summer held the phone up so that Dana couldn't see the screen, turned off the jammer, and waited until the phone in her pocket vibrated a few seconds later, letting her know the cloning was successful. Then she turned Dana's phone off and then back on again.

"What's your password?" she asked, turning the phone toward Dana so that she could see it was coming back on.

"08-12 – my due date," Dana replied without hesitation.

"Got it," Summer replied, typing in the number. *"Jesus, you're way too trusting."* Then she smiled and turned the phone to show Dana that everything was back in order and held it out to her. "I just forced it to reboot... sometimes these things get glitchy and you have to give them a timeout."

"Oh, thank you!" Dana gushed. "You're a lifesaver." She clutched the phone against her breast. "I'm right in the middle of a huge project, which is hard enough without being pregnant. A serious technology snafu would have sent me right over the edge."

"Glad I could help," Summer said. She noticed the hostess approaching, so spoke quickly. "Just in the right place at the right time, I guess. So, you're staying here because of work? What do you do?"

"I work for an art dealer who's setting up an exhibit here at the hotel," Dana replied.

"You've got to be kidding!" Summer said, her eyes wide with wonder. "I can't believe this. You work with Robert McNeal?"

Dana nodded, confused.

"I just earned my BA in Art History," Summer continued. "My aunt flew me down here to attend this exhibit as a graduation present and I wound up seated next to Robert on the plane. He gave me a ride here to the hotel, but when I offered to work as a free intern, he told me he already had more than enough help. I'll bet a lot of people are here working with you, right?"

The hostess waited patiently for Summer to stop talking, then asked, "A table for two?"

Dana coughed several times. "You can join me for dinner if you want, but I have to warn you... I'm catching a cold."

"I'll take my chances. I hate to eat alone."

"Good," Dana said. "You can listen to me whine about my boss and then we can discuss his decision to turn down free help from a technology wizard."

Chapter Five

Summer convinced Dana that one small glass of brandy wouldn't harm her baby, and it would help her get the rest she needed to fight off her cold. She hoped a little liquor would help loosen Dana's tongue, but never anticipated how well it would work.

"I guess I forgot to account for how tiny she is," Summer thought.

Even before their soup arrived at the table, Summer learned that Dana was about to become a single mother. She hadn't known the father of her baby was a married man until after their one and only night of unprotected sex had left her pregnant. Despite her circumstances, she was excited about becoming a parent. She had the support of her large family, as well as that of her life-long best friend and former college roommate – Robert's sister, Emma.

"Robert and Emma were orphaned when they were still just kids. An elderly aunt was appointed their legal guardian, but they spent most afternoons at my house. Emma preferred the chaos that comes with a huge family over the stony quiet of her aunt's empty mansion, and Robert – well, he just preferred to stick close to Emma."

"Poor kids," Summer murmured, only half-pretending her sympathetic tone.

"Yeah," Dana agreed. "Their parents were never around much, but it still sucked to lose them. Anyway, Emma has always believed that people usually have good hearts and intentions. Robert was eight years older than us, and much more worldly. He knew a lot of people would try to take advantage of Emma's innocence to get at her trust fund, so he appointed himself to be her protector. We understood his concerns, but geez..." Dana rolled her eyes. "If it had been up to him, Emma and I would have attended college on some isolated Tibetan mountain top."

Summer smiled, shaking her head. "Brothers."

"Yep. I have four brothers and two sisters. Two of my brothers are younger than me, but you'd never know it from the bossy way they act." She rubbed her tummy. "This little person isn't going to have so many siblings. I guarantee that. But it might be nice to have at least one more – if I ever find a man I want to marry, that is."

Summer smiled, faking the camaraderie of maternal instinct while thinking about how to best steer the conversation back to Robert. She knew about the trust fund from Robert's file. His family made their money in tobacco and retired well before anyone thought of suing the industry. Knowing he was worth more than several small countries had helped ease her guilt about participating in this con. But she hadn't known Robert was an orphan with a kid sister.

"Gordo probably left that out on purpose," she thought. *"Didn't want me to empathize with my mark."*

After the waiter returned with two deep bowls of steaming hot chicken noodle soup, and grilled cheese and bacon sandwiches, Summer tried again.

"So, did Emma go to school in Chicago where Robert could keep an eye on her?"

"No," Dana replied, as she spread her napkin over her belly. "After I earned an academic scholarship at Duke, Emma refused to consider going anywhere else. We stayed on campus, but Robert leased an apartment nearby. For about a year, he kept showing up all the time, serving as our unwanted chaperone." She took a spoonful of soup and sighed. "I swear, chicken noodle soup has medicinal properties."

Summer nodded. "So, what happened after that first year?" she prompted.

"Oh, yeah. Well, fortunately," Dana continued, "when Robert turned twenty-five, he came into his trust and began overseeing the family's McNeal Foundation in Chicago. At first, his advisors handled everything, but that didn't last long. After that, Robert was too busy to visit as often. He still flew to North Carolina at least every-other month, and whenever he was in town, he insisted on driving us everywhere, like we were still sixteen-year-olds with a curfew."

"I noticed that about him," Summer agreed. "He can't be more than seven or eight years older than me, but he made me feel like a backward child on the plane. He made me so nervous that I spilled a cup of coffee on his lap."

"No," Dana said, her eyes glowing with amusement. "You didn't! I would've paid good money to see that."

"Actually, there wasn't much to see. He jumped up and vanished into the bathroom, and when he came back, he looked perfectly normal. The worst part was that his seat was soaking wet, so he had to sit on a bright yellow life vest for the rest of the trip – and it squeaked every time he moved."

Dana was unable to hold back a snort of laughter. "It does my heart good to picture that. I mean, I adore Robert – don't get me wrong. But he sets incredibly high standards for himself and everyone who works for him. Plus, he's one of those guys who believes in being harder on friends and relatives, to make sure no one thinks he's showing favoritism."

"He's hard on you?"

"Yeah, but I usually find the challenge invigorating. I mean, not to toot my own horn or anything, but I'm normally a whiz with organization, multitasking, and I'm capable of handling even the *most* temperamental art collectors."

Summer arched her eyebrows. "Normally?" She said nothing else. She knew the best way to find out the most information was to pretend to be an interested, compassionate listener.

"Yeah," Dana said. "Since becoming pregnant, I consider myself lucky when I find my car keys in my purse rather than the freezer."

Summer feigned ignorance. "What does being pregnant have to do with finding your car keys?"

"It's called *momnesia*," Dana replied. "Apparently, your brain goes into a fog and there's really not much you can do about it until the baby's born. It has something to do with hormones, the lack of sleep that comes with not being able to get comfortable, and being drained of vitamins as the baby grows. And, as if that's not bad enough – in the last trimester, women actually produce fewer brain cells." She shook her head. "I'm six months, so now I have *that* to look forward to."

"I have a pretty good memory and..."

Before Summer could complete her sentence, Dana's phone rang. She glanced at the number and then held up her forefinger, signaling a pause in their conversation.

"Well, hello, Mr. Legatti," she enthused. "What can I do for you today?" Dana closed her eyes and frowned in concentration. "Certainly – we'd be happy to help you with both the procurements and sale." She nodded her head without opening her eyes. "Okay, so you're interested in jewelry from the early Romantic Period...particularly the jeweled Prince Albert wedding ring with the snake biting its tail..." Dana opened her eyes, balanced her phone against her ear with her shoulder, and fumbled through her purse while continuing to speak. "Hold on a second. Let me write this down." She extracted a worn, spiral tablet, pulled an ink pen out of the spiral and flipped to an empty page. "Okay, Prince Albert rings...or *acrostic* rings? I'm sorry – I'm not familiar with that style."

Dana scribbled furiously, repeating the customer's directions as she wrote. "Interesting...the first letter in the name of each stone spells out the word *dearest*? So then, a diamond symbolizes the 'd,' the 'e' is an emerald...got it...amethyst, ruby, another emerald, a sapphire, and a topaz. I'll do my best to find..." She shook her ink pen, which had started to skip. "Right. Secret compartments are a plus. And you're interested in auctioning some pieces as well?" She continued to scratch notes with her uncooperative pen. "Seven pieces total – three jeweled brooches and four *Mizph* rings from the Grand Period. Can you spell that? M. I. Z. P. H. Got it."

Dana glanced up, her expression of frustration turning into a smile when she saw that Summer was offering her a new ink pen. She took it, mouthing the words: "Thank you," before returning to her notes. "Hebrew – agreement between two men, made before God," she said. "Also signifies an emotional bond between two people who are separated by distance or death." She rolled her eyes at Summer. "Yes, between gay marriage being legalized and wars continuing to separate soldiers from their families for long periods, I think you're right – those rings might be quite marketable these days. And you have two necklaces and one ring from the Aesthetic Period?"

She continued on for several more minutes, describing each piece and jotting notes at a frantic pace. Finally, she hung up and shook her head. "Sorry about that, but he's an important client."

"Wow, you're really busy," Summer sympathized.

"You have no idea," Dana agreed, returning Summer's pen. "I'd better get back up to my room now. I don't even remember what dates separate one Victorian period from the next."

"Well," Summer said with a smile, "I can help you with that, at least. The Romantic Period covers the years between 1837 and 1861, the Grand Period picks up in 1861 and goes to 1880, and the Aesthetic Period starts in 1880 and ends in 1901."

Dana stared at her in disbelief.

"I just graduated with my BA from the School of Art Institute in Chicago, remember? I might not remember all that stuff in a few years, but..."

"You. Are. Hired!" Dana announced, clapping her hands together.

"That's great!" Then Summer frowned. "Unless you think it would make Robert angry, I mean."

"You let me deal with Robert," Dana said. "I know he comes off a little distant, but that's just because – well, because he got burned by someone he trusted and now he's a little gun shy of women... especially pretty ones. Listen, tomorrow morning I'm supposed to take a tour of this hotel, so I'll be prepared to answer customer's questions during our event. Could you come along with me and take notes?"

Summer jumped at the invitation. "What time and where do we meet?"

Chapter Six

After finishing their lunch, Summer and Dana stopped in the Promenade, preparing to part ways. Anyone observing their casual camaraderie would have assumed they were good friends rather than new acquaintances.

"Have fun touring the beach," Dana said, pushing the elevator button. "But don't drink too much. I'll meet you in the lobby tomorrow morning. The guided tour of the hotel starts at eleven, but I'll probably be there by ten-thirty. I'm kind of compulsive about not being late."

"Okay, see you then," Summer said. After turning away, she called back over her shoulder, "And try not to work too late – you need sleep if you're going to beat that cold!"

Dana coughed in response.

Summer had told Dana she was going bar-hopping along Clearwater Beach – the behavior a recent college graduate visiting Florida would be expected to exhibit. Truthfully, she had experienced enough of the bar scene to last a lifetime during the years when she, Dave and Edward were running their *Camp Sucker* scam. Instead, she skirted the outside walls of the huge hotel, memorizing all the exits and ground-floor windows, and whenever she was certain no one was watching, checking to see which ones were left unlocked.

After finishing the reconnaissance mission, Summer went clothes shopping. She returned to her hotel room late in the afternoon, shopping bags in tow, singing *Zip-a-Dee-Doo-Dah* under her breath. It was a relief to know she'd be able to report significant progress when Gordo called – progress she hoped would also encourage Justin. It still bothered her that her brother had suggested utilizing code two-hundred. She was positive he knew she'd *never* abandon him to save herself. Therefore, her concern was that he might try something stupid to take himself out of the equation.

She yawned as she crossed the threshold into her suite. *"That's strange – I wasn't tired a moment ago,"* she thought. A page from an internet health site flashed through her mind:

When confronted with fatigue, taking an honest inventory of things that might be responsible for it, is often the first step toward relief. Fatigue may be related to:

- Lack of Sleep
- Jet lag
- Stress
- Use of alcohol or drugs
- Excessive physical activity
- Anxiety

She spoke out loud, lecturing herself. "Hmm... let's do a quick review of your recent lifestyle, shall we, Summer? Lack of sleep? Check. You've had almost no sleep for two days. Jet lag? Check. You were stressed-out during the entire flight over your failure to get close to your mark. Then you drank two glasses of brandy to cozy up to a sweet little *pregnant* woman, and you followed that up with a long hike around the largest wooden structure in the world. Check. Check. Oh, and you did that because you were searching for unlocked doors that might help you carry out the theft of a *masterpiece*. And then you went shopping – all the while, hoping your brother doesn't go and get himself killed. No anxiety there." She sighed and yawned again. "Nope... can't be your lifestyle. Must be something else."

Summer pulled back the bedspread, kicked off her sneakers, grabbed one pillow from the six at her disposal, and sprawled sideways across the king-sized bed. The moment she closed her eyes, the strange mist from her earlier dream reappeared.

"What the hell is with these clouds?" she wondered. In her mind, she scanned page after page from books offering possible explanations, until she heard the familiar woman's voice, from just outside the fog.

"Your memory is quite unusual in the realm of the living but recalling every detail of our lives is normal here in the spirit realm," Margaret Plant said.

The clouds began to part, and Summer drifted down into the same chair she had occupied in her previous dream. Margaret was now attired in a high-necked, white blouse. Her puffy sleeves were gathered into wide cuffs of lace that extended from halfway down her forearms to her wrists, and the bustle of her black skirt filled the chair behind her. She continued, as if Summer and she had been chatting for a while.

"There are many differences between our realms, of course. However, I believe one of the biggest differences is that the living are able to rationalize their actions to excuse poor behavior, and incorporate their altered perception of events into their memories. This is not a luxury afforded to us who reside in the spirit realm. Our memories are perfect. They provide objective clarity about our behavior whilst we walked among the living. No one here possesses an overabundance of rosy memories, but it's a relief to no longer feel the need to justify every thought and action."

"You know, I've heard the dreamscape referred to as 'la-la land', 'Mr. Sandman's territory', 'the playground of your subconscious', and lots of other things – but never as the '*spirit realm.*'"

Margaret cocked her head and narrowed her eyes. "You're exhibiting some of that rationalization I just mentioned, darlin'. If you've never heard of the spirit realm, how is it that you're dreaming about it? Come, now. You're wise enough to recognize the difference between this experience and a dream, aren't you?"

Summer squeezed her eyes shut and massaged her forehead. "I'm under a lot of stress and this is all just a weird figment of my imagination."

"I can assure you," Margaret replied, raising her eyebrows, "that I am most definitely not a figment of *anyone's* imagination. I am a spirit, and while you're sleeping, your spirit and mine are connecting. I've done this many times before, so I will try to guide your interactions with the other spirits that have formed a connection with you since you've arrived at the Belleview."

"Spirits? Connections? What the hell..."

Margaret continued as if Summer had not interrupted. "The most important thing to remember is something that I suspect will be quite difficult for you to accomplish. That is, whenever a spirit is sharing a memory, you must watch and remain quiet. If you speak, the connection will be broken."

Before Summer could form her confused thoughts into questions, the clouds reappeared, carrying her away from Margaret. She tried to swipe the mist aside and return to the table, but she was powerless within this strange fog.

She recalled her earlier dream – when she was flying with a boy in a bi-plane. The instant she had yelled, "This is wonderful!" the dream and the fog dissolved. *"So, all I have to do is scream... or shout – and I'll wake up,"* she thought. But curiosity kept her quiet.

After what seemed like several minutes, the clouds began to thin. Summer squinted her eyes, straining to see beyond them. When the mist lifted altogether, she felt her stomach flip, as if she were in an elevator that had dropped too quickly. The feeling was disorienting, but not so unpleasant as to prevent her from experiencing a sense of amazement at the scene that appeared before her.

She was outside, and she was cold. There was snow, but it wasn't the pretty white kind reminiscent of Currier and Ives photos. This snow was covered with gray soot and did nothing to lighten the bleak landscape. She turned at the sound of heavy breathing and saw a young boy, struggling to carry two pails of water up a slick embankment. Looking beyond the boy, she saw that a small hole had been chopped into an ice-covered stream. Although she made no effort to move, Summer seemed to float alongside the child as he made his way down a muddy path, toward a row of identical houses that were little more than shacks.

Summer felt the urge to help the boy – maybe carry one of the buckets for him, but she recalled what Margaret said – watch and do not speak. She noticed that in place of gloves, the child wore dirty rags wrapped around his hands. Another rag encircled his head, covering his ears. She tried to guess his age, but it was difficult, since he was hunched over and kept his eyes on the ground.

He made an abrupt turn off the dirt path and followed footsteps in the snow toward the house that had the number *eleven* painted on its weather-beaten door. Three battered and warped planks of wood served as steps. There was no porch. As he reached the second stair, the door cracked open.

"Thanks," he said to the home's occupant, "but I can do this. Go stand by the stove, where it's warmer." Then, in what appeared to be a well-practiced maneuver, he quickly opened the door with one elbow, climbed the last step, set the buckets down inside, and shut the door.

It was an odd sensation. One moment, Summer was standing outside at the base of the steps and the next moment, she was inside the tiny house, with no understanding of how she got there.

"I emptied the hot water tank into the tub and covered it while you were out, Andy," a child's voice said.

Summer glanced in the direction of the voice, her eyes adjusting to the dim light. A thin girl, perhaps twelve years old, lifted a round, cast-iron lid from the back corner of the old stove.

"Thanks, Paige – you didn't have to do that," the boy replied as he shuffled over to her, being careful not to spill his cargo.

"Andy... as in Andy Turner, the soldier?" Summer wondered.

"Don't be silly. I was going to add a few scoops of coal, too, but the bin is almost empty again, so I thought I'd better save it for tomorrow."

Andy nodded his approval. "I'm sure the fire box is still hot enough to warm water." He set one of the pails down on the floor and poured the contents of the other one into a hot water reservoir, built into one corner of the cast iron stove.

The cold water sizzled and steam rose from the opening, but not as much as Summer thought it would have, if the fire box had been piping hot. When Andy poured in the second bucket of ice water, the stove made even fewer protests. The children exchanged a worried glance as Paige reclosed the heavy lid.

Andy removed the wet rags from his hands and head and draped them over a peg next to the stove to dry. He hung his coat on a second peg. Then he flipped the two buckets upside down in front of the stove to serve as chairs and slid a piece of oil cloth across a wire, revealing a small, grimy window. Paige retrieved their school books and the two studied side-by-side, lowering their eyes closer to their books as the daylight dimmed. When it finally grew too dark to see, Andy sighed and lit a kerosene lamp that hung from the ceiling.

Not long afterward, they heard the sound of footfalls on the steps outside. Both children jumped to their feet as the door opened. The man who stepped in was covered from head to toe in coal dust.

"Hello, Papa!" Paige exclaimed, rushing forward to take the lunch pail from his cold hand.

"There's my girl," the man said as he closed the door. When he smiled at the child, his teeth looked stark white against his blackened skin. "I stopped at the company store – there's some hard bread and a little chicken broth in my pail." He might have said more, but was interrupted by a fit of coughing.

In place of words, Andy and his father exchanged a nod of their heads. Andy held his hands out to collect the weary man's headlamp, wool cap, and coat.

"Paige started your bath," Andy said, glancing in the direction of a cast-iron tub, covered with a piece of plywood to keep the heat in. "I refilled the tank, but I'm not sure how hot the water is just yet. I'll check as soon as I shake your coat." He picked up the wire rug beater from its place by the door and stepped outside without bothering to put on his own jacket.

Once again, Summer was stunned to find herself standing next to the boy in the cold, watching him beat clouds of coal dust from his father's filthy coat. When he finished, Andy ducked back inside and hung his father's coat over his own, with Summer floating at his side like a shadow.

Paige was already busy dipping water from the hot water reservoir into one of the empty pails. When it was full, Andy carried the water to where his father, hidden from view only by a thin curtain, sat in the tub, scrubbing his head with lye soap. The way the man's vertebra protruded from his rounded back reminded Summer of pictures she had seen of starving people.

"It's not cold, but it's not very warm either," Andy apologized.

"It's all right, son – just pour it over my head."

An involuntary shudder ran through the man, as the lukewarm water rinsed some, but not nearly all, of the coal dust from his hair and body. He suffered another coughing fit, and spit black phlegm into the empty bucket two times before he was able to regain control of his lungs. Andy turned away with tears in his eyes, but wiped them on the sleeve of his gray shirt before Paige noticed.

The thick fog settled over Summer, carrying her away from the awful scene. Relieved, she didn't resist.

When the clouds faded this time, Summer was more subdued. She said nothing as she floated back into the chair at the table, facing Margaret.

Margaret summoned her teapot, filled two porcelain cups and slid one across the table. Summer immediately wrapped both hands around the little teacup. She was no longer cold, but felt oddly grateful for the sensation of warmth.

"It's a memory from long ago," Margaret said at last. "I believe Andy wants you to know that he understands poverty and what it feels like to lose one's parents at an early age."

"Yeah, right," Summer scoffed. "As if going hungry makes us the same. Andy's family might have been poor, but at least his dad was there, trying his best to take care of him. It's totally different when you're passed around from one stranger to the next, controlled by a government system that sets you up to fail."

"It's not as different as you might think," Andy said, materializing in the chair next to Margaret's.

Summer jerked back in surprise at his sudden appearance, nearly tipping her chair over. "Where the hell did you come from?" Then she gasped and slapped her hands over her mouth. She took a deep breath, squeezed her eyes shut, and stiffened her body, bracing for the over-Niagara-Falls-in-a-barrel feeling of hurtling through the clouds.

It didn't happen.

Chapter Seven

After a long moment, Summer dared to peek through the lashes of one eye. Margaret and Andy were studying her with a mix of curiosity and concern.

Summer turned accusing eyes on Margaret, indignation causing her cheeks to flush. "You said if I talked, the spirit connection with him would be broken and I'd go crashing back to reality."

"First of all," Margaret replied, with no sign of being cowed by the rebuff. "This *is* reality. To say otherwise is to suggest this isn't happening, or to imply the memories we share with you are fantasies."

Summer, unable to match Margaret's steady stare, shifted her gaze to the Victorian woman's wide-brimmed, black felt hat. Covered with short crimson feathers and white silk roses, it reminded Summer of the ridiculous bonnets worn by women attending the Kentucky Derby.

"Humph," Margaret said, as if she could read Summer's thoughts. She paused to stir three teaspoons of sugar into her teacup.

Summer silently chewed on her bottom lip for almost a full minute, impatiently waiting for Margaret to bring an end to the heavy silence.

"Perhaps you're in the habit of confusing *memorizing* with *listening*," Margaret continued at last. "Let me explain more clearly what I meant about the fragility of connections. There are differences between the moments we spend connecting. While your silence is always *preferred*, materializing in an existing space takes less energy and concentration than when spirits share a memory, wherein we must envision the entire location, as well as the event itself. Here at this table, we can tolerate small amounts of distracting communication without dematerializing. When sharing a memory, we can't. Therefore, I instructed you to remain quiet."

Not yet ready to concede the dispute, Summer folded her arms across her chest.

"The abrupt end of a memory connection doesn't adversely affect *spirits*," Margaret added. "It's the living who suffer intense discomfort when they pass from one realm to another without the benefit of a slow transition through the clouds. Besides, it would be prudent to make the most of our limited time together. Don't you agree?"

Summer narrowed her eyes at the rebuke but didn't speak.

"When I was coming up, jobs were scarce as hen's teeth," Andy said, ignoring the altercation. "My father considered himself damn lucky to have work, even though the mining company controlled almost every aspect of our lives."

Summer studied his starched, khaki-colored military uniform. A large, gold insignia was pinned on one side of his garrison cap – an intricate design with a war eagle at its center. His short, gold tie was tucked smartly into his shirt, just below the second button, and gold pins, stamped with the letters *US*, were fastened to both sides of his collar. Each shoulder was emblazoned with a blue, capsule-shaped epaulette that was edged in gold and had a matching gold band across its middle. A round patch was sewn to his upper sleeve, bearing the image of gold wings, sprouting from a white star with a red dot at its center, set against a blue background.

"My father never complained," Andy continued. "Even though he knew the long, dangerous hours in the mine were killing him, and the mining company was robbing him at every turn. Miners were only paid twenty-two cents for every ton of coal they wheeled from the mine, but the company weigh-man still tampered with the scale, shaving off about a thousand pounds from every coal bucket. They also forced the workers to accept company store script in place of real wages." Andy shook his head. "Prices at the company store were jacked up more than double what other stores charged, so everyone got so deep in debt, they couldn't afford to quit the mine. And that wasn't the worst of it."

The fog dropped over the table, carrying Summer away from the parlor. At first she wondered what Andy's final, cryptic statement meant, but then the clouds drew her attention. If Margaret was to be believed, her consciousness was in the process of transitioning to another location within the spirit realm. She wracked her memory, but knew she had never read anything about such experiences. It was interesting to experience an unusual event in the same manner she always imagined a *normal* person would. She swished her arms through the mist, enjoying the pleasant sensation of floating on air.

Most people confused having an eidetic memory with having a high IQ, but Summer knew her intellect was only slightly above average. Sure, she could ace any exam, as long as she had skimmed through books on the topic in advance. It was a simple matter of recalling what she had read and writing it down. But if she hadn't read about the subject, or if she were asked to describe something less black and white, like an emotion, she possessed no advantage whatsoever.

Margaret's comment echoed in her thoughts: "Perhaps you're in the habit of confusing *memorizing* with *listening*."

"Why do you care what a figment of your imagination says?" she wondered. *"Hell, even if she really is a spirit – who is she to judge me?"*

Despite her resentment, Summer's thoughts drifted to her lunch with Dana. When Dana told her she was concerned about pregnancy brain – momnesia, as she called it – Summer immediately recalled what she had read about the condition – that it's caused by lack of sleep and the fact that a pregnant woman produces as much as forty times more progesterone and estrogen than normal. She also recalled that there's a genetic instinct that forces a pregnant woman to adjust her priorities, shifting the care of her baby to the top of her list.

"But did you actually listen to Dana?" Summer closed her eyes, realizing that she had been so busy trying to manipulate Dana, she

hadn't paid attention to what was now blindingly clear. *"Her job is important to her and she's afraid that her pregnancy is making her mess up. And even though she doesn't want a lot of kids, she feels guilty that her child isn't going to be raised by two parents or be a part of a big family like the one she enjoyed growing up."*

Suddenly, she remembered the reason she had come to the Belleview and drew in a sharp breath. *"You're not here to listen,"* she silently argued with her conscience. *"You're not here to make friends. And you're certainly not here to make the most of your time in the spirit realm. You're here to save Justin's life and to do that, you better damn well not forget number fifty!"*

50: Never let a mark get under your skin.

She tried to convince herself to shout that out loud. To wake up. But the part of her that wanted to see what happened next won out. She felt chills as the fog began to clear, revealing the dusky interior of a barn and the sound of a hacking cough.

"I'm back, Pop," the younger version of Andy called to a blanket-covered form, resting on a small cot. "Let me get some wood into the stove to take the chill off. Paige is up at the house fixin' dinner. She'll be along with some soup for you real soon."

The only response was a wheezy gasp and another fit of coughing.

"I talked to Mr. Washburn today, but he says the goddamn mining company won't make an exception. They'll take me on, sorting coal from rocks in the dump piles for ten cents a day, but that's not enough to pay for a cabin, and they won't let me go down into the mine for two more years." Andy arranged twigs in the shape of a teepee inside of a rusty, pot-bellied stove. Then he blew a small flame to life on a piece of kindling and carefully placed it among the twigs. "Makes no sense. I may only be fourteen, but I'm bigger than most sixteen-year-olds and smarter than most of 'em, too."

Summer glanced around the room, which was about the same size as a stall, and smelled like one, too. She guessed the space normally served as a ranch hand's quarters and wondered why they were here. The cot, along with the small stove, a water bucket, and two milking stools, used up most of the room. Two straw pallets, each covered with a thin blanket, filled the remainder of the space.

"There, now," Andy continued. "That feels better already, don't it?" He carefully fed a few larger pieces of kindling into the fire, coaxing them to catch. Then he dipped water from the bucket into a tin cup and offered it to his father, using his other arm to help the sickly man sit up.

Summer's eyes widened when she saw Mr. Turner attempt to take a sip of water. His face was no longer covered with coal dust, but somehow the yellow pallor of his skin looked even worse. Just one swallow sent him into another coughing fit. Andy sat on the cot, allowing his father to lean against him until he recovered his breath at last.

"Mr. Beacon offered to take me up in his airplane tomorrow," Andy said, licking his dry lips. "He says if I can learn to fly his machine, he might let me help him with his crop-dusting business."

"Don't like the idea," his father wheezed. "Of being up so high. Ain't natural."

"Neither is spending your whole life underground like you was a mole," Andy replied.

The old man chuckled and then coughed. He took another sip of water. "That's true enough, I reckon."

"Mr. Beacon said he might be able to pay me a little cash money, in addition to the room and board I'm earning for milking his cows. But I'd have to quit school during the growing season, on account of crop-dusting takes all day."

"Might be best for now," his father conceded.

Just then a cold blast of air blew through the space. Andy jumped to the stove to close the door before the fire blew out. A moment later, Paige hurried in, her face red from the cold night. She carried a Dutch oven in her small hands.

"I made chicken broth and biscuits," she said, her face beaming with pride. "And there's plenty enough for all of us." She turned to Andy. "Mr. Beacon took to his bottle real early tonight. He barely ate anything before he fell sound asleep. I figure we'll eat this and I'll make him some more before I go to school in the morning."

"You're an angel, Paige," Andy said. He reached under the cot and pulled out a burlap bag, from which he withdrew three bowls and spoons.

As she watched the child ladle out the first helping, Summer heard an odd sound in the distance. The moment she turned her head, the clouds descended. An instant later, she woke in a panic – partly because of the rapid drop into her own world, but more so because she finally recognized the sound. It was the Imperial March – Darth Vader's theme song. It was the ominous ringtone she had assigned to The Broker's phone number.

Summer gasped and grabbed for her cell phone.

Chapter Eight

Summer shivered in the frigid hotel room, struggling to clear her muddled brain as she answered the phone. One dreadful thought surfaced: *"The Broker wouldn't call unless something is wrong."*

"Is Justin all right?" She squinted, waiting for her eyes to adjust to the light. *"Why is it still so bright outside?"*

"Your brother attempted to escape last night," The Broker said. He was never one to mince words.

His gruff voice made Summer's blood run cold. "Is he..." She couldn't bring herself to say the word.

"No. He's fine." The Broker paused. "But the terms of the deal have been altered."

"Wait – last night?" Summer's eyes shot to the clock on the nightstand, her mind racing. *"Nine-thirty? How can it be morning already?"*

All at once, things clicked into place. She had only intended to take a nap, but she had been exhausted. Without the *proof of life* call from Justin's captor to wake her at ten o'clock, she had slept through the night. Guilt formed a knot in her stomach. Her brother could have been killed while she was dreaming about strangers.

"But your deal with *me*, not Justin," she said. Her voice dropped to a whimper. "I'm working my mark just like I'm supposed to. Please – don't kill...don't...*Please.*"

"Nothing will happen to your brother, as long as he doesn't force my hand," The Broker replied. "But there are consequences for his

45

actions. Instead of warming the bench, he's going to join the team on the field."

"What does *that* mean?"

"Just what I said. He's replacing one of Gordo's men on the team. The deal I made with you hasn't changed. If you fail, your brother still dies. But now, he'll also be in danger of getting caught and sent to jail, just like everybody else."

The Broker hung up before she could ask any more questions.

"It's no big deal," she told herself as she pulled the quilted bedspread around her shoulders. *"Just a speedbump."*

But the tears welling in her eyes told a different story. Justin was working directly for Gordo now. And she knew better than anyone how hard it was to break away from Gordo once he had you in his clutches.

"Dammit, Justin," she muttered. "Why couldn't you, just for once, do as you were told?" She bit her lower lip, contemplating what part of the job he'd be assigned to handle, and wondering if anyone had informed her brother about the consequences of failure.

For now, there was nothing to do but stick with her plan and hope for the best. She shrugged off the covers and headed for the shower, surprised to discover that, despite her odd dreams and the horrific phone call, she felt more rested that she had in weeks.

Summer decided to stop at the restaurant for a cup of coffee and a bagel before meeting Dana for the tour of the hotel. She tucked herself into a corner of the large Terrace Restaurant, her back against the wall. Mostly hidden from view by white flowerboxes, overflowing with silk spring flowers on one side, and an intricately-carved, dark wood sideboard on the other, she was lost in her thoughts until a conversation on the opposite side of the flowerboxes caught her attention.

"Come on, Sharon," a man said. "I know what I saw, and you know very well that I'm not the only one who saw it."

When she peeked through the colorful silk flowers into the Promenade Corridor, Summer's eyes widened. The voice belonged to the desk clerk who had checked her into the hotel – Chris. The gullible young man had believed her when she claimed Robert McNeal was trying to take advantage of her – an innocent intern, so he had agreed to bill Robert for an additional suite in order to protect her virtue.

Sharon, the woman Chris was talking to, was a short, thin, middle-aged brunette. Summer pressed against her high-backed, upholstered chair, hoping they wouldn't notice her. Then she closed her eyes and continued to eavesdrop on their conversation.

"I don't doubt that you *believe* what you're saying, Chris," Sharon said. "But think about it. The Belleview Biltmore is more than one-hundred years old. When you're working the night shift at the front desk, you're *bound* to hear strange noises from time to time."

"It wasn't noise, Sharon – it was *music*," he argued. "*Old* music. And when I followed the sound to the ballroom, well, that's when I saw them. Two ghosts *dancing* together. And don't try to convince me that they were regular people. They didn't even have feet... and then they just up and faded away, along with their music. There's no *way* I imagined all of that."

"Really? I know the way you boys act when you're bored at night. Remember the time I caught you tossing tennis balls into the chandelier in the lobby?" Sharon sounded like a tolerant school teacher. "That time, you blamed your behavior on a cannabis-laced brownie that you were tricked into eating. So now, isn't it possible that you ate another one of those cookies last night and then your imagination just got the best of you?"

Chris chuckled. "Pot doesn't cause hallucinations, Sharon." He shook his head and frowned. "And no matter what you say, I know what I saw. It was ghosts. This place is haunted, just like everybody says it is." He shot a glance down the length of the wide corridor, as if he was worried that talking about ghosts might make them appear.

"I wish you'd change your mind," Sharon said. "After all, even if they were ghosts, they were *dancing*, for goodness sake. It's not like they were threatening you with an axe or anything."

"I'm sorry, but I just can't work here anymore. It creeps me out way too much."

"Well, I certainly can't force you to stay," Sharon conceded. "But I'll miss you." She smiled and gave him a gentle pat on his cheek. "Listen, I have to lead a tour right now, but if you stop by my office after lunch, I'll cut your final check."

"Thanks, Sharon. You know, except for the ghosts, I really liked working here."

When the pair turned and walked down the Promenade toward the lobby, Summer took a deep breath and blew it out. *"Just as well you're quitting, Chris... that way, you won't get into trouble for charging my room to the wrong credit card."* She waited a few minutes, then dropped ten dollars on the table and sauntered toward the hotel lobby to meet Dana.

As she approached the entrance, Summer spotted Dana, struggling to get up from a low chair. Her round belly was getting in her way. She smiled at the funny sight before, once again, code number fifty popped into her mind:

50: Never let a mark get under your skin.

Although it was subtle, Summer's smile tightened. She shifted her mindset and prepared to take the next step in gaining Dana's confidence. Just like all the great con artists before her, Summer took pride in her ability to gain a mark's trust. There was an art to it. It took a special talent to convince someone to share their secrets and hand over their money.

But this con was different. Dana wasn't a typical mark. She was a good person. And Gordo would use the information Summer conned out of her to steal money from people who hadn't even been involved in the con. Trusting Summer might even cost Dana her job. The thought of that left a sour taste in Summer's mouth.

Plus, it was one thing to con someone into giving you money or information – it was quite another thing to help steal a valuable painting, and stand by while Gordo set fire to the hotel to cover up the crime.

Summer did her best to put her concerns out of her mind. She raised her hand to wave at Dana, and ignored the guilt she felt when the pregnant woman grinned back and rushed over to give her a friendly hug.

"I'm so glad you made it," Dana gushed. "Here, I brought you a tablet and ink pen. Hopefully, with both of us taking notes on the tour, we should be able to answer most questions people will ask during the exhibition."

"Wow, you must feel a lot better today," Summer said, noting her lack of cold symptoms.

"Totally better!" Dana blurted. "It turns out I didn't have a cold. Apparently, oak pollen floods the air during the spring in Florida, so I had hay fever. Antihistamines fixed me right up."

Summer smiled. She was determined to stick to her resolve, but that didn't stop her from regretting that she couldn't be friends with Dana.

Sharon stepped into the center of the lobby and raised her arm. "If you are planning to take the tour, please gather around. If you haven't purchased your ticket yet, please go to the concierge's desk immediately and do so. And don't forget, for an additional eight dollars, you can enjoy a wonderful lunch in the hotel's lovely Terrace Restaurant, immediately following the tour."

A group of fourteen people assembled for the tour, eight of which were wearing bright red and purple hats, identifying themselves as members of the Red Hat Society. "Hello," the docent began. "My name is Sharon Delahanty. I'm an assistant manager and the resident historian here at the magnificent Belleview Biltmore Hotel, and I'm delighted that all of you will be joining me for a tour this morning."

Sharon shifted her glance to the ceiling and extended her open palms, encouraging the small crowd to look up. "We're standing in the newest addition to the Belleview Biltmore. It was built at the east end of the hotel in the early 1990s, while the hotel was under the ownership of the Mido Corporation. This addition made the Belleview *Mido*, as it was called back then, more accessible to disabled persons, and provided a modern entrance to its equally modern spa. This lobby also opens into the Promenade Corridor, connecting the *newest* section of the hotel to the *oldest*."

The docent highlighted the features of the modern lobby, including the high, domed ceiling, and giant aluminum chandelier, and she explained the significance of its round shape, copper pillars and koi ponds, with regard to the elements of Japanese feng shui. "But I must confess, the modern lobby has always had fewer fans than critics," Sharon said. "Folks around here usually refer to this lobby as the *pagoda*." She waited for the snickers to die down before adding, "The modern lobby will be replaced during the upcoming renovation, so you are some of the last people to ever witness this particular chapter of the hotel's history."

Recalling Sharon's parting conversation with Chris, Summer glanced up at the ornate and colorful chandelier, which resembled an open, upside down umbrella. *"I wonder how many tennis balls are up there?"* she mused. Then she glanced down the Promenade, thinking about what Chris had said about ghosts.

After the crowd admired the huge indoor swimming pool and spa, Sharon led them outside to sit in comfortable wooden rocking chairs on the wide, century-old veranda.

"When wealthy socialites and industrial leaders the likes of Thomas Edison and Henry Ford gathered on this veranda to enjoy the view, they were looking at the very same oak trees you see before you today," Sharon said.

"Wow," said one of the red-hatted tourists. "I get shivers thinking that I could be sitting exactly where Thomas Edison sat when he came up with his idea for electricity."

"He might have sat there thinking about other things," Sharon replied, "but he'd already invented electricity. As a matter of fact, the Belleview Hotel had electricity from day one, produced from a steam generator on the property. Each of the guest rooms boasted three electric lights, and the Tiffany glass panels in the dining room's ceiling were backlit with electric lights as well. Now, let's take a stroll down the famous Promenade Corridor."

The docent walked backward for much of the one-hour tour, pointing out the features of the various ballrooms and how changing social conventions had altered the way the rooms were used. The room that had once served as a Ladies Lounge, was converted into the Candlelight Speakeasy during Prohibition. And in later years, the same room was enlarged to function as an additional ballroom. She pointed out a door that had apparently been built by accident in the Promenade Corridor, since it never opened into any of the meeting rooms behind it. She unlocked the door to reveal a space less than a foot deep.

"No cleaning supplies were kept on this floor, so it wasn't a maid's closet. Historians speculate that it was probably just easier to close and lock the extra door than to take it out and plaster over the mistake," she said. "We call it the *Door to Nowhere.*"

Summer laughed along with the rest of the tour group, but she also made a mental note to come back and see if she could fit inside of the narrow space. It might make a handy hiding place while executing the more dangerous parts of Gordo's plan.

"Now," Sharon continued, "you must remember the Belleview was built during the Victorian Era, when women's fashion called for wearing hoop-skirted gowns. The reason the Promenade Corridor is so wide, is so those ladies could pass one another comfortably."

"This hallway makes me feel like I should be wearing one of those fancy dresses," Dana murmured.

Sharon smiled. "That's one of the many reasons the Belleview Biltmore is often referred to as *The Hotel That Time Forgot* – it embodies a true sense of history."

Summer half-listened as they toured the rest of the first floor, paying more attention to the narrow doorways that had been utilized by the workers to access the basement tunnels and work areas, than to Sharon's stories about the famous people who had frequented the hotel over the years. Dana, on the other hand, took endless notes and squeezed Summer's arm to reiterate points of interest, whispering, "We've got to remember this!" or "Can you picture me hanging out with the Vanderbilts in here?" and "Unbelievable...a hundred backlit panels of Tiffany glass on the ceiling. It's gorgeous! If not for all the windows, this would have been a perfect location for the exhibition, don't you think?"

When they walked downstairs to tour St. Andrew's Pub, the men's shoe-shine station, and the tunnels, Summer's senses switched to high-alert. This area, which was off-limits to guests unless they were part of a guided tour, would provide access to the various sections of the hotel, while keeping out of sight. Unfortunately, the tour only covered a small section of the tunnel labyrinth. She would have to explore the rest of it on her own.

Sharon pointed out a wooden staircase, used by workers so often that their feet had worn deep grooves in the steps, and a section of railroad tracks that had once coursed through the entire basement. Summer wondered if the small door that had once been used to offload ice blocks from the train, could be utilized to smuggle out the stolen painting.

"Henry Plant built railroad tracks right up to the doors of the Belleview Hotel," the tour guide said. "Guests entered by climbing the stairs to the grand entrance, while workers offloaded ice, luggage and supplies through freight doors like this one."

Sharon stepped aside to allow guests to move closer and take photographs. "Imagine men pumping rail carts along these tracks, taking supplies and luggage to the various sets of servant stairs. That really helped reduce the distance such items had to be carried." She pointed into the crawl spaces. "Look in there and you'll see some of the original knob and tube electric lines. This hotel served as an amazing example of the highest technology available in its day." She pointed to the remains of the boiler that had once heated water for the entire hotel, and a wheel that had been the lower gear of a cable-operated hoist – the predecessor of the elevator. She concluded the tour at the entrance to the Terrace Café, where those who had purchased lunch would be served.

Summer and Dana separated from the rest of the guests, choosing to sit several tables away from the boisterous, red-hatted group.

"Do you think Sharon would be willing to conduct a special tour for the guests attending the exhibition before the auction?" Dana asked, as she unfolded her napkin.

"I'll be happy to check," Summer replied. She eyed the menu. *"And maybe I'll be able to convince her to tell me more about those ghosts Chris saw. Who knows? Maybe I can figure out a way to blame them for stealing the painting."*

Chapter Nine

"So, how was the tour?"

The deep voice came from behind Summer. With her mind still on ghosts, she whipped her head around, half expecting to see a WWII soldier floating there.

She was only a little less surprised to see Robert McNeal pull out a chair at their table. *"What in the world is he doing here?"* She gave her outfit a furtive glance, concealing a grimace. Her loose-fitting, blue pullover, black slacks and walking shoes did nothing to accentuate her figure. And, as if that weren't bad enough, her hair was pulled back in a sloppy ponytail and she wore almost no make-up.

"Oh, no," Dana said. "By the look on your face, I'm guessing I forgot to tell you Bobby was joining us for lunch."

Struggling to regain her composure, Summer smiled. "Another attack of *momnesia?*"

"Afraid so," Dana admitted.

"How's that again?" Robert asked Dana. "You have amnesia?"

"You never listen." Dana rolled her eyes. "I've told you ten times that pregnancy can make you forgetful and that it's called pregnancy-brain – you know, *mom-nesia.* At least *I* have an *excuse* for forgetting stuff."

"Point taken," Robert said. He pulled out the chair next to Dana and sat without so much as glancing at Summer.

"What the hell?" Summer pondered. *"He acts like I'm invisible."* Smiling at Robert, she strove for a courteous tone. "It's nice to see you again."

Robert granted her a polite smile, nodded, and then returned his attention to Dana. He arched an eyebrow. "Should I be worried about the auction? If you don't think you can handle this one on your own..."

"Everything is fine," Dana replied, jutting out her jaw in indignation. "I told you, I'm perfectly capable of handling my job. I just have to make a few adjustments, that's all." She nodded at Summer. "That's one of the reasons I was so thrilled that this amazing intern fell into my lap yesterday. Between my checklists and her follow-up, I feel confident this year's event will be a huge success...just like they always are."

"Fell into your lap, did she?" Robert cast a suspicious glance in Summer's direction before returning his attention to Dana. "And pardon me for being a little worried, but this is the most important show we've held since I started managing the trust. You know that."

"Geez, Bobby, I..."

"It's Robert. We've talked about this. If we're going to have a professional working relationship, then you can't use my nickname at work." He glanced at Summer. "Sometimes Dana forgets we aren't little kids anymore. Since it looks like you got your wish to intern for this event, you can either call me Robert or Mr. McNeal."

"Oh, come on." Dana frowned. "She's not going to call you Mr. McNeal. You're not *that* much older than she is."

Robert eyed Summer as if trying to determine if that were true. His penetrating clear-blue eyes and nerdy black glasses made her catch her breath, just as they had on the airplane. "Robert it is, then," he said. He lifted his eyebrows. "So, exactly how *did* you two meet?"

"She happened to be standing nearby when my smart phone went on the fritz," Dana volunteered. "She saved me. It was an amazing stroke of luck that I ran into her, since *you* blew her off when she volunteered to help out."

"Yes. Extremely fortuitous," Robert replied, shooting another sideways glance at Summer. "You really *are* eager to get your feet wet, aren't you?"

Summer could tell he was still wondering how *accidental* their meeting had been.

"Give her a break, Bob... I mean, Robert. Don't you remember what it was like to graduate and want to put everything you learned into practice right away?"

When the waitress interrupted to take their orders, the two women realized they had forgotten to make a selection. Robert surprised Summer by ordering a cheeseburger while she and Dana were still skimming the menu. She had pegged him as a Caesar salad and sparkling water kind of guy.

"Maybe he's not as pretentious as he comes off," she thought. *"I wonder if he has me pegged as the Caesar salad type, too? Well, Robert, let's see if I can surprise you right back."* She gave the waitress a closed-mouth smile. "I'll have the same thing – with bacon on the burger and a side of fries," she chirped. From the corner of her eye, she saw Robert's head jerk up and turn toward her. He was trying to be discreet, but he was definitely checking her out. *"Well, it's about time,"* she thought.

"Darn it, you guys. I was going to be *good*," Dana pouted. "But I'm not going to sit here and watch the two of you scarf down burgers while I'm a nibbling on a *salad*. Cheeseburgers and fries all around."

When the waitress left, Robert picked up the thread of their previous conversation. "Are the exhibit pieces arriving on schedule?"

"Yep," Dana replied with a quick nod. "The lower-end pieces will begin arriving tomorrow, along with all of the display cases and the assembly team. The key acquisitions will be here in five days and of course, the *Bride On Stairs* will arrive the following day, giving us just enough time to set up and secure the showcase installation for the event."

"You guys need to remember that I just got out of school," Summer said. "I've seen tons of exhibits, of course, but I don't have *any* experience with setting one *up*."

Robert coughed. "Wow, nothing like jumping into the deep end – straight from the SAIC, to interning as second assistant in an exclusive, multi-million-dollar production."

"Don't let him scare you," Dana said. "It's true we're marketing some seriously high-end pieces, but this event has been in the planning stages for almost a year and I've hired crews to help us every step of the way. Robert is a worrier, but things almost always run as smooth as butter." Then she screwed up her face in thought. "Wait a minute. How is it that you attended the SAIC without interning for new exhibits somewhere along Chicago's Magnificent Mile?"

"An education at the SAIC doesn't come cheap. I worked two jobs to pay tuition and living expenses," Summer replied, lying with ease. "There was always a long line of students who were willing to volunteer their time to help with exhibits, and I couldn't afford to work for free."

"Two jobs, plus school?" Dana echoed. "That must have been tough."

"Shame your aunt couldn't have helped you out," Robert remarked. "You know, the one who's springing for this trip to Florida."

"So, you were paying attention on the flight down here, after all." Summer pretended confusion to hide her smug sense of satisfaction. "Oh, I'm sorry if I gave you the impression that my aunt is wealthy. She's not. She's not even my aunt, actually... she used to be my caseworker when I was in foster care. She covered the cost of my flight as a graduation present, but I'm paying for the rest of my trip with graduation gifts, savings bonds and my credit card. It's outrageously expensive to stay here, but as far as I'm concerned, it's worth it... even if I will have to eat Ramen Noodles for six months when I get back."

"Open mouth; insert foot, Robert." Dana shook her head. "He didn't mean to insult you. He just doesn't understand what it's like to be broke."

"Sorry," Robert said. "I do hope the experience you gain from interning for the McNeal Foundation's annual auction – and the boost it gives your resume – will reward your, um...persistence. The theme of this year's event is *Victorian Art*, so the pieces we are offering are all from that period – paintings, sculpture, antiquities, glassware, and jewelry. The centerpiece of the exhibit is James Jacques Joseph Tissot's, *Bride On Stairs*. As the first major event of the spring, we expect to draw a large crowd of collectors who were unable to win new acquisitions at Sotheby's or Christie's winter auctions."

Summer nodded, mentally scanning pages from the books Gordo had provided on the subject of art dealers.

"Our auctions are on par with theirs, if I do say so myself," Dana interjected. "The McNeal Foundation event is catered – hot and cold hors d'oeuvres, wine, champagne...why, we even plan to host a costume cocktail reception the night before. We'll dress in keeping with the Victorian theme and we're encouraging our patrons to do the same. I'll help you pick out an outfit to rent for the exhibit. There's a fantastic costume shop nearby, called *The House of Make-Believe.* It's huge."

Robert cleared his throat. "Yes. That should be great fun." His expression didn't match the sentiment. "Now, as I was saying, we will be showcasing a wide assortment of antiquities, which are divided according to anticipated value. Items worth less than one thousand dollars will be displayed and sold on the day of the event. Our more expensive offerings are already being advertised to prequalified collectors and we're accepting silent bids online. The highest silent bid on a given item becomes the starting point at the live auction."

Summer perked up. The banking account information of those prequalified collectors was *exactly* what Gordo had sent her to acquire. "I'm pretty good with spreadsheets and checking background information." She swallowed, trying not to sound over-eager. "I worked primarily for accountants and attorneys while I was in school."

"Thanks," Robert said. "But I handle all the confidential client information myself. Your job is to help Dana with her tasks."

"I don't understand," Summer said. This was true. She had assumed Dana did all of the bookkeeping for the enterprise. "Isn't accounting usually a major part of the first assistant's job?"

"I can't be trusted with confidential financial information," Dana admitted, without an ounce of embarrassment. "Not because I'm dishonest. It's just that somehow secrets seem to leak out of me like I'm a rusted-out bucket. I've always been that way, so I'm not offended that Robert holds onto that part of the job. I have plenty of other valuable skills to offer."

The waitress arrived and distributed the three, thick burgers, each accompanied by a pile of French fries. Then she set a large bottle of ketchup next to Dana's plate. "Need anything else?"

Summer shook her head, still reeling from disappointment. She had thought getting close to Dana was the key to completing her role in this con, but she had apparently hitched herself to the wrong cart. *"How in the world am I going to get a look at those financial records within six days?"* She decided to try again. "You know, Robert, I could do the financial work without talking to Dana about it. I'm pretty good at keeping my trap shut."

"Thanks again," Robert said. "But when we were kids, we used to say the three best ways to broadcast news were: *Television, Telephone,* and *Tell-A-Dana.* I'd worry she'd wheedle the information out of you."

Dana rolled her eyes but didn't deny the accusation. "Don't worry, you'll get plenty of great, hands-on experience working with me, Summer."

"That's right," Robert agreed. "Dana is at the top of her game when she's organizing events and coordinating with people to make sure stuff gets done. And nobody is better when it comes to keeping people informed about event details, or socializing with clients during an exhibit." Robert nodded at Dana's belly. "But because *Little Junior* there is messing with her brain and all, she needs a little extra help right now. I don't."

If she pushed any harder, Summer was certain Robert would become suspicious.

"Oh, man!" Dana cried, as she noticed a large blotch of ketchup on her swollen tummy. She dipped the corner of her napkin into her water glass and began to rub at the stain.

"I better to go back to the original plan – seduction," Summer decided. She gave Robert a sexy smile and looked into his eyes. "That makes sense, but if you change your mind, give me a call." She glanced down only long enough to write her phone number on a sheet of her notebook paper and tear it off. Then she returned her gaze to Robert and licked her lips. "I'm really good. I'm just down the hall. And I'm always up late."

"Thanks," Robert said. Barely glancing at her, he took the scrap of paper she held out to him. He tucked it into the breast pocket of his crisp, white shirt and then reached for his sandwich. Less than a minute later, his phone buzzed. He pulled it from a pocket in his pleated, gray trousers, glanced at it, and announced. "Sorry, but I'm going to have to finish this in my room." He got to his feet and picked up his plate.

"Another late submission?" Dana asked.

"Yeah, but it's a sweet, old woman and a good customer, so I don't mind." He turned to Summer. "Now, I have total faith in Dana and I'm sure you'll be a big help to her, but if something happens and *either* of you think you're getting in over your heads, just remember – letting me know sooner is *way* better than later."

"We've got this," Dana said.

Robert smiled at Dana's red-tinted belly with the genuine affection of a big brother. "Please do me a favor." He jerked a thumb in Summer's direction. "Don't let her carry liquids *anywhere near* the art."

They all chuckled, remembering the coffee spill on the plane. But as his smile faded, Summer also recognized a flicker of interest in Robert's eyes. Her stomach turned with the realization that she was feeling the same thing. *"Don't let yourself fall for him. Not even a little bit,"* she thought. *"Remember, he's going to hate your guts when this is all over."*

Chapter Ten

"You're pretty lucky to have a boss who lets you speak your mind," Summer said, watching Robert disappear down the Promenade Corridor with his lunch stowed in a Styrofoam box he had obtained from the waitress.

"That wasn't me speaking my mind as much as it was me acting out. Ever since Robert hired me, we've worked hard to keep our professional lives separate from our personal ones. I'm usually pretty good at it, but lately my crazy pregnancy hormones seem to be connected directly to my big, fat mouth." Dana shook her head and gave the ketchup stain on her belly one last rub before giving up. "I feel like I have to point out every little mistake he makes – like misjudging you the way he did. Probably, so I don't feel like I'm the only one who's goofing up lately."

"He didn't misjudge me, you did." Summer thought, ignoring another twinge of guilt. "I'll do whatever I can to make you look good. You just tell me what you need me to do."

As they ate, they chatted about the Foundation's past auctions, and Dana's desire to make this year's event stand out. Finally, Summer patted her stomach. "I'm stuffed. If I eat any more, I'm going to look pregnant, too."

"Yeah, right, Miss Perfect Body." Dana laid a hand on her round bulge. "Truthfully, my figure was always sort of average, even before I got pregnant." A peculiar expression crossed her face. "I think that's why I was so flattered when Martin picked me out of the crowd the night we met."

"Martin is the baby's father?"

Dana nodded in mute response.

"If you tell me this is none of my business, I promise I won't be offended," Summer said. "But, don't you think your baby will want to know its father?"

"You sound like Robert."

"Sorry. It's just that my mom never wanted my dad around, and I think that made me miss him *more*. I never understood how two people could care about one another enough to sleep together and make babies, but then change so much they couldn't even tolerate being around one another long enough to share special moments with the kids they created."

Tears pooled in Dana's eyes.

"Never mind," Summer blurted out. "I'm poking my nose where it doesn't belong. I'm sure you have your reasons."

"He doesn't even know I'm pregnant."

"Oh, Dana..." Summer instinctively reached out and covered Dana's hand with her own. "Don't you think he'd want to help?"

"No, I don't." Dana closed her eyes a moment and then leaned closer, lowering her voice. "You know, when I first realized I was pregnant, I debated whether or not to keep it. After I made my decision, I dreaded the thought of telling Bobby – um, Robert. I mean, I'd worked so hard to convince him to quit treating me like I was his kid sister – to recognize that I was a grown-up, capable of taking care of myself and making my own choices. And then I went and made this huge mistake, proving he was right all along. Left on my own, I *do* screw things up." She bit her lower lip.

"The ability to have sex without getting pregnant isn't a measure of a woman's success, you know. And besides, it appears you were able to convince Robert to accept your decision. So it looks like everything is working out just fine."

"Robert doesn't think I made the right decision, but he's agreed to keep his opinions to himself – for now, anyway."

"How *big* of him to agree not to make judgments about how his *employee* chooses to live her *personal* life." Summer's words dripped sarcasm. *"What a haughty prick. He deserves whatever happens to him."*

Dana gave her a wry smile. "It might not sound like a big deal when you say it like that, but trust me, it's a major step in the right direction. When Robert first found out I was pregnant, he wanted to go find Martin, drag him back to Chicago, and force him to marry me."

"And let me guess – you didn't want to get married in a shotgun wedding?"

"No. But it's way more complicated than that." Dana blushed, suddenly nervous. "I haven't even told Emma the whole story."

"Well, you can tell me, if you want," Summer assured her. "Sometimes it's easier to talk to someone when you don't have a long history together. And, believe me. I've made more than my share of huge mistakes. I promise not to judge."

Dana fidgeted in her chair, frowning. "I really do want to tell somebody. Swear you can keep a secret?"

"I promise."

After taking a long drink of water, Dana began in hushed tones, "I met Martin at a nightclub where a group of us used to go on Friday nights. I usually sat with Emma and her husband, Ole, but Emma wasn't feeling well, so they had decided to stay home that night. Ironically, it turned out Emma was three months pregnant." She chewed on her bottom lip a moment. Then the rest of her story gushed out, like the rush of air escaping from an untied balloon.

"Martin swept me off my feet. I don't think there's any other way to describe it. He was *so* handsome – tall and well-built – like a blond body builder or something. We were drinking and laughing. And he totally ignored my other girlfriends – even though most of them are better looking than me. It was as if we were the only two people in the club – maybe in the whole world."

"I think you tend to sell yourself short with regard to your looks, but keep going," Summer encouraged. "What happened next?"

Dana's chin trembled and she teared up again. "That's the problem. I don't know what happened. The next thing I remember was waking up in my bed, naked, with him lying next to me." She wiped her eyes. "I was so embarrassed. I didn't even remember leaving the bar with him. But I must have. I mean, otherwise, how would he know where I lived? Anyway, he woke up, acting all in love...telling me how great we were together and how I rocked his world. Then he rolled on top of me, wanting to do it again. It was awful. He was a *stranger*. I tried to wiggle out from under him, but...well, since we'd obviously already had sex, I guess he thought I was teasing. He laughed and before I knew it, he had me pinned down and was inside of me. I was so confused, I didn't tell him to stop. I just lay there and let him..."

"It's okay." *Camp Sucker*, the scam she and her former partners operated, flashed through Summer's mind. She recalled how Dave and Edward used to slip roofies into their marks' drinks. *"I wonder if Martin drugged her?"* She squeezed Dana's hand. "Having a one-night-stand with a stranger isn't the end of the world."

"Not one night. He stayed with me most of the weekend," Dana continued, her voice soft. "And he barely let me out of bed the whole time. At first, I kept thinking about how happy I was when we first met. I kept trying to recreate that feeling, but it didn't take long for me to realize the cover didn't match the book. He...well, he turned out to be someone I didn't want in my life. I don't know why I didn't just admit that I had made a huge mistake and ask him to leave."

"But you *did* ask him to leave, right?"

"I did, but not until after he found out what I did for a living and tried to convince me to help him steal from Robert."

"What do you mean, he wanted you to *steal* from Robert?" Summer asked. *"Damn it, if someone just tried to rip-off Robert, he might still be on high alert. That will make it even harder to pull off this job."*

"At first, he just asked a bunch of questions about the value of the art we sold and what security measures we took to protect it. Then he wanted me to give him Robert's banking information, so he could transfer funds out of his account. He said Robert was so rich, he'd never miss it. Of course, I refused to help him."

"Does Robert know why you kicked the guy out?" Summer sneered with genuine disgust. *"I might be a grifter, but I've never forced someone to do something against their will."*

"No, Robert doesn't know anything about that – or what happened next."

"There's more?"

"Yeah," Dana raised her glass of water to her lips with a trembling hand.

Summer scooted her chair a closer to Dana's. "Tell me."

"Well, when I refused help him, Martin got so pissed off that he started screaming at me. I was really scared that he was going to hurt me. He was so big and strong...and so *mad*. Fortunately, I have a great landlord who's built like a linebacker. When Jake heard Martin yelling at me, he pounded on my door and said if I didn't open up, he was calling the police."

"Would he have done it?"

"I think so. Martin must have believed him, too, because he didn't try to stop me from opening the door. And the second I did, Jake pulled me out into the hall and stepped between Martin and me. He was holding a baseball bat, and he looked like he was prepared to use it. He asked me if I wanted Martin to leave. I think I was too shaken-up to speak, but I must have nodded, because he stood in front of me and told Martin to get out and never come back. Jake said if he ever caught sight of him hanging around me or the building, he'd be sorry."

"So Martin left?"

"Yeah, but not without throwing a few insults at me first. He said he was doing me a *favor* sleeping with me and I wasn't worth the trouble of getting his hands dirty fighting Jake. And he told Jake that he should count his lucky stars that he didn't have time for a fight today."

"You poor thing. What an ordeal. You must have been terrified."

"I was. In fact, for a few weeks afterward, I thought my nervous jitters were making me queasy. Then it dawned on me that it might be morning sickness." Dana shrugged her shoulders. "So now you know why I don't want Martin anywhere near me or my baby."

Summer nodded. "And he's never tried to come back?"

"Nope. Haven't seen hide nor hair of him since then. I think he probably prowls nightclubs looking for someone he can take advantage of, and I was an easy mark. I'm sure he's found someone else by now."

Summer shifted uncomfortably in her chair. During the course of her life, she had known countless Martin's. She could easily visualize him targeting sweet, innocent Dana. If her landlord hadn't come to her rescue, there was little doubt Martin would have stolen everything she owned.

"So, what did you tell Robert to get him to give up on the shotgun wedding idea?"

"I told him I found out the guy was married."

"So, he just gave up and accepted the fact that you're going to be a single parent?"

"Not exactly," Dana rolled her eyes. "I mean, he bought my story, but then he proposed to me himself."

Summer drew in a breath. "I didn't realize you and Robert were..."

"Oh, God, no! *Ewww!* We're not... I mean, *yuck!* He didn't expect us to have a *physical* relationship. He was just offering to give my baby his *name*. Of course, I said *'no way.'* It would have been like marrying one of my brothers. Still it was sweet of him to ask, don't you think?"

"I don't think 'sweet' covers it. I mean, *wow.* Are you sure Robert isn't a time traveler from the days when knights in shining armor searched the land for damsels in distress?"

Dana giggled, her mood lifting now that her dark secret was out. "Maybe so, but you can understand why I don't ever want him to learn the *real* story, right?"

"Never fear...noble Sir Robert will learn nothing from me." She grinned, enjoying Dana's friendship, despite the warning bells sounding in her head.

"Thanks, Summer. Now, let's get to work." Dana sat up straight, sucked in a deep breath and flipped her notepad back to the first page. "Let's start by going over our agenda for the rest of the day. First, I want to introduce you to Maxwell, our production manager and then..."

Chapter Eleven

By the time she returned to her hotel room that evening, Summer had developed a new respect for people who organized massive public events and made it look easy. Although some of the cons she had orchestrated in the past had been complex, her objective had always been to keep everyone, except her partners, in the dark about their plans. This art exhibit and sale was just the opposite. According to Dana, the key to a successful event is keeping the public informed and excited about being invited to attend, and the hotel staff informed about the housekeeping details.

Struggling to keep her heavy eyelids open, Summer barely managed to kick off her shoes and eat a tuna salad croissant before she drifted off to sleep on the fainting couch in the parlor. As the thick fog bank dropped over her, she began to hear voices from just beyond the mist.

"I don't disagree," Margaret said. "But there are numerous tangles in this ball of yarn and I'm not sure we'll have enough time to work all the knots out."

"I understand," Andy said. "I'll try to move things along."

Summer, concentrating on the conversation, didn't realize the fog was lifting until she found herself seated at the small round table in her parlor, across from Margaret and Andy. She glanced across the room and was unnerved to see herself laying on the couch a few feet away, sound asleep.

"Hello, my dear," Margaret said. Her hair was wrapped in a thick coil on top of her head, and her cobalt and white floral print dress had a high neckline and puffy sleeves, trimmed in lace. She glanced at Summer's sleeping form. "Don't worry. If your body begins to wake, your consciousness will return to it instantaneously."

Summer bit her tongue. She wasn't used to being the least knowledgeable person in the room and didn't like the feeling one bit. Her instinct was to even the score – perhaps tell Margaret her dress made her look like a delftware vase. She cast a glance at Andy, who was dressed in the same khaki uniform and garrison cap as before. The realization that he couldn't have been more than twenty or so when he died, squelched her petty concerns. "Why am I dreaming about you guys again?"

Margaret raised her eyebrows, but then smiled. "Given your memory, I'm quite certain you remember this is the spirit realm, so why do you insist on calling this a dream?"

Summer shrugged a shoulder. "It's just easier to think about this as being a dream as opposed to being a connection to a realm I never knew existed. But I guess it doesn't matter. I'll be leaving in a few days and..."

Before Summer could complete her sentence, the clouds gathered around her, pulling her from the scene. *"Impatient much?"* she jeered silently. Then she heard Andy's disembodied voice in the mist.

"After my father died, my sister Paige and I stayed on at Mr. Beacon's farm. I milked cows and flew the crop-duster, while Paige cooked and cleaned. Times were hard, but every Saturday we woke up early and got our chores out of the way, so we could spend the whole day at the movies. The matinee always started with the Movietone News, which usually involved a correspondent discussing the war in Europe. Sometimes they played a short film from the battlefront. Bombings were loud and scary, but the war was far away, so we didn't worry about it too much. As a matter of fact, whenever the newsreel camera was filming from inside the bomber, I liked to pay close attention to the instrument panel and pretend that I was the pilot."

"I guess news took the place of previews back then." Summer wanted to ask questions, but she kept quiet as Andy continued.

"After the news, we watched cartoons and then a segment of a serial, like *Buck Rogers in the 21st Century* or *The Lone Ranger.* Next came a short comedy, followed by the movie of the week. By the end of the afternoon, most of us had forgotten all about the war, let alone our personal hardships."

"Yeah, I get that. Justin and I had a crappy childhood, too. We used to spend our Saturdays in the arcade."

"The attack on Pearl Harbor changed everything. After that, the war was just about the *only* thing anybody thought about. Even at the movies."

As the mist faded, Summer found herself in an old-fashioned movie theater, seated next to a young version of Andy. His short, light hair was slicked back, and he wore a checkered shirt, tucked into a pair of dark wool pants. Paige sat on his opposite side, dressed in a dingy white blouse and plaid skirt, with her tawny hair pulled into a ponytail. She studied Andy's hands as he carefully broke a package of Necco Wafers in two, and handed her the slightly larger half.

The lights dimmed and their attention was drawn to the screen, where a black and white movie, titled *Winning Your Wings*, began to play. An airplane landed and a military pilot walked toward the camera, pulling off his goggles and helmet. Several people in the audience gasped when they recognized the famous movie star, Jimmy Stewart. When he asked if anyone in the theater had questions about the Army Air Corps, a mock theater audience appeared in the film. While the women in the simulated theater audience looked on with admiration, various men took turns asking questions about the mustering-in process, medical exams, and cadet flight training, all of which Jimmy Stewart answered in a way that encouraged the members of the audience to sign up right away.

As the short film ended, the mist engulfed Summer, carrying her from the scene and once again, Andy's voice floated through the clouds.

"A few weeks before my eighteenth birthday, I happened to run into Mr. Washburn, the mine supervisor. We both knew I'd be called up to serve in the war effort real soon. I told him I wanted to join the Army Air

Corps, but I needed a high school diploma to qualify for flight school. He admired my patriotism and knew I'd been flying a crop duster for years, so he agreed to give me a diploma from the mine's high school. Tom Beacon said he'd look after Paige, as long as I sent a hefty monthly allotment for her upkeep, so I joined up on my eighteenth birthday and was sent to Montgomery, Alabama, for air cadet testing and flight school."

The fog began to lift once more. This time, Summer found herself standing next to Andy in a small, drab green office. He wore the same khaki uniform, except the insignia on the left side of his garrison cap was a pair of wings sprouting from a propeller. Behind a metal desk, a middle-aged, barrel-chested man reviewed the top sheet on a stack of paperwork. Although she didn't know what all the emblems on his uniform meant, Summer was certain the man was a high-ranking officer.

"At ease, Mr. Turner," the man said.

Andy spread his legs apart and clasped his hands behind his back, but remained rigid as he continued to stare straight ahead.

The man removed his glasses and glanced up. "Congratulations, son. You've managed to graduate at the top of your class and are being promoted to the rank of Second Lieutenant."

Andy fought to keep from grinning. "Thank you, sir."

"No thanks are necessary. You've earned it. Your pay will be adjusted to $166.67 a month, starting January first." He picked up a white handkerchief and rubbed a lens of his glasses as he spoke. "But there's something else. You won't be shipping out with your fellow graduates. Your trainers agree that you possess a real knack for instruction, so you're being sent to Florida to help organize and operate a new pilot training program there."

"Sir?" Andy's exhilarated expression morphed into one of disappointment. "Thank you, sir, but if it's all the same to you, I'd rather join my brothers in the fight."

"Top of your class or not, it's not your place to question orders, son."

Andy frowned and set his jaw, anger blazing in his eyes.

"Jesus Christ. Don't act like I just shot your dog, Turner. Most men in your position would be thrilled to be sent to Florida instead of the South Pacific theater." The man held his glasses up to the light, then huffed a breath on the lenses and rubbed them some more. "Look, I know you're all fired up to go bomb the enemy, but you need to remember, there's only so much one pilot can do. By overseeing the training of others, you'll help send hundreds of well-trained bomber pilots into battle." He held his glasses up again and, apparently satisfied, put them back on. "Besides, your record states you're the sole support for your sister, and since the Sullivan brothers' tragedy, my orders are to keep sole surviving males out of combat whenever possible."

The fog dropped over Summer again, but this time, Andy didn't speak. She floated in the clouds thinking about his situation. *"Why would anybody be pissed off about being sent to Florida instead of going to fight in a war that was killing hundreds of people every single day?"* she wondered.

After what felt like a long while, Summer drifted through the mist to the round table, where Margaret sat, still dressed in the blue and white dress. This time, Summer made a conscious effort not to look at the couch.

"I've always believed there would be fewer wars if women were in charge of the government," Margaret said. "Men tend to believe a large number of things justify risking their lives and the lives of others, while most women would endure almost anything to avoid losing the lives of their children."

"Maybe," Summer quipped. "But then again, I've seen women hold grudges for *years* over really stupid stuff, so you never know."

Andy materialized at the table with no warning, causing a shiver to run down Summer's back. Although neither he nor Margaret looked completely solid, Andy was far more transparent than his counterpart. Neither spirit seemed to notice the disparity in their appearance.

"Some wars are worth fighting," he said, frowning. He watched Margaret stir three teaspoons of sugar into her hot tea and he continued staring into her cup as if it were a window to the past. "It was almost Christmas time. I was supposed to go home for two weeks before reporting to my duty station, but I was embarrassed that I was being given kid glove treatment. I opted to go straight to Mac-Dill Air Station instead. When I arrived, the place reminded me of a circus that traveled through our town once – so many things happening at one time, it was hard to make sense of things. They weren't ready to receive personnel, so I was instructed to report to Colonel Timothy Huck at the Belleview Biltmore Hotel, where I was to be bivouacked."

As the clouds engulfed Summer, she heard Andy say, "It's just bonkers how one decision can make things go so terribly wrong. If only I'd gone home for a couple weeks and reported for duty along with everybody else..."

This time, Summer didn't drift along on fluffy clouds. Instead, she felt as though she was falling down a smoke-filled laundry chute. Her heart raced and her breath came short and fast. Suddenly, her descent slowed and she drifted into the front seat of a Jeep as it pulled up to the Belleview Biltmore. Her heart still pounding, she noticed the guardhouse at the entrance was empty and the gate was open. Army trucks lined the long hotel driveway and soldiers milled around in groups under the shade of huge oak trees.

"I feel like I just entered the Twilight Zone," Summer thought. Everywhere she looked, trucks and soldiers resembled those she had heretofore, only seen only in books and old movies.

"I never imagined a building could be so dad-blamed huge," Andy said.

Summer started to answer, but since Margaret said it was imperative that she remain silent, she pressed her lips together instead. A split second later, she realized Andy had been talking to himself, not to her.

"Hey, fellas," he called to a small group of soldiers smoking cigarettes nearby. "You have any idea where I can find a Colonel Huck?"

One of the men took a long drag on his cigarette, then pinched off the ember and ground it out beneath the toe of his shoe, while simultaneously dropping the butt into his pocket. He sauntered over before noticing the gold second lieutenant's bar and blue flight officer's badge on Andy's uniform.

"Yes, sir," the man replied, as he saluted.

Unaccustomed to his new rank, Andy hesitated before returning the salute.

The soldier grinned and jabbed his thumb toward the hotel. "The Colonel's in the lobby, having a meeting with Mr. Kirkeby, the fella that owns this white palace. I don't know how the old fuddy-duddy expects us to turn this place into barracks and training rooms without taking down all his fancy thingamabobs, but he's in there bustin' the Colonel's chops about it."

Andy glanced at the hotel doors but didn't take his hands off the steering wheel.

"Sir," the soldier continued, "if you don't mind me saying so – on days like this, I'm glad to be a junior officer in this man's Army – it's a lot easier for us cadets to pass the buck."

Andy gulped. "Do you suppose it's all right to leave my Jeep here until I get signed in?"

The man gave him a curious glance. "Heck, sir, next to the Colonel, you're the highest-ranking man here. You can leave your vehicle anywhere you want to."

Summer suddenly gasped. *"I'm not just observing this memory. I know exactly what Andy's thinking and feeling. How can that be?"* She felt the heat of his reddened cheeks as he stepped from the Jeep and exchanged another awkward salute with the cadet, and then the flutter of butterflies in his stomach as he walked up the stairs to the entrance of the grand hotel.

As he crossed through the entrance, Andy's jaw dropped. Everywhere he looked were examples of Victorian grandeur, the likes of which he had never imagined: crystal chandeliers, elegant furnishings, gilt mirrors, brocade and lace draperies, flocked wallpaper, ornate crown molding, marble statues, and huge, brightly-painted porcelain urns.

The sound of a man's high-pitched voice brought him out of his reverie. On the far side of the wide lobby, two men were having a heated discussion. One of the men was dressed in an Army uniform bearing a colonel's insignia.

Andy approached the two men cautiously, the scene reminding him of a baseball coach yelling at an umpire over a perceived bad call. Colonel Huck was rather short, with a clean shaven round face and close-cropped sandy hair, while the red-faced man had a receding hairline and a bushy mustache. The Colonel treated the ranting man with respect, however it was clear that he was in the process of taking charge of his command. The moment he caught sight of Andy, he turned to him and smiled.

"Finally," said Col. Huck, relaxing his posture. "It looks like my staff has arrived."

Andy cast a nervous glance over his shoulder, wondering who the Colonel was talking about. When it dawned on him that Col. Huck was talking about him, he gulped. Snapping to attention, he saluted. "Second Lieutenant Andrew Turner reporting for duty, sir."

The Colonel squinted at Andy. "Aren't the rest of my officers with you, Lieutenant?"

"No, sir," Andy replied. "It's just me. And actually, I'm reporting in two weeks early." He handed his orders to the Colonel.

Col. Huck's face paled, but he quickly recovered. After studying the orders for only a moment, he returned his attention to Andy. "Well, I guess that makes you my second in command for now, Lieutenant Turner. This is Mr. Arnold Kirkeby, the owner of this fine establishment, which has been requisitioned by the Army. Obviously, it can't serve its purpose in its current condition, so our first task is to remove all the finery and place it in secured storage. As of this moment, I'm turning that responsibility over to you. Additionally, you'll be in charge of the new arrivals. They can handle on-line training assignments like this one until slots open for them in flight training classes over at MacDill."

"On-line training?" Andy asked.

"On-line training," Col. Huck repeated. "Easy jobs that anyone can do, like on an assembly line – back home, you probably called it *busy work*. Idle soldiers tend to get into trouble, so we make 'em earn their pay doing whatever needs to get done. Once they clean this place out, you can put them to work painting the walls Army green."

The color drained from Mr. Kirkeby's face as Col. Huck outlined his plans for the grand hotel.

Although she couldn't hear Mr. Kirkeby's thoughts, Summer knew *exactly* what he was thinking. The fabulous Belleview Biltmore Hotel was going to be occupied by the Army, whether he liked it or not. Rather than operating as a winter playground for the world's wealthiest travelers, the hotel's opulent rooms would serve as home to thousands of soldiers who would not otherwise have been able to afford to stay at the hotel for even one night.

"Here, take these," Col. Huck continued, handing Andy a large ring with three keys on it. "They're for the locks on the storage buildings out yonder. Once the fancy hotel furnishings are moved over there, you'll need to make sure those buildings stay locked. And post guards to keep Mr. Kirkeby's possessions safe until the war's over. Then he'll be able to turn this place back into a fine hotel for the rich folks who *belong* here."

The Colonel turned to the red-faced man, who was tugging at his bowtie, obviously irritated by the interruption. "It's been a pleasure meeting you, Mr. Kirkeby. You can provide any further directions to Lieutenant Turner here. I'm sure he'll carry them out in fine order." He extended his hand for a shake and then turned on his heel, before Mr. Kirkeby had time to object.

Andy watched Col. Huck depart, too stunned to speak.

Chapter Twelve

Mr. Kirkeby didn't try to hide his contempt about being passed off to Col. Huck's underling, especially one who had just arrived at the Belleview Biltmore. He worked himself into a frenzy, ranting about the necessity to protect and maintain the lavish hotel while occupied by soldiers.

"How can I expect someone like *you* to appreciate the significance of this establishment?" Mr. Kirkeby hissed, working his jaw in a sawing motion as if trying to keep worse insults from spewing forth. "For almost fifty years, this hotel has been welcoming great men, the likes of Thomas Edison and Henry Ford – the Vanderbilts – the Duponts – Babe Ruth...and now you propose to slather its walls with paint the color of moldy bread? It's preposterous! It's..." His voice trailed off as he glanced over Andy's shoulder. He gulped hard and attempted a smile.

Following the direction of the man's gaze, Andy turned and saw a girl approaching, her honey-blonde hair pulled into a ponytail. She wore a red sweater with sleeves pushed up to her elbow, and baggy black dungarees that were rolled up to expose white bobby socks and saddle shoes. Newspaper ink stained her hands, forearms and one of her cheeks, making it difficult to take her worried expression seriously.

"Maybe you can talk some sense into the Army, Violet," Mr. Kirkeby continued, struggling to ratchet his voice down several octaves. "I want them to cover the hotel's walls with plywood to protect them, but these dullards insist on *painting* them."

"I understand that it's upsetting," Violet said, her warm, low voice sympathetic. "But I tend to agree with the Army on this one. If the Belleview is to do her part in the war effort, she has to dress in uniform. We can't expect men to feel like soldiers if they're living in a castle, and besides, it would take acres of plywood to cover all these walls."

Mr. Kirkeby's eyes glistened with emotion. "They're going to ruin her."

"Nonsense," Violet replied, giving the man a tender smile. "They aren't tearing down the walls, they're just painting some of them. We'll remove all the Belleview's swanky decorations and once this horrible war is over, we'll bring everything back in and decorate her like a Christmas tree. You'll see. The White Queen of the Gulf will be good as new in no time at all."

Violet turned to Andy and winked. "Isn't that right, soldier?"

Andy cleared his throat, trying not to stare at her cornflower blue eyes and praying his voice wouldn't crack. "Yes, ma'am. I'm sure the Army won't need to be here long. Just until we train enough pilots to bomb all the Japs back to hell, where they belong."

Despite the newspaper ink stains, Andy noticed a blush creeping into Violet's cheeks.

Flustered, he scooped his garrison cap from his head. "Sorry for the salty language, ma'am. It's been a while since I've talked to a lady." He turned his attention back to Mr. Kirkeby. "You and your daughter can rest easy, sir. We'll take good care of your hotel."

Mr. Kirkeby drew back in surprise. "*Daughter?*" He glanced at Violet. "This isn't my daughter. Violet is one of the Barnes girls. Her father owns the Rosery Farm."

Andy raised his eyebrows to remind Mr. Kirkeby that he had just arrived and had no idea who was who, let alone how they were connected to the Belleview Biltmore.

The man scowled. "For your information, the Rosery has been supplying fresh cut flowers to this hotel for a good twenty years. And Harry Barnes always sends a few farm hands over to get the orchid and rose gardens ready for the winter season, to boot. I told him that he could store his flower vases and what not, with the rest of the valuables we're removing for safekeeping. Violet, here, volunteered to help supervise the packing – to make sure the hotel's property is treated with the care it deserves."

"I'm sure you have nothing to worry about, sir," Andy said. "I'll make sure the men who are assigned to clear this place out are careful with your, um – valuables. But if it makes you feel better, you and Miss Barnes are welcome to observe their work." He gave Violet a half-smile. "You've been packing your vases in newspaper, right?" He pointed to her hands and then tapped his forefinger against his cheek.

Violet's eyes widened. "Yes." Clearly embarrassed, she rubbed a clean section of her forearm against her cheek, smearing the ink into a larger stain. "I mean, I did. The vases are all packed, so I started working in the kitchen – crating dishes." Gathering herself together, she turned to Kirkeby, who was tugging at the edges of his bowtie again. "Mr. Kirkeby, there's no reason for you to watch the hotel be taken apart. I'll stay. And I promise to ring you right away, if I spot any funny business."

Andy glanced toward the hotel's entrance and the soldiers milling around outside, and then glared at Kirkeby. Summer heard his thoughts as clearly as if he had spoken out loud. *"Are you nuts? You can't leave this little cookie alone in a hotel with a bunch of flight cadets!"* He stiffened his back and turned to Violet. "I'm sorry, ma'am, but it was one thing when I thought you were here in the company of your father, but..."

"He's quite right, Violet," Mr. Kirkeby interrupted. "It wouldn't be appropriate to leave you unchaperoned with strangers – not even honorable men in uniform." He extended his hand toward Andy for a shake.

Andy took the offered hand, breathing a sigh of relief as Kirkeby continued talking.

"I must insist that you stay close to Lieutenant Turner whenever you're here." Then Kirkeby shifted his gaze to Andy. "And you don't have to worry about Violet, Lieutenant. She's level-headed – not like those khaki-wacky girls who hang around down at the drugstore."

For the second time in less than twenty minutes, an important man had dropped tremendous responsibilities into Andy's lap and then walked away. And once again, Andy stared after the man, mute with astonishment.

"Lieutenant Turner?"

Andy wasn't sure how long Violet had been trying to attract his attention. He shook his head, trying to clear his thoughts. "Miss Barnes, I don't know…"

"That's okay, I do," Violet replied. "Two of the storage buildings are behind the servants' dormitory and the other one is a warehouse at Weaver's Grocery store. I'll take you there."

"No…I mean…thanks, but that's not what I was talking about, Miss Barnes."

"You can call me Violet."

Andy sized-up the lanky girl, trying to appear less like a fish out of water. "What I was trying to say, Miss Barnes, is that this is no place for a woman."

"Perhaps not," she replied. "But until everything is packed safely away, you're going to need my help. I'm the only one who knows which items are to remain in the hotel, which are to be stored, and which are going to Weaver's, to be sold or shipped to Mr. Kirkeby's other hotels."

Andy grimaced at the truth of the matter. "You can stay long enough to write me a list."

"Don't be silly. There are four-hundred and twenty-five rooms in this hotel in need of packing."

"Wait – how many rooms?"

Summer smiled at Andy's attempts to imagine a such an enormous building.

"I didn't count the one-hundred and fifty rooms in the servants' dormitory because all that's over there are beds and dressers, and they're staying put," Violet explained. "But the main hotel building has four-hundred and twenty-five rooms, not counting the ones in the basement." She smiled at the expression of disbelief etched on Andy's face. "Yep. People say it's the largest wooden building in the world, and it belongs to the Army now – well, at least until the war is over."

"Fantastic," Andy muttered. "It serves me right. What was I thinking reporting in two weeks early?"

Violet continued talking as the fog settled around Summer, tugging her away from the memory.

"It's not all bad news," Violet said, hiding a smile behind her ink-stained hand. "The Colonel chose Sunset Cottage as his quarters, and for now, all the cadets are housed in the servants' barracks, so you have the entire hotel to yourself for a while. Not even Thomas Edison can make that claim. Come on. I'll give you a tour."

As the mist settled over her, Summer suddenly felt the odd sensation that she was teetering at the edge of the clouds, about to tumble off. *"Not again,"* she moaned. *"Wake yourself up before you fall!"* She forced her eyes open and discovered she was about to roll off the narrow couch in her parlor. She sat up and glanced up at the round table, half expecting to see Margaret Plant seated there.

"Okay, no more sleeping on the sofa," she mumbled, getting to her feet.

Chapter Thirteen

Summer had barely tumbled into her bed before she was asleep again, floating atop the billowy clouds. *"Margaret said watching these memories would help me, but I don't see how – unless I can use Andy's knowledge about the hotel to help pull off this job."*

"Don't be absurd!" Margaret's icy voice cut through the peaceful fog like a lightning bolt. "Spirits don't form connections with the living in order to assist them with criminal endeavors."

Like all good con artists, Summer had practiced for years to master the art of hiding her thoughts, emotions, and nervous tells. No one but Justin ever knew what was going on in her head unless she wanted them to. Until now.

Goose flesh rose on Summer's arms as the mist faded and she floated down into what had become a familiar scene – the parlor table, sitting opposite Margaret Plant. "Can you read my thoughts the same way I was able to read Andy's when I was watching his memories?"

"We would never help you do harm to the Belleview!" Margaret continued, ignoring her question. She stirred sugar into her steaming tea with such vigor, it sloshed over the back side of her cup. Then she dropped the spoon into her saucer with a clatter, lifted the dainty, pink rosebud-covered teacup to her lips and took a long drink.

"That must be her version of doing a shot of tequila," Summer thought.

By the time she returned her cup to its saucer, Margaret had not only regained control of her temper – she looked amused, confirming Summer's suspicion that she could read her thoughts.

Summer took a deep breath and tried again. "Okay, if you aren't trying to help me do my job, then what's the purpose of all of this? Why do you keep bothering me...forcing me to watch Andy's memories?"

"Andy's story and his reasons for forming a connection with you are his alone to share," Margaret said. "In the meantime, I suggest you learn to exercise patience. It's a skill that might help you begin to make wiser choices."

"It must be nice to feel all superior about how you chose to live your life." Summer balled her fists. "But then again, you've probably never gone to bed hungry – or had your life threatened – or been responsible for someone else's life."

"I've been in all of those situations," Margaret replied. "Multiple times. But I've always believed that an intelligent woman with allies can accomplish anything she sets her mind to. Therefore, I've always managed to get myself out of such pickles without breaking the Ten Commandments...well, other than telling a few falsehoods from time to time. And I've managed to do so *without* possessing any special gifts."

"You believe my eidetic memory is a gift?" She balled her fists. "My entire life, people have been misusing me because of my *gift*. I'd give it away in a heartbeat."

"At times, everyone who has a special gift or talent is tempted to blame it for their hardships, when in fact, it is more than likely the person's own decisions that created the situation."

"Bull..."

Margaret raised her eyebrows. "I'm not saying evil-hearted people won't try to take advantage of you from time to time. I'm merely pointing out that you can choose whether or not to submit to their will."

Before Summer could object, she caught a glimpse of Andy's apparition, looking even more transparent than he had before. An instant later, the fog engulfed her, but this time, the clouds were thinner. After only a few seconds, the mist disappeared altogether, and she found herself standing at the young Lieutenant's side in a field of scrub grass. Summer closed her eyes as a strong wave of nausea passed over her. She recalled what Margaret had told her about the cloud buffer, and how it made the transition between the world of the living and the spirit realm a less jarring experience.

"Okay, Margaret... you made your point," Summer silently conceded. *"If I feel like this after traveling through a thin mist, I don't ever want to know what it would be like to go through with no cloud buffer at all."*

"These two buildings used to house the steam generator and supplies, back when the hotel made its own electricity."

Recognizing Violet's voice, Summer opened her eyes and was surprised to discover that she and Andy had crossed the field and were now standing with Violet in the shadow of a large, white building. Andy used one of the keys Col. Huck had given him to remove a padlock and chain that held the doors closed.

"After the steam generator was removed," Violet continued, "they used this building to store excess furniture and supplies. The hotel's chandeliers and other wonderful trimmings will be safe and sound stored in here."

Andy dropped the thick chain to the ground and swung the double doors open. The arched building resembled a barn, except there were remnants of machinery scattered about, in place of stalls.

Violet pointed to a small stack of cardboard boxes near one corner. "Those are the vases and other equipment my pop uses when he works here. I figure as long as we stack boxes away from the walls and tend the rat traps, everything we store in here should keep just fine."

"Rat traps?"

Before the words were out of Andy's mouth, Summer knew exactly how the spirit felt about rats, and why. They had been a constant, unwelcome companion during the long months when he and his family had taken shelter in Mr. Beacon's barn, back home in West Virginia. Just before his father died, Andy had caught a rat chewing on one of the gravely ill man's toes. The memory of his father's pitiful moans still rang in Andy's ears. Summer drew in a sharp breath but somehow, she managed to remain quiet.

"Mostly just little fruit rats," Violet explained, holding her thumb and forefinger about six inches apart to demonstrate their size. "As long as you keep your soldiers from bringing food and water out here while they're standing guard, pests shouldn't pose much of a problem."

Andy cast a nervous glance around the dimly-lit building. "How do you know your way around this place so well? I thought you just came here to help your father put flowers in vases."

"This was my playground when I was a kid," Violet explained. "During the winter season, my father spent most of the day here. After school, we'd wait for him to finish his work, so we could hitch a ride home in his truck. Daisy and Iris liked to make friends with the rich kids who stayed here with their parents, but I preferred to wander around the grounds on my own."

"This place is usually locked up all summer, right?" Andy asked.

"Yep. This will be the first time it's ever been open during the summer...at least, officially," she said with a coy smile.

"Officially?"

"Some of us local kids knew how to get inside the hotel. We used to run through the halls and play hide and seek in the basement. Whenever I wanted to be alone or I got annoyed with my sisters, I'd come out here."

Andy raised his hand, which still held the padlock. "How did you get in?"

"The doors were locked, but no one ever gave a second thought to the coal chute." Violet grinned and pointed toward a dark corner of the large building. "It was easy for me to come and go with no one being the wiser."

Andy chuckled. "I'll have to remember that." He glanced around the large, mostly empty space. "What did you do in here all by yourself?"

"I'd usually curl up on an old couch to read or do my schoolwork." Violet smiled at his quizzical expression. "I know. Not very exciting. I guess I've always been a strange little duck."

They exited the storage room and Andy chained the doors again before escorting Violet back to the kitchen to continue crating the Belleview Biltmore's fine china. Afterward, Andy decided to walk over to Sunset Cottage, one of twelve large cottages dotting the perimeter of the hotel. "I sure hope Colonel Huck will consider changing my orders," he muttered.

$$\sim$$

"They call this a cottage?" Andy wondered with awe, as he approached the white, two-story building. *"It's even bigger than the mine supervisor's house, back home."*

Summer had read about the twelve cottages on the hotel's property. The green-shingled roof and white siding on the 3,000-square-foot Sunset Cottage matched the hotel, but it's architectural features were even more ornate. Arches formed a scalloped pattern at the outer edge of a wide veranda that wrapped all the way around the structure.

Hoping he was following proper protocols, Andy hesitated and then tapped lightly on the door.

An attractive woman answered the door, wearing a blue plaid dress, hemmed just below her knees. A wide belt wrapped around her narrow waist, and over each ear, a part of her curly, shoulder-length brown hair was fashioned into a victory roll. She smiled at the sight of Andy's worried frown. "You must be looking for my husband, Colonel Huck."

Andy managed a nod. "Yes, ma'am. Can you tell him Second Lieutenant Turner would like to meet with him please?"

The woman opened the door and took a step back, still smiling. "Come on in, Lieutenant. I'll show you to his office."

Andy gulped, wiped his shoes on the mat, palmed his garrison cap, and then stepped inside. With its polished pine floors, crystal chandeliers, elegant woven carpets and Victorian furnishings, the interior of the cottage looked like a miniature replica of the hotel. Across from the front parlor was a library, which Col. Huck had commandeered to serve as his office.

"Tim, darling," Mrs. Huck said, "I believe this young man is looking for you."

Andy stepped inside and drew himself to attention.

"Thank you, Mary." He smiled at his wife and then turned to Andy. "I was wondering how long it would take you to hunt me down. Have a seat, Turner."

"Can I bring you gentlemen some ice tea?" Mary asked.

"I guess you had better, dear," Col. Huck said. "This soldier looks like he's close to fainting dead away." He gave his wife a good-natured wink as she turned toward the kitchen.

Andy flushed, embarrassed to realize he had licked his dry lips at mention of iced tea, and sank into one of the two leather arm chairs that faced Col. Huck's massive mahogany desk.

"Sorry to bother you, sir, but this is my first assignment and..."

"And you're mighty confused. It's understandable." Col. Huck locked his fingers behind his head and leaned back in his chair. "First off, you need to know that this is only a temporary assignment for me," he explained. "To win this war, the United States needs more soldiers than ever before, so the Army is requisitioning large hotels in coastal towns from Florida to California to house all those soldiers. My job is to turn those hotels into stations, fit to house and train recruits. Once that part's done, I turn the post over to another officer, who will assume the task of training thousands of young men to fight – or in this case, train thousands of fighter pilots."

Andy nodded, still confused about his role in the effort.

When his wife returned with the iced tea, Col. Huck leaned forward and took the glass she offered. "Thank you, dear," he said.

She handed the other glass to Andy, smiled at his mumbled thanks, and then exited, closing the door behind her.

Andy wanted to guzzle the cool drink down in one swallow, but to be polite, he restrained himself. After downing half the sweet tea, he lowered his glass, and concentrated on what the Colonel was saying.

"I usually spend about ninety days at each location, but because this hotel is so damned enormous, this assignment will take twice that long," he said.

"You mean we won't be training flight crews for another six months?" Andy asked, trying not to let his dismay show.

"That's right, Turner." Col. Huck rubbed his forehead. "Look, son, I know you're all jazzed up and full of piss and vinegar – ready to fight. And I know you didn't sign up to oversee a squad of painters and movers." He picked up a roster and handed it to Andy. "But that's the job that needs doing right now. At the first of the year, three more lieutenants will be here to help get this place shipshape, but for now, my staff consists of you and thirty air cadets. And every one of those cadets is just as excited about this assignment as you are. I need you to get them organized and keep them moving forward until the other officers arrive to help."

"Sir, I grew up in a miner's shack and then I lived for a time in a barn, sleeping right next to the milking stalls. I flew a crop duster. Then I joined the Army. They sent me to pilot training and then they shipped me here. I don't know one single thing about packing up finery or paintings or – well, any of this stuff."

Condensation began dripping down the side of the glass and over his fingers, but Andy barely felt it.

"Then I suggest you get busy figuring out which cadets do know how to do some of those things and put them in charge of teaching the others. And don't give 'em a chance to figure out you're scared shitless."

Andy started to protest, but the Colonel stopped him with a wave of his hand. "Go on now – I need to meet with the civilians we've hired to cook and whatnot, and I need to check on a shipment of bunks I've ordered. I'll expect a report on your progress every evening, an hour before sunset. The missus likes me to sit on the porch with her to watch the sun go down and I try not to disappoint her." He reached for the heavy, black phone on his desk – a clear indication that their meeting was over.

Andy jumped to his feet and started to salute before he realized he was still holding a half-empty glass of iced tea. Just before the glass hit his forehead, he managed to shift it into his opposite hand and raise his wet fingers in a salute.

"Relax, Turner." Col. Huck's lips curled into a half-smile. "No need to salute indoors. And you best finish that iced tea. If you don't, Mary will fret all evening that you didn't like it."

As Andy lifted the glass to his lips, Summer was distracted by a strange beeping sound. When she turned toward the noise, she fell backward into the mist and woke thrashing in her bed. She bolted to a sitting position before she realized the beeping was coming from her alarm clock. She slammed her open palm against the top of the clock to shut it off, her heart still racing from the fall.

"Oh, man," she moaned, "I'm supposed to meet Dana in the Starlight Ballroom first thing this morning."

Putting thoughts of Andy out of her mind, she raced for the shower. Twenty minutes later, she opened the door to the hallway, still frustrated that she still hadn't figured out a way to gain access to Robert's computer.

Summer paused in the hallway, her hand resting on the glass doorknob, and glanced back at the small round table in the parlor, thinking about what Margaret said about making better choices. *"It's not like I want to do any of this,"* she told herself.

An odd sensation suddenly tingled through her fingers and raced up her arm. She yanked her hand from the doorknob and stared as the door closed itself. *"What the hell?"*

Stunned, Summer rubbed her hands together, staring at the door, trying to convince herself that she had imagined the sensation of other hands – hundreds – perhaps thousands of them – turning that same doorknob for more than a century and stepping out into this hallway. In that same instant, she had heard a cacophony of echoes from past generations – wealthy travelers chatting about the warm Florida winters, as well as workers who busied themselves with hotel operations and tried to oblige every whim of its guests.

"This is crazy!" She walked on unsteady legs to the elevator and pushed the call button, still feeling as though she was surrounded by visitors from the past. As the doors slid apart, she caught a momentary glimpse of an elderly black man, wearing a doorman's uniform, pulling open a steel mesh door – the kind used in old-fashioned elevators. She blinked and the image was gone.

"Going down?" asked the only person in the elevator – a man wearing a normal, modern business suit.

Summer managed a weak, "Yes," as she stepped inside.

When they reached the first floor, she moved down the Promenade in a daze, continuing to sense the history of the hotel permeating from its walls, almost as if its past was a tangible thing. She avoided looking at the huge, framed photographs that lined the walls, for fear the people in the scenes might come to life before her eyes. At the entrance foyer to the Starlight Ballroom, she stopped next to the grand fireplace and gazed into the enormous gilt-framed mirror hanging above the carved oak mantle.

"Okay, Margaret, you win." Summer had no doubt the powerful spirit was responsible for her mystical experience. *"I'll try to keep Gordo from destroying this magical place."* She took a deep breath and straightened her shoulders. *"Now, get out of my head!"*

Forcing a smile, Summer strode into the ballroom, spotted Dana, and raised her hand to wave. Then she froze; her knees turning to jelly. Time moved in slow motion. Her hand drifted down to her side as her mouth tried in vain to form words. Dana was standing in the middle of the ballroom, carrying on a lively conversation with *Justin*. Unharmed, grinning, perfect *Justin*. The other half of her whole from the moment of their birth.

Flooded with more emotions than she could process – relief, confusion, love, happiness, worry, nervousness – she continued to watch slack-jawed, as Justin flirted openly with Dana, until one question filled her thoughts:

"What exactly is Gordo forcing him do?"

Chapter Fourteen

Summer's stomach churned as she fought the urge to run to Justin. To hug him. To shake him. To demand an explanation. Ever since The Broker had called to let her know Justin had violated the terms of Gordo's deal by trying to escape, she had been worried about his new role in the operation.

"Has Justin been sent to seduce Dana?" Summer wondered. She knew that would be a smart move on Gordo's part. Her brother might be able to get information out of Dana that she had failed to obtain or, at the very least, keep the pregnant woman distracted throughout the heist. And if things went sideways, Gordo would probably set Justin up to take the fall. Summer tried, but couldn't visualize an outcome where Dana or Justin didn't get hurt – or worse.

"Hey," Justin called out as he caught sight of his sister in the wide doorway. He gave her a half-wave, half-salute. "See?" he turned to grin at Dana. "I told you she'd be shocked." He raised his voice so that Summer could hear what he was saying. "When we were *five*, I accidentally set our kitchen on fire and when we were *eleven*, I accepted a dare to eat a bug. She had that same look on her face both times!"

Summer's mind immediately deciphered his coded message.
5:Back up my story; 11: Don't worry; I've got this.

She narrowed her eyes, certain his high level of confidence wasn't warranted. "You were *nine* when you set that fire and *fourteen* when you ate the bug," she answered, knowing he would understand.

9: I need to talk to you in private; 14: The plan isn't going well

"And on our *twentieth* birthday," she added, "you promised you wouldn't keep showing up on my doorstep, unannounced."

20: The person next to you is an innocent

Justin cocked his head, the glint of curiosity in his eyes. "For *one* thing, this isn't your doorstep. And *one* more thing, I believe I said I'd stop popping in on you by the time we're *fifty.*

1: I love you. And he said it twice. *50: Never let a mark get under your skin.*

Summer closed the distance between them, her joy at seeing her brother outweighing all other concerns for the moment. "Fifty is too late." All she could do was hope that he would understand. Although she had tried not to care about Dana, she felt an overwhelming urge to protect her.

Justin held out his arms and enveloped her in a bear hug, lifting her off her feet and swinging her in a circle. Then he put her down and stepped back. "You look great! I thought for sure somebody would spoil my surprise and tell you I was coming."

"Wait. I thought her trip was a last minute, spur of the moment thing," Dana said, looking back and forth between Summer and Justin. "How did you know she'd be here?"

"Watch this," Justin said. He placed his fingertips on either side of his head in mock concentration and closed his eyes. "Summer can read my mind. It's a twin thing. I just have to think of the name and she'll say it. She's done it dozens of times before."

12/Dozen: You take the lead.

"Not much of a mystery," Summer said. She rolled her eyes. "You sat next to Aunt May during my commencement exercises at the SAIC. You left before the ceremony was over, but I'm guessing, not before she told you she planned to surprise me with an airplane ticket and that my flight would leave early the next day."

"Busted!" Justin said, continuing to weave their story, Mad Libs style. "I thought I'd fly down to surprise you, but just as I arrived, I happened to overhear Maxwell freaking out about how his exhibit installation specialist broke his arm. He was worried he couldn't find a skilled replacement on such short notice, and well, you know, I've been setting up art shows all around Chicago…"

"So you volunteered to take his place?" Summer wondered whether the man had been paid to say he broke his arm, or if Gordo's thugs had decided to make sure that Maxwell really *did* need a replacement.

"You got it!" Justin gave her a sad, puppy dog look. "Of course, that means that we won't get to spend as much time together as I hoped, but I figured you'd understand. I couldn't leave Maxwell hanging in the breeze. And besides, just before you came in, this young lady told me you managed to land an intern gig with one of the big-wigs running this show. Very impressive!" He glanced around and then lowered his voice. "Hey, do you think your boss would notice if you snuck out for an early lunch?"

"Um – you're talking to my boss. Ms. Big-Wig, in the flesh." Summer smiled, going along with Justin's ruse. She was certain Gordo had given him the lowdown on all the players, including Dana.

As she expected, Justin pretended to be embarrassed. "Wow, sorry... you didn't look...I mean, when I saw you in here, I thought you were another intern. I mean, you're so *young* and *pretty*. None of *my* bosses has ever looked as good as you, that's for sure! I mean, damn!"

Summer let him ramble on until she was certain his flattery had endeared him in Dana's eyes. Then she gave her head a slow shake and turned to Dana, smiling. "Enough already! Let's start over, shall we? Dana Cooper, I'd like you to meet my brother, Justin Tyme, your newest employee."

Dana giggled. "No way. Your parents named you Summer Tyme and Justin Tyme? They must have a good sense of humor."

Justin shot a meaningful glance at Summer. She returned an almost imperceptible shake of her head, indicating that the topic of parents had never come up.

He surprised Summer by wrinkling his nose. "I guess that's one possibility. Unfortunately, they bailed on us before we were old enough to ask."

"Oh, you poor things," Dana murmured, resting a protective hand against her belly bulge. "I'm so sorry..."

"No worries," Justin continued. "We managed to stick together and watch each other's backs. That was the most important thing."

Summer eyed her brother. He was telling Dana the truth, more or less – his way of showing her respect. *"He must have taken a liking to Dana, just like I did."*

"Besides," Justin continued, lightening the mood. "I'm pretty sure they left because of her, not me." He jabbed a thumb in Summer's direction and grinned. "She was always a troublemaker. As for me, I was born with a halo."

"Yeah, right…" Summer retorted. She wrinkled her nose at Justin and then chuckled.

"OMG!" Dana sputtered. "Your brown eyes have the same flecks of gold and your facial expressions are exactly the same! And so is your hair color. Are you sure you're not *identical* twins?"

Justin flexed his muscles and then pointed a forefinger in the general direction of his crotch. He wasn't a bodybuilder, but he had done enough construction work to develop a strong, lean body. "Yep, I'm *damn* sure we're not identical," he teased.

Dana scrunched her face into a grimace and smacked her forehead. "Oh my God! I can't believe I said that! You must think I'm dumb as a stump."

"Actually, I think you're kind of cute, boss lady," he replied. He tapped the tip of Dana's nose with his forefinger and smiled.

Summer cleared her throat, feeling oddly voyeuristic and left out. "Geez, Justin, you've been here for less than sixty-three minutes, and you're already messing up our schedule. Dana and I have at least seventy-one things to get done this morning. Why don't you and I catch up over lunch?"

63: Stop grandstanding; 71: Play it cool till we get a chance to talk

"Sounds good, and for the record," Justin shot back. "I've been here for *eighty-seven* minutes. But you're right – I'd better get back to Maxwell. He probably thought of at least eleven more things he wants done before lunch, and I haven't finished one thing yet." He grinned. "Then again, I *am* one of those amazing guys who can do the job of something like forty-eight *regular* men."

87: Quit acting so bossy; 11: Don't worry, I've/we've got this; 1: I love you; 48: The Tyme Twins can't be stopped

Summer raised her eyebrows and then smiled. "Of course! *How* in the *world* did I forget that you can do the job of *forty-eight* regular men?" She bumped Dana with her elbow. "You and I better be really careful where we walk in here. It's getting *awfully* deep."

"Now, now," Justin said with a good-natured grin. "Hey, I've got a great idea. Why don't we all go out to dinner together? It'll give me a chance to ease Robert's mind – let him see that I know what I'm doing."

Summer glared at her twin before twisting her face into a smile for Dana's benefit. *"Dinner with our marks? Have you lost your mind?"*

Chapter Fifteen

"I don't know why you went and got all pissy, Summer," Justin said, as he slid into the booth across from her at Jazzy's BBQ. "You told me to take the lead and I did."

"I wouldn't have, if I'd known you were going to invite Dana and Robert to dinner! Christ, Justin, we need some time alone to figure out how we're going to get out of this mess alive."

"You worry too much. We've been stuck in the middle of crap storms lots of times before and we always manage to come out smelling like roses."

"This time's different." Summer bit her lip. "You don't know these people like I do. I crossed them before, remember? They're sadistic monsters."

"You said they made you work off your debt and then you had to leave town." Justin smiled at the waitress who was walking toward their table and lowered his voice. "Doesn't sound too bad to me. We help them pull off this job and I have to agree to stay out of Vegas, too. No big deal."

"Sorry, but that's *not* how this is going to play out." Summer unfolded her napkin, avoiding Justin's gaze. "Gordo hates my guts. He wants me gone – permanently. And he's going to do his best to make it happen."

Justin didn't respond because the waitress had arrived with menus. He glanced at the menu cover and then at the young girl's nametag. "Thanks, Michelle. Listen. We're just visiting the area, so... what does the staff at Jazzy's BBQ recommend?"

"Everything's great, but our barbequed ribs are our most popular item," Michelle answered as she placed two glasses of ice water on their table. "Everybody loves our collard greens, too."

Justin turned to Summer. "Ribs sound good?"

"Not for lunch," she said. "I'll just have a house salad with ranch dressing."

"Seriously?" Justin pretended shock. "No barbeque?"

Summer shrugged. "We have a dinner date, *remember*?"

"Yeah, yeah." He rolled his eyes and switched to an exaggerated southern drawl. "But that ain't gonna stop me none! I'll take a big ole' platter of them ribs, collards and mac n' cheeeese, pleeease."

Michelle granted him an indulgent smile as she scribbled down the order.

Summer glanced at the waitress. "Please excuse my idiot brother. He likes to pretend he's a comedian."

"I understand." Michelle gave her a wink. "I have brothers, too."

Justin shook his forefinger at the two women. "Hey, now – I'm just trying to get my overly serious sister to lighten up. But it looks like I need to bring out the big guns, so please bring us a bottle of your house zinfandel, Michelle." When the chuckling waitress retreated to the kitchen, he returned his attention to Summer. "Maybe now would be a good time to tell me the truth about your last run-in with these guys."

"Yeah." Summer nodded. "I didn't tell you before because I figured the less you knew about it, the safer you'd be. But now I think the opposite is true." She took a few sips of water. "The most important thing you need to know about Gordo is that he's vindictive as hell. He never forgives anybody who crosses him. The only thing that's kept him from killing me already is his fear of The Broker."

Justin leaned forward. "What makes you think he wants you dead?"

"You remember the con I used to run? The one I called *Camp Sucker*?"

"Vaguely. You had a couple of guys working with you, right?"

"Dave and Edward." Summer closed her eyes to the painful gush of memories flooding her brain. "It was a marriage counseling scam.

It was pretty profitable, so we traveled around having fun until funds ran low and then we'd run another game."

"Until..." Justin prompted.

"Until we decided to run our game in Vegas." Summer gulped as she continued to dredge up long-buried memories. "Normally, I phished the internet for a few rich, insecure trophy wives, and then *Pastor* Dave and his assistant, *Deacon* Edward, arranged a chance encounter with each of the women. They'd sell them on *Camp Unity* – a wilderness retreat, aimed at saving troubled marriages in just one weekend. Dave had a brilliant pitch about the camp's amazing success record. Almost every woman we targeted wanted to attend."

"So, as soon as the desperate housewives paid for camp happy matrimony, you guys skipped town?"

"I wish, but no. After Dave gained their trust, he told them there was a last-minute cancellation for the camp session that was scheduled to take place that weekend. Since they were joining at the last minute, he'd insist they pay cash. Most trophy wives are given well-funded personal shopping accounts, so Dave also convinced them to keep the retreat a surprise from their husbands."

"Surprise marriage counseling camp?" Justin shook his head. "Didn't that make the women suspicious?"

"Not really. Dave would tell them that all husbands tended to resist the *idea* of camp, but wound up loving the *experience*. He gave each wife some GHB to slip into her husband's drink before bedtime."

"GHB – the date rape drug?"

"Yep – Liquid Ecstasy. Once the husband was knocked out, Dave and Edward collected the cash, and then loaded the sleeping men into wheelchairs and rolled them into a transport van. Then, on the way out of town, they offered the wives glasses of champagne to kick off the weekend.

"Let me guess," Justin said, crossing his arms over his chest. "Their drinks were *also* spiked with GHB."

Summer nodded.

"And then you parked the van and took off with the keys?"

"Sort of. We dropped them off in a remote area, next to a campfire. We always wrapped each couple in a blanket and left them a map, snacks and water, but no phones or electronic devices. We were long gone by the time they figured out what happened and found their way back to civilization."

"So what went wrong in Vegas?"

"I hacked into the bank account of a woman who was desperate to save her marriage. She was so dumb, she didn't even know there was over a million dollars in her account. Anyway, Dave convinced her to pay him $500,000 dollars, in exchange for holding a private camp session for her and her husband."

"Score!" Justin exclaimed, holding his forearms up to represent football goalposts. When she didn't smile, he refolded them across his chest. "So, why wasn't that a good thing?"

"It turned out that her husband laundered money for the mob. Whenever money was in transit, he stashed it in her account for a few days, knowing she never checked the balance." Summer took another drink of water. "We were skiing in Sundance, Utah when a couple of Gordo's goons caught up with us. Dave managed to get away, but they tied me and Edward up, stuffed ball gags into our mouths, and blindfolded us. Then they shoved us into the back of Edward's cargo van and drove us into the desert. When the van stopped, they dragged Edward out. I could hear him screaming, but there was nothing I could do." Tears stung her eyes. "When it finally got quiet, I knew he was dead."

"Jesus, Summer, how did you get away?"

"I didn't. They stuffed me into the trunk of a black Caddy and drove me to Gordo's ranch, just outside of Vegas. I was in pretty rough shape by the time they tied me to a chair in the barn. Then, the worst of his goons started acting all nice and shit. He took off my blindfold, pulled out my gag, and gave me a drink of water, while the other guy set up a folding table next to me."

Justin stared at her without making a sound.

"I was going crazy," Summer continued. "You know – wondering what they were going to do to me. But they just walked out and closed the door – left me tied up out there, all alone. It was getting dark, so it took me a few minutes to figure out what they had dumped all over the table. At first, I thought it was a pile of raw meat, but then I realized it was Edward's fingers... his hands, his feet, eyes... teeth..." She closed her eyes. "The barn was so isolated, I guess they weren't worried about anyone hearing my screams."

"Good God, Summer. What... how..."

"I figured they were going to do the same thing to me that they had done to Edward – maybe worse. I kept wondering how much pain he felt before he died. I thought about it all night long. The next morning, Gordo came in and gave me a choice – to work for him or take a ride back out to the desert."

All color had drained from Justin's face. "Doing what kind of work?"

"Mostly computer hacking – a few cons. They didn't know about my memory, and I managed to keep it a secret. I became Gordo's golden goose, which was good, in a way. His goons weren't allowed to touch me because Gordo was worried I wouldn't be able to concentrate on my work if I was getting raped all the time. I started creating files and hiding evidence against Gordo in every computer system I hacked. Eventually, I collected enough evidence to ensure he and his cohorts would all go to jail for life. Then, I hired The Broker to negotiate a deal for my freedom."

Justin took her hand and squeezed it. "Christ – the whole year that I was bouncing around Europe, having a great time, you were..."

"Paying the price for my own screw-up." Summer interrupted, pulling her hand back. "I knew there was something wrong about that bimbo having so much cash in her bank account, but I got greedy." Summer glanced up and watched as the hostess seated another couple, several tables away. "Listen, Justin," she said, lowering her voice even further, "They usually kept me and a few of their prostitutes locked up in a shabby house with no Internet access, and Gordo was constantly threatening to sell me or have me killed. The thought of you being out there having wild adventures was the only thing that kept me going sometimes."

"Did you ever hear from Dave?"

Summer gave her head a single shake. "Dave turned himself in to the police, hoping to confess in exchange for protection, but he was *accidentally* put into the general prison population before meeting with the DA. They found him hanged in his cell, after having been tortured, beaten and raped."

Justin gasped. "This Gordo creep has that kind of reach?"

"Yes, he does. Listen, Justin – I didn't want to tell you any of this, but you need to know what kind of monster we're dealing with."

"A monster you escaped from." Justin covered his eyes with his open palms and groaned. "Until I messed up and gave him an excuse to drag you back."

"It's not your fault, Justin. You didn't know. Besides, Gordo is like a dog with a bone. I knew he'd never give up until he had me back in his stable or put me in the ground."

When Michelle suddenly appeared at the table with their wine and food order, the twins slipped on cheerful expressions that were so convincing, anyone would think they had been sharing a funny story rather than discussing a living nightmare.

"Sorry it took so long," Michelle said as she pulled the cork from a bottle of Beringer. She filled their wine glasses and set the open bottle in the middle of the table before serving Summer's salad. When she set a platter of ribs in front of Justin, he drew back, barely managing to hide his revulsion.

"I'm sorry," he said, staring at the ribs, slathered in barbeque sauce. "But I think Summer had the right idea. I should have gotten a salad."

Michelle hesitated, obviously unsure whether to leave the dish or take it away.

"Don't be a goof," Summer said, raising a warning eyebrow at Justin. She reached across the table and helped herself to a rib. "You'd never survive on just a salad and these look delicious."

Justin gave the waitress a broad smile. "I'm kidding! Geez, you guys sure are gullible."

Michelle frowned. "Very funny. Now, seriously, can I bring you anything else?"

"Not a thing," Summer assured her. "Thanks."

After the waitress left, Summer took a bite of the barbeque. "These ribs are excellent, Justin. Eat."

Justin eyed his plate and took a tentative bite of mac n' cheese. "What exactly are you supposed to do to pay off my debt, Summer?"

"Well, now that Gordo knows I have an eidetic memory, I'm supposed to get close to Robert, hack his computer and memorize his clients' bank account information. But that's not all." Summer grimaced. "During the auction, they're going to set fire to the hotel. They figure it will go up like a tinderbox and panic the crowd, providing a distraction while they steal the painting – and whatever else they can get their hands on."

"Damn shame to burn the place down," Justin said. "But none of that sounds too hard."

"It might not *sound* hard, but so far, I haven't been able to get anywhere near Robert's computer and I just promised Margaret I'd do whatever I can to save the hotel. And on top of that, now you're involved in the scam, too. By the way, I don't know what you're planning, but I saw you flirting with Dana. You need to know that she's a sweetheart, who doesn't deserve another hit and run guy in her life."

"I'm not planning on hurting Dana. I like her. And who the hell is Margaret?"

"She's a spirit who haunts the Belleview Biltmore."

"A ghost? And, what... she just appeared to you and asked you to save the hotel?"

This was Summer's favorite thing about Justin. There was no judgement or doubt in his voice. No indication that he thought she might be hallucinating. He simply accepted whatever she told him as fact. He listened, drank wine, and gnawed his way through the rack of tender ribs, while she nibbled on her salad and told him everything she had experienced in the spirit realm.

Chapter Sixteen

Although it had been a relief to talk everything over with Justin at lunch, they hadn't been able to resolve any of the issues that weighed heavily on Summer's mind. Upon returning to the Belleview Biltmore, the twins spent the remainder of the afternoon "in character." Justin, as Maxwell's installation specialist, began assembling display cases and made preparations to install additional security measures, while Summer and Dana reviewed authentication documents for more than five dozen pieces of antique jewelry that had arrived for the show.

"Is Justin, you know...attached or anything?" Dana asked, after securing the last of the jewelry in the hotel's vault.

Summer eyed her, feigning surprise. "So it wasn't my imagination – you two *were* flirting earlier!"

"We were not," Dana protested, even though her pink cheeks said otherwise.

Summer offered an exaggerated eye roll in response. "Sure... whatever."

"It's just that, well, he's nice and Junior here didn't seem to freak him out." Dana patted her belly. "The minute most guys find out I'm single and pregnant, they start acting as though I have leprosy. It's like they're worried I'm on the hunt for a baby daddy or something." She sighed and turned her mahogany brown eyes toward the floor. "I'm not, you know – looking...I'm just lonely."

Summer used the tips of her fingers to lift the girl's chin back up.

"There's nothing wrong with flirting, Dana...or even continuing to look for a more serious relationship, for that matter. Becoming a mother doesn't mean you stop being your own person." A grin suddenly split through her serious expression. "I just think you can do a lot better than my dumb brother. You don't know him like I do. He can be a real pain in the butt."

Both women chuckled.

"If we're all done here, I guess we'd better go back to our rooms and get gussied up for dinner," Summer teased. "I mean, we don't want you to be late for your *first date.*"

Dana's eyes widened and she gave Summer a light slap on her arm. "Stop that *right* now," she insisted. "It's not a date. And *promise* you won't tell Justin I like him!"

"You know, he uses more hair products than I do," Summer continued. "And, oh yeah, just wait until you see him eat. It's like he was raised by wolves."

They laughed again.

"Come on," Dana pleaded, crooking her little finger. "Girlfriend pinky promise that you won't say anything!"

Not for the first time, Summer felt a stab in her heart. Her lifestyle didn't permit her the luxury of having close friends. No matter how she felt about Dana, there was no getting around the fact that the sweet, pregnant woman would be hurt, disappointed, angry, and perhaps even humiliated when the con was discovered.

Summer pasted on a smile. "I promise," she said, knowing these sacred words meant nothing in her world.

Stifling a yawn and struggling to keep her heavy eyelids open, Summer sat on the edge of her four-poster bed, resisting the urge to lay down for a quick nap. She pointed her toes and slipped her feet through the legs of her snug-fitting white slacks, ignoring another yawn. "Sorry, Margaret," she said, recognizing the insistent pull of the spirit realm, "you guys are going to have to wait until after dinner." She stood, yanked her slacks up, and then sucked in her breath to close the zipper. "And by the way, I want to lay my cards out on the table here, so to speak. I won't help you save the hotel if doing so involves me or Justin joining you in the spirit realm. But I am trying to think of a way..." Her voice trailed off.

"Who am I kidding?" she thought. *"Gordo knows The Broker will kill me and Justin if we don't honor the deal he negotiated between us, so there's no incentive for him to change his plan."* Summer continued to contemplate the situation, while pulling a clingy, sleeveless turquoise blouse over her head. *"Besides, Gordo hates my guts. If he found out that I want to save the hotel, he'd probably make me light the fire myself. Hell, even if I help him pull off his scam without a hitch, he'll probably keep looking for an excuse to end me."*

She checked her makeup, wishing for the umpteenth time that she was just a normal girl, going out to dinner with friends rather than a con artist with a freakish eidetic memory. She repeated her personal mantra, "It is what it is, and you are who you are," and then turned away from the mirror. She sighed, slipped on a pair of strappy, high-heeled sandals, and left her room.

Her straight blonde hair, parted in the middle, swung softly around her shoulders as she stepped off the elevator and into the Promenade. She absently brushed it back, her thoughts still spinning in circles. *"If the hotel burns down, what will become of Margaret, Andy, and the rest of the spirits that haunt this place?"* She bit her lip. *"Maybe I can come up with a better way to pull off this heist – one that doesn't require the use of fire."*

As she approached the Terrace Café, Summer cleared her mind and glanced around the restaurant, her nerves on edge. She spotted Justin and Dana, sitting next to one another at a table. Their heads were closer together than she would have expected them to be, and they were smiling as if sharing a private joke.

"Oh, God, what's Justin thinking? I told him not to flirt with her anymore. This is going to be a disaster." Just then, she heard Robert clear his throat right behind her. She spun around, disconcerted, a tiny squeal escaping before she regained her wits.

"Sorry," Robert said. "That was me attempting *not* to startle you."

"Good job."

"Yeah, but it's the thought that counts, right?"

When he pushed his glasses up, Summer noticed uncertainty in his clear blue eyes for the first time.

"And I really am sorry."

"Don't be silly. I probably would've done the same thing," she said.

"Yeah – and it would have been a lot more embarrassing if *I* had yelped like that." His mouth twisted into a half-smile.

"Most definitely," Summer agreed, nodding her head with mock seriousness. She pointed in the direction of their table. "Dana and Justin are already here."

Robert glanced over to the couple, and then surprised Summer by taking her arm, escorting her to the table, and pulling a chair out for her. When Dana saw Robert approaching, she sat back and blushed like a teenager caught kissing on the couch.

Unabashed, Justin looked up and grinned. "Well, don't you two look nice," he said. "Sorry we didn't wait for you to get seated. I wanted to get Dana off her feet."

"Thanks," Summer said, shooting a warning glare at her brother. "I'm surprised you're here already. I thought I was twenty-five minutes early."

25: Be Careful

Gold sparks flashed in Justin's eyes, signaling his annoyance. He glanced at his watch. "You're way off. Technically," he said with a smirk, "you're not early. You're actually somewhere between four and eight minutes *late* – but who cares?"

Summer narrowed her eyes as her mind instantly translated his message.

4: Mind your own business; 8: I'm happy with this person.

"You're right," she said, keeping her voice light. "I guess I was having a flashback. Remember when we were living with that foster family – the *Gordons* – and Mr. Gordon always threatened to *kill* us? He hated when we were late for supper. Sometimes I feel like he's still watching my every move – ready to kill us if we mess up."

"Wow," Dana said, "he sounds awful." She leaned toward Justin. "I've heard terrible things about some foster homes out there, but I've never met anyone who actually *lived* in one."

"It got bad sometimes," Justin admitted. "Guys like Mr. Gordon are the reason I decided to start living in the moment. I mean, if you're always worried that every minute might be your last, you can't ever *enjoy* life, you know?"

"Dammit, that's the exact attitude that got us into this mess," Summer thought. She picked up her menu and hid behind it, swallowing her anger.

"Oh, by the way – I ordered drinks," Justin said as the waiter arrived with three martinis and a lemonade.

Summer peeked around the menu and watched as Justin took Dana's lemonade from the short, stocky man and handed it to her as if she were a princess. Dana's emotions were an open book. The elfin woman beamed at Justin, obviously thrilled with his attentiveness and the respect he demonstrated for her pregnant condition.

Summer's heart melted, watching them evolve into a couple before her eyes. How could she object to anything so sweet? She picked up her martini, envying her twin's optimism. As she raised her glass to her lips, she noticed the same envious look flash across Robert's face.

"I saw that," she thought. *"You're almost as good at hiding your emotions as I am, but not quite. Then again, I've probably had more practice."*

Then she remembered why she wore armor on her emotions. Gordo's plans would undoubtedly crush this budding romance. *"Please, Margaret,"* she prayed silently, *"If you help me stop Gordo from hurting them, I swear I'll do everything I can to stop him from destroying your home."* She hoped Margaret could hear her prayers. She was certain God never had.

"Who knows?" Robert said, obviously uncomfortable with the mounting silence at the table. "Maybe the Gordons were just trying to keep you safe. I'll bet Dana told you I was a tyrant while she and Emma were growing up." He turned to Summer. "The truth is, all I did was try to warn them about dangerous people and situations. They never listened, so I had to repeat myself a lot, but it was for their own good."

"Ha!" Dana cried. "Seriously, you guys, he might not have been a *brutal* tyrant, but he was *unbelievably* old fashioned. Once, when

Emma and I wanted to go to a frat party, he threatened to slap us into chastity belts and lock us in our rooms until we were thirty! No kidding. He acts so old, Junior will probably want to call him *Grandpa* instead of Uncle."

"Very funny," Robert said. "And in case you've forgotten, you two were the prettiest girls on campus, and that frat was a pigsty full of horny wolves." He shook his head. "And since you decided to attend college out of state, I had to fill in for your parents *and* your brothers *and* your sisters. *Jesus.* I'm lucky my hair didn't turn gray from watching out for you guys."

"Oh, poor Bobby." Dana giggled. "Forced to hang out with us and all of our girlfriends at college – it must've been *so* hard on you."

Robert grinned. "Okay – maybe it wasn't *all* bad. But just you wait – when Junior gets to be a hand full and you start freaking out about everything, I'm gonna just sit back and laugh."

"I'll bet you'll change your tune after our babies get here. You'll probably run yourself ragged trying to make sure they're safe. I can see it already...checking to make sure their bath water isn't too hot and that they're eating enough vegetables. When they start learning to walk, you'll probably tie pillows to their butts!"

"No way... I plan to be the uncle who brings drums, puppies and sugar whenever I visit."

Dana laughed. "Okay, but just remember what they say about payback, Bobby. When you have kids..."

"All right, all right," Robert said. He grinned and held his hands up in surrender. "You win. I'll help watch out for them. But no potty training."

Dana laughed again, and they toasted to the deal – his martini against her lemonade.

Justin and Summer exchanged a look of amazement. They'd always believed family interactions like this only took place on TV shows, and that loving families were the stuff of fairytales – no more real than magic beans or unicorns.

Summer felt a lump growing in her throat and picked up her martini. She hated knowing that these bright, beautiful lives would soon be smeared with the ugliness of the criminal underworld. She shifted in her chair, lost in thought and fighting an almost over-whelming urge to slink away from the table. It took her a moment to realize Justin's solution to the discomfort had been to change the subject.

Summer gave her brother an incredulous stare, hoping she had misunderstood him.

"Did you say *ghosts*, Justin?" Dana asked.

"Yep – my sister says this hotel is haunted with all kinds of ghosts. Tell them, Summer."

"I knew it!" Dana blurted, without waiting for Summer to reply. "I haven't seen any, but I sure can feel them around me sometimes – it's like they're watching me – not scary or anything, just, I don't know – maybe *curious*."

Flabbergasted, Summer laid her arm on the table and stared at Justin. At lunch, she hadn't told him not to talk about the spirits, but that was only because she assumed it was obvious. After all, she reasoned, it's difficult to gain a mark's trust, if they think you're crazy.

"I – I think Justin may have – *exaggerated*," she said, searching for another explanation.

"Did they touch you?" Dana interrupted, enthusiasm bubbling in her voice. "Because when we went into the basement on that tour, I could have *sworn* I felt a child's hand touch my belly." She gave her stomach a light pat to demonstrate what she meant and then smiled at Justin. "Who knows? Maybe a ghost child was, you know – saying hello to Junior."

Robert slid his warm hand on top of Summer's and gave it a gentle squeeze. "It's okay – you can tell us. I actually think I might have seen – well, not seen, exactly – but I think I *heard* some."

Summer didn't move. Her role in the con called for her to pretend to enjoy Robert's attention in order to get closer to him, or to be more precise, his computer. She wasn't supposed to experience *real* desire.

Chapter Seventeen

Summer sucked in a deep breath and forced herself to look at Robert. *"Damn those gorgeous eyes,"* she thought.

"Tell me what you *saw* and then I'll tell you what I *heard*," he said, giving her hand another light squeeze.

She ignored the pleasant tingle that ran up her arm and focused on deciding what, if anything, she should tell them about Margaret and Andy. Her eidetic mind recorded every moment she had spent in the spirit realm, but those visits – especially the time she spent revisiting Andy's memories – felt private.

"They're spirits," she said, her voice barely a whisper. "Not ghosts." She cleared her throat, still trying to regain her composure. "And I honestly don't know if I'm seeing them or just dreaming about them."

"There's a difference between ghosts and spirits?" Robert asked.

"Damn – why I did I tell him that?" Summer glanced at his hand, still covering hers. "According to Margaret there's a difference – Margaret Plant, that is. I think she's kind of like the head spirit here. Or, more likely, I dreamed that she is. Anyway, she said a spirit retains its memories and personality, but a ghost is just a fragment that got left behind when the rest of a person's spirit was drawn into the light."

Robert kept his penetrating blue eyes trained on her and spoke as if they were alone. "What else has she told you?"

"She just gives me advice – like I need to listen more and talk less. She drinks a lot of hot tea. And she loves this hotel. Her husband, Henry

Plant, is the guy who built the place. But like I said, I'm probably dreaming."

Summer gulped, worried she would continue to answer every question Robert asked. Her mind flashed to a training manual on interrogation:

> ...Tender physical contact can act like a truth serum, especially when the individual hasn't experienced much kindness in recent memory...

Another chapter in the training manual listed techniques used to counteract truth serum or beat a polygraph test. One suggestion was to use pain as a distraction. She bit the side of her tongue. *"That's better – keep focused on unrelated stimuli..."*

"Well – *my* encounters weren't dreams," Robert said, interrupting her thoughts. "I'm positive I was awake." He leaned back in his chair and crossed his arms.

When Robert lifted his hand from hers, the warmth vanished like a puff of smoke. Much to her chagrin, Summer discovered she wanted him to put it back. She bit her tongue again – harder.

"Well, don't keep us in suspense," Dana urged. "What happened?"

"I heard children – maybe half a dozen or more of them," Robert said to no one in particular. "A couple nights in a row. They were in the hallway outside my door – running and laughing – lots and lots of laughing."

"Little children?" There was a catch in Dana's voice that suggested she was thinking about children dying at the hotel.

"*Laughing* children," Justin repeated, resting a comforting arm across her shoulders. "And children don't laugh unless they're happy, right?"

"Yeah," Robert agreed. "They seemed to be having a ball. At first, I thought some kids had gotten away from their parents or babysitter. But when I opened the door, the laughter stopped and I didn't see a single kid anywhere in that hallway. And it's not like the noise faded away or anything. It just stopped – *so* weird. Finally, I convinced my- self somebody must've been holding a door open or something and went back to work. I'd almost forgotten all about it, until the next night, when I heard them out there *again.*"

"The same little kids?" Justin asked.

"I think so." Robert shrugged. "Anyway, I decided to call the front desk to report them to security – not that I wanted to be an old grouch or anything, but it was really late and they sounded so young..."

"Bobby has always taken curfews *very* seriously," Dana said. "I mean *Robert*," she corrected, shooting him a teasing smirk.

Justin leaned forward, intrigued. "Did the security guy hear them, too?"

Robert scrunched his face at Dana in a silent sibling-like retort, before responding to Justin. "Nope. A few minutes after I called the front desk, it suddenly got quiet again and then the security guard knocked on my door. He said he hadn't heard or seen anything unusual, but he also told me that I'm not the first person to report invisible kids playing in the halls late at night. Anyway, he said he'd patrol the hall more frequently to make sure everything stayed quiet, and I guess that worked. At least, I didn't hear anything last night." He took a sip of his martini and turned to Summer. "Now I kind of wish I hadn't spoiled their fun. Who knows? Maybe they would have visited my dreams, too."

Summer started to give him a scowl, but then realized he wasn't mocking her. She picked up her martini and tapped her glass against his. "Well, then, here's to Margaret, Casper and the rest of the friendly ghosts that apparently haunt this place."

"Spirits, not ghosts." Robert took a drink in an unsuccessful attempt to hide his smile.

"Here, here," Justin said, lifting his own glass to join the toast. "And here's to making new friends and lasting relationships. And I do mean *lasting* – get it? Even after we turn into ghosts...or spirits."

Summer rolled her eyes.

"And to a successful auction," Dana added, raising her lemonade.

The conversation gravitated to the display cases for the art exhibit, and soon Justin and Robert were discussing security measures, including the pros and cons of requiring people to stand behind velvet ropes to view the exhibits.

"I agree the art would be more protected," Robert said, "but I think we should nix the ropes. Collectors are usually more likely to buy if they feel a personal connection to the art, and distance might keep those connections from forming."

Justin rubbed his chin. "We could hang ropes from stanchions and only unhook them for serious lookers – sort of like presenting them with backstage passes."

"Let me give that some thought," Robert said.

"Enough, already," Dana pouted. "Let's order some food and talk about anything *except* the exhibit."

"Good call," Justin agreed, picking up his menu. "I'm starving, and you need to feed your little man."

Dana giggled. "That's sweet, but Junior is a she, not a he."

"Junior is a strange name for baby girl," Summer said.

"Look who's talking about strange names," Robert teased.

"Ha! He's got a point there, Summer Tyme," Justin agreed, laughing.

"Really, Justin Tyme?" Summer shot back. "Talk about the pot calling the kettle black..."

"Stop it, you guys," Dana said, suppressing a giggle. "The reason I call her Junior is because I didn't know she was a girl until just before we came to Florida, and I haven't had time to think of a girl's name yet."

"How about Alice?" Justin suggested, flipping his open palms out, as if to say *ta dah.*

"Alice Cooper?" Dana laughed. "I don't *think* so."

"Okay, then, how about Jackie?" Justin continued.

"Saved by the bell," Summer told Dana, pointing toward the approaching waiter. "Food always shuts him up."

Her comment proved to be true. Despite his big lunch, Justin devoured a thick steak and baked potato, while Robert, Dana, and Summer each enjoyed a large portion of chicken and broccoli Primavera. Throughout the meal, the foursome discussed topics ranging from favorite movies, to whether it would be better to own a tropical island or a log cabin in the middle of a forest. Then, while Dana and Justin split a serving of apple pie à la mode and Summer sipped on a Bailey's Irish Cream, Robert paid the check, claiming they talked about the exhibit enough to justify calling it a business dinner.

"Who's up for a walk?" Dana asked. "If I don't waddle around in the fresh air for a while, I won't be able to go to sleep."

"Sounds good to me," Justin said.

"Not me." Summer shook her head. "I'm about to fall asleep right here at the table."

"I agree with Summer," Robert said. "Besides, I have to get up at the crack of dawn to make some international calls."

Justin stood and helped Dana to her feet. He shook Robert's hand and gave Summer a hug before guiding Dana through the double doors of the restaurant that led to the outdoor café and the gardens beyond. Once again, Robert took Summer by the elbow. This time, he escorted her back down the Promenade toward the elevators.

"Looks like your brother and Dana really hit it off," Robert said.

"Yep, looks that way," she agreed, concealing her envy and her concerns. For a few seconds, she considered following her brother's example – throw caution to the wind and find out if Robert felt same rush she had when their hands touched. *"Let your guard down and people will die."* The grim reminder jolted her back to reality. When the elevator doors opened, she moved to the far side of the lift and pushed the button for their floor. "I understand why you enjoy hosting these art exhibits," she said, adopting a professional tone. "It's a privilege to see so many rare antiquities up close. Pictures in books don't do them justice."

"No, they do not." Robert smiled. "And just wait until *Bride On Stairs* arrives. She's absolutely stunning."

When they reached the fourth floor, Summer stepped out, making sure to put some distance between herself and Robert in the wide corridor. "I read that whenever they replace the carpet here at the Belleview Biltmore, they order it by the mile, rather than the yard," Summer said. "I wonder if that's true."

Robert shot her a sideways glance, but didn't say anything about the abrupt change in her demeanor. "I don't doubt it," he said. "The manager told me they'll be closing in a few months for a complete renovation. Can you imagine the salesman's response when they call to place an order for a couple miles of carpet?"

They reached his door before hers and Robert hesitated. Summer thought he was trying to decide whether to walk her to her door and perhaps even attempt a good night kiss. She waved a hand and continued down the hallway. "Thanks again for dinner," she called over her shoulder. "See you in the morning." She felt his eyes on her, but didn't look back. Instead, she pulled the antique key from her clutch, unlocked the door, and slipped inside.

Summer kicked off her high heels and threw herself onto her bed, closing her eyes against the sting of tears. "It's the right thing to do," she mumbled, ignoring the chill of the mist settling over her.

"Bull feathers!" Margaret scoffed. "None of what you're planning is the *right* thing to do."

Summer made a futile attempt to stay awake, but the pull of the spirit realm was too powerful to resist. "I don't have a choice."

"Yes, you do," Margaret said as the fog dissipated and the round table in the parlor came into view. "What you don't have is control over *other* people's choices." She poured a cup of hot tea and slid it across the table to Summer. "And you're letting your fear of what they *might* choose determine the choices you make."

"If I don't do what they say, they'll kill Justin and me."

Margaret stirred three teaspoons of sugar into her cup of tea. "Perhaps," she agreed. "But death isn't the end of the journey. The choices you make throughout your life follow you into the spirit realm and beyond."

"So, you're saying I should let them kill us rather than help Gordo steal a painting?"

"No. I'm saying life is all about making choices. The afterlife is about earning redemption for the choices you made. You must decide which burden you prefer to carry throughout eternity – the burden that comes from taking action or failing to take action."

"Is there a third option?"

Margaret took a sip of her tea and paused to study the rosebud design on her cup before returning it to its matching saucer. "An intelligent woman with allies almost always has the ability to create more choices."

"What the..." Summer wheeled her head around as Andy materialized at the table, and next to him, flashing in and out like a television picture with poor reception, was Violet Barnes.

Chapter Eighteen

"You can do it, Violet," Andy encouraged. "Just focus on sitting here at the table with me and Margaret, like you've done a hundred times before."

As the temperature in her suite continued to drop, Summer's sleeping body burrowed under the comforter, while her consciousness watched Violet's ghostly image blink in and out of the parlor – appearing as a child one instant and an adult the next. When Violet finally managed to stabilize her adult apparition, Andy beamed and Margaret nodded her approval.

The spirit's pale blue eyes and blonde ponytail looked exactly as they had in Andy's memories, but seeing Violet as a child reminded Summer that the Barnes girls used to play in the Belleview Biltmore during the off-season. "I guess that explains the ghost children Robert heard playing in the hall late at night," she mumbled.

"My, oh my," Margaret replied, "you *do* possess a strong mind." She glanced at Violet. "You're doing well, darlin'. Take a moment to rest while I explain this." She returned her gaze to Summer. "The ability of spirits to travel wherever we went while we were alive, is linked to our ability to alter our appearance. As you surmised, Violet can appear as a child because she visited the Belleview as a youngster. Andy and I were both grown before we came here, so we aren't able to appear as children here."

"Robert heard *several* children."

"I'm not surprised. Many spirits return here to relive some of their happiest childhood memories...running through the halls and playing hide and seek in the basement."

"So, no children actually died here?" Summer relaxed into her chair, picturing Dana's round baby bulge.

"I didn't say that," Margaret said, reaching for her teapot. "Despite the best efforts of spirits to protect all of the children who come here, a handful of youngsters have been lost over the years. Violet likes to keep them company until they're ready to travel the lighted path."

"I never had children of my own," Violet explained. "So I watch over them." She smiled at Andy with victory in her eyes.

"See?" Andy reached over and took her hand. "I knew you could do it. Showing her your memories is just as easy. Trust me."

"I believe Violet's desire to help protect the hotel is what allowed her to form a connection with you," Margaret said.

Before she could analyze this new development, the fog dropped over Summer, pulling her from the parlor table and tumbling her, head over heels, into the mist. Ignoring her flip-flopping stomach, she swallowed hard and stretched her arms and legs out, as if floating on her back in water. Her efforts paid off and soon she was floating like a bubble on the surface of the sea.

After a long while, the mist began to clear, revealing a rainbow of color. As Summer drifted into the scene, she realized she was standing on a narrow path within an enormous field planted with row after row of asters, chrysanthemums, roses and gladiolas. An orange orchard grew at one edge of the field and on the opposite side stood four of the largest greenhouses Summer had ever seen.

"We leave the windows of the greenhouses open during the spring and summer," a woman said.

Summer turned toward the unexpected voice and found Violet standing behind her, along with two other blonde women and three soldiers. *"This must be one of Violet's memories,"* she thought.

"The bees fly in to help with pollination," the woman continued.

She had a coy smile and wore more makeup than Violet, but the resemblance was unmistakable. *"These must be her sisters,"* Summer thought.

One of the soldiers gave the woman a smirk. "If you ask me, Iris, those are some lucky bees – gettin' to pollinate as many gorgeous stems as they want to all day long."

Iris giggled. "Don't be fresh, Lieutenant Murphy. Daisy and Violet are too young to hear such talk."

"Please, call me Gus."

Something about the way the man allowed his eyes to roam over Iris gave Summer the creeps. *"He's as slimy as a Holiday Inn lounge lizard,"* she decided.

"What the hell is that?" the tallest of the soldiers interrupted in a high-pitched voice, pointing overhead.

The whole group looked up as a large bird flew from a tree in the orchard to the rooftop of the white farmhouse behind them.

"A flying turkey?" suggested the most muscular soldier of the trio.

"That's just one of our peacocks, coming home to roost for the night," Daisy said, stepping closer to the well-developed man.

"Are they good to eat?" Gus asked.

"They taste a lot like turkey, but we don't usually eat them unless the flock has too many males. The real benefit of raising peafowl is that they rid our fields of bugs and snakes."

Just then, the bird let loose a shrill "Caw," followed by an equally loud, rapid series of "Ah's."

The big man chuckled. "Sounds just like you, Squeaky."

"You're a real comedian, Lumpy," the thin man retorted. "But I'd rather sound like me than be stuck with your musclebound brains."

"Knock it off, boys," Lieut. Murphy said. "The Barnes family was kind enough to invite us to Christmas dinner, so the least we can do is to behave like gentlemen while we're here."

"Sorry, ma'am," Squeaky said. He stepped closer to Violet, in an obvious attempt to pair up the group.

"Speaking of dinner," Violet said, "I'll bet Mama could use a little bit of help right about now." Without waiting for a response, she stepped across a row of red chrysanthemums and onto another narrow path.

Summer smiled and followed Violet toward the white, two-story farmhouse, admiring her polite maneuver to escape the soldier's advances. As they approached the house, she was surprised to see Andy, resting on a wooden porch swing. The closer they got to the house, the more she could sense his emotions, as well as Violet's.

"You came!" Violet raced up the wide, wooden steps to the porch, as Andy stood to greet her.

A shy smile crossed Andy's face at her warm greeting. "I'm sorry I'm late. I had to get a few soldiers squared away before I could leave, but I wasn't about to pass up a home-cooked Christmas dinner."

"My sisters are giving the other soldiers a tour of the flower fields, but I came back to help Mama get the meal together. You're welcome to go out and join them if you want. Just follow the path." Without taking her eyes from him, she pointed in the general direction of the field.

"I can't. I already agreed to help your father before dinner. We're going to deliver honey and flowers to each of the neighbors who have service stars in their windows. He's checking with your mother to find out which gifts go to the blue star service families and which ones are for those who, um, have had to replace blue stars with gold ones."

"Really? Goodness, he must have taken a liking to you awfully fast," Violet said, a shy smile lighting her face.

"I don't know about that." Andy shifted his focus to his shoes. "He gave me the impression I was the odd man out, since three soldiers had already arrived to entertain his three daughters."

"Well, that's the most muddled thinking I ever heard." Violet stomped her feet, as if to knock off some nonexistent dirt. "Iris invited those soldiers on her own, and as far as I'm concerned, she can darn well entertain them on her own." She lowered her voice. "I invited *you*."

Andy stood up straight, smiling as the meaning of her words sank in. "Well, then, I'd best have a talk with your pop while we're out. And when we get back, I promise to do my best to entertain you."

The screen door opened and Harry Barnes, who possessed the physique of a pro wrestler, stepped onto the porch. "Vi – you best get on into the kitchen to help your mother." He walked to the steps, and without looking back, called over his shoulder, "Come along, son. You'll have plenty of time to moon over my daughter when we get back."

Andy flinched as Violet dashed through the door, leaving him alone with her father. Summer felt herself being tugged in two opposite directions, but Andy's pull was the strongest, so she followed him.

"You don't miss much, do you, sir?" he asked, trailing after Harry Barnes as he strode around to the side of the house.

"A man with three blonde daughters, living in a town that's full-up with soldier boys, can't afford to miss much," he replied. He pulled open the driver's door of his dusty, red cargo truck.

Andy nodded and opened the passenger door. They climbed inside, and as the truck doors banged shut, the fog engulfed Summer, pulling her away from the memory.

As she floated in the mist, Summer thought about how the military had commandeered the Belleview Biltmore Hotel to house three-thousand Army Air Corps soldiers. She knew the military had occupied several other large hotels in the area for the same purpose. Now, for the first time, she thought about the drastic impact the influx of so many men in uniform, along with the coinciding departure of most local young men, must have had on the small community and the lives of everyday people, like Violet's family.

When the fog cleared again, Summer found herself with the Barnes family and their guests as they gathered for their Christmas feast. The elegant polished oak table ran almost the entire length of the dining room. Six matching, high-backed chairs, plus three plain white kitchen chairs, surrounded the table.

Harry Barnes took his seat at the head of the table while the ladies scurried about, filling the table with a wide assortment of dishes. Gus started to pull out the chair at the opposite end of the table for himself, but stopped short when he noticed the scowl on Harry's face.

Gus stepped gallantly aside, pretending he had meant the chair for the lady of the house. "Here you go, Mrs. Barnes," he said as Rose

Barnes entered the room, carrying a huge turkey on a platter, garnished with a ring of caramelized orange slices. "Your well-deserved chair awaits."

"Thank you, Lieutenant," she replied, panting from exertion, "but I'm not ready to be seated just yet."

Andy stepped over to Rose. "Allow me," he said, lifting the heavy platter from her shaky hands.

"Thank you, son," she said, her gratitude evident in her smile. "The bird goes over there – in front of Harry." She wrung her hands together until Andy placed the crown jewel of the meal safely in its place and then let out a sigh of satisfaction. "You can go on and sit if you like," she said, before returning to the kitchen.

"If you insist," Gus said, settling into the high-backed chair next to hers.

When Squeaky started to take the chair next to him, Gus gave him a quick elbow in his ribs. "I believe Iris wants to sit in the middle," he said.

Since there were only three chairs on that side of the table, Squeaky had the choice of sitting next to the girls' imposing father, or moving to the other side of the table, where four chairs were squeezed close together. He charged around the table, obviously hoping for the first chair in the row, but Lumpy beat him to it. Squeaky grudgingly moved down to the third seat.

Andy frowned at his fellow soldiers' antics and held the kitchen door open for the ladies, who paraded back and forth, filling the table with more delectable dishes than he had ever witnessed in one meal. In addition to the turkey, there was oyster dressing, sweet potato casserole, green beans, buttered squash, mashed potatoes, sliced tomatoes, cranberry sauce, thick-sliced bread, and giblet gravy. They also filled the sideboard with apple, pumpkin and pecan pies.

When at last the ladies were ready to be seated, Gus jumped to his feet and stepped in front of Andy to pull out a chair for Rose and then Iris. Meanwhile, Daisy slipped into the chair between Lumpy and Squeaky and Violet sat between Iris and her father. Andy ignored Gus's childish behavior and squeezed into the only open chair – the one across the table from Violet and next to Harry Barnes.

Andy tried to give the big man as much room as possible, but still managed to bump into him every time he moved more than a few inches.

Once everyone was settled and had paid homage to the magnificent presentation of the meal, Rose asked Harry to say the blessing. Everyone bowed their heads, reminding Summer of a Norman Rockwell scene. After Harry finished giving thanks for the feast, he asked God to watch over those fighting to save the world from tyranny and to bring peace to those who had lost loved ones in the battle. He wrapped-up by asking God to keep his family and their guests safe from harm and to instill pure and righteous thoughts into all of their hearts and minds.

"Good luck with that," Summer thought, as she watched Gus and Iris playing knees-ees under the table.

After Harry carved the turkey and everyone passed around the various dishes, Rose poured each of them a goblet of orange wine and told the story of how she and Harry had purchased their land right after getting married. They named the farm The Rosery, which was a combination of their names – Rose and Harry, and the girls, of course, were named after some of their favorite flowers.

"Before the war," Rose said, "we furnished fresh flowers to the Japanese Gardens and the Belleview Biltmore every day. Now they're both closed, so most of our flower orders are for weddings and, unfortunately, funerals."

"But we've got no complaints," Harry said. "We grow more than enough food to meet our needs and we earn extra money from the orange grove and bee hives."

"That's true," Rose agreed. "Plus, we're able to trade ration coupons with our neighbors – homemade wine and jars of honey in exchange for gas and sugar coupons, and so forth." She took a deep breath and looked at the young faces around her table. "But enough about us old folks," she said. "I'd like to learn a little bit about you boys."

Gus got the ball rolling. "I'm Second Lieutenant Gus Murphy, from Chicago. I'm temporarily assigned to the Fort Harrison Hotel, getting it ready for occupation – at least for a little while longer. I'll be transferring over to the Belleview Biltmore at the first of the year. It's so big, they need more officers to oversee the men who've been assigned to get it ready to house troops. Not to brag, but I'm an ace pilot, so once the cadets start arriving in a couple of months, I'm sure I'll be reassigned to turn them into fighter pilots."

"My goodness," Iris said. "That sounds like a difficult job."

"Not for me," Gus said. "I plan on standin' my squad at attention on their first day and sayin', 'lookee here, boys, if you want to live, you best learn *Murphy's Laws* real quick.'" He held up two stubby fingers. "Then I'll tell them, 'Murphy's Law Number One: Never question your squad leader's orders, and Law Number Two: Never forget Law Number One.'"

Lumpy and Squeaky snickered, even though Summer was certain they'd heard the joke more than once.

"Gee, I'd love to watch you fly sometime," Iris said, her eyes glistening with admiration.

"Oh, please," Summer thought, repulsed once again by the man's cocky, self-centered manner.

"What about you, Sergeant Wilkins?" Rose asked, gracefully preventing Gus from continuing his personal missive. "Where do you hail from?"

Lumpy said that he too, was raised in Chicago. "I'm a gunner. My real name is George Walter Wilkins, but they call me Lumpy because of my muscles. I don't mind the nickname, though. I never liked the name George Walter, and I couldn't stand the son-of-a-bitch I'm named after." Harry Barnes' scowl melted the grin from his face. "Oh," he said, realizing his mistake. "I'm sorry. I shouldn't call my father a son-of-a-bitch in front of church-going broads – I mean *ladies*." He smiled and returned his attention to his plate, scooping up a heaping fork full of mashed potatoes.

Next, Squeaky announced he was Sergeant Sabastian Crawly, from Louisiana. "I joined up with the Army for just two reasons," he said, holding up two fingers the way Gus had done. "First, I wanted to get away from my crazy family. Second, a navigator gets to tell smart-alecky pilots where to go. And third, because I want to kill Hitler, even though it won't be easy to get my hands on the beady-eyed son-of-a – um, gun – here in Florida."

No one bothered to ask him how he acquired his nickname. The more excited he got, the more often his voice cracked and squeaked.

Summer, still listening to Andy's unspoken thoughts, swallowed a laugh at his assessment of Squeaky. "*The dumb bastard can't even count to two, but he believes he can take on Hitler single-handed. Lord save us.*"

Rose smiled at Squeaky. "Well, I'm sure you'll do your part with gusto, no matter what job you're called on to handle," she said. Then she turned to Andy. "I suppose that brings us to you, Lieutenant Turner. Tell us a bit about yourself."

Andy struggled to swallow a bite of turkey. "There's not much to tell, really." He paused for a sip of wine. "I learned to fly a crop duster on a farm in Pennsylvania, just outside the small mining town where I was raised. My little sister still lives there. She's the only family I have left, so I do my best to provide for her. As for my military duties, well, I guess I'll be doing pretty much the same thing as Gus – training our boys to fly for Uncle Sam." He shrugged and took another drink of wine.

"You're being too modest," Violet gushed, letting her gaze sweep around the table. "I happen to know that Andy graduated at the top of his class, and Colonel Huck personally entrusted him with securing thousands and thousands of dollars' worth of property that had to be removed from the hotel. He's in charge of packing up priceless antiques and keeping an inventory of everything that's being stored in the old generator building." She lifted her chin. "Andy put a huge padlock on the doors and makes sure guards are posted around the clock to protect everything, so the hotel can be put back together once the war is over."

"You don't say?" Gus said, a spark of interest glowing in his eyes. "Maybe I can help take some of the load off when I get there. Maybe help out with the guards."

"I think I can handle the job," Andy said, feeling better about his assignment now that he knew Violet thought it was important. "But there's tons of other work that needs doing, and I'll sure welcome your help. We're supposed to install a fire sprinkler system and paint the whole inside of building before the cadets start arriving. Frankly, I don't think we have a prayer of getting it all done."

Summer felt a shiver run down her spine at the way Gus was watching Andy – an alligator sizing up a meal.

Chapter Nineteen

"What a slimy asshole," Summer thought as the fog blanketed the scene and carried her away. *"I sure hope Andy is smart enough to stay away from him."* She chewed on the inside of her cheek as she floated along, worrying. *"This is ridiculous. Why should I care what happens to a dead guy?"*

When the fog lifted a moment later, Summer was floating at Andy's side as he made his way through a wide, open section of the Belleview Biltmore Hotel.

In the book Gordo had given her to study about the hotel, early pictures portrayed this area as the lavishly appointed lobby. Back then, its decor included a hand-carved mahogany registration desk, plush circular couches, crystal chandeliers, and enough art to fill a museum. When a modern lobby was built in the 1990s, this space had been converted into the upscale *Lobby Lounge*, with a high-top mahogany bar on one side of the room and several cozy seating areas punctuating the opposite side of the space. But here in Andy's 1942 memory, the cavernous lobby space, painted drab Army green with no decor in sight, was barely recognizable.

"No wonder they didn't include pictures of this era in the book," Summer thought. It took a moment for her eyes to adjust to the unusually dim space. *"Jesus – they painted all the windows black!"* An instant later, her brain reminded her about the WWII practice:

The theoretical purpose of a "blackout" during wartime was to minimize outdoor light as much as possible, and block light from escaping through windows. Doing so was intended to prevent crews of enemy aircraft from being able to identify targets at night, and protect ships along the shoreline from being seen in silhouette by enemy submarines. Streetlights were not lit, car headlights were shaded, and store signs were turned off. The most commonly used methods of blocking light from escaping through windows included: heavy blackout curtains, black paint, and tar. In reality, "blackouts" did little to impair navigation by bombers and caused a significant increase in traffic and rail accidents. However, they did engage the entire civilian population in the war effort and made sure everyone became conditioned to obeying rules.

The center of the lobby was filled with rows of pine benches, and metal desks and chairs lined the three walls. In place of the grand chandeliers, hung dull, cone-shaped pendant light fixtures, reminiscent of the type used in police interrogation rooms. The mahogany registration desk was draped with heavy canvas and buried under stacks of books, maps and paperwork.

Andy walked to the left of the bar and stopped at the entrance to a large office. Summer peered inside, trying to wrap her head around the fact that a space that served as a small billiard room in her time, had once been a busy communications room, complete with a telephone switchboard, telegraph station and post office – all staffed by members of the Women's Army Auxiliary Corps.

A stern-faced WAAC marched to the doorway, where a ten-inch wide board had been nailed across the opening, forming a narrow counter.

"Good afternoon, ma'am." Andy twisted his Garrison cap in his hands, beads of perspiration dotting his forehead. "I was told you're holding a cable message for Second Lieutenant Andrew Turner."

A younger WAAC, her dull brown hair twisted into a tight bun at the base her neck, glanced up at the sound of his name, but then quickly averted her eyes. The subtle action reminded Summer that during WWII, most people feared telegrams so much that bicycle messenger boys were nicknamed *Angels of Death.*

"Dread," Summer thought, *"that's what Andy's feeling."*

The stern-faced woman turned and walked to a rack of small square boxes that lined one wall of the office. She snatched a white envelope from the box marked with the letter "T" and then returned to Andy. She removed a clipboard from a nail in the wall and laid it on the makeshift counter. "Sign here," she said, her soft voice at odds with her rough appearance. She pointed her ink-stained forefinger at the signature line of a form and handed him a fountain pen.

Andy licked his dry lips before accepting the pen and signing his name.

When he was finished, the woman collected her pen and clipboard. "I'll pray for God's mercy," she murmured as she turned away, leaving the small envelope on the counter.

He eyed the telegram for a moment and then picked it up, handling it gingerly, as if it might bite. Then he slid it into his pocket, unopened, and turned away.

Summer sensed Andy's emotions as though they were her own – his certainty that something terrible had happened, and his desperate attempts to convince himself otherwise. He fumbled with the ornate brass handle on the lobby door and then hurried across the wide porch and down the steps, into the clear, crisp winter afternoon. He didn't stop until he reached the back side of the storage building. Being careful to avoid a clump of sand spurs, he sat cross-legged in the dirt, withdrew the envelope and laid it on the ground. He lit a cigarette and examined his name, hand-written in a feminine script under the Western Union logo – resisting the urge to set the cable on fire without reading it. After taking a few deep drags of tobacco smoke, he finally opened the thin envelope and removed the typewritten message.

It was from Thomas Beacon, the farmer who taught Andy how to fly and agreed to care for his sister after their father died, freeing him to join the Army Air Corps. The short message dashed Andy's last flicker of hope:

Sister mortally ill – TB. Come quick. Need cash for doctor.

Andy closed his eyes, struggling to hold back his tears. He didn't move a muscle until the cigarette burned down to his fingers. Startled, he dropped the butt to the ground and stood. While grinding the cigarette into the dirt beneath his shoe, he slipped the telegram into the envelope and tucked it back into his pocket.

"Oh my God," Summer thought, tears glistening in her eyes, *"Andy's trying to figure out how to save his sister and I'm trying to save Justin. Is that why he feels so connected to me?"*

Before she had time to consider the possibility, Summer was engulfed by the fog.

Violet's voice floated through the clouds. "They say God has a plan," she said. "But I still don't understand why he felt the need to test Andy with so many hardships. We could have been so happy together."

When the sound of the Andrew Sisters singing *Boogie Woogie Bugle Boy* began filtering through the mist, Summer tried to swim toward the music. As the fog cleared, she found herself seated next to Violet at a soda fountain. Violet tapped her toes to the music and smiled at a young couple as they plunked nickels into the Wurlitzer jukebox in the corner. When a tiny bell tinkled behind her, Violet grinned and spun her barstool toward the door.

"What's wrong?" she asked, the moment she saw Andy.

He tried to smile at Violet as he dropped onto the stool next to hers, but Andy's eyes were dull and his shoulders slumped as though he was carrying the weight of the world. "Two root beers, please," he called to the soda jerk. He glanced at Violet's cornflower blue eyes and blonde curls before fixing his gaze on his hands and the countertop beneath them. His fingers were locked together so tightly that his knuckles had turned white. "I'm sorry, Vi, but there's no way around it. I'm not going to be able to take you to the picture show tonight."

"That's okay, Andy. The Capital Theater is still showing *The Flying Tigers*, and we've already seen it twice."

Andy nodded and placed a quarter on the bar to pay for their drinks.

"Please tell me what's wrong, Andy," she coaxed.

He set his jaw, pulled out the telegram and slid it in front of her. "I got this today. It's about my sister, Paige. She's sick." When the fountain boy returned with the drinks and his change, Andy pressed his lips together and picked up the nickel. "I need to send her all the money I can pull together. That means I can't afford to take you out anymore. If you want to start seeing other..."

Violet sat up straight. "I haven't been dating you because you spend money on me," she said, her nostrils flaring with indignation. "I thought I made that clear. If I was only after a good time, I'd be hanging around Coe's Casino and accepting dates with different men every night of the week, like Daisy and Iris do."

Andy flushed with embarrassment, but before he could respond, the little bell over the door tinkled again and Gus Murphy walked in, wearing summer khakis, even though spring had not yet arrived. He made a beeline for Andy and gave his shoulder a brotherly squeeze.

"I just heard about your sister," he said. "Damn crappy break, but I have an idea to make some pennies rain down from heaven." He eyed Violet's figure and then gave her a wink. "Sorry to rain on your parade, dolly, but I need to take dreamboat here someplace private, so we can talk business."

"Hold on a minute there, hotshot," Violet demanded. "How do you already know about his sister, when Andy only found out a little while ago?"

"Whoa there," Gus said with a smirk. He ran a forefinger over his Clark Gable style mustache. "Was Shrinking Violet just *pretending* to be shy at Christmas?" He squeezed Andy's shoulder again and chuckled. "I guess Squeaky's lucky you two hit it off. He's not man enough to handle a pistol like her."

Andy frowned. "Answer the lady's question. I didn't tell you about Paige."

"Paige? That's your sister's name?" Gus laughed. "Paige Turner?"

Summer's eyes grew wide, recalling her first day at the hotel, when she heard voices in the elevator. A woman had been talking about how the man's sister had a strange name like hers. *"That must have been Margaret and Andy talking about Paige and me,"* she realized.

"How did you find out about my sister?" Andy repeated.

"Don't get excited, fly boy." Gus chuckled again. "Let's just say a little birdie keeps me well informed, and in exchange, she doesn't have to worry about buying her own nylons."

"The young girl in the communications room," Summer thought.

Andy and Violet exchanged a wary glance.

"So, do you want my help, or not?" Gus asked.

"Don't..." Violet said, placing her hand on top of Andy's.

"I need to hear what he's got to say," Andy replied. "Please don't worry. I'll call you tomorrow."

"Yeah, don't worry, dish," Gus sneered as he opened the door. "I'll take good care of our boy."

Summer wanted to scream as the fog rolled over the scene, carrying her away. *"Stay away from him, Andy! Gus is bad news. Can't you see that?"*

Margaret's voice drifted through the mist. "He knows, but desperation smothers intelligence every time."

Chapter Twenty

Summer expected to drift through the fog to join Margaret at the parlor table, but all at once, her slow descent stopped and she began to roll over and over in the clouds, in the opposite direction from where she had been headed. When the mist finally dissipated, she was surprised to find herself in the basement of the Belleview Biltmore. It took a few moments to shake off her dizziness, but then she recognized the shoeshine station, located just inside the men's bathroom, near St. Andrews Pub.

Gus Murphy climbed onto the platform and sat in one of the two white, wooden, throne-like chairs and motioned for Andy to sit next to him. Then he looked down a young black man, seated on a stool at his feet and demanded, "Gimme' a spit shine."

The young man opened a can of brown shoe polish and got to work, while Lumpy checked to make sure the bathroom stalls were empty.

"Lap dogs pretending to be pit bulls," Summer thought, as she watched Lumpy step into the hallway with Squeaky and close the door.

"Turner, you might have noticed that I'm a natural born wheeler-dealer," Gus began, smirking at Andy. "Been that way since I was a kid." He glanced down and shook one of his feet. "Hey! A little less spit and a lot more polish there, boy."

The young man jerked his head up with fire dancing in his atypical green eyes, but an instant later he shifted his gaze down and mumbled,

"Yes, suh, boss. Whatever yo says, boss." He picked up the open can of polish and rubbed his rag across the surface before getting back to work.

"That's right, nigger," Gus said, a smirk twisting at the corners of his mouth. "Don't forget who's in charge around here."

Summer's jaw dropped at the racist slur. She studied the striking young man, waiting for him to react, but he kept his eyes trained on his task, vigorously brushing and buffing one shoe and then the other. His curly short hair was as black as coal, but in addition to having light eyes, his skin tone was the color of caramel. He wore a clean, short-sleeved white shirt, tucked into a baggy pair of black dungarees, and well-worn, but polished shoes.

As Andy shifted in his chair, Summer sensed his discomfort and shared his thoughts – memories of his own childhood, reminding him that wealthy white people tended to believe that poverty and inferiority were synonymous. *"I guess they feel the same way about colored people as they do about poor folks,"* he thought. A sour taste filled his mouth with the sudden realization that he had been elevated into the elite white ranks when he graduated from flight school at the top of his class. He had been proud of that accomplishment, but now the thought that people would assume he and Gus were cut from the same cloth sickened him.

"As I was sayin'," Gus continued, unaware of Andy's emotional turmoil, "I meet a lot of people who have *access* to things, and a lot of other people who want to *buy* things. I do my best to bring these people together, and they reward me for my help, so things work out great for everybody."

"So, what's that got to do with me?" Andy asked, the inside of his mouth turning to cotton.

"I like you, Turner." Gus grinned at Andy. "And I figure you can use a friend like me right about now – what with your sister being so sick, and you needin' extra cash and all."

"I'm doing all right," Andy lied, remembering Violet's warning. "I figure I'll take some leave and work out payments with the local doc when I get back home. Besides, I don't own anything that you could sell."

"Well, maybe you can help me out in other ways," Gus said. "Accept my help or don't. No skin off my nose, either way."

When the shoeshine man rocked back on his heels, signaling that he was finished, Gus stood up, examined the gleam on his leather shoes, and then flipped a quarter off his thumb, tiddlywink fashion, into the air. The young man caught the spinning coin with ease.

Gus stepped down from the platform and paused. "If things don't work out back home, well...you come see me. Who knows? Maybe we can do some biz together." Then he pulled a second quarter from his pocket. "Boy, you take good care of my friend, here. His shine's on me." He flipped it to the man, who again, snatched the flipping coin out of the air.

Andy opened his mouth to protest, but Gus stopped him with a wave of his hand. "It's nothing. Murphy's law – take care of your friends. Remember that." Then he pointed at the shoe shiner. "And as for you, boy...you remember to keep quiet about what's said in here or I'll have to teach you Murphy's law about what happens to squealers." He slid his forefinger across his throat in a cutting motion to clarify his threat and then yanked the door open.

"Okay, you knuckleheads, let's blow this joint," Gus said, sliding between Squeaky and Lumpy. "I've got a taste for some Gold Star whiskey and a game of poker. Squeaky, you go liberate us a jeep from the motor pool so we can head over to Coe's Casino. Lumpy, you go call those wacky dames we met..." His voice faded and then disappeared altogether as he and his minions climbed the stairs to the hotel lobby.

"You don't have to shine my shoes," Andy said, once he was sure the trio was out of hearing range. "Just keep the quarter."

"It's no trouble at all, sir," the man said, taking Andy's left shoe in is hand. "I'm waiting to escort my mother home after she finishes her shift in the laundry. Shining shoes helps pass the time and besides, I'm hoping you'll allow me to ask you some questions about navigation."

Andy yanked his foot back in surprise. "What the...who the...you sure don't talk like a...a..."

"I know." He smiled. "All educated colored men know it's best to pretend to be a bumpkin from the boondocks whenever we're around *that* sort of white folks." He jabbed a thumb in the direction Gus and his cohorts had gone.

Andy nodded, trying to regain his composure. "Are you really a shoeshine man?"

"Nope," he confessed. "This has been Big Tom's station since I was knee-high to a grasshopper, but he signed up with the infantry after the attack on Pearl Harbor. When you fly boys arrived, I bought these supplies and started making use of the station in my free time, learning about aviation while polishing shoes for officers who *appreciate* a good spit shine. I was just about to leave when you gentlemen arrived, and like I said...I have some time on my hands."

"Well, I'll be damned. You know, my father worked shoulder to shoulder with lots of colored fellas in the coal mine, but none of them had schoolin'. Then again, neither did my father." Andy furrowed his eyebrows. "Name's Andy Turner," he said, extending his hand.

The man gave Andy an easy grin – wiping his hands before accepting his handshake. "I'm Alexander Washington."

"Washington, huh?" Andy asked, rubbing his jaw. "I never saw a colored person with green eyes before. Where you from?"

"My family is French-Carib from Trinidad. Shortly after my grandfather died, the elderly French baroness they worked for decided to spend the winter in Florida and she brought Granny Millie and my mama along. That was almost fifty years ago – back when this hotel first opened. Anyway, not long after they arrived, the old woman died, and my family decided to stay on here, working in the laundry."

"Well, you sure don't *sound* like the son of a colored maid."

"That's because I was educated along with the wealthy kids in the little school house here at the hotel."

"Where I'm from, the rich folks wouldn't have stood for that. Hell, they didn't even let poor *white* kids into their schools."

"The parents never knew," Alexander said. "You see, all the rich kids liked playing in the basement, where my mother worked. When I was a baby, she kept me with her, in an empty laundry basket. She told me all the little girls liked to make a fuss over me and play with my nappy hair. I guess they got so used to seeing me around, they didn't find it strange when Miss Burkholder, the schoolteacher, asked me to sit in the back of the class to fetch water, feed wood into the stove, wipe the chalk boards and such. Nobody suspected that she was going over the lessons with me after class."

"So, how much schooling did you get?" Andy asked.

Alexander grinned. "The colored schools around here only teach trades and they stop at the eighth grade, but Miss Burkholder saw to it that I earned a high school diploma, and then Mama and Granny Millie insisted that I attend Florida A&M University, up in Tallahassee. They had their hearts on me becoming a doctor, so they're none too happy with me right now."

"Why's that?"

"Because, I made up my mind to head up to Alabama and join up with the Tuskegee Airmen as soon as I learn a little bit more about navigation."

"Why navigator instead of pilot?"

"I figure I can learn navigation by asking questions and studying the maps and such that you fellas have hanging in the training rooms." He shook his head. "I can't learn to fly that way."

"I could teach you," Andy said without thinking. "I mean, I need some teaching practice before the cadets get here anyway, so may as well practice on you."

As the fog dropped over Summer, she frowned. *"Andy's a nice guy, but too naive. I've known a hundred Gus Murphys. He wants something from Andy and he's not going to let him go that easy. Alexander has the right idea –keep your head down and steer clear of snakes like him."*

Beyond the mist, she heard the loud roar of a motor come to a sputtering halt. The clouds were still too thick to see through them, but Summer heard a second engine start up. A few minutes later, she flinched at the sound of a man's angry voice.

"What were you thinking, trying to get away with a boneheaded stunt like this, Turner?"

Chapter Twenty-One

Summer strained to see through the mist, fearing she recognized the man's voice and hoping she was wrong. As the mist began to dissipate, she searched the scene, trying to determine where they were and what was happening.

She was standing near the open entrance of a Quonset-style hangar that contained two twin-engine airplanes. Mechanics working on the plane that was parked furthest from where she stood were responsible for the deafening racket. Two men revved the plane's engines, while a third man tinkered with some wiring near the landing gear.

"MacDill Airfield?" Summer wondered.

Next to her, stood Andy and a second man, both dressed in full flight gear. It was easy to deduce that they were attempting to avoid a confrontation with Gus Murphy and his minions, muscle-man George Wilkins, known as Lumpy, and twitchy Sabastian Crawly, nicknamed Squeaky.

Gus's voice cut through the chaos like a stiletto knife. "Answer me, Turner! What do you have to say for yourself, letting a cadet taxi a *Widow Maker* into a hangar?"

The noise made it difficult to hear Andy's reply, but Summer understood his thoughts. He was scared. In an attempt to gain control of the situation, he nudged the other pilot toward the door. "Go on. It's all right. Don't pay them no mind." Andy was still issuing instructions to the cadet when one of the mechanics switched off the airplane's engines. "Change your clothes and get back to the car," he shouted in the sudden silence. Then, more quietly, he added, "I'll be along shortly."

"You stay put," Gus hissed. "Nobody's goin' anywhere until we get a few things straight around here." As he studied the cadet, a dangerous smile lit his face and then vanished. "Tell me it ain't so, Turner." He sneered and shook his head. "May as well take off the helmet, boy. I can see you're colored."

"A nigger?" Wilkins echoed in disbelief. "Dressed in flight gear?" He lurched toward the cadet, but Andy blocked him. "Goddammit, Turner, get out of my way!" he yelled, "I'll teach him what happens to niggers who try to..."

Summer clenched her fists at her side, biting her tongue. *"I know I can't speak, and I know I can't change the past, but that doesn't stop me from wanting to kick that racist bastard right in the nuts."*

"Back off, Lumpy," Gus ordered. "Let's hear what Turner has to say. Maybe he just wanted to play dress-up with his pet monkey. Is that right, Turner?"

"Come on, Gus..." Andy tried to sound friendly. "Let this go. We weren't hurting anybody."

"That's Lieutenant Murphy to you," Gus sneered. "Only my friends call me Gus, and you didn't accept my offer of friendship now, did ya?"

Andy glanced around, searching for an escape and hoping for witnesses, but the men on the far side of the hangar were too busy working to notice the escalating situation.

"You know, Turner," Gus continued. "I don't think nobody'd stop me if I decided to take the colored boy back up in that Marauder and make 'im swim home." He glanced at Lumpy and Squeaky, sharing a maniacal grin. "Whadda' think, fellas? Should we drop him into Tampa Bay?"

"Can you swim, boy?" Squeaky jeered.

"Okay, you've made your point," Andy said. He closed his eyes and took a deep breath. "What do you want?"

Gus cocked an eyebrow. "What do I want?" he repeated, feigning disappointment. "All I've ever wanted is to be friends, Turner –

friends who could help one another out of tight spots like the one you've gotten yourself into here."

"Okay," Andy grumbled. "We can be friends – but only if you let him go." He glanced at the cadet. "And if you don't get in the way of his training."

Gus chuckled, ignoring Andy's requests. "You're seriously trying to teach a colored to fly a B-26? A *Flyin' Coffin*?"

"This man has the makings of a damn fine pilot," Andy replied.

"Take off the helmet, boy." Gus spit on the concrete floor near the cadet's feet.

The cadet glanced at Andy, who gave him a nod. He pulled off his gloves, revealing caramel-colored hands, and then proceeded to un-coil the scarf from around his neck. Next, he unfastened the chin strap and removed the brown leather helmet and dark aviator goggles.

"Well, I'll be damned," Gus said. "If it ain't the green-eyed shoe-shine boy. Why, if it weren't for that kinky nigger hair of yours, you could almost pass for a white feller."

"Let him go," Andy repeated.

"No skin off my nose," Gus replied. "Just remember you owe me." He turned to Alexander Washington. "Now, you listen here, boy. Do you know why they call the B-26 the *Widow Maker*? Tell 'em, Squeaky."

Sabastian Crawley cleared his throat. "It's because the Marauder is the most finicky bitch Uncle Sam ever bolted together." His shrill voice rose and cracked. "She's fast, but her wings are short and her body's shaped like a fat cigar – kind of like colored women." He cackled and glanced at Gus for approval. "Take-offs and landings are real killers, too." He snickered again.

"That's right," Gus said, finishing Squeaky's thought. "If you're not moving one-hundred and forty miles per hour at take-off or landing, then one – or both – of the engines stall and you crash." Gus grinned, cupped his palm and made a diving motion. "While you were polishing the shoes of *real* pilots, maybe you heard on or two of 'em say '*One a Day in Tampa Bay.*' They say that because so many B-26s crash into the water...and that's when they're being flown by good, *white* pilots, who are a *hell* of a lot smarter than some *colored* boy."

"He knows that flying a Marauder is dangerous business," Andy replied. "So do I. That's why I take over the controls for takeoff and landing."

Gus returned his gaze to Andy. "If you and this dumbass nigger boy want to kill yourselves, that's fine by me. But you're violating the law, lettin' a colored boy fly out of a white base. If the brass finds out, you're gonna lose your wings and be sent to the infantry...maybe even get court-martialed." He smiled and held his hand out to Andy for a shake. "But since we're gonna be friends now, I might be persuaded to keep my mouth shut."

Summer understood the conflict going through Andy's thoughts all too well. After all, how many times had she been driven by desperation and helplessness to do the will of others even though she hated what she was being forced to do?

Before she could hear Andy's response, the fog filled the hangar, sweeping her away from the scene. As she floated in the misty clouds, Summer searched her eidetic memory for information about WWII fliers and the Tuskegee Airmen. To her chagrin, she discovered she knew little about either topic, outside of Hollywood movies on the subjects.

She knew only slightly more about Jim Crow laws, which designated separate public facilities for people, based on their race – separate schools, drinking fountains, entrances, seating sections, waiting rooms, and so on. *"I didn't realize Jim Crow laws existed in the military, too. That must have sucked. You can't eat together, but you can fight for the same cause and die together, no problem."*

Andy's voice began to filter through the mist. "Of the men who joined up with the Army Air Corps to become pilots, over sixty percent washed out during their first nine months of training. By the time they reached advanced training stations like MacDill and Drew Air Fields, every Aviation Cadet had undergone preflight instruction and had nearly one-hundred and fifty hours of single engine air time under his belt."

The clouds thinned until Summer could see through them. Margaret and Andy sat at the little parlor table, watching as Summer floated into her seat.

"And only twenty of the sixty-five cadets who started advanced training, would ever qualify to pilot multi-engine planes," he continued.

"Interesting, but what the hell has any of that got to do with me?" Summer wondered.

"I believe," Margaret said, responding to her unspoken question, "that Andy is attempting to underscore the magnitude of young Mr. Washington's accomplishment. But I understand your confusion." She turned to Andy. "Given our limited time together, perhaps you should move things along, dear boy."

"Alexander learned to fly in a bird that was made to carry a seven-man crew and a four-thousand-pound payload. A twin-engine bomber with a bad reputation for crashing." Andy shook his head. "He was flying the Marauder solo within three months. But none of that mattered to Gus or the Army brass. They only cared about the color of his skin."

"What became of him?" Summer asked. "Did he make it to the Tuskegee Airmen?"

Andy frowned. "That didn't matter. I taught him to fly because it was the right thing to do, even though I had nothing to gain and a lot to lose. And here," he thrust his arms out with open palms, as if to encompass the entire spirit realm, "where I'm forced to recall *every single moment* of my life with perfect clarity, it's one of the *few* things I'm truly *proud* to remember."

"Yes, darlin' boy," Margaret quipped, as she reached for a steaming pot of tea and began to fill three cups, "that's all well and good. But if you want her to learn from your *mistakes*, you're going to have to show *those* to her."

Andy let out a heavy sigh. "I received three more telegrams about Paige in the weeks following that day in the hangar. My sister was deathly ill, but I couldn't take leave to go home. The war was being fought in the air like never before, which meant we had to train thousands of pilots in record time. Cadets were starting to arrive for advanced flight training, and thousands more were expected to report within the next few weeks." His hazel eyes glistened with unshed tears. "I sent my paycheck home to pay for her care, but she needed more than money. She needed a miracle."

To avoid looking at Andy's tortured expression, Summer focused her attention on Margaret, watching her stir three teaspoons of sugar into her tea. She was familiar with the gut-wrenching pain of being kept from the side of a sibling in serious trouble. *"I guess it hurts just as much, whether you're held back by the Army or the mob."*

Margaret slid the sugar bowl across the table to Summer, drawing her attention back to the discussion. She stirred a single teaspoon of sugar into her own cup, but as she raised the hot liquid to her lips, the fog dropped over the parlor, pulling her from the scene. *"Just as well. I can't stand tea."*

She was getting the hang of giving herself up to the mist, floating in the clouds without resistance. Relaxing minimized the nauseous rollercoaster feelings that came from moving through years of Andy's memory in mere minutes.

"Maybe Andy's trying to teach me that I need to do whatever it takes to save my brother." She pictured Justin lying deathly ill someplace, waiting for her to come to him. *"If it were me, I'd do anything to get there."*

After what felt like a long time, she began to see images appearing at the edges of the fog. She rolled onto her side to see more clearly. It was as if she was watching short video clips, as Andy searched through his memory. She saw him crumple a telegram in his fist and pound it on the narrow shelf that served as a counter in the doorway of the communications room at the Belleview Biltmore. She sensed his agony and felt as helpless as the WAACs, whose job it was to distribute telegrams that, more often than not, contained terrible news.

As the memory clip faded from view, another appeared in its place. This time, Andy twisted his Garrison cap in his hands as he stood before a metal desk, watching a Sergeant review his request for emergency leave. "Sorry Lieutenant," the Sergeant said, "but orders are orders. The Colonel says that until we turn the tide on Hitler, the Army needs every aviation instructor to stay on task." The Sergeant rolled a rubber stamp across his red ink pad and then stamped the word *Denied* across the request. "Try to think of it this way," he said, as he dropped the request on top of a stack of similarly rejected pleas. "Your work is preventing a lot of other families from having an angel of death show up at their door with a telegram." With nothing more to say, he waved his hand, signaling Andy to move along. "Next?" he said, craning his head to the side, focusing his attention on the line of men waiting behind Andy. The next man gently nudged his way to the desk.

The moment that memory disappeared, another came into focus. This time, Andy stood in a long line of soldiers, waiting to make use of three tiny phone booths, tucked into a nook at the end of a hallway. It took Summer a moment to orient herself. Then she recognized the boxed spiral staircase nearby and realized the reason everything looked so different was because the hotel's modern lobby wouldn't be constructed for several decades yet. When Andy and the rest of the soldiers had been housed here, the short flight of stairs leading to the East Wing of the hotel was located at the end of the Promenade corridor. One minuscule phone booth was to the left of the stairs, and two newer, but equally tiny booths had been wedged in on the right.

Several of the waiting soldiers chatted and joked among themselves, but Andy stood with his arms folded across his chest, staring at his shoes. Summer felt the weight of his thoughts. He was trying to figure out how he could break the news to Paige that her brother – her only living relative – was going to let her die alone. A small part of his heart hoped she had already fallen into a coma and would be spared the devastating news, but the rest of him longed to hear his kid sister's voice one more time.

There were still at least ten soldiers in front of him in line, eagerly waiting their turn to call home – looking forward to hearing hometown gossip from their folks or the sweet sound of their best girl's voice, promising to stay true blue. Andy balled his fists, doing his best to hide his mounting jealousy.

"Hey! You there – Turner!"

Andy automatically swung his head toward the sound of his name. Gus Murphy was leaning over the rail at the first landing of the boxed spiral staircase. "Come on over here," he called.

Andy glanced at the line in front of him and then at the even longer one behind him. He shrugged. "What do you want? I'm waiting to ring my sister."

"Hey fellas," Gus shouted to the group. "I need to talk to the Lieutenant upstairs for a few minutes. When he gets back down there, anyone who doesn't let them back in line is going to get a knuckle sandwich from me, got it?"

Andy's face reddened. "I don't recall asking for your help, Gus."

"Yowser, Turner! Stop bein' so damned touchy and come on up, so we can discuss a little biz." Gus straightened and started back up the stairs, stopping only long enough to call over his shoulder, "Ya play your cards right and you'll be at your sister's bedside come morning."

Gus's words hit Andy like a punch to his heart. Ignoring the warning bells clanging in his head, he stepped out of line and turned to the short, stocky soldier behind him. "Don't worry. I don't expect you to hold my place," he mumbled.

He hesitated at the bottom of the spiral stairs and looked up to the fourth floor. Gus was already up there, waiting by the entrance to a separate staircase that connected the fourth and fifth floors. Violet had explained to Andy that the fifth floor wasn't deemed suitable for guest rooms because rich hotel guests objected to traversing so many steps. Instead, the top floor housed nannies and servants who traveled with their wealthy employers. He suspected Gus had chosen quarters on the fifth floor for similar reasons. His room at the far end of the East Wing was the most difficult part of the hotel to access, and therefore the most private.

"What in the hell am I getting myself into?" Andy mumbled under his breath. "I should turn around right now."

But his feet began to climb.

Chapter Twenty-Two

Summer floated at Andy's side, his mood darkening with every step, as two questions spun in his mind like a tornado. *"Can he really do what he says he can?"* and *"What will he want in exchange?"*

"Christ, Turner," Gus said, watching Andy trudge up the staircase. "You act like there's a hangman's noose up here instead of a ticket home."

"You sending me home out of the goodness of your heart there, Gus?"

"Like I said, I'm always willin' to help my friends, Turner." He held the door open for Andy.

Andy gave him a dubious glance and then stepped into the narrow stairwell. While the boxed spiral staircase was wide and boasted elegant railings and carpeted steps, these stairs were narrow, bare and worn, with a plain iron pipe for a hand rail.

The duo emerged at the front end of the East Wing. While the other floors of the hotel hummed with activity, this one was eerily quiet. Their footsteps clicked against the floorboards as they walked down the corridor, passing a common bathroom and several rooms that were equipped to serve as quarters, but were still unoccupied. On the other four floors of the hotel, quarters consisted of four men per room, each with a bunk, a shared closet and eight men to a bathroom. Up here, the ceiling was lower – no more than eight feet at the highest point and, because one side of the gabled roofline resulted in a slanted interior wall, the rooms were only large enough to accommodate three men – two in bunks and one on a single cot. Footlockers were positioned at both ends of the bunks and at the foot of the cot. Despite the tight quarters, the open windows at this height allowed a sea breeze to circulate through the floor, even in the dead of summer.

They walked all the way to the end of the corridor and then stepped into a room that overlooked the aqua-blue waters of the Intracoastal Waterway. Andy would have whistled at the view, had his mouth not been so dry. Then he noticed the bunks were occupied. Wilkins, known as Lumpy, sprawled across the bottom bunk and Crawly – the one they called Squeaky, was up top. Both were thumbing through girly magazines and barely glanced up when they entered the room.

"What's buzzin', cousin?" Squeaky asked, without taking his eyes off his magazine.

"You two goons take a powder," Gus ordered. "Go find somethin' useful to do. I told you, you can't be up here whistlin' Dixie all the time or somebody's gonna notice."

Summer glanced around the room. Nails in the walls served as makeshift hooks near the bunks, holding starched uniforms on wire hangers. She figured Gus had claimed the room's only small closet for himself. Several pin-up graphics of young, voluptuous women, perched half-naked atop huge bombs, or posing on the wings of war planes, and adorned with quips like *bombs away* or *big guns*, filled the remaining wall space. A black and white poster of Betty Grable, clad in a swim suit and stiletto heels hung over Gus's bed. The air smelled of sea salt, sweat and testosterone.

"What's eatin' you?" Lumpy grumbled as he rolled to a sitting position and tucked his magazine under his pillow. He stood to straighten his blanket, ducking just in time to avoid being kicked in the head by Squeaky.

"None of your beeswax," Gus replied. "And if you gimme any more lip, I'll see to it you're put to work bubble dancin' for a week or two."

"Don't get touchy." Squeaky put his palms up in protest. "No need to threaten us with dish washin' duty." He gave Lumpy a knowing smirk as he crossed the room. "You know, I wouldn't be opposed to paying a visit to the mess right about now. Maybe *inspect* the rations."

Lumpy grinned and lurched toward the door. "Yeah, we could sample 'em, too. Make sure the chow's good enough for hard-workin' soldiers."

"Close the door on your way out," Gus called after them.

Andy watched the wooden door click shut as though it were the slam of a jail cell. He sighed. "So what's this noise about me being able to visit my sister?"

"Take a load off, Turner," Gus said, pointing toward Lumpy's bunk. He sat on his cot and slouched forward, resting his forearms on his legs. "It just so happens there's a situation brewin' that might interest you."

Andy sat, still uneasy. He knew Gus was trying to tempt his curiosity, but was determined not to bite.

Like schoolboys in a staring contest, they sat silent for a few moments, each waiting for the other to speak.

Gus caved first. "I'm thinkin' about becoming friends with a certain Sergeant," he began. "The poor fella got himself into a scrape last night – went and got soused while on guard duty. But he might be in luck because the penguin Sergeant who filed the skin owes me a big favor. He's a carrier pigeon for the Colonel, but likes to act like a BTO, so..."

Andy ran a hand through his short hair and frowned. "A penguin? Skin? BTO?"

"Jesus Christ... you really don't know bupkis, do you, Turner?" Gus shook his head. "A penguin's a soldier in the Airforce who doesn't fly – and this *particular* penguin is an eager beaver errand boy for the Colonel, but he likes to pretend he's a big-time operator – a BTO."

It wasn't the first time Andy felt like the men who grew up in big cities spoke a different language than the one he learned in the small mining town where he was raised. Embarrassed, he nodded to acknowledge he understood.

"Anyways – when I met the penguin at Coe's Casino, he was pretending he *was* the Colonel. After he made the mistake of lettin' me buy him too much to drink, he told me about a little rendezvous he had planned with a certain dolly later that night. Turns out the broad was a dimwit who didn't even notice the Colonel's hat didn't match his uniform. Anyway, by the time I happened along to their secret meet-up spot down by the oyster beds on the bluff, her landing gear was wrapped around his back and she was squealing *'ooohhh Colonel'...*" Gus waggled his eyebrows. "Do you need me to explain that part to you, too, Turner?"

Andy blushed and shook his head, still trying to figure out how any of this had anything to do with him.

"Get on with it, asshole." Summer narrowed her eyes and pressed her lips together to stop herself from vocalizing the thought.

"Now, if we weren't buddies, that Sergeant would have been in all sorts of hot water...impersonating an officer, let alone what that girl's daddy would have done to him. But luckily for him, I waited until he shot off his guns and then came runnin' up, actin' like he was this big honcho who I had been sent to find right away. The dame was downright impressed... who knows? Maybe she's still hoping to hear weddin' bells."

Andy shifted in frustration. "So what's a Sergeant's love life got to do with me, Gus?"

Gus lit a cigarette and reached for a half-clam shell that he was using for an ash tray.

Andy wanted to remind him that no indoor smoking was allowed until the sprinkler system was installed – another project that was way behind schedule. But he bit his lip instead, waiting for Gus's reply.

Gus blew out a series of smoke rings. Then he smiled. "That penguin happens to have access to the personnel records. He can pull the skin – um, that's a reprimand – stands for *skin 'em alive* – out of the other Sergeant's jacket. No skin in his jacket means he'll probably get to keep his cushy desk job when the new Colonel reports for duty in a couple weeks." He blew out another smoke ring. A single one this time. Bigger.

Andy puffed up his cheeks and blew out a long breath. "Why do I care about that?"

"Because," A sly smile spread across Gus's tanned face. "that Sergeant's job is to process leave request paperwork."

Andy recalled the dispassionate Sergeant who had stamped the word *denied* on his leave request, and finally understood the way Gus operated. *"A favor for a favor...for a favor."* He balled his fists, disgusted by his own vulnerability. "Alright, so suppose you called in these favors to help me out and the sergeant approves my request for leave. What would you want from me in return? I can't pay you. I don't have any money... and I..."

"I'd only need a teeny tiny favor in return, Turner... hardly anything at all." Gus smiled.

Summer gasped when the clouds dropped over the scene, carrying her away from the memory. *"Damn it. What's the favor?"*

She didn't remain in the mist for very long. When it cleared, she was back at the parlor table, surprised to discover her teacup still in her hand. She hastily returned the cup to its saucer and stared at Andy, who was so transparent that she could make out the shape of the chair behind him.

"These are difficult memories for Andy to share," Margaret explained, drawing Summer's attention.

Summer had become accustomed to the Victorian woman's attire, but remained fascinated by the variety of her wardrobe. This time, the spirit wore a bright blue dress with puffy leg-o-mutton sleeves, trimmed with white lace, along with a large blue felt hat, festooned with a long, white egret feather.

"I'm afraid he's used up all the energy he can draw for now. He won't be able to share any more tonight," she continued.

"Can't *you* tell me what happened?" Summer asked.

Margaret shook her head. "It's not my story to tell – only Andy can access his memories."

Suddenly, Violet materialized next to the table, wearing a modest, mid-calf navy skirt, paired with a white, short sleeved blouse and saddle shoes. She had tied a light blue scarf into a bow on top of her head. It seemed to accentuate her pale blue eyes, but did little to keep her fat blonde curls from swirling around her shoulders.

"I can help tell it," Violet said. "After all, our stories had become one by that time." She floated into the chair next to Andy and took his hand.

Andy closed his eyes and faded even further from sight. Summer could barely make out the outline of his form – as if he were turning into mist.

"Andy met me at the Japanese Gardens to tell me what that awful man wanted him to do. I ..."

A sudden tapping noise caught Summer's attention. The moment she turned toward the sound, she plunged through the fog, feeling like she was falling from an airplane without a parachute. She clawed at the air – grabbing for anything that could stop her fall. She tried to scream, but no sound came out. Gulping back panic, she forced herself to focus on what Margaret had said. "When the living move between memories or leave the spirit realm, floating in the clouds eases the transition." Summer covered her face. *"Wake up!"* she commanded. *"It's just a bad transition. Wake up and you'll be in your bed. Hit the ground and the shock of the fall might kill you!"*

Chapter Twenty-Three

When Summer's flailing hand struck the top corner of her four-poster bed, she was finally able to force her eyelids open. Although the logical part of her brain knew the fall hadn't been real, her heart was pounding and adrenaline surged through her veins as she struggled to get her bearings.

Someone was knocking on her door.

She threw back the down comforter, embracing the frigid air to erase the lingering nightmare from her thoughts as she swung her legs over the side of the bed. "I'm coming," she called. She hoped she didn't sound as shaky as she felt. Jittery with adrenaline, she stood and immediately tripped over the heels she had kicked off a few hours earlier, stubbing her toe. "Ouch! Goddammit!"

Summer hopped on one foot back to the bedside lamp and turned it on. She squinted her eyes to focus on the clock. One-thirty a.m. *"Jesus Christ – who's knocking on my door at this hour? Justin? Dear God, please don't let it be Gordo or one of his minions."*

Her hand trembled as she turned the glass doorknob. She was still dressed in the tight, white slacks and clingy, sleeveless turquoise blouse she had worn to dinner.

Her mouth dropped open at the sight of Robert. His sky-blue eyes sparkled as he shifted from foot to foot, looking more like a small boy anticipating a rocket launch than a calm and serious art dealer.

"What the..."

"Did you hear them?" he blurted. Then his eyes drifted over her. It was his turn to drop his jaw.

Summer glanced down and noticed her chilled nipples poking through her thin blouse. She ran a hand through her hair, wishing it was long enough to provide a modesty shield, then folded her arms across her chest.

"I'm sorry," Robert mumbled. "Were you sleeping?"

"No," Summer lied. She didn't want him to know she had been upset about the way they parted and had fallen asleep in her clothes. Then, realizing her bed-hair and wrinkled blouse were dead giveaways, she lied again. "I mean, I wasn't in bed. I...must have...dozed off on the couch."

"I'm sorry," he repeated. "I was just hoping you heard the ghost children running in the hall." He shifted his gaze to the carpet and rubbed the dark stubble on his chin. "I should have known it was too late to knock. I'm an idiot."

"Jesus, he's got no idea how good-looking he is." Summer blushed and bit her lower lip. *"I wonder what he'd think if I told him I didn't hear the children because I was busy with a bunch of other spirits?"*

Robert's shoulders slumped as he glanced up and attempted a smile. "Sorry to have bothered you. I guess I should probably get some sleep, too." He shoved his hands into his pockets and started to turn away.

Summer shivered, not sure if it was caused by the temperature in her room or something else. *"Remember you have a job to do,"* she chastised herself. *"Keep your focus or people die."* The mantra worked.

"Wait," she said. Slipping into her con-artist persona with less ease than usual, Summer added a tender lilt to her voice. "Maybe you can only hear the ghosts from inside *your* room. I'm not tired and it might be fun to listen for them, if you wouldn't mind some company."

Robert jerked upright as if he were a marionette and a puppeteer had pulled his strings. "Really? That would be great...I mean, if you're sure you wouldn't mind."

"Just give me a minute to change into something more comfortable."

Robert shuffled his feet, licked his lips and cleared his throat – tell-tale signs of confusion and hesitation. Summer smiled. *"Not much of a poker player,"* she thought. "Nothing to worry about – I'm just cold. I figure the thick hotel robe in my closet would feel pretty good right about now."

Robert nodded, still looking as though he had swallowed a swarm of butterflies.

"Come on in. It'll just take me a sec to change." Summer turned and raced down the hall that separated the parlor from the bedroom before he had a chance to respond – or back out.

After closing the bedroom door, she slipped into a short, light-pink nightgown with matching panties and then wrapped herself in the oversized terry bathrobe and slippers that came with the suite and were each emblazoned with the bright green Belleview Biltmore logo.

"Options," she recalled from a book she had read about spy techniques.

When going undercover, a good agent gives himself options that will allow him to transform into the person he needs to be, regardless of how a situation unfolds.

Summer ran a brush through her silky blonde hair and returned to the parlor, her hand on the rope belt, ready to reveal the nightie. But when Robert smiled, obviously pleased by her innocent, well-covered appearance, she tightened the belt. "Do you have coffee in your room?"

"Yeah, but given the hour, maybe we should forego the caffeine. I'd almost forgotten that tomorrow is a big day."

"The auction doesn't take place until the day *after* tomorrow," Summer said, hoping he wasn't changing his mind.

"No, but *Bride On Stairs* arrives tomorrow. Wait till you see it. It's a fabulous painting."

"With a beginning bid of four-million, it ought to be. I did almost forget about the welcome reception for the major players tomorrow evening," Summer lied. She wondered what it would be like to *really* forget something.

"You mean the costume party." Robert wrinkled his nose.

"Come on. It should be fun. And it's sure to get the big spenders in a good mood. Don't people make more purchases when they're happy?"

Robert nodded grudgingly as she picked up her key and stepped to the doorway. "Now, let's go listen for some ghosts."

As they strolled down the hallway to the Presidential Suite, Summer recalled the memories Andy had shared with her, and his resolve to do whatever it took to be at his sister's deathbed – even make a deal with Gus Murphy. *"The lesson Andy has been trying to teach you is that you have to do whatever it takes to help the people you love, no matter the cost. So I have to do this. If I don't get those records, they'll kill Justin."*

The knowledge of that certainty did little to relieve Summer's guilt. She felt sick to her stomach, thinking about how fast Robert's fondness for her would morph into hate when he discovered what she'd done. When he unlocked the suite and held the door open for her, she tensed.

"Game time," she thought. She snatched a bottle of red wine from the rack on the entrance table and then walked down a long hallway to a grand parlor, where she plopped down on the couch. Kicking off her slippers, she crossed her legs, allowing a sliver of the nightie to peek through the opening in her robe. "Can we share a drink while we wait?" She held up the bottle by its neck, rocking it back and forth, a teasing smile on her lips.

"I really did invite you here to listen for ghosts," Robert said, chuckling appreciatively. "But yeah, a glass of wine sounds pretty good." He took the bottle from her and walked across the spacious parlor, through an equally large dining room, and into a small kitchen, where she lost sight of him.

"This is some suite," she called after him. "Mind if I look around?" She stood and began her tour without waiting for a reply. In addition to the rooms she could see from the main parlor, there was a master bedroom with an en-suite bathroom. The Victorian-style bathroom was similar to the one in her own room, but the bedroom was huge – furnished with a king-sized mahogany four poster bed, floor to ceiling mahogany built-ins, a small sitting room with sliding pocket doors, and access to a balcony. She turned and dashed down the entrance hall, where she found two more bedrooms. It was obvious that Robert used the guestroom closest to the front door as an office. His laptop computer was open on the desk.

Summer's eyes grew wide as she creeped toward her target. *"Could it be this easy?"*

"Hey, where'd you go?" Robert called from the parlor.

Sucking in a sharp breath, she backed out of the room and smiled. "Giving myself the fifty-cent tour. This place is incredible."

"In my opinion, the best part is out there," he said, waving a glass of wine toward the glass doors and balcony beyond. "Unless there's a full moon, you can't see much at night, but during the day, I have an amazing view of the golf course and the water."

As she settled back on the couch, he offered her a goblet of merlot. *"I wish I could just steal the computer and be done with this damn job,"* she fretted, careful to hide all traces of her true emotions. She took the glass and then patted the seat next to her, signaling him to sit. "So, how does this work?" she asked. "Do we have to be super quiet to hear the laughing ghosts, or what?"

Robert sat at the far end of the couch, his back rigid. "No. I mean; I don't think so. I had music playing earlier."

Summer curled her legs under her body, casually leaning closer to him. "What kind of music?"

"Mostly old stuff from my collection – Heart, Journey – a little R.E.M."

"You have good taste," she said, hoping his music was stored on his computer. "Why don't you turn it back on?"

She frowned when he stood and walked over to the built-in. She hadn't noticed the CD player next to the TV. He pushed a button and the *Eagles* song, *Take it Easy* filled the room.

"Whoa," he said, adjusting the volume dial down. "I was in the office. I doubt I would have heard them from out here with the music cranked like that."

Summer perked up. "Were you in the office every time you heard the ghosts?" she asked, fighting to maintain a casual tone.

"Hmm...yeah, I guess I was," he admitted.

"Well, then, I suggest we move our little ghost-hunting party into that room." She uncurled her body and stood, picking up the wine bottle in one hand and her glass in the other. She sang the well-known lyrics to the *Eagles'* tune as she hurried down the hall toward the office. *"Come on, Robert. Follow me."*

Chapter Twenty-Four

The small room was lit by a lamp on the desk where Robert's laptop rested. Ignoring the office-style chair, Summer perched on the edge of the queen-sized sleigh bed. She smiled when Robert appeared in the doorway. He leaned against the doorframe and took in the sight of her on the bed before shifting his gaze to his wineglass. He swirled the dark red liquid and then lifted the glass to his lips without speaking.

"So, do you think the mini-spirits are reliving some fun they had in this hotel when they were kids?" Summer asked, determined to keep the mood light. *"And do you have any idea how sexy you look, backlit in that doorway?"*

He bit his lip and shuffled to the chair, spinning it around to face the bed before sitting. "Maybe." He stretched out his long legs and crossed his ankles. "I guess I'm not totally convinced that I'm even hearing ghosts. When I showed up at your door, I was hoping that you had heard the sound and would tell where it was coming from...that it was something normal...you know – something other than ghosts."

"Me? What makes you think a girl who has been dreaming about spirits since she got here could convince you that the ones *you're* hearing don't exist?"

"Good point."

"So, while we're waiting, tell me more about yourself," Summer said. "All I know is that you're a top-notch art dealer who appointed himself to serve as an overly strict chaperone to his sister and her college roommate. Surely there's more to you than that."

"*Allegedly* overly strict chaperone." Robert grinned. "It's clear that you get all your information from Dana. In her mind, I've always been Emma's overprotective big brother, who likes bossing everybody around. The truth is, Emma and Dana have acted like they're joined at the hip ever since elementary school, so I usually got stuck watching out for both of them. And I really am pretty demanding, so I can understand why Dana thinks I'm a hard-nosed boss. But you're right – that's a pretty narrow view of me."

"So tell me the rest of your story," Summer encouraged. "Did you always love art?"

"Not really. Before my parents died, I was your typical spoiled little rich kid. Our parents traveled a lot, but Emma and I were fine. Our nannies and servants were kind, and we had every material thing we could ever ask for. I *liked* art, but truthfully, I resented having to attend foundation functions and I *hated* being lectured about how I was expected to live up to the McNeal ideals and carry on our family's legacy."

"When did things change?" Summer asked.

"When our parents died, we moved into the home of our elderly spinster aunt, in River North, Chicago, where we were pretty much left on our own. After a few years, I guess you could say I rebelled – drinking, carousing...putting myself at the center of the universe – typical coming-of-age stuff."

"And Emma?"

"I was too self-absorbed to notice that we were growing apart until after Emma had been unofficially adopted by Dana's massive family. When I finally realized how much I missed her, I had to hang around the Cooper's house, just to see her. One day, Dana's parents sat me down and told me it was time for me to stop feeling sorry for myself and get my shit together."

"They really said that?"

"Well, they used nicer words, but that was the gist of it. They reminded me that our aunt wouldn't be around much longer and then the two of us would be all that was left of our family. Once I understood that, I decided to become a role model for my kid sister. I settled down, graduated from the University of Chicago and then started learning about the job I was preordained to hold."

"Director of the McNeal Foundation?"

Robert nodded. "By the time Emma was ready to graduate from high school, I had discovered for myself why our parents had been so passionate about art and was honored that it would be my job to carry on the family legacy. But I hadn't forgotten my wild college days and I was determined to keep Emma away from frat parties, filled with guys like me."

"So you protected them. And apparently, you did a great job."

"Not really. I turned out to be a piss-poor chaperone," Robert said. "Despite all my hovering, Emma met her husband at a frat party when she was *supposed* to be at the library, and hell, I didn't even know Dana was *dating* a married creep until she told me he got her pregnant." Robert frowned and took a deep drink of wine.

Dana had confessed to Summer that she had been date-raped, but Summer had promised to keep her secret, so she said nothing. *"I hope those two know how lucky they are to have someone like you in their corner."*

"As it turns out," Robert continued, "I wasn't even smart enough to look after my own love life. I fell for a beautiful woman with a cash register in place of a heart."

"Dana told me you had a bad experience with a gold digger."

"Yeah. Finding out the truth about Lisa nearly did me in. I really loved that woman – or at least I thought I did. Maybe it doesn't count as true love since she was pretending to be someone else, but it still hurt. It was as if the woman I fell in love with had died or something and left a stranger in her place."

"Okay – seduction is off the table." Summer pulled the belt on her robe tighter. *"It might not be much, but at least I can spare you the pain of feeling like that again when you find out what I've done."*

As the night wore on, Robert relaxed and spoke more freely. Summer kept the focus of the conversation on him and his family, art, childhood pets, and everything from favorite bands to favorite numbers, hoping to tire him out while also collecting clues about his computer password. When his glass was empty, she refilled it, and when the bottle was empty, she got another. She made subtle shifts until she was reclined, with her head resting against the pillows. When Robert began to yawn, she seized her opportunity.

"Maybe you should join me over here," she said. "We can try being quiet for a little while to see if our conversation is what's keeping the ghosties away." She ignored the guilt gnawing at her gut. *"You have to go through with this,"* she silently reminded herself. *"If you don't honor the contract, either Gordo or The Broker will kill Justin – and maybe you, too."*

Robert yawned again. "That might be a good idea, but listen…if you want to go back to your room, I'd understand."

"No, I'm good for a little while longer," she replied. *"God, I really hate that I have to do this."* She wished she could keep him from finding out, but she knew he was too smart. The moment Gordo hacked the bank accounts of the art collectors, Robert would deduce what happened. The trail of the compromised financial data would lead right back to this room.

Summer swallowed the lump in her throat as she watched Robert use his toes to kick off his loafers, letting each shoe thump to the floor. She hugged herself and closed her eyes, wishing he hadn't turned out to be such a good person. *"If only things were different…"* Summer slammed the door on the wishful train of thought. *"If things were different, you never would have met him in the first place. And besides, he deserves the love of someone who's a hell of a lot better than you."*

Robert's gentle snoring brought an end to her mental beating. She slipped from the bed with the agility of a cat and scooped up the laptop computer. In the bathroom, she went to work, using her hacker skills and eidetic memory to sort through every detail of their conversation, searching for likely passwords.

"He keeps reams of notes and relies on Dana to research the details of the art pieces and keep them organized," she thought. *"That means his password will be something he can remember easily. And he's not the least bit self-centered, so it won't be about himself. Maybe Emma's birthday?"* She typed it in and instantly got an incorrect password message. *"I guess that was too much to hope for."*

Robert hadn't been especially enthusiastic about any specific band and he said it would be impossible to narrow down his list of favorite artists, let alone choose one favorite, so Summer eliminated those categories as password possibilities.

Then she remembered the story he told her about how his sister had chosen the name for the Persian kitten he got her for her thirteenth birthday. Emma and the cat were both Capricorns. Summer began to type. After a few more failed attempts, the password *Capricorn13* was accepted. She couldn't resist a fist pump – deciphering Robert's password had taken less than ten minutes.

Finding and opening the confidential client files was simple. Every client was required to provide a link to a bonded account that could be immediately accessed for payment each time a collector won the bid on a piece of art. A skilled hacker could use the financial data from that account to worm his way into additional accounts.

"Geeze, Robert – you really need someone like me to overhaul your computer security."

If only Gordo would be content to hack just one or two of the accounts, fraud investigators might never discover how the victim's information was compromised. But Summer knew that restraint and caution were not in Gordo's vocabulary. The con would be uncovered and when it was, Robert would piece everything together.

Summer only had to study each page for two seconds in order to lock it into her mind forever, but there were dozens of files. She clicked through file after file, page after page, never looking away from the screen. The process took the better part of an hour. Finally, she shut down the computer and crept back to the room, where Robert's peaceful and rhythmic snoring assured her that he hadn't noticed her absence. She placed the computer exactly where it had been on the desk, reconnected the charger, and then slid back into bed.

Robert stirred, but only enough to roll onto his side and flop an arm across her ribcage. Summer took in a sharp breath, surprised by the sense of longing his touch evoked. She bit her lip. *"What I want doesn't matter."* She reached for his arm, intending to gently free herself from his grasp, but when her fingertips touched his flesh, he gave her a gentle squeeze.

She paused. *"Oh, what the hell."* With her hand still resting on the warm flesh of his arm, she squeezed her eyes shut tight against welling tears and sighed. *"This might be as close to love as I ever get."* She didn't notice the temperature dropping or the fog settling over the room until she heard Violet's voice in the mist.

Chapter Twenty-Five

"The day started out so beautifully," Violet's ethereal voice began.

Summer expected the fog to part, allowing her to float into her seat at the parlor table, but instead she remained ensconced in clouds, as Violet's voice drifted over her in an odd, surround-sound fashion.

"When I was just a little girl, Mr. Dean Alvord and his wife, Miz Nellie, bought about sixty-five acres, at the end of Rosery Road – near our farm, and turned it into an attraction called the Japanese Gardens. He built a bamboo tea room overlooking Clearwater Bay, where Japanese women dressed in kimonos and served dishes from the Orient. They built a little red bridge over a stream that ran through the property, and added paths throughout the flower gardens, leading to a pagoda and all kinds of statues and sculpted trees. It was tremendous. Father and Kawa – Mr. Hawakawa, that is – the lead horticulturist at the Japanese Gardens – well, he and father were great friends and they really enjoyed working together. But then..."

The long pause made Summer uncomfortable. *"Something bad happened,"* she thought. *"Because no one ever says, 'but then – things got even greater!'"*

"Soon after Mr. Alvord died, the Japanese attacked Pearl Harbor. After that, folks got pretty itchy about anything Japanese. Donald, Mr. Alvord's son, closed the gardens. Most of the Japanese workers were sent away, supposedly for their own protection, but Donald took responsibility for Kawa and his family, so they got to stay and continue tending the gardens. Nobody minded that I liked to come around, so the attraction became my special hideaway. When Andy told me he wanted to talk to me in private, I thought he was going to… Anyway, I told him I'd meet him there. I curled my hair and put on my favorite blouse – the one that matched my eyes. I wanted everything to be just so."

As the mist began to clear, the scent of flowers filled the air. A moment later, Violet and Andy appeared, strolling down a grassy path that was lined on both sides with lush gardens filled with clusters of flowers in various shades of orange, purple, white, red and yellow. An elderly Japanese man was busy pulling weeds a few feet from the path.

"Hello, Kawa," Violet called.

The old man wore light cotton pants, a work shirt with sleeves rolled up to his elbows, and a pith-helmet styled hat. He smiled and bowed his head before returning his attention to his weeding.

"There it is, up ahead," Violet said, tugging on Andy's hand. "The teahouse! Oh, how I miss Mimiko's homemade miso soup – not to mention her fried dumplings and rice cakes."

The teahouse had a thatched roof and bamboo walls, with long windows and a wrap-around porch, decorated with Japanese lanterns. They walked around to the rear veranda, overlooking Clearwater Bay, and leaned against the bamboo railing to take in the view.

"It's nice here," Andy said. "I sure wish the Japs would of stuck to building places like this instead of turning into a nation of hellish murderers."

Summer flinched at Andy's use of the slur. *"I guess it was a common term back in his day, but still…"*

"They're not all like that," Violet replied, as if she and Summer were of one mind on the issue. "If you want my two cents worth, I think Japan is probably filled with mostly good folks, just like we have here at home."

"That's just crazy," Andy snapped. "I mean, I know you have a soft spot for a couple of them who work here, but believe me – most Japs are blood-thirsty animals. Just look what the cowards did to Pearl Harbor." He rubbed his chin, as if fighting back a slew of additional insults.

"I know, but like I said, I don't think most Japanese are like that," Violet insisted. "Just the soldiers."

Andy squeezed the handrail with both hands and worked his jaw back and forth, focusing on the Bay and beyond, toward Clearwater Beach. "Well, then it's a good thing you aren't in the Air Corps," he replied. "Because, trust me, those bastards deserve everything our bombers unload on them. I'm only sorry that it won't be me dropping eggs on them until not one Goddamn teahouse is left standing."

Violet turned and darted from the veranda before Andy had time to collect himself.

He squeezed his eyes shut for a moment. "God damn it," he hissed. Then he turned and chased after her.

Violet was a swift runner. Andy didn't catch up with her until after she had crossed the little red arching bridge and almost reached the largest pagoda on the property. The tower had five tiers of red eaves, with rice paper windows separating each level and a red demon-arrestor spike rising from the top point of the roof.

Andy caught Violet by her arm and pulled her to a stop. She was trembling and her cheeks were wet from tears. "I'm so sorry, Vi." He bit his lip. "I don't know what gets into me sometimes, letting my dad-blamed mouth run off the way I do." He wiped her tears with his thumb. She sniffled. "I didn't mean to bust your chops. You're probably right. A lot of Japs probably do get a bum rap."

"I'm not addlebrained, you know." Violet gulped. "I know their army has done ghastly things – but I've met so many good Japanese people here that I just can't believe that they're all terrible."

"Let's not talk about it anymore," Andy said, relaxing his shoulders. He lifted Violet's chin and they gazed at one another as if they were the only two people in the world. He bent and kissed her, and for one moment, the world was perfect.

"Ouch!" Andy slapped a mosquito on the back of his neck. "Damn blood-suckers." He rubbed at the itchy spot. "I don't think I'm ever going to get used to how many bugs there are out here in the boondocks."

"Daddy says mosquitoes are drawn to excited blood. If you don't want to get bit, you just have to stay calm." She glanced at the double door to the pagoda. "Come on – kick off your stompers and let's go inside."

Andy glanced warily at the building. "That's another thing – why do Japs always take off their shoes before going inside?" But he sat on the small, ornate bench outside of the door and removed his shoes before padding inside after her.

"Whoa," he murmured, glancing around at the intricate wood carvings covering the walls, many of which were painted in bright colors, accented with gold leaf.

Summer nodded in silent agreement, eyeing the carving of a golden dragon that covered the length of an entire wall.

"Isn't it magnificent?" Violet asked. "They have lots of weddings in here – or at least they used to. Personally, I always thought this would be a fine place to say wedding vows."

"Yeah, it's... nice, but I think I need some fresh air."

Summer was aware that Andy had grown uncomfortable in this sacred building. She understood. *"I've always been nervous in churches too,"* she admitted. *"But at least this one has a lightning rod in case God tries to strike him down."*

Violet followed Andy outside, where they sat side-by-side in wide, rattan chairs with bright, floral cushions.

Summer glanced at Violet and then at Andy, aware of both of their emotions. Violet was excited, eagerly anticipating Andy's question. Andy, on the other hand, dreaded the confession he was about to make.

"Violet, I hope you know how precious you are to me and how much I want you to be at the center of my life always."

Violet bobbed her head, making her blonde curls bounce.

"And I always want to be truthful with you." Her wide, blue eyes were aglow with innocence, shaming him. He shifted his gaze to his stocking feet and twitched his toes. "Gus Murphy got my leave approved," he said. "I've got two weeks to say goodbye to Paige, so I'm heading home on the afternoon train."

The color drained from Violet's face as his words – the ones that were so different than she was expecting – sank in. "But – but, he's a

wise guy – a real bad apple," she said, knitting her eyebrows in confusion. "Why would somebody like that help you?"

Andy closed his eyes, unable to look at her.

"What have you done, Andy?" she whispered. When he didn't respond, she raised her voice. "Tell me!"

"I made a deal with him, okay?" he said, without looking up. "Turns
out some bigwigs over in Tampa have it in mind to turn MacDill into a
permanent military base after the war. They think it will go a long way
in swaying the opinion of local politicians and top brass if they build
barracks and housing for officers. One of them – a general..." Andy
tried to swallow the lump in his dry throat, to no avail. "Well, he's got a
fussy wife who demands a lot of finery in her home – like crystal chandeliers. So Gus and I made a deal. I'm letting him take two chandeliers
from the warehouse in exchange for leave and a ticket home."

Violet gasped. "You're stealing from Mr. Kirkeby? From the
Belleview Biltmore?"

"Come on, Vi," he urged, "try to understand. Paige is all the family
I've got left, and she's dying. I need to be with her. This was my only
option other than taking a French leave."

"I might have *understood* if you had gone AWOL." She trembled.
"But if you go through with this other *option* as you call it, then
you're not the man I thought you were, Andrew Turner." Violet
crossed her arms and leaned back in her chair, distancing herself
from him. "And not a man I would want to spend my life with."

"Ease up, Violet. It's not like I don't know it's wrong, but..."

Summer felt his anger flare, but couldn't tell if he was angry with
Violet or with himself.

"But, you know the cost of a couple chandeliers is peanuts to
someone with megabucks like Kirkeby," he continued. "He probably
won't even notice they're missing."

"*I* would know."

The chill in Violet's voice sent a shiver up Summer's spine.
*"That's the voice of someone who's just learned the ugly truth about
someone's character. It's the same way Robert's going to sound when
he learns about me."*

"I grew up in that hotel and I treasure every inch of it," Violet continued, "including every one of its chandeliers. But that's not the point. Colonel Huck entrusted you to guard the warehouse because he thought you were an honorable man, worthy of that trust. Frankly, so did I."

"Well, I'm *sooo* sorry to disappoint you and Colonel Huck!" Andy slammed his fist on the arm of his chair, causing a small cloud of dust to rise. With immediate remorse, he cowed. "I'm sorry, Vi, I really am. But the deal is done and can't be undone. There's nothing I can do to fix it now."

"The same can be said of us," Violet said, standing on shaky legs. She stepped to the pagoda's door, snatched up her shoes and dashed down a grassy path, tears streaming down her cheeks for the second time in what she had hoped would be the happiest afternoon of her life.

Summer was pulled along with Violet as Andy grappled with his shoes and called after her.

"Please, don't go!" He glanced at his wristwatch. "Goddammit," he muttered, struggling to get his second shoe on. Violet was running in the opposite direction from the entrance. "I've got to go or I'll miss my train! I'll figure out a way to make this right when I get back. I promise!"

She didn't reply or even look back.

Chapter Twenty-Six

As the fog descended over the scene, Violet's disembodied voice began wafting through the air. "It was just as well that Andy didn't ask me to marry him that afternoon. If I'd said 'yes' and then learned about his dishonest dealings with that horrible Gus Murphy, I'm sure I'd have broken off our engagement. As it was, I just ran from the gardens, leaving him standing there, calling after me."

The soft clouds dissolved, returning Summer to the parlor table.

"Nothing good ever comes of rushing to judgment," Margaret said. She picked up a steaming teapot and poured four cups, even though she and Summer were the only ones at the table.

A moment later, Violet began to appear in the chair opposite from her. Although still semi-transparent, she picked up a cup of tea and took a long sip. Summer pretended not to notice that she used the pinky of her opposite hand to dab her tears.

"Then again," Margaret continued, "the same thing could be said of making rash, desperate decisions. It's easy to convince oneself that one will never have to pay the piper. And yet…"

"The piper always demands payment plus interest," Andy said, finishing her thought.

Summer's hand jerked at Andy's unexpected appearance, knocking her teacup over. In an instinctive attempt to avoid getting a lapful of hot liquid, she lurched backward in her chair and jumped to her feet. She gaped with amazement when she realized the full cup of steaming tea had returned to its saucer, leaving no evidence of a spill.

"How..." she began. Unable to form a coherent question, her voice trailed off.

"Close your mouth, darlin'," Margaret said. "It's not sorcery. I manipulated energy to create this parlor space, which I choose to share with my guests. That means I maintain a good deal of control over the inanimate objects in the space. Well, as long as there's not too much outside interference, that is."

"Like if I talk too much?" Summer suggested.

"Chatter does make it difficult to concentrate, as do other disturbances outside of my control."

"Like if someone knocks on my hotel room door?" she asked.

Margaret nodded. "That's right. And unfortunately, I have extremely little control over objects in the living realm. Although I've tried many times, I can do little more than open windows or drawers and move objects short distances. That's why I require your assistance to save the Belleview from destruction."

"Well, I'm sorry, but I can't stop Gordo from setting the fire – I mean, not if I'm going to honor the terms of the deal we made with the Broker." Summer frowned. *"And if I break the deal, they'll kill Justin."* She started to lift her teacup but, remembering the earlier spill, thought better of it. "Besides, Andy's memories sent me a clear message – to do whatever it takes to save my brother's life, no matter the cost to me or anyone else, right?"

"That's not..." Margaret began.

"Even when we were kids," Andy interrupted, "Paige always knew whenever I lied or did something I wasn't supposed to. So when I showed up at Tom Beacon's farm without so much as a phone call, she knew something wasn't right. She was fading fast, but she rallied long enough to badger me into telling her what I'd done to get a two-week leave."

"But you only did it because you loved her," Summer said. "The same way I'm doing what I'm doing because I love Justin."

"Yeah, well, Paige didn't see it that way. She was mortified to learn that she was the reason I had become a thief." Andy rubbed his open palm over his face as if to erase the memory of her disappointment. "She was on her deathbed, coughing up blood and struggling for every breath, but her only worries were about *me*." He glanced at the teacup, frowned and then raised his eyebrows at Margaret.

"Very well," Margaret said with a sniff of mild disapproval. She waved a hand as if sweeping away the teacup. It disappeared and, in its place, a shot of whiskey and a beer chaser materialized.

Andy gave her a nod as he picked up the shot and tossed it down his throat. Then he lifted the beer and downed half of the glass without saying a word.

Summer bit her lip, resisting the urge to speak. *"That looks way better than hot tea. Maybe I should ask her to switch my drink, too."*

"Ladies drink tea," Margaret stated, as if it were an indisputable fact. "Plus, when a spirit relives a memory, it's as if that moment in time is happening all over again. With memories as painful as these, a bit of the Devil's brew is warranted."

"It was just an idea." Once again, Summer wished the Victorian spirit couldn't read her thoughts so easily.

"Anyway," Andy continued, "Paige made me promise I'd figure out a way to undo the deal I made with Gus Murphy and return those chandeliers to the storage room at the Belleview Biltmore. I couldn't refuse her dying request, so I promised I would." He gulped down the rest of the beer and then wiped his lips with the back of his hand. "For the next few days, my sister struggled for every breath as she slipped in and out of consciousness – kept mumbling about beautiful flowers, and how Mama and Pop were waiting for her and such. All I could do was sit by her bed and hold her hand. I was as useless as her doctor." He shook his head.

"You did plenty," Margaret cooed. "You helped her transition to the next step on her eternal journey."

Andy gave her a weak smile before returning his attention to Summer. "At sunrise on the fourth day, Paige woke up with her thoughts as clear as a bell. Between her fits of coughing, we reminisced about doing our homework next to the stove and how I took her flying in Tom Beacon's crop duster. I told her I was going to ask Violet to marry me. She smiled and said she hoped we'd have a bunch of kids, and live a long, happy life – said she'd be watching from heaven."

Violet reached over and wrapped a loving hand around Andy's bicep. He slid his hand over hers and patted it.

"Looks like Violet forgave him," Summer thought.

"It was wonderful to have my sister back," Andy said. "But before the sun had even burned off the morning dew, she lost consciousness again. That was the last time I ever talked to her. She died the next day. I buried her in the church graveyard, next to our parents, and planted a red rose bush on her grave."

Summer swiped away a tear as the fog dropped over the table. *"I can't even imagine how horrible it would be to have to bury Justin. Wait. Is that my connection to Andy? Do we both lose our siblings?"* When the clouds began to dissipate a few moments later, she heard the lonely sound of a train's whistle. Grateful to escape her dark thoughts, she focused on getting her bearings.

She was floating next to Andy as he stepped off a train and into a bustling crowd of men and women from all walks of life, including dozens of soldiers. A small sign on the stone building nearby read: *Clearwater Depot*. She turned a slow circle until she recognized enough of her surroundings to identify the location. *"I know where we are. This is downtown Clearwater – the train station at Court Street and East Avenue."*

Before she had time to contemplate how much downtown Clearwater had changed over the years, she heard someone calling Andy's name.

"Lieutenant Turner!" a young man called from the edge of the crowd.

To her dismay, Summer realized the depot building was divided into two sections. The voice was calling from just outside the open door marked: *Colored Waiting Room*.

Andy waved at the black man and began making his way through the mass of humanity to reach him. "Ho, there, what brings you to the depot, Alexander?"

Summer recognized Alexander Washington, the young black man with bright green eyes that Andy had taught to fly the B-26 bomber. His short-sleeved white shirt, buttoned all the way up to his neck, was tucked into a pair of high-waisted, wide-legged black pants, and his brown leather shoes were polished to a rich gleam.

"I come lookin' for you," Alexander said. "Brought you a letter."

"But, I'm home almost a week early," Andy said, confusion etched on his face. "How'd you know I'd be here?"

"I called your sister's house. A man there told me what happened. I'm deeply grieved for your loss, Lieutenant." Alexander turned an envelope over in his hands and bit his lip.

"You tried to call me? Why? What happened?" Andy's confusion morphed into concern. "Is everything all right here? Gus isn't giving you trouble again, is he?"

"I'm fine," Alexander said. "But I figured you'd want to know..." He shifted his weight from one foot to the other as he spoke. "Your girl left town. She stopped by the hotel and asked me to give you this letter when you got back." He held out the envelope, the ink slightly smudged from being gripped with sweaty hands.

Andy stared at the letter as if it contained an order for his execution.

"Damn," Summer thought, *"a Dear John letter. That sucks."*

"Hundreds of cadets have arrived every day this week," Alexander continued. "They're filling up the hotel, so it's time for me to head on up to Alabama. But I didn't trust anyone else to deliver this letter to you. Besides, I wanted to thank you for everything, and let you know that I scored a ninety-seven on my pilot training entrance exam." He moved the letter a few inches closer to Andy's hand.

When Andy still made no move to take the envelope, Alexander flipped it over to reveal an address printed on the back. "She told me where she was headed, so I wrote it down for you." He winked.

Andy continued to stare at the dreaded envelope.

"Holy mackerel! How can a man be such a gorilla in a bomber, but be scared to death of a little sheet of paper?" Alexander chuckled and shook his head. "I know this particular situation might be above my pay grade, but the way I figure it, Miss Violet wouldn't have said nuthin' unless she was hoping you'd chase after her. And you've got what, four more days before you have to report back here for duty?"

Andy nodded as Alexander's words sank in. "Five days, actually." He took the letter and held his hand out for a shake. "Thanks, buddy.

The next time I see you, I expect you to be all decked out in a Tuskegee pilot's uniform, with a whole fruit salad of hero ribbons tacked on your chest."

"Wouldn't that be something?" Alexander grinned. "My Mama and Granny Millie would probably burst from sheer pride."

As the mist dropped over the scene, Summer was surprised to hear Violet's voice rather than Andy's.

Chapter Twenty-Seven

"Thinking about that day in the Japanese Gardens still upsets me," Violet's disembodied voice lamented. "I was so disillusioned and heartbroken. I hadn't experienced the loss of anyone I loved before, so I couldn't comprehend Andy's despair at the thought of losing Paige, his last living relative. And talk about naïve – I just refused to believe that an officer in Uncle Sam's Army could be as deceptive and evil as Gus Murphy."

When the fog faded, Summer recognized Rosery Flower Farm, Violet's home. They were in an alcove off the living room of the main house. Violet sat at a telephone table, staring at the bulky, black, rotary-dial phone that rested on the small, attached shelf. Her eyes were still puffy from crying.

She took a deep breath, lifted the clunky handset off the receiver, and glanced at a note by the phone. Then she dialed a number, using her forefinger to wind the dial around for the first number, then waiting for it to rewind to its original position before dialing the next number in the sequence. When she finished, she raised the handset to her ear, stiffened her back, and waited for someone to answer the call.

"Hello," she said, "My name is Violet Barnes. I was told to ask for Mr. Farris, the staffing manager. I'm the girl who's being interviewed about completing Jane Long's summer employment contract. She's getting married and..." She paused, listening. "Yes, ma'am." She twisted the telephone cord around her finger. "No, ma'am." Her eyes widened as she dropped the cord. "Yes, ma'am, I can be there to-morrow." She picked up the pencil and scribbled additional information on the note. "Yes, I've got it. Thank you, ma'am."

Curious, Summer eyed Violet's hastily written note as the fog engulfed the memory. It was the address for the Sea Cliff Inn, in Cape Cod, Massachusetts. Summer's thoughts drifted to the Cape. When she and Justin ran away from their last foster home at the age of seventeen, they wound up there. The attractive and well-built twins quickly discovered easy pickings among the rich tourist-season residents. By embellishing the details of their awful childhoods, they had been able to con residents into giving them everything from food and shelter, to designer clothing and even cold, hard cash. That is, until one father found his daughter's growing affection for Justin unacceptable. He had paid them enough to make it worth their while to take the ferry back to the mainland and never return.

Violet's voice interrupted Summer's musings. "Jane Long and Joe Constantine were school chums of mine. Joe came from a good family that owned a gladiola farm on Highway 60, but Jane's father wanted her to wait until after the war to get married. She agreed to work at the Cape for the summer, but as they say, distance makes the heart grow fonder. The day after I broke things off with Andy, she called, asking if I'd be willing to take her place at the inn for the rest of the season, so she and Joe could get married. I agreed to interview, never expecting to get hired. But when I called, I learned they were in something of a panic because three girls had just quit without notice. The woman who answered the phone asked if I was a healthy, Christian girl, and if I had plans to get married in the near future. When I said *yes* to the first question and *no* to the second, she said I was hired and asked if I could start work immediately."

When the mist began to clear, Summer found herself trailing behind Violet and a thin, middle-aged woman, as they mounted a narrow flight of stairs.

"The hist-aw-ric Sea Cliff Inn fust opened in 1886." The flat tone in the older woman's Bostonian accent suggested she had recited these instructions more times than she cared to count. "Because the inn's only open faw fawteen weeks in the summer, we almost always operate at full occupancy. That's three-hundred guest rooms." When they reached a small landing, she paused before opening the door. "Yah will be rooming in the attic dorm on our right, with the rest of owa' female workers. They's thurty open cots and a communal bathroom in this section. The boys have the same set-up on the left."

The heavy wood door opened with a creak, and Violet cast a wary glance around the narrow, dimly-lit space. The shiplap walls were painted yellow, but the ceiling appeared to be raw wood. To her left, a young man leaned against a wall near an open window, smoking a cigarette. Near where he stood, the words *Male Staff Quarters* were painted on a closed door in large, black letters. Violet turned and saw a nearly identical closed door centered on the wall to her right. The only differences were that this door bore the designation: *Female Staff Quarters* and there was a lock on it.

"Mr. Prescot," the woman scolded, "I believe yah've been instructed not to smoke in the hallway."

"Indeed I have, Mrs. Perkins," the man replied. He grinned and attempted to smooth a wayward curl into his wave of dark brown hair. Refusing to cooperate, the curl fell back onto his forehead. "But judging by the smell in there, I think some of the boys must have eaten skunk for supper. You wouldn't bust my chops over needing a breath of fresh air, now would you?" He took a long drag on his cigarette and blew it out the window before grinding the butt into a clam shell.

Summer bit her lip to keep from giggling. Violet coughed for the same reason.

"That's no excuse faw wearing unmentionables in the corridor," Mrs. Perkins replied. "Go back inside immediately."

"Unmentionables?" It took Summer a moment to remember that a tee-shirt was deemed to be underwear in the 1940s, even if it had sleeves and was tucked into a pair of slacks.

"Geez, don't flip your wig," the young man mumbled. As he reached for the door handle, he winked at Violet. "Hey, there, doll face. Are you rationed or single?"

"That's none of yahr business, Mr. Prescot." Mrs. Perkins placed her balled fists on her hips. "Now, scoot!" She huffed. "I *strongly* advise owa' young ladies not to consort with the male staff."

Although the advice was clearly meant for Violet, Mrs. Perkins continued to stare after the young man until he entered the men's dorm and closed the door.

"If yah're caught in there," Mrs. Perkins said, shaking her finger at the door, "yahr parents will be informed and yahr employment will be terminated." She turned her attention to Violet. "Stay away from that one, in particular." She jerked her head in Prescot's direction. "Kingsley Prescot is bad news. He hails from a wealthy, powerful family, and they have political aspirations faw him." She took out a key, unlocked the women's dorm, and lowered her voice. "As we discussed, room and board are included in yahr compensation, as is a small weekly stipend. But the majority of yahr earnings will come from the tips yah receive from yahr assigned guests, so the harder yah work, the better yah will make out."

She escorted Violet down the center aisle to an open cot. "Fresh linens are provided each week."

Violet nodded at the folded pile on the unmade bed and then looked around the room. A small, rectangular lamp table separated each cot from the next. Most of the beds were occupied by sleeping women, but here and there, girls were reading by lamp light. A few nodded at the new arrival, but no one spoke. At the far end of the dorm, a light glowed in the opening to the bathroom. Two ironing boards stood just inside, creating an entrance of sorts.

"Yahr table is the one to the left of yahr cot," Mrs. Perkins continued. She pointed at the clothes draped over Violet's arm and the compact valise in her other hand. "Yah were issued two uniforms, which yah're expected to keep washed and pressed. Every time yah report for work in a dirty or wrinkled uniform, yahr pay will be docked fifty cents." She pointed at four pegs, nailed above each cot. "Yah can hang yahr uniforms up thaya and keep yahr personal belongings in the draw of yahr table or beneath yahr bed." She narrowed her eyes. "But be warned. Valuables left unattended often come up missing." She turned and pointed to a sleeping form on the cot next to hers. "That's Helen Kurtz. Yah will be working with her in the morning, so she'll show you around. Now yah best get some sleep. Breakfast is served in the staff dining hall at 5:30 sharp."

The moment the mist dropped over the area, carrying Summer from the scene, Violet began speaking again.

"The next morning, Helen, a chubby redheaded girl from Missouri, escorted me to the dining hall, which was aptly named. It was narrower than the Promenade Corridor at the Belleview Biltmore, with long, wooden tables and benches on either side. We each picked up a bowl and stood in line, waiting for the kitchen staff to serve us oatmeal and hardtack, which is what people in Massachusetts call dry biscuits. After we choked down our breakfast, Helen showed me around and introduced me to several of the guests we were assigned to care for. We worked all day long, cleaning guest rooms, doing laundry and helping-out in the formal dining room, making sure our assigned guests wanted for nothing. Before bed, we were served a bowl of thin, fish stew that smelled like hog slop."

When the mist faded, Helen and Violet were in the bathroom, washing their uniforms in a galvanized tub.

"I'm still hungry," Violet said. "I guess I should have asked more questions about the room and board part of our compensation."

"I'm sorry. I should have warned you about that," Helen said. "If you're brazen enough, you can try swiping a little food from your guests' supper plates before serving them. But most of us salvage the uneaten food while we're clearing the tables – or do favors for Kingsley Prescot in exchange for extra food. He's always well-fed. I think the cooks hope to impress his father."

"Mrs. Perkins warned me about Kingsley Prescot. She said he's trouble."

"I don't know a whole lot about him," Helen said as she wrung water from her uniform. "The girls say his father is some big-wheel who's friends with the owner of the Sea Cliff. He's making Kingsley work here for the season because he believes it will help him become a well-rounded businessman."

Helen dipped her wet uniform into a starch solution and then draped it over a hanger. "I can tell you one thing for sure. He's well-named. Most folks around here treat him like a king. They do most of his work, hoping he'll help them find other jobs when the season is over. But not me. I don't think it's a good idea to get too friendly with rich boys." Helen grinned. "But maybe I'd feel differently if I was a dish like you." She paused to study Violet, who was still scrubbing her uniform. "You know, I caught him watching you several times today. Who knows? You could be his Cinderella."

"Horsefeathers!" Violet said. Although still hurting from her break-up with Andy, she blushed at the thought of attracting the attention of someone so important. "I'm just a Florida farm girl. He couldn't possibly be interested in the likes of me."

The duo hung up their wet clothes, and then pressed their alternate uniforms. Afterward, they rolled their hair around soup cans and fastened them with bobby pins, before tumbling onto their cots. As Violet reached out to turn off her lamp, the fog dropped over the scene, carrying Summer away.

"When I woke up the next morning," Violet said, her voice wafting through the clouds, "my pressed uniform was missing. Helen helped me search for it, but it was gone – stolen. There was no time to iron my other uniform, so I had to wear it damp and wrinkled. Mrs. Perkins fined me fifty cents and informed me that a replacement uniform would cost me an entire week's pay. I was so upset, I ran outside to collect myself. Kingsley must have overheard. He followed me out and promised me he'd find the culprit. And he did! One of the other girls had stained her own uniform and had taken mine in a moment of desperation. When Kingsley informed her I was a close friend of his, she returned it post haste."

This time, when the mist faded, Violet was in the hallway outside of the dorm, talking to Kingsley.

"If you really want to thank Kingsley Prescot," he said, "you'll come out tonight after everyone goes to sleep. A bunch of us are planning to ride bicycles to the beach for a party and a midnight swim."

Violet agreed immediately, excited to be invited to a secret beach party, but then frowned. "But how will we get out? They lock our dorm door."

Prescot grinned and pulled a key from his trousers pocket. "No problem, doll. I've got connections."

As Summer watched the memory, time sped up as if watching a movie in fast-forward mode, so that the remainder of the day passed in mere seconds. Time slowed down again that night, just as Violet was climbing out of the small window where she had first set eyes on Prescot. She and a few others took turns climbing down a ladder, and then snuck over to where the guest bicycles were stored, to join the rest of the group.

There were fewer participants than Violet had anticipated. Perhaps eight or ten people all together. Violet rode next to Kingsley, who had strapped a flashlight to the handlebars of his bicycle. Another boy pulled a wagon behind his bike. When they reached the beach, they constructed a makeshift privacy curtain by tying a blanket between two thin trees, and then the girls took turns changing into their swimwear. Violet wore a modest one-piece suit, with wide shoulder straps and a short, full skirt. The other girls wore strapless suits with no skirt at all. One even wore an almost scandalous two-piece suit that showed several inches of bare skin between her waist and bra-styled top. Once changed, most of the group waded into the cold water, laughing and splashing around in the shallows, but Violet stayed on the shore.

Summer could read Violet's nervous thoughts as clearly as if she were speaking out loud. This beach party was nothing like the ones she remembered from her childhood. There was no fire. No music. No snacks, and no drinks, except the keg of beer that had been in the wagon. And although she liked to swim, Violet was used to considerably warmer water and the thought of swimming late at night, when dangerous creatures might be lurking beneath the dark surface, terrified her.

One of the boys handed out cups of beer, as increasing cloud coverage choked out the last of the moonlight. Everyone spoke in hushed tones as they listened to the cold waves crashing in the distance. Violet didn't care for the taste of beer. She took only a few bitter sips, while everyone else refilled their glasses, laughing about having to grope around in the dark.

Kingsley shined his flashlight at her. "You need to drink faster, baby-doll," he goaded.

Violet flinched and held her hand up to shield her eyes from the bright light. "In Florida, a beach party involves a bon fire and roasting marshmallows," she said, trying to calm her mounting discomfort.

"Here on the Cape, we make our own heat," Kingsley joked.

The more everyone drank, the more they flirted with one another. Violet trembled as the group began pairing up. Before long, necking couples began disappearing behind sand dunes, trying to hide from the beam of Kingsley's flashlight.

When she and Kingsley were the only couple left on the beach, he scooted next to her and gave her a clumsy embrace. She turned her head as he began raining sloppy, beer-breath kisses on her cheek, searching for her mouth.

"What are you doing?" Violet cocked her head, trying to read his expression in the dark. "Certainly you don't expect me to..." She shoved him back, trying to make sense of what was happening.

Kingsley chuckled. "Don't play innocent with me. You know what we came down here to do."

"I'm sorry if you think I led you on, but I'm not that kind of girl," Violet said. "I thought we were going to have a *real* beach party." She put one stiff arm on the sand and pushed herself up. "I'm going back to the inn."

"Buullll shhhit," he slurred. "Kingsley Prescot could have had any one of these girls tonight, but he chose you, and now you're the only woman left on the beach. You're crazy if you think he's going to let you back out now. You Goddamn tease."

Before Violet could get her balance, he grabbed her by the arm and pulled her back to the ground. Pinning her down with his body, he gave her a rough kiss. Violet fought the urge to panic, wishing with all her heart that she was back home at Rosery Farm. Then she realized that all those years of hard work in the flower fields had probably made her as strong as Kingsley, who had never done an ounce of manual labor in his entire life. She shoved him to the side with all her might, catching him by surprise. She rolled in the opposite direction, then leapt to her feet and ran down the beach as fast as she could.

Kingsley laughed and got to his feet to give chase, enjoying the game. "Kingley's coming for you, doll face," he shouted. Her screams, muffled by the crashing surf, seemed to tantalize him. "Fight all you want, but Kingsley's gonna win this battle – and wait till you see what happens to Kingsley's prisoners!" He laughed.

He was gaining on her. Violet knew she couldn't outrun him on the beach. He was only a few feet behind her when she turned toward the cold surf, her eyes wild.

Summer didn't feel the cold water as she waded in at Violet's side, but she could sense her emotions and read her thoughts. She remembered reading about how a gazelle would run into a river filled with crocodiles to avoid a lion's attack, and now, sensing Violet's fear, she understood what drove the gazelle.

Chapter Twenty-Eight

The icy surf and soft sand beneath her feet slowed Violet's movements as she struggled to reach deeper water. Fortunately, these obstacles had the same effect on Kingsley. She could hear him splashing behind her, getting closer with every step.

"This is great," he cackled. "Kingsley prefers the smell of the sea to the smell of cleaning powder anyway." Then he stopped laughing. "Come on, baby doll," he growled. "Let's get out of this cold water and warm each other up. My balls are freezing!"

Violet ignored him, swimming with all her might toward deeper water, with no real destination in mind. She thought about the sign on the beach next to the inn – the one that read: *3,000 miles to Spain.* She wondered how long it would take to swim three-thousand miles.

"Don't be stupid," Kingsley yelled. His voice sounded farther away. "You'll drown if you keep going!"

Violet knew he was right, but the gazelle in her continued to swim toward the crocodiles until she could no longer hear the lion behind her. She kept swimming even after she knew Kingsley had turned for shore, panic and adrenaline driving her arms to continue their churning motion.

Eventually, a new fear washed over Violet. With no moon or stars for guidance, she had no idea which direction she was swimming. She came to a halt, treading water – moving in slow circles, searching for anything that could offer her the tiniest bit of hope for safety.

She could hear the waves crashing in the distance, but on the open water, her ears deceived her, refusing to pinpoint the direction of the sound. A dozen dangers taunted her frazzled thoughts – cramps – sharks – Davy Jones' locker – dehydration – sea monsters – exhaustion...

She swam first in one direction and then another, second-guessing herself over and over. Was the sound of the waves crashing on shore becoming louder or softer? Then she felt the pull of the tide. Certain she was being drawn out to sea, she fought against it, but the force of nature was far too powerful. Another wave washed over her, filling her nose and mouth with saltwater. She bobbed to the surface, sputtering.

Summer could feel the Violet's growing desperation. *"Is this how she died?"* she wondered.

Finally, Violet remembered what the swimming instructor at the Belleview Biltmore had taught her about swimming against the tide. *"Never try to fight the sea. You'll lose every time."* She flipped over and floated on her back, trying to conserve her strength, allowing the tide to carry her wherever it chose. She shivered, colder now that she had stopped moving, and wondered if Kingsley would alert anyone that she was missing. *"I doubt it,"* she mused. *"Kingsley Prescot won't care what happens to a maid who rebuffed his advances."* Thoughts of Andy began filling her mind with longing, as tears rolled silently down her cheeks, saltwater into saltwater.

After what seemed like a long time, she remembered overhearing soldiers talking about dying at sea. They said that once a person quit fighting for breath, drowning was a painless way to die. Regardless, she resolved to float as long as she possibly could before sinking into the depths of the cold water. Her thoughts turned to her family and she wondered what they would do when they were told that her lifeless body had been found on some shore. Perhaps she wouldn't be found and her parents and sisters would never learn what had become of her.

When exhaustion set in, Violet tried to coax herself into giving up, but her drive to live was stronger than her resolve to let go, so she remained on top of the water. From time to time, she would struggle to an upright position and glance around, hoping to see something – anything. But it was too dark. She was so tired of seeing absolutely nothing.

Then it happened. Violet saw a light in the distance. She closed her tired eyes and rubbed them, trying to determine if it was real or imagined. When she reopened them, the light was still there. She started swimming toward it, uncertain whether it was a light on the shore or Heaven's gates. To her exhausted mind, one was as good as the other.

All at once, the light disappeared from view. Violet froze, holding her breath and trying not to move. A full second went by before the light reappeared. She fought her rising terror and refocused on the small, glowing beacon in the distance. Again, it disappeared for a moment. It was a long moment. Long enough to realize that something had blocked the light from view. Long enough to recognize the dorsal fin of a shark. She stayed as still as she could and watched the monster circle her once more.

"I will not die without a fight," Violet whispered. She decided to swim toward the light with every ounce of strength she could muster, while trying to splash as little as possible. With each turn of her head her eyes searched wildly for the light and for the fin. She wondered if the shark was beneath her, it's jaws open, ready to feed. She contemplated how much it would hurt to lose an arm or a leg, and whether she would be able to keep swimming afterward. She focused all of her attention on the light. It was getting closer. Then her fingertips brushed against something hard.

She yanked her hand back and made a fist, certain the shark had begun its attack. To her amazement, her knees struck sand. Traumatized, she struggled to her feet. The water was only knee deep. Thankful the shark had not followed her into the shallows, she dragged one foot after the other, feeling her adrenaline drain out of her body with every step. By the time she reached dry sand, her other senses began to return. Instead of her own heartbeat, she could now hear the waves crashing behind her, and the taste of sour spittle filled her dry mouth. She shivered as the chilly night air blew over her wet skin and through her dripping hair.

Feeling lightheaded, she stumbled toward the light, still wondering what it was and hoping beyond hope, that Kingsley wasn't still waiting for her to return.

When she reached what she finally recognized to be a bonfire, Violet collapsed onto her knees and cried, holding her arms as close to the flames as she dared. She saw no one, but next to the fire was a small pile of wood, an Army blanket, a towel, and a canteen. Numb, she wrapped herself in the towel and opened the canteen, praying it didn't contain beer. She choked on her first swallow of tepid water, but she couldn't stop drinking. She coughed and drank and coughed some more, until finally, the taste of saltwater was gone from her mouth. Only then did she close the canteen. She dried herself the best that she could, wrapped the damp towel around her hair, and then added several pieces of wood to the fire, causing it to blaze. Afterward, she wrapped herself in the blanket and lay down close to the fire. The warmth of the itchy blanket felt like Heaven as she passed out, exhausted.

Summer noticed the mist settle around her, but before she had time to react, it melted away again. She was still with Violet on the beach, next to the roaring fire. The waves crashing in the background, which had once been one of her favorite sounds, now sent a shiver up Summer's back.

Violet woke to a familiar voice, chanting the mantra, "Thank God, thank God, thank God..." A warm hand caressed her cheek. She struggled to open her eyes and focus. In addition to the glow of the fire, a beam of light shined on her. She put a hand up to block the glare, trying to remember where she was.

"Oh, I'm sorry," the gravelly voice whispered. The light moved away from her face. "I've been searching the beach for hours. I lit three fires, hoping you would see one of them, but I was so afraid..."

"What? Who..." She murmured. The events of the evening came back to her, but she was still confused.

"It's me, Andy," a hoarse voice whispered. He shined the flashlight at his face, so she could see him. "I think I lost my voice shouting your name." He turned off the light and stood to add more wood to the fire.

Violet was too stunned for words. *"Am I hallucinating?"* she wondered. *"Is this what happens when you die?"* She finally managed to whisper, "Andy?"

"Don't you remember me?" he asked, mistaking her bewilderment for lack of recognition. "I'm Andy – Andy Turner – the soldier from the Belleview Biltmore. We were..." he paused, choking on his words. "We were – seeing each other – dating – we met at Christmas..."

"You can't possibly think I forgot you," she mumbled, still trying to determine if this was a hallucination or reality. "My dear, sweet Andy – I couldn't forget you if I lived ten lifetimes."

Her body began to convulse with shivers, despite the warmth of the fire. Andy dropped down next to her, tears in his eyes, and took her into his arms. "I – I was so afraid. I thought I'd lost you."

Summer knew Violet was thinking about how terrified she had been to be alone on this beach with Kingsley. But now, alone with Andy, she felt safe and content beyond words.

"This can't be real," Violet said, leaning against Andy. "You can't be in Massachusetts. And how could you know I was lost in the water?"

Andy pulled her closer. "I came here to apologize and beg you to forgive me," he explained.

In the warmth of the roaring bonfire, Violet slowly regained her strength.

"It was late when I arrived at the inn," Andy explained, too nervous to stop talking. "But thank God I was able to coax your dorm supervisor into fetching you. When you weren't in your bed, Helen Kurtz told her that you and some of the others had gone to the beach for a party. She thought you might be with Kingsley Prescot, but we found the bastard asleep in his bed. When we questioned him, Prescot said that you had been playing in the water and swam out too far. He said he tried to warn you, but you just kept going. He finally gave up, figuring you drowned." Andy shook his head. "The supervisor of the men's dorm had to pull me off to keep me from throttling the little prick."

"I swam out to escape Kingsley's um...carnal overtures." Violet sniffled. "And he...he left me for dead?"

Andy gave Violet a squeeze. "If it makes you feel any better, I think I loosened his front teeth before they pulled me off of him...and now everyone at the inn knows what a lousy creep he is."

Violet managed a half-smile.

"Anywho, I remembered you bragged you could swim a hundred laps in the Olympic-sized pool at the Belleview Biltmore." Andy got up to add the last of the wood to the fire. "I was sure you were still alive, so I made Prescot show me where he last saw you. Helen and the dorm supervisors helped search for you for a while, but then they decided that Kingsley was probably right. They headed back to notify the authorities, but I stayed and kept searching. I knew you wouldn't give up."

"I was so cold and lost, I thought about it," Violet admitted. "But then I saw the fire. You saved my life, Andy." She opened the canteen, took another drink and then recapped it.

"You wouldn't have come here in the first place if it weren't for me." He sat next to her, suddenly overcome with emotion. "I'm so sorry, Violet. Do you think you'll ever be able to forgive me?"

"Of course, I can, Andy," she said. "You made a serious mistake, but you're a good man and I know that no matter how long it takes, you'll find a way to make amends. And once you've earned your re-demption, turn around and you'll find me right here, waiting for you with open arms."

He smiled, glancing around the beach in mock amazement. "You'll be right here?"

She blushed. "Well, not *right* here, of course, but..."

His kiss put a stop to her rambling. "I love you, Violet," he whispered. "I promise to set things right, if it's the last thing I do. And I promise to spend the rest of my life proving that I'm worthy of your love."

As the mist engulfed Summer, she heard Violet promise to love Andy, "forever and always."

Chapter Twenty-Nine

"Shit," moaned Summer, as she drifted in the misty clouds. "Andy and Violet are trying to tell me their relationship worked out, only because he agreed to confess and make things right, no matter what it cost him. Goddamn Dudley Do-Right. He's trying to teach me that to be worthy of a man like Robert's love, I'd have to confess about being a con artist and spoil the scam. That might save the hotel, but it would get Justin and me killed, so what's the point?"

Her eidetic memory began racing, flashing images of old friends and lovers. Other than Justin, she had destroyed every relationship she'd ever attempted. *"Besides, Robert would never forgive me the way Violet forgave Andy. Not once he realized that I was trying to con him from the moment we met."*

She rubbed her hands over her face, allowing her horrific memories to chase one another through her brain in a tangled symphony. She recalled doing whatever it took to survive in crappy foster homes, then running con after con, until it became easy to swindle people. Those chapters of her life ended with Dave and Edward's gruesome murders, but the next chapters were no better. While living under Gordo's absolute domination, she witnessed troubled women being forced to become drug-runners and prostitutes. Her motivation to escape his clutches had been driven, not by her desire to save those poor women, but to save herself – and now she was willing to do whatever it took to save herself and Justin. *"Even if I changed, how could someone like Robert ever love someone with my history and twisted sense of right and wrong?"*

Eager to ignore her mounting dilemmas, Summer breathed a sigh of relief when the clouds parted.

"What do you mean I'm not authorized to go in?" Andy demanded.

Summer concentrated, attempting to get her bearings as the remainder of the mist cleared and the surroundings took shape. When she noticed the Belleview Biltmore a short distance away, she realized she and Andy Turner were standing in front of the old steam-generator building, where the hotel's artifacts were stored.

"Orders, Sir," the pimply-faced soldier said. "Nobody goes in except the officer who has the key." His voice still contained a shaky, adolescent quality – as if it might crack at any moment.

Andy reached for the keys he wore on the chain with his dog tags, but stopped, remembering that he had turned them over to Colonel Huck before departing to visit Paige for the last time. He eyed the cadet. "You must be new here. Otherwise, you'd know that I *am* the officer who's in charge of this building," he said. "I've just been away for a couple of weeks."

The boy soldier frowned, fiddling with the butt of the M1 Garand rifle he clutched against his chest. "I reckon you'll have to work all that out with the Colonel, Sir. Until you do, I hope you won't cause a ruckus, because my orders are to stop anyone who tries to go in there."

"No problem, Private," Andy said. "I'll head over to Colonel Huck's quarters and get this straightened out right now."

"Colonel *Huck*?" The private cocked his head to one side. "He left a couple days ago. Colonel *Lindley* is in command of the Group C Replacement Training Center now."

Andy frowned, disappointed he hadn't had a chance to wish Colonel Huck farewell. Then he nodded and refocused on the private. "So, do you know where I can find Colonel Lindley?"

"No, Sir," the boy mumbled. He glanced at the gold pilot's wings on Andy's uniform and then dropped his gaze to the ground. "I washed-out yesterday, sir. They assigned me to the Goon Squad and stuck me out here, guarding this door. Truthfully, you're the first person I've talked to all day, Sir."

"Wow, a lot has happened while I've been gone. They've already begun sorting cadets." Andy shook his head. "Listen, Private, washing out

of aviation training must be disappointing as hell, but it doesn't mean you're a goon. You're still a soldier in the Army Air Corps, so keep your chin up and do your part. There's no rule that says you have to fly to be a hero."

"Thank you, Sir. I'll try to remember that, Sir."

Andy returned the private's awkward salute and set off in search of the new Commanding Officer. Everywhere he looked, the hotel grounds bustled with activity.

"Jesus Christ, it's one thing to read that three thousand soldiers were bivouacked at the hotel," Summer thought, amazed at the spectacle. *"Seeing it is something else altogether."*

Floating along at Andy's side, Summer couldn't help recalling historic facts she had read about the hotel in the book Gordo had given her to memorize. Dozens of soldiers marched in unit formation across the hotel's famous golf courses. The swimming pool that hosted the 1924 USA Olympic trials was now filled with soldiers, struggling to swim laps with sandbags strapped to their backs, to simulate the weight of a pilot's gear. Along the bluff, where for decades, people had gathered to admire the beautiful Intracoastal Waterway and watch glorious sunsets, guards were posted with binoculars to watch for signs of enemy submarines lurking nearby. Elsewhere on the bluff, an obstacle course utilized sandspur filled gullies and steep, muddy banks to train soldiers to watch for hidden dangers.

"Excuse me, soldier." Andy's voice brought Summer out of her reverie. "Can you tell me where I can find Colonel Lindley?"

The lanky, dark-haired soldier drew himself to attention before speaking. "The commander's office is attached to the hotel lobby, Sir. He usually works there during the heat of the day."

"Thanks," he replied, returning the man's salute. "As you were." He turned toward the hotel's main entrance, climbing the broad stairs to the wide veranda two at a time.

The lobby had also been altered in his absence. The vast open space still housed administrative personnel, but their desks had been rearranged to form rows, and at each desk, a man sat typing test results and transfer orders. Andy glanced to his left and flinched at the sight of the communications room. The memory of receiving the telegram about his sister's illness threatened to reopen the fresh wound of her loss. He turned and strode toward the parlor on the opposite side of the room. A Sergeant sat at a desk outside of the Colonel's office, eyeing his approach. Andy swiped the garrison cap from his head, reached behind his back, and tucked it into his belt.

"Sergeant..." he momentarily shifted his gaze to the man's chest in search of a name. "Birmingham," he continued, "I'm Lieutenant Andrew Turner. Please ask Colonel Lindley if he has a moment to speak with me about resuming my responsibility for guarding the hotel's artifacts."

"Guarding the what, Sir?" the Sergeant asked.

"Colonel Lindley's predecessor, Colonel Huck, had assigned me to oversee the security of the artifacts, removed from the hotel and stored in the old generator building. I had to take an emergency leave a couple of weeks back, so I gave him the key until I returned. Unfortunately, while I was away, the command was turned over to Colonel Lindley, so I need to speak to him to get it back."

"Colonel Lindley is *extremely* busy, as you can imagine, Sir," the Sergeant replied. "I doubt he has any idea where Colonel Huck might have put a key to a *storage* room."

Summer felt the heat creep up Andy's neck as he swallowed his anger. "It's not just any old storage room," he tried to explain. "It's the building where all the paintings, chandeliers and antiques are stored – all the things we took out of the hotel before you men arrived. It's incredibly valuable stuff, so I need to get in there and make sure everything is safe."

The Sergeant looked dubious, but stood and tapped twice on the commander's door.

"I'm on the phone, Sergeant," a gruff voice called back. "Is it urgent?"

"No, Sir," he replied, opening the door about a foot. "A Lieutenant Turner is here to see you. Something about a key he thinks Colonel Huck might have given to you to hold for him."

The Colonel chewed on a cigar while holding his hand over the mouthpiece of a black desk phone. A galvanized metal fan oscillated on his desk, partially obscuring his expression, but Andy could still make out a buzz-cut of gray hair, thick, curly eyebrows and the jowls of a bulldog.

Andy bit his tongue to keep from interrupting the Sergeant, but wanted to better explain the situation.

"What kind of key?" the Colonel asked.

"It has something to do with the valuables they took out the hotel for safekeeping," the Sergeant replied.

"Check my assignments folder, Birmingham. Don't you remember? I made a list of all the duties that involve dealing with civilians and divided them among my officers. Holding onto a key sounds like something that would be included in that list."

"Yes, sir." Birmingham pulled the door closed. Without acknowledging Andy, he strode to the wall and opened a metal filing cabinet. After thumbing through several folders, the Sergeant withdrew one and laid it on top of the other files in the drawer. He opened the folder and ran his forefinger slowly down the left column. Each time he reached the bottom of the page he flipped it over and began the same process on the next sheet. He paused midway through sheet number four. "I think I found what you're looking for."

Andy took a step toward Birmingham, but the Sergeant closed the folder and dropped it back into the drawer before he could read the text.

Summer could feel Andy's growing frustration.

"So, what did you find out there, Birmingham?" he asked.

"The task of keeping the hotel property secure has been reassigned to a Lieutenant Murphy."

Summer could tell Birmingham knew Gus Murphy by the way the man tugged at his tie. She was equally certain the Sergeant had helped the Colonel distribute these assignments and wondered how much he had been paid to let the fox have the run of the hen house.

"You can't...be serious," Andy stammered, his heart sinking. "You need to get that key back. Lieutenant Murphy can't be trus...he uh, can't handle that kind of responsibility."

"Anyone who can handle the responsibility of training cadets to fly Marauder bombers should be able to look after a little crystal and silverware," the Sergeant replied.

Andy closed his eyes and pressed his lips together as the fog dropped over Summer. *"I know Gus is up to no good,"* he thought. *"But without proof, I'll be the one who winds up in jail for stealing those chandeliers."*

Chapter Thirty

Summer considered the parallels between Andy's circumstances and her own as she floated through the mist. *"Andy must have formed a connection with me because we both want to be good people, but we got mixed up with criminals and lost control of our lives."* She closed her eyes. *"And if we don't correct our situations, we'll never be worthy of anybody's trust... or love."*

The fog suddenly dissipated, catching Summer off guard. She flailed her arms to gain her balance as Andy and the lobby of the Belleview Biltmore came into focus. She could hear Andy's unspoken thoughts, but she hardly needed to, since his emotional tells were so easy to read.

He winced as he read the monthly assignment schedule posted on the lobby wall. He had been absent when pilot instructors were assigned to the current class of cadets, so he would have to sit out this cycle of flight training.

He knew that more than half of the Air Corps cadets were expected to wash out during the seven months of aviation training – many of them during their first few weeks at the Belleview Biltmore. The pimply-faced kid guarding the warehouse flashed through his mind. He had no desire to witness such failures, let alone be the one who had to break the news to the cadets.

"Six weeks on the ground," he muttered, "teaching zombie-brained cadets how to use radio equipment and chart a course to Germany, with the added joy of crushing their dreams if they don't pass muster."

Those who survived the grueling physical and mental demands of initial testing were divided according to their natural skills and abilities, to fill the various slots necessary to form bomber crews. Although most cadets dreamt of earning their pilot's wings, the vast majority would become enlisted navigators, bombardiers, radio operators, gunners, and mechanics. After assignments were made, training became job-specific, and the balance between ground and flight training shifted from mostly classroom to almost entirely flight training. Meanwhile, another group of cadets would fill the classroom seats and the overlapping process would start over again.

Each bomber crew was required to receive two hundred flight training hours. Pilot instructors began by co-piloting takeoffs and landings, but cadets quickly learned to fly increasingly difficult solo missions. By the end of their training, they would be locating and bombing practice targets while fighting mock battles in the air. Successful cadets graduated and were transferred to combat units, where their heroic conquests would bring honor to the men who trained them.

Seething with jealous indignation at being grounded, Andy kicked a nearby trash can so hard it almost tipped over. Several men looked up from their typewriters at the loud bang, but Andy ignored them and climbed the ornate box-spiral staircase to his quarters on the second floor.

Summer felt Andy's anger melt into depression. He couldn't stop thinking about how he'd have to teach in a hot classroom, while his contemporaries spent their days flying. *"They'll probably come back here every night and torture me with stories about their thrill-packed adventures."*

Andy stomped over to the large calendar hanging on the wall of the room he shared with three other Lieutenants, now that the hotel was full. He scowled at the caricature of a pretty, scantily dressed woman waving at a plane flying overhead, with the Air Corps insignia in the background. He licked the tip of a pencil and began to x-out the June days that had already passed. Then he flipped up a page and circled the date when the next batch of cadets would leave the classroom to begin flying. "I'll be flying again in no time," he said, trying to bolster his mood. *"And besides, this will give me a little time to make good on my promise to Violet."*

He rubbed the bridge of his nose and stared out the window at the blue-green waters of the Intracoastal Waterway, trying to formulate a plan. *"I have to convince Gus Murphy to return the chandeliers. I'll promise to pay back every cent of the money he gave me, plus interest... over time, of course. Once they're back in the warehouse, no one will ever be the wiser."* He chewed on his lower lip and imagined Gus's less-than-enthusiastic reaction. *"If Gus makes a big stink about it, I'm going to have to go to the Colonel and confess."* He winced again. *"He'll probably make me sit out another round of flight training... or worse."* He shuddered at the thought of more severe punishments. *"Hell, Violet was prepared to sacrifice her life to protect her honor. I guess I should be willing to go to jail if that's what it takes to earn mine back."*

Andy climbed the stairs to the fifth floor and made his way to the end of the East Wing, where Gus Murphy bunked with his two minion sergeants, Lumpy and Squeaky. Enlisted men were supposed to be housed separate from officers and in much tighter quarters, with eight bunks per room. Andy had no doubt that Gus finagled this exception for his two loyal flunkies by employing a combination of lies, bribes and threats.

Squeaky was alone, reading a girly magazine on his bunk while tapping his toe to the music of Glenn Miller's Orchestra on the radio.

"Where's Gus?" Andy asked.

Squeaky barely glanced at Andy over the top of his magazine. "Flight training."

Already in a foul mood, Andy narrowed his eyes at the Sergeant's insubordination, but since Squeaky knew about his part in the theft of the two chandeliers, he opted to ignore it. "When will he get back?"

"How should I know? I'm not his secretary."

"You're right," Andy said, his temper flaring. "You're not his secretary. You're a numbskull who's too stupid to realize that he's poking a stick in a hornet's nest." He strode over to the radio and yanked the cord from the wall socket. "Now get your ass off that cot and report back to your post."

"Dang!" The Sergeant's voice cracked, proving his nickname was a good fit. "Don't go blowin' a fuse, Lieutenant."

Andy lowered his voice to an ominous hiss. "Get out of here, and I mean right now. Don't come back until you're off-duty!"

Squeaky got to his feet, straightened his tie and saluted in an obvious attempt to get back into Andy's good graces. "Geez, Lieutenant, I was just takin' a little break while the cadets are busy working on some navigation charts."

Andy looked the thin man over before returning the tardy salute. "Yeah, I'm sure they're learning a lot from the likes of you. As of tomorrow, I'll be overseeing the navigation training, so you can plan on me reviewing every damn one your lessons."

As he edged toward the door, Squeaky shot a glance at Gus's bunk and then at Andy's angry scowl, like a pathetic dog caught between two masters. "Gus usually gets back here around four or five," he mumbled.

Andy frowned, moving to the side only enough to let Squeaky pass. "Tell him that I need to talk to him as soon as he gets back today."

"I don't mean no disrespect, Lieutenant," Squeaky whined, "but there's usually a line of fellas waitin' to talk to Gus when he gets back here." He eyed Andy warily. "If you tell me what's it's about, I could maybe help speed things along."

Andy chewed on the inside of his cheek for a moment, considering the Sergeant's rather reasonable suggestion. "Okay," he finally said. "Tell him I've changed my mind and can't go through with our deal. We need to put the stuff we took back into the warehouse before someone notices it's missing."

"That's crazy talk." Squeaky's voice cracked again. "All of it?"

Andy's stomach soured as he took a step back. "What do you mean, 'all of it'?" He leaned against the wall, no longer sure he could trust his legs to keep him upright. "Have you taken more than the two chandeliers?"

"You're acting bonkers, you know that?" Squeaky shook his head and took another step toward the door.

"You're about see what bonkers looks like, if you don't tell me what the hell is going on this minute, Sergeant."

Squeaky shifted his gaze to his shoes. "Listen, Lieutenant, I don't know bupkis about bupkis, so please don't bust my chops about this." He shuffled through the door and started down the hallway, but then he paused and looked back. "No matter what the Colonel thinks, Gus is the one who really runs things around here, and he's not a guy you want to cross. Me and Lumpy – we just keep our heads down and follow orders, just like 'most everybody else. If I was you, I wouldn't stir the pot, Sir." Without waiting for a response, he turned and hustled down the hall.

Andy ran a hand through his hair. *"What have I gotten myself into? And what the hell has Gus done while I was gone?"* He considered his next move. *"I need to have a look around that storage room. But how can I get in without a key?"*

All at once, he remembered Violet telling him how, as a child, she would sneak into the steam generator building during the summer months when the Belleview Biltmore was closed. *"Even though the generator is gone, the coal chute was never sealed off!"*

He raced down the steps, out of the door, and across the lawn, working his way around to the back of the old building.

Summer glided along at Andy's side, reading his thoughts and feeling his emotions. He hoped the hotel's treasures were still safely stored inside, but he knew better.

"How many of the hotel's treasures are already missing... and what will it take to convince Gus Murphy to bring them back?"

Chapter Thirty-One

The heavy steel door of the coal chute had not been used for years. Andy worried the rusty hinges would make so much noise when he wrenched it open that it would alert the half-sleeping guard posted at the front door. Fortunately, when the door finally gave way, the obnoxious screech was masked by the racket of shooting practice on the nearby bluff.

He breathed a sigh of relief as he slid two cotter-pin latches into metal rings on opposite sides of the opening, designed to keep the heavy door from slamming shut. When he caught sight of the coal smears on his hands, memories of his father flashed through his mind.

"You were a good man, Pop." Andy hung his head. *"No matter how miserable your life got in the coal mine, you never lied, cheated or stole. I'm sorry I haven't lived up to the fine example you set, but I promise to try harder from now on."*

To keep his uniform from getting stained with coal dust, Andy stripped down to his underwear and clutched his balled-up clothing to his chest like a football as he scooted down the rough iron ramp and landed in a wheeled coal bin at the bottom of the chute. He dropped his shoes onto the floor and then tucked his uniform inside his undershirt to free up his hands so that he could climb out of the enormous, coal-blackened bucket.

Enough daylight filtered through the opening to allow Andy to make his way across the large warehouse relatively unscathed. His spirits rose as he passed dozens of crates on his way to the light switches. In the gloom, everything appeared to be intact. *"Goddamn Squeaky. Had me worried over nothing."*

He smiled as he flipped the panel of switches that controlled suspended incandescent lights throughout the warehouse. The grin fell from his face when he turned around and saw gaping holes in every aisle, where crates and cardboard boxes had once been numbered and stacked one against the next. Then he spied his inventory ledger, resting on the table beneath the switches, where he had left it before he went on leave. He dropped his uniform onto the table and picked up the book, his hands shaking.

When Colonel Huck had put Andy in charge of preparing the exquisite Belleview Biltmore Hotel to house military personnel, he had used the ledger to meticulously record the details and location of every treasure that was removed, packed and stored in this building. His heart sank as he flipped through the pages of his own handwriting. About a quarter of the items in the inventory had been lined out.

As if living a nightmare, Andy stumbled up and down the aisles in his stocking feet, confirming that each of the items that had been lined out was missing. Ten of the crystal chandeliers were gone, in addition to the two he already knew about. Several statues had also been stolen, as well as a few ornately carved mahogany china cabinets and dozens of large mirrors and paintings, all mounted in elaborate gilt frames. *"This is all my fault,"* he thought. *"If I hadn't opened the door to Gus, this would never have happened."*

Watching Andy's horrified reaction to the theft shamed Summer. She had always tried to accept W. C. Fields's philosophy, "You can't cheat an honest man," but in her heart, she knew her cons had tempted scores of mostly honest people to take actions they never would have taken, had they not had the misfortune of crossing paths with her.

"I don't want to see this." She closed her eyes, but couldn't help wondering how many of her victims felt like Andy after they had discovered they'd been deceived. *"It's exactly how Robert will feel when he finds out what I've done."*

Andy's muffled sobs brought her attention back to the memory. He had dropped to his knees and covered his face with his hands in an attempt to silence his emotional outburst, but there was no way to conceal his tears. "What have I done?" he whispered between ragged breaths. "Oh, God, what have I done?"

Summer wondered if it would comfort Andy to understand how people like Gus Murphy operated. *"He probably arranged to have Andy's leave request denied in order to convince him that he had no choice but to participate in the black-market ring if he wanted to see his sister before she died."* She flinched at how easily she had been able to visualize the various aspects of Gus's con.

Andy rubbed his eyes with the back of his hand. "I have to get it back," he mumbled. "All of it."

Even though she knew these events had transpired several decades in the past, Summer had to bite her tongue to keep from warning Andy not to do anything stupid. The stolen treasures were worth many thousands of dollars, even in 1942. A guy like Gus Murphy wasn't about to roll over and return property worth that kind of money, just because one of his marks felt guilty.

Summer was grateful when the clouds descended over her, carrying her away from the uncomfortable scene. She tried to relax and float in the mist but she couldn't quiet her mind. *"Gus Murphy and Gordo Adolphus may not be the same person, but men like that are all cut from the same evil cloth."*

Summer heard Andy shouting even before the mist cleared.

"Oh yeah? Well, you can tell Gus to kiss my keister, Squeaky!" he yelled. "And you can tell him not to bother trying to crack wise with me, either."

As the scene came into focus, Summer watched an outraged Andy poke Squeaky in the chest with his forefinger as he railed on. "I know he's smuggling hotel property alongside those replacement parts he's delivering to Georgia tonight. If he doesn't return everything he's stolen, I swear I'll report him to the Colonel and sink his whole operation."

At first Summer didn't know where they were, but then she recognized the dark room. Only the stained-glass panels covering the back-lit vaulted ceiling made it possible to identify the grand Tiffany Ballroom. In the present, this ballroom was one of the most sought-after wedding reception venues in the Tampa Bay area, but in Andy's memory, when the room wasn't being utilized as the dining hall, it served as a classroom. The gorgeous ivory ballroom that Summer was accustomed to seeing, had been painted a drab olive green, and the huge, elegant floor space was filled with row after row of long, rectangular tables and plain wooden chairs.

She knew that all seventeen-hundred of the hotel's windows, including several of the interior Tiffany glass panels, had been slathered with thick, black paint as part of its blackout protocols. The Army's efforts to keep light from leaking out, also kept the sunshine from coming in through the floor to ceiling windows. If a door to the veranda hadn't been propped open, she might not have even known it was daytime.

"You wouldn't be acting so high and mighty if Gus and Lumpy were here," Squeaky shot back. "Besides, you can't prove *you* didn't steal all of that stuff before Gus ever took over. Maybe *you'll* be the one who goes to jail, and maybe he'll make it look like that pretty, blonde babe of yours was involved, too."

Summer thought the skinny man might break glass if the pitch in his voice rose any higher, but she took his threats seriously. *"Be careful, Andy. Squeaky might be a chihuahua but his buddy is a pit bull."*

Andy balled his fist and threw a punch, intentionally hitting the wall, right next to Squeaky's head. The Sergeant crouched down and crossed his arms over his face as if to ward off Andy's next blow.

"Stand up, you sniveling coward," Andy growled. "I'm not going to hit you – my beef's with Gus."

Squeaky stood, but retained his defensive posture, dropping his guard only to chin-level.

Andy ignored him and turned to pick up an armload of charts he was using to train the navigator cadets. "I'll be in my room, looking over this week's lessons. You tell Gus that he has until this time tomorrow to either agree to return everything he stole, or agree to pay Mr. Kirkeby everything that's owed to him. If he refuses, then I'm going to the Colonel to confess my part in the operation and tell him every-thing I know about it." He paused in the doorway before stepping into the Promenade Corridor. "And if you and your boss know what's good for you, you'll never, ever threaten Violet Barnes again."

This time, the fog dropped over Summer like a blanket. She thought about Andy's situation and wondered if he was trying to teach her to stand up to her tormentors. *"I don't know about Gus, but Gordo isn't a schoolyard bully – he's a murderous bastard who wants to keep me and everyone I care about under his thumb. If I try to fight back, he'll put me in the ground."*

"Maybe he's trying to tell you that dying isn't the worst thing that can happen to you."

Summer jerked her head toward the edge of the fog, surprised to hear Margaret Plant's voice. She waited for the fog to carry her to the familiar parlor table, actually looking forward to having tea with the Victorian spirit. *"Maybe dying's not the worst thing,"* she thought, *"but it's definitely in the top ten."*

Margaret chuckled. "Those in the living world have so much to learn. Dying's not even in the top fifty worst things that can happen to you, darlin'."

Summer strained to see through the fog, but the parlor table didn't appear and Margaret Plant didn't share any more pearls of wisdom. Instead, Summer continued to float for what felt like hours. She made a mental list of things that might be worse than death. Most of the items on her list involved the deaths of people she cared about, or a multitude of other bad things happening to them. She was trying to decide if she would have chosen death over spending that horrific night in Gordo's barn, tied to a chair next to Edward's dismembered body parts, when the fog suddenly dissipated.

She was floating down a corridor of the hotel at Andy's side, when a young soldier ran up to him. Andy appeared to be carrying the same charts he had been holding in the last memory, but now the breeze blowing through the open doors at either end of the cor-ridor carried the scent of fresh morning dew.

The wild-eyed soldier stopped short and saluted. Andy frowned, glancing at the armful of charts. Rather than risk dropping them to return the salute, he nodded. "As you were, soldier," he said, expecting the boy to rush on past.

"There's an emergency in the fourth-floor lobby, Sir. You need to go there right away. They've got Alexander Washington, Sir. He's mighty scared."

Summer felt a chill run down her spine, knowing without a doubt that Gus Murphy and his minions were holding Alexander hostage in response to Andy's threats.

Andy raced to the elevator and pushed the button for the fourth floor. Normally, an iron mesh gate would have been attached to the elevator cab, but it had developed a nasty habit of jamming shortly after the Army arrived at the hotel. With the war effort needing every scrap of metal it could acquire, the decision was made to simply remove it. Andy had become accustomed to standing in the open elevator, watching the inside walls of the shaft glide by as the cab quickly rose from one floor to the next. But today, the lift felt as though it was traveling at half-speed.

He peered through the stationary safety gates as the elevator passed the second and third floors, but he saw no one in either lobby. By the time the elevator reached the fourth floor, Andy had imagined a dozen different scenarios and outcomes, each more frightening than the last. When the elevator finally came to a stop, Squeaky was there, waiting.

"Oh, please, allow *me*, Lieutenant," he said with exaggerated politeness. He pulled the safety gate all the way to one side and then gave Andy a deep bow; his poor imitation of a doorman.

Andy surveyed the lobby as he stepped out of the lift. Alexander sat on a bench seat beneath an open window, directly across the elevator lobby. His face glistened with perspiration and his unblinking green eyes were wide with terror. Gus Murphy stood next to him, his mouth turned up in a nasty smirk. When Andy took a step toward the pair, he realized Gus had a pistol aimed at the back of the young man's head.

"Stop right there, Turner," Gus commanded.

"This is between you and me, Gus," Andy said. He let the navigation charts fall into a pile at his feet. "Let the kid go."

"Not so fast," Gus said. "Me and this shoe-polishing nigger were just having a nice conversation, weren't we boy?"

Alexander didn't respond. He squeezed his eyes closed and pressed his trembling lips together as tears, sweat and snot dripped down his face unattended.

Squeaky dropped a lit firecracker at Andy's feet, snickering when the pop made him flinch. He snorted and lit several more, tossing them behind Andy. "Not so full of beans now, are you Mr. Big Wheel?" he taunted, circling Andy by stepping into the elevator on one side and back out again on the other. "Who's the coward now?"

"Careful, Squeaky," Summer said to herself. *"You're acting like one of those cats who enjoys teasing a chained dog – prancing around just out of reach. Don't forget, it's only fun until the chain breaks."*

Andy didn't move a muscle, refusing to cover his ears as more firecrackers popped, or even acknowledge Squeaky's presence. "What's the plan here, Gus?"

"Did you hear your flight training paid off?" Gus said, intentionally ignoring Andy's question. "Yep, your boy got accepted to go fly with those other nigger boys in Tuskegee, Alabama." He shook his head in mock wonder. "I just don't know what those Alabama folks are thinkin' – allowin' a bunch of coloreds to run amok with valuable airplanes. Maybe they figure they can train them to fly like them monkeys in the *Wizard of Oz.*" He shook his head with disgust. "It ain't the natural order of things."

Andy struggled to keep his voice calm. "I hear the Tuskegee Airmen are doing good work – escorting bombers into battle – maybe even protecting some of the pilots who earned their wings right here with us."

"Well, this *particular* flyin' monkey has a tough choice to make this morning," Gus continued. "He can choose to be my *friend*, or he can become my *enemy*." He moved his gaze from Alex to Andy. "I put a lot of stock in friendship and loyalty, remember? I told you all about it the day *you* decided to become my friend."

Andy frowned, recalling Gus's twisted definition of friendship. He granted favors and kept secrets, but his *friends* usually paid a steep price whenever he decided to call in his markers. "The price of our friendship was two chandeliers, Gus – not a warehouse full of treasure."

Alexander moved his lips, trying to speak, but his voice was little more than a whimper. Gus rapped the butt of the gun against the young man's head, hard enough to make him wince. "Are you listenin' to this bullshit, boy? It's not very friendly to go makin' threats against your friends, now is it? But that's exactly what your precious Lieutenant went and did."

When Andy started to take another step forward, Gus shook his head and placed the barrel of his gun against Alexander's temple. Andy carefully placed his foot back where it had been.

"That's good," Gus said. "Now, as I was sayin', it's important to think our choices through. If this here boy decides to be my friend, well then, he goes off to Tuskegee with letters of praise from not one, but *two* officers. But if he's *not* my friend, well, then, I've got no incentive to watch his back. I'd be obligated to inform the brass that this here colored boy dressed up like a white cadet and flew planes that were intended for white pilots. I'd also have to tell them that he did so with your full knowledge – with your help, even. That kind of scandal might or might not cost you your cushy job as a stateside flight instructor, but it would definitely disqualify the boy from flight training at Tuskegee. I'm told they're only willin' take a chance on the top of the breed up there in Alabama – any hint of illegal behavior and he'd be out. Isn't that so, Squeaky?"

"You bet it's so," Squeaky agreed. "If we told on him, well...the closest the poor boy would ever get to a pilot's wings is when he was polishin' a white pilot's shoes." He snickered, pleased with his own wit.

"And who would believe anything he had to say after we proved he was a deceitful cuss? For instance, if he tried to claim I'd done something wrong, well, it would be obvious to everyone that he was just tryin' to get even with me. On the *other* hand, he could agree to be my friend and tell *my* version of what's been going on in that warehouse, and then everything would work out all right for him. Either way, things will turn out just fine for *me*. Now, if I were a *bettin'* man, I'd bet the boy's going to choose to be my friend, but we'll have to wait and see."

"What makes you think I'll let you get away with any of this?" Andy asked.

Gus grinned and gave a nod of his head. "That's the beauty of this plan," he said. "You won't be around to stop me!"

"That's right, you asshole," Squeaky threw a firecracker into the pile of navigation charts, drawing Andy's attention.

Alexander let out a short, strangled cry, earning him another whack on the head from the revolver.

Andy snarled, first at Squeaky, then at Gus.

Too late, he saw Lumpy charge at him from his blind side, his arms locked straight out in front of his body. In that same instant, he realized that Squeaky and Gus had intentionally kept his attention focused away from the oncoming danger, and that Alexander had been trying to warn him.

Lumpy hit him square in the chest, knocking him off his feet.

Andy fell backward into the elevator as if moving in slow-motion. His feet kicked, searching for purchase on the floor of the elevator cab as his arms wind-milled, fighting to stay upright – a pilot attempting to stay aloft without an airplane.

The cab wasn't there.

Somewhere in his frenzied mind Andy realized that Squeaky hadn't just circled behind him in the elevator to taunt him. While he was too distracted with the firecrackers to notice, the bastard had pushed the button, sending the cab to the first floor.

Time lost all meaning. After her initial fright, Summer experienced the fall as a floating sensation, vaguely similar to the one she felt each time she moved from one of Andy's memories to the next. She remained connected to Andy's thoughts.

Although grief-stricken that he and Violet had been cheated out of the beautiful life they planned to live together, Andy felt an irresistible magnetic force pulling him toward a dazzling lighted path. He recognized his sister at the opposite end of the path, reaching out to him – smiling at him – welcoming him into her world. He started to drift toward her but something nagged at him, holding him back.

"How can I join Paige in Heaven when I've left such a mess of things behind?" he reasoned. *"I intended to earn my redemption, but I*

waited too long. And isn't the road to hell paved with good intentions?" He hesitated and looked around, trying to decide what to do.

The instant Andy turned away from the lighted path, he plummeted into an inky black, endless void. As he fell, he became aware of a voice in the darkness and tried to focus on it. Was Violet calling to him? Crying? Begging him to stay?

Horrified by the dark abyss, Summer screamed and tried to claw her way back toward the light.

Chapter Thirty-Two

"Whoa there, Summer," Robert said as he gently shook her shoulder. "Wake up! You're having a nightmare."

Summer woke, still thrashing and moaning, unable to shake the horror of the endless fall. *"Is that what Andy has been trying to teach me all this time? That if I don't earn my redemption before I die, I'll turn out exactly like him? That I'll be lost in the darkness – stuck between two worlds forever?"* She shivered, squinting her eyes to block the light of the bedside lamp.

"Jesus, no wonder you're shaking," Robert soothed. "It's freezing in here and we're both lying on top of the blankets. Here – get under the comforter."

"I'm...okay," Summer said, her voice shaking even more than her body. "Just a...bad dream."

"That's an understatement. It must have been one hell of a nightmare."

He reached over and pulled the comforter down far enough that she could slide her legs inside the cozy pocket. The sudden warmth made her tremble even more.

Robert pulled the comforter up to her chin and tucked it around her body. "Do you want to talk about it – or would you rather I make some hot coffee?" He brushed a wisp of hair from her face.

"Please stop being so nice to me," she thought, filled with remorse. *"I just stole your client files, for God's sake."* She closed her eyes and tried to remember the last time a man had been so kind to her.

Once in a while, after pulling off one of their *Camp Sucker* cons, she and Dave would have sex. He had always been sweet, but it had been so easy for him to don his con artist persona of *Pastor Dave* that she could never tell whether his emotions were genuine or part of his act. At the time, it hadn't mattered.

But Robert wasn't making sexual advances. His gentle touch reminded her of the thirteen times her father had tucked her into bed before her mother had murdered him in a drug-induced rage. Summer automatically made a mental correction. *"Twenty-one times, not thirteen."*

Keeping track of numbers had become important to Summer when she was a child. She had been excited on the first Saturday afternoon of every third month, because that's when her father knocked on their door with cash for their mother and candy for them. He'd take her and Justin to the park or the zoo, buy them hot dogs for dinner and tuck them into bed before he left that night. When Summer realized that her memory hadn't been eidetic for the first two years of her life, she reasoned that her father had probably begun his quarterly visits when she and Justin were born. That meant he had probably tucked her in *twenty-one* times, not *thirteen.*

She tried to avoid contemplating whether her life might have turned out differently, had her father lived long enough to tuck her in fifty or even sixty times. *Real* numbers were all that mattered. For instance, she knew her strung-out mother had been convicted of shooting her father eight times, then reloading her pistol and shooting him eight more times, because his quarterly payment had been fifty dollars short. She knew that he died at nine o'clock at night, fifteen minutes after he tucked his five-year-old twins into bed for the thirteenth, or perhaps, the twenty-first time. And she knew that her mother was killed in an altercation with another inmate, after serving only thirty-four days of her life sentence, before even one visit with her children could be arranged.

Her desire to learn more about her family had sparked Summer's initial interest in computer hacking. But as far as cyberspace was concerned, her mother had no living relatives and her father never existed. She wasn't even sure she and Justin spelled their father's last name correctly when they changed theirs to match his. Eventually, Summer gave up and decided it was a waste of time to ponder questions for which there were no answers.

That philosophy had served her well until she saw Andy turn away from the lighted path and fall into an inky black void. *"He died without earning his redemption. Just like Dave did. And Edward. And me too, most likely."* A single tear pushed through her closed eyelids and trickled down her cheek. *"Where are they spending eternity? Where will I go?"*

"Hey, everything's okay," Robert said, brushing the tear away. "It was only a dream. You're safe now."

She couldn't bear to look at him. A muffled sob escaped her throat.

"Aww, poor Summer," he murmured. "Come here."

He slid an arm beneath her shoulders and cradled her head against his chest. "Shhh," he said, patting her back.

The tender gesture turned out to be the proverbial straw that broke the camel's back.

Summer began to cry.

She cried for Andy. She cried for the father she barely knew and for the mother who loved drugs more than her children. She cried for the little twins whose various foster parents had abused them – trotting them out like circus animals to entertain guests with their amazing memories, and later, renting them out to those who could profit from their unique ability. She cried for the loss of every lover and friend who passed through her life, for Dave and Edward, and most of all, for the wretched person she had become – a victim who now victimized others.

Robert continued to hold her close, murmuring words of comfort until she cried herself out.

"Jesus," Summer mumbled, finally catching her breath. "I have no idea what *that* was all about." She rolled away, sat up and dabbed beneath her eyes, hoping her expensive waterproof makeup had lived up to its advertising claims. She glanced back at Robert in time to catch his skeptical expression. *"Yeah, I wouldn't believe me either."* She snatched a tissue from the cardboard box on the nightstand, wiped her face and then opted to tell him a partial truth.

"The reason it's so cold is because the spirits were here. They have to zap the heat energy to do their thing. That's one of the details that got me thinking that I wasn't just *dreaming* about ghosts."

"Really?" Robert propped a pillow against the headboard and leaned back, all ears.

"Yeah. They hack into my subconscious while I'm asleep and show me some of their memories." She paused to take another deep breath. "Tonight I watched a soldier fall down an elevator shaft to his death."

"Sounds scary," Robert said as he settled his gaze on her. "But not scary enough to make you *that* upset. What else is going on?"

Summer winced. *"I guess it was too much to hope that he'd be so distracted by talk of ghosts that he'd forget all about me losing my shit."*

A part of her wanted to confess everything, but she pressed her lips together, resolute. Telling Robert would just make him hate her sooner than later, and besides, Justin's life was at stake. Robert remained silent, waiting for her to continue.

"An uncomfortable silence tends to make guilty people talk. It's Interrogation 101." Summer fidgeted, trying not to talk first. Then she decided to try another stab at distraction. "The soldier did something he was ashamed of and then died before he could set things right. He haunts this hotel. It's horrible. I think his soul is trapped in limbo – maybe forever."

"Come on, Summer," Robert countered. "I don't know you all that well yet, but you don't strike me as a girl who would cry her heart out over some ghost's personal issues."

"You're right – you don't know anything about me," Summer shot back, surprising them both with the force of her words. She swallowed and softened her voice before adding, "I've made lots of bad decisions in my life, just like that soldier did."

"I think you're being too hard on yourself," Robert said. "I mean, you had some tough breaks as a kid, what with your parents running out on you and your brother, and then the two of you having to live in foster homes and all..." He laid his open palm against the small of her back. "But you should be really proud of yourself, Summer."

She started to scoff at the ridiculous idea, but didn't want him to think she objected to his touch. Instead, she focused on the warmth of his hand through her robe. "For what?"

"Think about it. You pulled yourself up by your bootstraps and earned a degree from a prestigious university. And although I was against hiring an intern, you managed to figure out a way to get hired. That took a lot of spunk. That, along with the quality of your work, has convinced me that you've got what it takes to have a successful career in the art industry."

Summer shrugged off the undeserved compliments. *"All I am is a good liar with a great memory. Yay me."*

"And even if the social worker you call your aunt couldn't take you in as a child," Robert continued, "she wouldn't have flown you to Florida as a graduation gift if she didn't love you. And how about your brother? He flew down here just to hang out with you for a while. That kind of devotion from your family doesn't just *happen.* You *earn* it. So I'm pretty certain you've already made up for any bad things you might have done."

Summer bit her lip. *"Except that I don't really have a loving social worker, and Justin was sent here by the mob to help me swindle you."* She shook her head. "It's not that simple, but thanks for the vote of confidence."

"You forget, I'm speaking from experience," Robert said. "I used to be a spoiled rich kid who screwed up all the time."

"That's pretty hard to imagine."

"Yeah, well, trust me. I was a real mess until I finally figured out that the way I'd chosen to live my life wasn't making me happy. I decided to make some changes – be a better role model for Emma. After all, what's the point of living if you're miserable all the time? I accepted the fact that I'd probably still screw up a lot, but I also realized I'd have a billion or so chances to make amends."

Summer nodded, intrigued. *"He's right. Why continue to do the bidding of horrible people just to survive, when I'm so miserable all the time?"*

"Eventually, doing the right thing became easier – even when other people didn't follow my example. So my advice to you is: don't be so hard on yourself. Just try to do as much good as you can every day and accept that you're going to screw up sometimes. You'll enjoy life a lot more that way."

"Sounds like an excellent philosophy," she said. *"Of course, I'll never live long enough to make amends for all the crap I've done."*

"It works for me," he said. "Not to mention, it makes it easier to face myself in a mirror."

"Okay, I'll give it a shot," Summer said, warming to the idea. *"Since it looks like I'm about to get myself killed anyway, I may as well go out trying to do the right thing, like Andy did. Besides, getting stuck between worlds still beats an eternity in hell."*

She gave Robert a broad smile.

A genuine smile.

Then she licked her lips and leaned toward him, allowing the robe to slip off her shoulder, exposing her pink nightie. *"And in the meantime, I'm going to enjoy every sweet moment life has to offer."*

Chapter Thirty-Three

As Robert's lips neared hers, Summer fought her eidetic memory, but it was no use. As if watching through the window of a bullet train, kisses from the past flashed through her mind. While bouncing between foster homes, she had endured numerous clumsy kisses from young, would-be Casanovas, always in search of love, or at least acceptance. Since aging-out of the foster care system, her quest had resulted in more than a dozen disastrous affairs. She had come to believe that relationships were like sand castles built within easy reach of the tide. Sooner or later, her past, her abnormal memory, or both would rise up like a cresting wave to break them apart.

Robert's soft moan snapped her back into the moment. He cupped the back of her head with one hand while pulling her close with his other hand. She saw the desire burning in his blue eyes, but just before their lips touched, he gulped and turned his head, nestling her head on his shoulder and rubbing his cheek against her hair.

Summer's senses sharpened with every second that ticked by. She smelled the starch in his pale peach shirt and the slightly musky scent of his skin beneath. His warm hand slid down the side of her head, covering her ear, while his fingertips continued to fondle her hair. The delightful sound reminded her of listening to a seashell.

She moved her head in small circles, like a purring cat enjoying a scratch. Then she began nibbling at his neck while fumbling to unbutton his shirt. A fleeting smile crossed her lips when she heard Robert catch his breath – a sure sign that he was turned on.

"Stop," he whispered. He covered her hand with his – a half-hearted attempt to stop her from undressing him. "Come on, Summer. You're obviously upset about something. It would be wrong for me to take advantage..." He sucked in air as her cool fingers slid inside of his shirt and tweaked his nipple.

"I'm fine," Summer murmured as she slid down and kissed his chest. She tasted him with the tip of her tongue. Salty, with a hint of soap. "I just let a bad dream get to me. It reopened a few old wounds, that's all." Determined to enjoy what could be the last pleasurable moments of her life, she unfastened the last button.

"I'm all right now – really," Summer said, hoping he'd believe her. She pushed his shirt aside, then pulled away long enough to shrug off her robe. She rolled on top of him so that her ample chest mashed against his, with only her flimsy nightie between them.

"Oh, God," Robert whispered as he kissed her hair.

He wrapped his arms around her so tight that Summer felt the heavenly sensation of becoming a single entity. In that one moment, nothing else mattered. She relaxed and let him roll her onto her back, expecting him to take her, but instead he pushed her hair back and gazed into her honey-brown eyes.

"You're absolutely beautiful," he said, as if noticing for the first time. "But I don't want to do anything that you might regret in the morning."

"Then kiss me, because I'm positive that I would regret it if you don't."

Robert chuckled, then let the smile fade as he lowered his mouth to hers.

His lips were softer than she imagined, made to feel even softer by the contrast of his scratchy five o'clock shadow. *"Does he feel this amazing because I'm in so much danger?"* Summer wondered, *"Or is it because he fell for the woman I'm pretending to be – the one I wish I was?"* She pushed the thoughts away. The only thing that mattered was that his lips delivered the tender, loving kiss she had always hoped for. She would treasure the memory of it for the rest of her life – no matter how long that would be.

They fed on one another's passion, tongues merging in an urgent dance, unable to satisfy their hunger. She panted, unwilling to stop even to take a deep breath, as he ran his hand down the length of her back and then tugged the spaghetti strap of her pink nightie off one shoulder. Eagerly, she bent her elbow so that he could slide it off and bare her sensitive nipple.

Summer arched her back and gasped as he cupped her breast and massaged it with strong fingers. "Yes, yes," she murmured as he slid down and repositioned himself to take her swollen nipple into his mouth. She raked the back of his shirt with her nails, longing to touch his skin.

Either sensing her desire or wanting the same thing, Robert raised himself to his knees long enough to tug off his shirt and toss it toward the nightstand. Summer pulled her nightie over her head. Her nipples stiff, she held her breath as he lowered himself back down. As their naked upper bodies pressed together, she whimpered with pleasure.

"This is the one," she thought. *"This is the moment I'll choose to remember when Gordo and the Broker come for me."* The realization that she would be gone before this relationship had a chance to fade gave her more comfort than she could have imagined possible. She was free to make love to this man, with no concerns about what would happen a month, or even a week, from now.

She writhed beneath him, letting her hands glide over each contour of his back, memorizing every touch. She hesitated at his waistband for only a moment before pushing her hands between their bodies to unzip his pants.

Robert rolled to the side to help her free his bulging penis from the uncomfortable confines of his khakis. After a few determined tugs and kicks of his legs, the pants dropped off the end of the bed, landing in a heap on the floor. An instant later, he heaved himself back on top of Summer's willing body. They explored one another, amazed by the way they seemed to fit together so perfectly, and thrilled by the tantalizing suspense of being separated only by two strips of silk – her pink panties and his short, black boxers.

Summer pushed against the heel of his hand as he cupped her mound, wanting him to touch her, to fill her, and yet not wanting the ecstasy of desire to come to an end. She was certain he felt the same way as she fondled his long, straight erection through his silk underwear.

Just as Robert slid his hand inside her panties and began exploring her, the moment was shattered by someone knocking on the hotel room door.

Their reactions to the interruption were telling.

Summer froze, terrified that Gordo had been listening – that he somehow knew she had decided to sacrifice her life rather than help him steal the painting and destroy Margaret Plant's home. *"Please, God. Just this once. Be on my side. Don't let me get caught. At least not before I've gotten Justin and the others out of harm's way."*

"Damnit," Robert muttered. "Maybe whoever it is will go away." When another loud knock made it clear that wasn't the case, he gave her a quick kiss. "Don't move," he said, without realizing that she hadn't so much as twitched a muscle. "Someone's got the wrong room number – or maybe those ghost kids are playing a prank on us." He pulled on his pants and zipped them while crossing the room.

As he reached for the glass doorknob, another fear clutched Summer. *"What if Gordo decided to steal everything the old-fashioned way – with a gun?"* Adrenaline surged as she sat up. "Wait," she cried, scrambling to put her robe back on. "What if it's... you know, a bad guy... this could be a hotel invasion."

Robert grinned. "You've got quite an imagination, there, Summer. You really think a thief would sneak past the guard gate and through a manned lobby, take an elevator to the fourth floor, walk all the way to the end of the corridor and knock on the door, all on the off-chance that I might have something worth stealing in my room? Trust me, it's somebody's drunk husband with the wrong room number."

When he pulled the heavy bedroom door open, sunlight flooded the room.

"What the hell?" he said. "What time is it?"

Summer shot a glance at the window. Not a spec of light penetrated the hotel's black-out curtains and Robert's crumpled shirt covered the clock on the nightstand. Her mind flashed back to the night before. She came to his suite on the pretense of helping him listen for ghost children, so the only thing she brought with her was her room key, and even that was on the table in the foyer, next to his phone. She groaned, realizing their mistake. They had assumed they had been asleep for only a brief period of time when he woke her from her nightmare. Obviously, they had slept much longer than that.

The knock repeated. This time, a man's voice called out, "Mr. McNeal? Are you in there?"

Robert screwed up his face, dumbfounded. "Maxwell?"

"Maxwell – your Production Manager?" Summer asked, already certain it was true.

Without answering, Robert walked down the short corridor to the entrance of the suite and opened the door. "What's wrong, Maxwell? And what time is it?"

"It's nine o'clock. And *Bride On Stairs* arrived four hours early, that's what's wrong." The frazzled man wailed like a diva encountering paparazzi without makeup. "The extra security men I hired won't be here for *three more hours* and the feckless guards who accompanied the delivery couldn't stay." He swiped the back of his hand across his forehead and through his salt-and-pepper hair. He was clearly exasperated by the morning's events, but still struggling to appear as though he'd been torn from the pages of a GQ magazine.

Robert was instantly alert. "If they left and you're up here, then who the hell is down there guarding *Bride On Stairs*?"

"The new chap, Justin, uncrated the piece and is beginning the installation. I tried to call you, but..."

"You left him alone with the Tissot? Why didn't you just call me?"

Maxwell stiffened with indignation. "I also called the agency and asked them to send the guards earlier than originally requested. They said they'd do their best. Meanwhile, I pulled the security man from the video room to stand guard at the door to the exhibit until they arrive. As for calling you, I tried, but your phone went straight to voice mail. And your room phone is off the hook, *as usual*."

Robert spied his cell phone and eye glasses on the table in the foyer. He snatched up his glasses and put them on, then checked his phone. "Damn – forgot to charge it last night." He frowned and narrowed his eyes. "Why didn't you send Dana or Justin up here to get me, Maxwell?"

Maxwell looked over Robert's shoulder to where Summer stood in the open door of the guest room. "When Miss Dana couldn't locate Miss Summer this morning, she decided to go to the *House of Make Believe* costume shop on her own, to pick up everyone's costumes for the cocktail reception. And when Justin, Miss Summer's *brother* learned that she wasn't in her room or answering her phone, he was…well, he was reluctant to knock on your door for fear she and you were, um…" He waved his hand in the direction of the bedroom. "It might have been awkward."

Robert coughed. "All right. I understand. You get back down to the exhibit hall now and make sure Justin does a good job with the installation. I'll be down in a few minutes." He started to close the door, but stopped. "You're a good man, Maxwell," he said. "I appreciate your discretion. Please tell Justin and Dana that I sent Summer on an errand earlier this morning."

The manager gave Robert a polite nod, turned on his heel, and strutted toward the elevator.

By the time Robert closed the door and turned to Summer, he had transformed his scowl into a sheepish smile. "I don't know about you, but those are the best damn room-darkening drapes I've ever seen. Honest to God, I thought it was, like, three or four in the morning."

Summer nodded. "I just about fell over when I saw the sun was up." She started toward him, suddenly feeling shy. She pulled at her belt, even though it was already so tight that it was biting into her waist. "I guess I'd better run back to my room and get dressed."

"I hate to let you go, but…"

"You don't have to say it." Summer smiled, though her heart felt heavy. "I understand. The exhibit is a huge deal, so you probably don't have time to get involved with anyone right now. It's okay if you think last night was a mistake."

He circled her in his arms and kissed her hair. "Mistake? No. I'm crazy about you, Summer. Don't you know that?" He dusted her forehead with his lips. "But you're right about this show being a huge event for the Foundation. I need to get down there to put out some fires this morning, and I probably won't be able to spend much time with you until the auction is over. But what's a few days when we've got a whole lifetime ahead of us to figure things out? I promise I'll make it up to you."

Summer closed her eyes and hugged him back. *"I wish that was true,"* she thought. *"Andy and Violet thought they'd have a whole lifetime together, too. I guess some people are just born unlucky."* She gave him one more kiss, then stepped back and faked a smile, already thinking about how to keep everyone safe. "Sounds good to me," she said. She picked up her room key, looked out the door to make sure the coast was clear, and then dashed down the hall. *"Besides, I have a fire of my own to put out, right, Margaret?"*

Chapter Thirty-Four

"I don't have time to sleep right now," Summer cried. Exasperated, she muffled another yawn and stared into the bathroom mirror, willing her eyelids to remain open. As she reached for her toothbrush, she felt a familiar wave of cold air pass over her.

"Time is short, darlin'."

Summer recognized Margaret's voice. With gooseflesh rising on her arms, she spun around to face the long-dead Victorian woman, but no one was there. In the split second it took for her to turn around, even the chill in the air had dissipated.

"What the hell?" Summer's mind immediately presented a passage from a book on mental illness:

Auditory hallucinations aren't necessarily an indication of mental illness. They can be the result of many situations, including exhaustion or periods of extreme stress.

"Auditory hallucination," she murmured. But before she could contemplate that possibility, she remembered that soon after she had checked into this hotel, she heard voices in the elevator, and shortly after that, a male voice whispered to her in this very bathroom.

The second time it had happened, she had been admiring the hotel's historic elegance and commented that it was a shame Gordo planned to burn it down, when someone said, "Our sprinkler system would put the kibosh on that kind of stupidity." At the time, she thought Gordo had managed to plant a bug on her and she soaked all of her clothes in the sink to destroy it. But that was before she knew about the spirits.

Summer swayed, feeling as though her knees were turning into melted wax. "Come on, Margaret," she pleaded. "Not now. I've got less than twenty-four hours to come up with a plan to keep Justin alive." She yawned. "And protect Robert and Dana from getting tangled up in this mess." Another yawn. "And keep Gordo from setting this place on fire."

"Life is all about making choices," Margaret's voice said. "The afterlife is about earning redemption for the choices you made."

"You already told me that." Summer snapped her lolling head upright. "I'd love to discuss that philosophy some time, but right now, I'm supposed to help Dana with costumes. Wait...I'm supposed to pretend that I'm out running an errand for Robert."

Confused, she realized she had stumbled to the side of her bed, which was still turned down from the night before. "All right, Margaret. You win," Summer said, sinking onto the soft mattress and closing her eyes. "Just for a minute."

Summer was adrift in the clouds an instant later, with Violet's voice filling her ears.

"After coercing Alexander Washington into telling the military police that he had witnessed my sweet Andy's *accidental* fall to his death, Gus Murphy and his thugs let him go. They assumed he'd high-tail it to Tuskegee, happy to still be alive, but they'd underestimated his character. Alexander hoofed it straight to The Rosery, to tell me and my father the truth about what had happened."

Images began to appear at the edges of the mist. It was like watching short, silent films of Violet's memories. Tears sprang to Summer's eyes as she watched the first heartbreaking scene unfold. Alexander found Violet and her father inside one of the farm's large greenhouses. When she heard the horrific news, Violet fell to her knees, sobbing.

"Alexander feared that Gus had arranged for *me* to have a fatal accident, too, but he couldn't go to the authorities," Violet's ethereal voice explained. "They would *never* take the word of a negro over that of an Air Corps officer. Unless Alexander agreed to say that

Andy's death was an accident and then leave town, Gus said he'd kill him and make it look like he'd been caught in the act of trying to steal more art from the warehouse."

The silent memory faded away, replaced by one of Alexander and Violet climbing into her father's red pick-up truck.

"Thankfully," Violet continued, "Daddy was always cool-headed when the chips were down. He gave Alexander the keys to his truck and told him to take me to the Japanese Gardens. He trusted Mr. Hawakawa to keep me hidden until it was safe to come home. He said Alexander should drive the truck on up to Tuskegee, where brave men like him were needed to help win the war."

The image at the edge of the mist faded from view. "I was zombie-brained with grief," Violet said, her voice quivering. "As Alexander drove past the last of The Rosery's flower fields, I screamed for him to stop. Then I jumped out of the truck and started pulling stalks of purple gladiolas. Alexander probably thought I had gone bonkers, but he didn't try to stop me. When my arms were full of flowers, I climbed back into the truck and ordered him to take me to the Belleview Biltmore. He tried to talk me out of it, but when I threatened to walk there by myself, he stopped arguing."

Another scene appeared at the edge of the clouds. Summer watched Alexander sneak Violet through the hotel's basement and up the hidden servants' staircases until they reached the elevator lobby where Andy had fallen to his death. When she opened the safety gate and stared down into the empty shaft, Alexander took a firm hold on her arm.

"I think Alexander was afraid I planned to kill myself, but I just wanted to say a proper goodbye and figured this was the closest I could come to that. But when I looked down the elevator shaft, I couldn't help imagining how horrible it must have been for him – falling into that dark pit. I started to cry and I called out to God, begging for it to be a mistake – begging him to send Andy back to me."

"Andy must have heard her," Summer realized. *"That's why he turned away from the light."*

"Yes, Andy did hear me," Violet agreed. "Perhaps that was God's way of answering my prayers."

Summer winced, still uncomfortable about the spirits' ability to hear her thoughts.

"Alexander insisted we leave before the soldiers returned from the air fields, so I said my goodbyes and tossed the gladiolas down the elevator shaft...a ritual I would repeat often over the years. I found shelter at the Japanese Gardens, where Mr. Hawakawa hid me with several Japanese people that I thought had been taken to the holding camps. It turns out that young Mr. Alvord and my Daddy had been keeping secrets of their own."

As the images of Violet faded from the edge of the clouds, Summer was surprised to hear Andy's voice.

"After hearing Violet call to me, I stepped off the lighted path and fell into the dark space between worlds, with no concept of space or time. Then I heard Gus's voice in the distance. I think I was drawn toward him because he and Squeaky were discussing what they should do about Violet. I floated into his quarters, still feeling as uninvolved in his world as a speck of dust floating in a sunbeam. But when I realized they were talking about hurting Violet, it was as if electricity surged through me, waking me from a deep sleep."

At the edge of the mist, Summer saw an image of Gus and Squeaky sitting on Gus's cot. She didn't see Andy.

"I became enraged, thinking about everything Gus Murphy had taken from me – my life with Violet – our future home and children. I didn't want to be dead. I didn't want to go to heaven. I wanted the life he had stolen from me. I hauled off and punched the bastard, but my fist went right through his jaw. That infuriated me even more."

Summer noticed the two men in the memory looked up before going back to their conversation and wondered if they had sensed the presence of Andy's spirit.

"I heard Squeaky tell Gus that he had talked to Violet's father," Andy continued. "He said she was working in Connecticut for the summer. I knew that wasn't true but was glad her family understood she had to be protected from Gus. I don't know what I would have done if Margaret Plant hadn't appeared just then."

In Andy's next memory, Summer saw the Victorian woman's spirit appear. She was by no means solid-looking, but Summer was still surprised Gus and Squeaky didn't notice her. Summer assumed she was talking to Andy, even though she couldn't see him.

"Margaret told me that only a few people had died at the hotel over the years, and most of those had traveled the lighted path immediately. Usually, spirits visited the Belleview Biltmore only after becoming aware of their altered existence. Since I knew zilch, she proceeded to teach me all about the spirit world."

In strobe light fashion, short clips of memory began blinking in and out in rapid succession – brief images of the elevator shaft, the mess hall in the Tiffany Ballroom, the soda shop and many other local locations.

"I learned that I could go anywhere I had gone while I was still alive," Andy's voice continued. "Margaret also taught me how to concentrate and absorb energy, then use that energy to influence people's dreams. She even showed me how to focus energy to move objects in the world of the living. I decided to listen in on as many of Gus's conversations as possible while adjusting to my new world."

Memory images, mostly from within the hotel, continued to appear and then disappear at the edge of the mist. The speed of the images would have been too difficult for most people to absorb, but this time, Summer's eidetic memory worked to her advantage. She gobbled up each image, confident that she could recall every one of them if necessary.

Many of the memories involved Gus conducting his illegal businesses on the grounds of the hotel. She watched him move several valuable items from the warehouse and stash them in covered trucks late at night. He cheated his fellow soldiers out of their hard-earned pay in crooked poker games, blackmailed a good number of vulnerable people, and hid wads and wads of cash beneath a loose floorboard under his cot. After a while, Summer began to make out Andy's transparent shape in the scenes.

"As the months passed, I discovered that Gus tricked a lot more suckers than just me into going along with his crooked schemes. He collected dirt on lots of the fellas and did favors for others. Lots of guys, like me, *believed* he was doing them favors when in fact, he actually *caused* the problem that needed solving. I learned that the

Red Cross could have arranged for me to go home when Paige was dying, but since most of the Sergeants in the administrative pool were beholden to Gus for one thing or another, they didn't tell me that. Also, lots of the top brass between here and North Carolina were in his pocket. Whenever he needed to move stolen goods to another location, he'd just arrange to haul plane parts to another base or oversee some long-distance flight training. I hated Gus's miserable guts more every day."

When the rapid-fire images finally faded from the mist, Summer lay back on the bank of clouds. *"What has any of this got to do with me and the mess I'm supposed to be fixing right now?"* she wondered.

"When I overheard Gus making plans to set fire to the hotel and warehouse to cover his tracks, I knew I had to do something to stop him. I also hoped that if I saved the hotel, I could earn the redemption that I had been seeking before my death."

"Wait, Gus planned to set fire to the hotel way back then?" Summer bit her lip to keep from talking out loud. *"Is that what I had to learn? How you stopped him? So I can prevent Gordo from doing the same thing?"*

When Andy continued as if he hadn't read Summer's thoughts, she bit her lip harder.

"I started visiting the dreams of the soldiers charged with building the sprinkler system here at the hotel. I suggested the system wasn't nearly good enough – it needed larger pipes, more runs, and lots more sprinkler heads. I made them realize they needed to work harder. Faster. I also suggested they conduct scrap metal drives and trade the metal for the extra galvanized pipes needed to build the huge sprinkler system. They listened."

Images began appearing at the edge of the mist again. This time, the clips of memories depicted soldiers hosting scrap metal drives at the hotel. It appeared as if everyone in community had become involved.

"Soldiers cut apart the old boiler in the basement and salvaged the train track rails that hadn't been used at the Belleview Biltmore for more than a decade. Town folk donated everything from old radiators and farm equipment, to tin cans, pots and pans, toys and even bottle caps," Andy said. "The soldiers took pride in the sprinkler system, building it with care and making sure no areas of the hotel were left unprotected. They loaded every room, closet and even the basement with thick water pipes and thousands of sprinkler heads."

Summer recalled reading that when a fire marshall had been questioned about the adequacy of hotel's antiquated sprinkler system, he had replied that the system was so massive, it took two of his inspectors a solid week every time they inspected it. In fact, it far exceeded even the most current sprinkler system requirements, especially since the long-since petrified wood of the hotel wasn't nearly as flammable as it once was. The fire marshall had gone so far as to express the opinion that hotel guests at the Belleview Biltmore should be more concerned about *drowning* than dying in a fire there.

"I'll bet Gordo doesn't know about all those sprinklers," Summer thought, feeling a glimmer of hope. *"But wait... if Andy stopped Gus from destroying the hotel, why didn't he earn his redemption?"*

"Eighteen months after we occupied the hotel, the air strikes paid off," Andy continued, again ignoring her unspoken question. "We and our allies were winning the war. Word came down that the Army Air Corps didn't need nearly as many pilots, and quarters had been built at MacDill Air Field for those who had already been trained. We were to close up operations at the Belleview Biltmore immediately. The night before Gus put his arson plan into action, he, Lumpy and Squeaky decided to make one last flight, to smuggle the last of the valuables to Cuba, where he could hide them until after the war. There weren't many planes available for an unauthorized flight, so unfortunately for Gus, he got stuck with the same temperamental Marauder that I used to fly."

Summer knew the short-winged B-26 was so hard to control on takeoffs and landings that the pilots claimed that one a day crashed into Tampa Bay. Her jaw dropped as she watched a clip of Andy's shimmering spirit working at the knots that held the antique furniture and other valuable treasures in place in the cargo bay of the airplane.

"Having a load of stolen property suddenly shift during takeoff would have made for a few interesting minutes in the cockpit, no matter who was flying that bird," Andy said. "I figured he'd be forced to circle around and land, but it turns out Gus wasn't the ace fly boy he claimed he was. He let up on the throttle, which was exactly opposite of what he should have done to get control of the Marauder. He realized his mistake, but it was too late. Gus froze-up when the left engine stalled. Squeaky started screaming, making it hard for anyone to think, while Lumpy jumped up and tried to secure the cargo, causing even more sudden weight shifts. In the end, the plane earned her nickname, *The Flying Coffin*."

Stunned, Summer watched as the spirits of Gus, Squeaky and Lumpy left their broken bodies and floated toward a bright path of light. Squeaky and Lumpy disappeared into the light, but at the last moment, Gus turned around and saw Andy's spirit. His face contorted into an expression of terror. He turned back and shot toward the light, but just as most his spirit disappeared, a large black cloud emerged and remained behind.

"As far as the living were concerned," Andy continued, "Gus Murphy and his two buddies made an unscheduled flight and never returned. They were marked AWOL in a stolen aircraft and eventually, dishonorably discharged from the Army Air Corps. No one ever thought to look for them at the bottom of Tampa Bay."

The short clips of memory switched back to the Belleview Biltmore's empty warehouse.

"When the brass discovered the warehouse was empty, they suspected Gus had stolen everything, but that would have made the Army Air Corps look bad, so they paid old man Kirkeby to cover up the whole thing. After a while, most folks forgot about the missing treasures. And because the overbuilt sprinkler system was never needed, I didn't earn my redemption. Even worse, I had caused the death of three men, so the debt my soul owes multiplied several times over."

"*What happened to the cash Gus Murphy was hording in his room?*" Summer wondered.

"That black cloud you saw is Gus's ghost. It still haunts his quarters, protecting that loot he hid beneath the floorboard," Andy said.

"*Glad you finally chose to answer one of my questions,*" Summer silently chastised. "*Wait – his ghost – not his spirit?*" Summer recalled Margaret telling her that a ghost was a fragment that broke from a spirit that traveled down the lighted path. Most often, it was the most evil part of a spirit's energy. She shivered, remembering the stories she heard about an evil specter on the fifth floor of the hotel. It was easy to imagine that it was Gus.

"With your help," Andy said, once again choosing to ignore her silent questions, "we'll finally put that cash and this overbuilt sprinkler system to good use. Maybe I'll earn my redemption, to boot."

"There's even more at stake here than Andy realizes." It was Margaret Plant's voice again. "But first things first, darlin'. We'll help as much as we can, but for now, you need to wake up and get moving."

Chapter Thirty-Five

"So that's it. My mind's made up. I'm going to renege on the deal." Summer stepped into the shower and closed her eyes, relishing the caress of hot water cascading down her body. *"As soon as Gordo and The Broker realize I've decided not to honor the terms of our deal, they'll kill me."* She sighed. *"That means I need to keep up appearances until I can figure out how to save Justin, prevent a hotel fire, stop Gordo from stealing a multi-million-dollar painting, and protect Robert's clients from financial disaster. So, no pressure or anything."*

A wave of cold air suddenly dropped over her as if the door to the bathroom had opened. In the instant it took for Summer to react, she heard Margaret's voice.

"You aren't as alone as you think. And darlin', an intelligent woman with allies can accomplish *anything.*"

"What?" Summer squeaked, wiping the water from her eyes.

There was no reply, but Summer wasn't surprised by the silence. She could tell by the return of the warm air that the spirit was gone.

"Thanks for being my ally, Margaret, but I doubt there's much you and the other spirits can do to help me." She closed her eyes again, determined to enjoy the warm shower. *"Now, how can I make sure I live long enough to lead the bastards on a chase far away from this place? Away from Justin. From Robert."*

She rubbed a soapy washcloth over her breasts and down her abdomen, recalling the sensation of Robert's body pressed against hers, the taste of his kiss. *"God, how I wish we hadn't been interrupted this morning."*

She caught herself before slipping too far into the sexy fantasy. "Knock it off, damn it. Focus!"

Summer turned the faucet to cool the water and concentrated on the memories she'd witnessed during what had turned out to be a twenty-minute nap. *"Pretend you're doing reconnaissance for a scam. What useful information did you pick up?"*

She made a fist and then lifted one finger for each item she counted. The hotel had an overbuilt sprinkler system. The hidden servants' staircases and tunnels provide shortcuts through the hotel. A stack of cash is hidden beneath the floorboards of Gus's old quarters. His creepy ghost haunts that section of the hotel. Margaret taught Andy how to function in the spirit world, so they both know how to untie knots and move things.

"It's not much, but it's a start." When thoughts of Robert began to tease the corners of her mind again, Summer's heart sank. *"I finally found a man I care about – maybe someone I could spend my whole life with, but it's too late. If I play my role in the con, I might live, but Robert would hate me. If I don't, I'm dead."*

She turned off the water and reached for a towel. "I finally get it, Margaret. When Gus killed Andy, he destroyed the potential for Andy and Violet to spend a lifetime together in *this* world." She wrapped a fluffy white towel around her body and another one around her wet hair. "So, even if Andy earns his redemption and they both travel into the light, they'll still feel cheated out of a lifetime of memories they hoped to take with them to enjoy throughout eternity."

Summer continued to talk out loud as she dried off and then slipped into a tee shirt and jeans. "I understand that. I mean, I wouldn't want to die, even if I hadn't fallen for Robert. But now it feels like Gordo will be stealing more than my *life*. He'll be stealing an entire lifetime of memories Robert and I might have created together."

She narrowed her eyes with hatred for Gordo. *"I know it was my own scam that brought that pig into my world and got my partners killed. I'll never forgive myself for that, but I earned my freedom back fair and square, Goddammit. I can't believe that psycho still holds a grudge. When Justin crossed his path, I'll bet he was absolutely thrilled to have a chance to get back at me. He probably hopes I'll rabbit so The Broker will kill me."*

She removed the hairdryer from its hook on the wall and turned it on. "Margaret, I think I might be able to get the last laugh, no matter what else happens," she said, her voice muffled by the noisy dryer. "After all, I learned a thing or two during my three years of doing research work for one of the best law firms in Seattle. I should be able to plant a pretty solid trail of evidence for the police to follow right to his door." She grinned.

After applying some light make up and gathering necessary gear from her pack, Summer sat in one of the high-backed chairs at the parlor table. *"I should be able to stay awake in here."* She held a mini recorder, the size of a thin flash drive, in her palm. With her eyes closed, she visualized the financial files she memorized the night before and reread every word and number into the recorder. Then she opened a cheap, disposable laptop and, using an anonymous sender account, addressed an email to the group of art collectors, warning them that their bank accounts had been hacked. She hastily set a timer to release the email as the auction was coming to a close. *"The deal says I have to hand over the client's account data, but it doesn't say I can't tell them what happened. So technically, I haven't broken the deal yet."*

Just as she finished, her phone chimed, indicating she had a text. She hadn't heard it go off while she was in the shower, but now noticed a waiting text from Justin in addition to a new one from Robert.

Justin's message incorporated their special number code.

"6, 35, 9, 1"

Summer read the message as:

6: Are you okay?; 35: Change of plans; 9: I need to talk to you in private; and 1: I love you.

Summer frowned, wondering which part of the plan her brother was talking about. Before sending a reply, she read Robert's message:

"Meet Gloria Burton in hotel restaurant at 10:30. Take possession of her cameo necklace for the sale. Told Dana I sent you to Tampa to pick it up as favor to Gloria. Everything's cool. See you in ballroom afterward."

Summer couldn't help but grin at Robert's chivalrous gesture as she thumbed her reply:

"Will do. And thanks!"

Then she replied to Justin's text.

"Agree 35, 13, 9 at reception, 15, 24, 1, & I mean it, 24!"

She had no doubt he'd be able to translate the message to:

35: I agree there's been a change of plans; 13: Follow my lead; 9: We need to talk in private at the reception; 15: We need to escape; 24: Don't do anything stupid; 1: I love you. And I mean it, 24: don't do anything stupid!

Summer checked the time on her phone. *"Ten-fifteen. Best change and get going."* She slipped into a grey silk blouse and her favorite black slacks. Then she peeled back the corner of her cell phone's protective silicone case and slid the miniature recorder inside, where it wouldn't be detected. Afterward, she tucked the phone into her back pocket, and left for the restaurant.

Walking down the wide hallway, she focused on the hotel's sprinkler system for the first time. The pipes of the fire prevention system were painted the same white color as the ceiling, making them much less noticeable.

"I'll bet Gordo has no idea the sprinkler system was overbuilt," Summer mused as she stepped into the elevator. The moment she pushed the first-floor button, images of Andy filled her thoughts – his eyes filled with terror as he fell backward into the empty shaft.

Summer didn't realize she was holding her breath until the lift came to a smooth stop. Exhaling, she stepped into the Promenade Corridor and leaned against the wall, pretending to admire the design of the elegant walkway while composing herself. In addition to the wainscoting, wallpaper, and wide crown molding, dozens of huge pictures and shadowboxes decorated the corridor. Summer was certain these decorations usually kept visitors' attention. If anyone happened to look up, their eyes would be drawn to the high carved arches that punctuated the walkway and the beautiful chandeliers suspended from them.

"I doubt most people notice the sprinkler system running the length of the corridor on either side." Summer craned her neck to examine the system. *"But there really are an awful lot of sprinkler heads."* Still trying to figure out how she was going to stop Gordo and his goons from burning down the historic hotel, she tested doors along her path, noting which ones were locked. *"Gordo doesn't know how to pick locks, so he probably won't plant fire starters in there. But how am I supposed to inspect all eight-hundred and twenty-thousand square feet of this hotel for incendiary devices?"*

When she reached the Terrace Restaurant, Summer paused to look around. The breakfast rush was over, so most of the tables were vacant. The dining room, furnished with elegant, Victorian Era high-backed chairs, white linen tablecloths, gold chandeliers, and walls lined with intricately carved China hutches and sideboards, reminded Summer of the treasures Gus Murphy stole from the warehouse. Glancing up at the boxed spiral staircase on the far side of the room, Summer wondered if his ghost could cause her physical harm if she took his money and used it to get Justin to safety.

She gulped and shifted her gaze to the occupied tables, keeping an eye out for a woman who looked like she might be named Gloria Burton. Near the entrance, a young couple stared at their smartphones, oblivious to the elegant surroundings. An elderly black man caught Summer shaking her head at the couple and smiled. The man reminded her of someone, but before she could place him, an equally old woman waved at her from the table next to his. *"Betty White's clone,"* Summer thought. *"Even her hairdo screams 'Golden Girls!'"*

Summer returned the woman's wave and strode to the corner table, where she extended her hand. "You must be Mrs. Burton."

The old woman had a mischievous glint in her eyes as they shook hands. "And you, my dear, must be the stunning Miss Tyme who has stolen poor Robert's heart clean away."

Summer was caught off guard. "My name is Summer Tyme, but I don't know about the *rest* of that description."

"Summertime? What an interesting name. Please, have a seat, my dear." Mrs. Burton tapped her forefinger against the lip of her cup. "Care for some tea?"

"No, thanks," Summer said, "I've had more than my share of tea recently."

Mrs. Burton reached into a large, Louis Vuitton tote and removed a navy-blue velvet box. "I've been doing business with Robert for years, yet when I called him to arrange to drop this off, he asked me to postpone my spa appointment because he wanted me to meet you." She held up the box and winked. "That's the act of a smitten man, my dear."

Summer felt her cheeks flush as a rush of emotions flooded her senses. It pleased her to think Robert had feelings for her, but it also broke her heart to think she wouldn't live long enough for a relationship to develop. "He's just really busy this morning," she said, not meeting Gloria Burton's eyes. "I don't know if he told you, but Tissot's *Bride On Stairs* arrived several hours earlier than expected, throwing his schedule for a loop."

"Yes. I'm sure that's it," Mrs. Burton said, making no attempt to disguise the knowing smile playing across her lips. She flipped a gold latch on the box and opened it to reveal a cameo and diamond pendant, suspended from a thick chain of white gold.

"Oh, my," Summer said. "That's exquisite."

"Yes, she's a beauty – circa 1897," Mrs. Burton agreed. "I'd hoped to pass it down to one of my daughters, but I'm afraid they don't share my appreciation for antique jewelry." She shook her head. "Whenever *I* wore it, I always felt a special connection to the women who owned it before me. I couldn't stand the thought of one of my daughters tossing it into the back of her jewelry box after I'm gone, so I decided to sell it instead."

"I'm sure whoever buys it will treasure it always," Summer said.

"I just hope they enjoy wearing it as much as I have." The old woman closed the box and passed it to Summer. "Now, dear, as much as I'd love to stay and chat, I'm already late for my appointment at the spa. Perhaps we can talk more at the reception this evening."

"That would be nice. Are you planning to wear a costume?"

"Absolutely. I can hardly wait to show it off. I'm even wearing a powdered wig." She frowned and shot a glance toward the kitchen. "Well, it seems my waitress has disappeared."

"You go on to the spa. I'll wait for the check. It's the least I can do."

"Thank you, my dear," Mrs. Burton said. She gripped the arms of the chair with her thin, wrinkled hands, pushed herself to her feet and took hold of a bright red walker. She dropped her Louis Vuitton tote into a large pouch attached to the front of the walker, blew Summer a kiss, and tottered off.

Summer watched her leave, amazed the woman was willing to entrust a five-thousand-dollar necklace to her care without so much as a receipt, just because Robert had asked her to. *"Other than Justin, no one I've ever known has been worthy of that level of trust,"* she thought.

She felt proud of Robert's sterling reputation, for reasons she didn't quite understand. Even though she was planning to double-cross Gordo and knew she'd never see Robert after tomorrow, she didn't want him to ever discover the real reason she had come to Belleair. She hoped he would always believe that she was the person she was pretending to be.

When she noticed a young, plump waitress burst through the kitchen door, Summer raised an open palm, but failed to attract the girl's attention. The waitress beamed as she approached the elderly black man.

"Betty insisted I bring you a helping of peach cobbler, on the house," the waitress said. "She said to tell you she still uses your Granny Millie's recipe." She placed a dish on the table in front of the man.

"Well, goodness, me," he replied. "Isn't that special." His face broke into a wide grin. "She's a good woman, that Betty." He scooped a fork full of cobbler into his mouth. "Mmm, mmm! And a damn fine cook, too." He waved a thin forefinger at the dish. "You know, I've been eating cobbler made from this recipe ever since I was a nappy-headed tyke, hiding under the counter in that very kitchen." He shook his head slowly. "Almost ninety-four years. Imagine that."

"She said your grandmother used to be a cook here," the waitress replied. "That's amazing."

"Granny Millie worked as a maid in this hotel from the time my mama was a little girl. But then, one night they needed extra help in the kitchen and she volunteered. After the head cook tasted her cobbler, he had her reassigned to work with him. You know, my mother worked here, too – in the laundry." He grinned. "So, you might say this hotel was my childhood home. Why, I even attended school in a little one-room schoolhouse they used to have out back."

"You used to work here, too, didn't you?"

The old man nodded. "Sure did. I helped restore this wonderful old hotel after the war. I guess we helped heal each other back then. Anyways, when my mother died, I took her home to be buried with our ancestors in Trinidad. I thought about staying there, but I missed my home." He grinned. "Over the years, the world has changed so much, the Belleview Biltmore is the only place I recognize anymore – the hotel that time forgot."

"You ought to write a book about your life, Alex," the waitress said. "No kidding. Heck, I bet someone would turn it into a movie."

Summer's eyes widened. He had aged a great deal, but his sea-green eyes were just the same. *"I'll be damned. It's Alexander Washington."*

Chapter Thirty-Six

Summer squirmed in her seat, unable to take her eyes off Alexander Washington. The waitress noticed she was eavesdropping and gave Summer a wink.

"I could listen to your stories all day, Alex," the waitress said. "But unfortunately, I have other customers to tend to." She patted him on the shoulder and moved to Summer's table. "Can I bring you anything else?" Then she glanced at the table and noticed Mrs. Burton's lipstick-stained tea cup and the untouched place setting in front of Summer. "I'm sorry," she said, poking her finger against her temple. "I don't know where my head is at today. Let's start over. Can I bring you something to drink and warm up your friend's tea?"

"Mrs. Burton had to leave," Summer said, forcing herself to look away from Alex. She held up the check. "Could you charge this to my room please?"

The waitress gave her a curious look. "No problem, but don't you want to order something for yourself?"

Summer started to shake her head but thought better of it. "You know, I think I will. I'll take a cup of black coffee and a helping of that peach cobbler."

"I thought I saw you eyeing that cobbler," the waitress teased. "You know, girls as thin as you don't usually get to eat stuff like that. You must have a really high metabolism." She grinned and slapped herself on her broad hip. "Lucky for you I'm not the jealous type."

"This treat will cost me an hour in the gym," Summer lied, "but it just looks too good to pass up."

The waitress chuckled. "Trust me, it's worth *two* hours in the gym." Then she turned and sashayed back into the kitchen.

"Margaret, is Alexander one of the allies you were talking about?" Summer chewed on her bottom lip. *"I guess there's only one way to find out."* She picked up the blue velvet box and got to her feet. Resting her hand on the back of her chair for emotional support, she cleared her throat. "Excuse me," she said, not sure how to begin the conversation. "But is your name Alexander Washington?"

"Nobody has called me Alexander since I was a boy. I go by Alex these days." He cocked his head to one side. "But tell me, now – how does a pretty young thing like you know the name of an old geezer like me?"

"I'd be glad to tell you as long as you promise to hear me out before calling the guys in white coats to come and put me in a straitjacket."

Alex smiled. "Sounds like I'm in for a mighty interesting story." He stood and pulled out a chair for her. "Have a seat, young lady."

"I know this sounds crazy," Summer began, "but we have a mutual acquaintance." She sat and sucked in a deep breath. "His name is – was – Lieutenant Andrew Turner."

Alex dropped into his own seat and stared at her, his green eyes growing misty. "I didn't know Lieutenant Turner had any family, other than a kid sister that died."

"I'm not a relative." Summer glanced up as the plump waitress returned with her order.

"So...you two...decided to eat together?" the server asked, her tone indicating a mix of confusion and surprise.

Summer glanced at Alex, hoping he hadn't changed his mind.

"Why, yes we have," Alex said. You know, it's not often that an old man with one foot in the grave receives attention from several lovely ladies during the course of one meal." He gave the waitress a broad grin and rubbed his palms together. "This must be my lucky day."

The waitress rolled her eyes and shook her head, amused. "One foot in the grave, my butt. I'll bet you'll live long enough to dance on all of our graves." She placed Summer's cup of coffee and cobbler on the table.

Alex laughed as the waitress patted his shoulder and walked away. The moment she was out of earshot, he stopped smiling and returned his attention to Summer. "Perhaps you should start at the beginning."

Summer nodded. "The first thing you need to know is that my twin brother and I got ourselves into some trouble. We're being forced to participate in a scam that's supposed to take place in this hotel tomorrow night. The second thing you need to know is that I've decided to try and stop the bad guys, but they're more evil than you can imagine, so I doubt I'll live to tell about it. And the third thing you need to know is that this hotel is haunted by many spirits, including that of Lieutenant Turner. That's how I know you're a trustworthy man."

Alex took a sip of his coffee and then slowly returned his cup to the saucer. "I believe I'm going to require a lot more details about each of those three things," he said. "But first, why don't you tell me your name?"

Keenly aware she had little time to spare, Summer complied. Then she rushed through a synopsis of the events that brought her to the Belleview Biltmore, as well as the odd dreams that she had eventually realized were visits to the spirit realm. At first, Alex leaned back in his chair and listened with his arms folded across his chest. By the time Summer finished describing the events surrounding Andy's death, the old man was leaning toward her with his forearms resting on the table and his mouth hanging open.

Summer drank some coffee to soothe her dry throat and then continued. "Andy felt so guilty about helping Gus Murphy steal those two chandeliers that he tried to get them back. When he discovered Gus was stealing all sorts of treasures from the hotel, he thought the only way he could find redemption was to stop him. Even after Gus murdered him..." She paused, realizing she must be dragging up horrific memories for Alex.

"Tell me everything," Alex said as he rubbed his jaw. "I need to hear this."

Summer nodded. "Well, Andy's spirit kept on trying to stop Gus and make amends. He haunted a bunch of soldiers into building a fantastic sprinkler system because he knew Gus planned to cover his tracks by burning down the hotel and warehouse." She bit her bottom lip again. "But Gus never carried out that plan because he and his two evil sidekicks, Squeaky and Lumpy, died."

"Wait – those bastards *died*?" Alex sat up straight, his eyes wide with surprise. "When? How?"

"Gus and his minions were trying to fly the last of the stolen treasures to Cuba in a B-26. Andy – well, Andy's spirit, untied the ropes securing the stolen cargo. When everything shifted during takeoff, Gus lost control of the plane and crashed."

"That's right." Alex nodded and rubbed his chin. "The Marauder had a reputation for crashing on takeoff. The boys used to have a saying: 'One a day into Tampa Bay.'" Suddenly, he smacked the table and grinned. "Well, I'll be damned. All these years, I thought those sons-of-bitches made a clean getaway and were living the highlife on a tropical island somewhere. But, hallelujah and praise the Lord, they've been burning in hell this whole time."

To avoid having to explain the difference between spirits and ghosts to Alex, Summer decided not to mention the fact that Gus's ghost still haunted the Belleview Biltmore.

"Andy wasn't trying to kill those guys, but he still believes he needs redemption for the role he played in their deaths," she said. "I think they got what they deserved. How about you? You must have hated them for making you watch Andy's murder."

"And then lie about what happened," Alex added. "When I first joined the Red Tails in Tuskegee, I hoped I'd die in battle, just so I could quit having nightmares about that day. Then I started imagining those bastards were sitting inside every enemy airplane that crossed my path. I felt a little better every time I shot one of them down. My imaginary vendetta helped make me one of the fiercest pilots in the Corps." He took a sip of coffee and made a sour face. "Cold." He swirled his cup and watched the black liquid within, losing himself in thought.

Summer picked up her own cup and took a sip. It was lukewarm, but she didn't mind. She settled the cup back onto the saucer and then studied Alex, who remained transfixed, staring into his coffee cup as if it contained a portal to the past.

"After the war ended," he finally said, without looking up, "I came back home to rebuild my life. But I could never stop searching the faces of tourists, always looking for those men – hoping they'd return to the scene of the crime, I suppose. At least, a part of me hoped they would. The other part of me was afraid of what I would do if I ever saw them again." After a moment, he lifted his gaze to meet hers. "I wish more than anything that I could have saved the Lieutenant's life that day."

"Maybe you can still help save Andy. That is, you could help him earn his redemption – and help me too. It would be dangerous, but I sure could use an ally who knows his way around this hotel."

A look of steely determination filled Alex's green eyes. "I think all three of us can use a little redemption. What do you need me to do?"

Summer felt a tiny flicker of hope. Was it conceivable that she could double-cross Gordo, but still fulfill the literal terms of the deal she made with The Broker?

Chapter Thirty-Seven

Fifteen minutes later, as Summer raced into the foyer of the Starlight Ballroom in search of Robert, she almost ran over Dana, who was sitting in the middle of the floor. At the last moment, Summer jumped over her like a sprinter clearing a hurdle, clutching the blue velvet box to her chest.

A startled cry escaped Dana's lips before she realized what had happened. "Oh my God," she squealed. "You almost sent me into labor!"

"You're lucky I have such good reflexes," Summer shot back. "What in the world are you doing on the floor?" Trying to discern a logical explanation, she glanced around the large foyer.

Restrooms occupied one wall of the space. The opposite wall was filled with an enormous, ornate fireplace and next to it, a narrow door led to a small, sunken conference room, which had once served as the children's dining hall and dance studio.

Dana pushed out her bottom lip like a pouting child and held up her open palm, which was filled with loose pearls. "I forgot I was wearing the stupid necklace that goes with my costume." She nodded toward the closed, massive doors leading into the Starlight Ballroom. "It got caught on the doorknob and snapped. The little beads rolled all over the place and I couldn't pick them up because I couldn't see them over my belly, let alone reach them. So, like an idiot, I sat on the floor to pick them up and then I couldn't get back up."

Despite the dread of her looming confrontations with Gordo and The Broker, Summer couldn't stop herself from chuckling. "I'm sorry," she said, unsuccessfully trying to keep her giggles from erupting into gales of laughter. "I know...it's not funny, but..." The more Summer tried to stop, the harder she laughed. "You just...look so adorably pitiful...sitting on the floor."

"Oh, just you wait. One of these days, *you're* going to be all pregnant and get momnesia and *you'll* forget you can't do normal things like get up off a floor – and I'm just going to laugh and laugh."

Summer covered her mouth until she regained her composure. "How long have you been down there?"

"Too long."

"Why didn't you call for help?" Summer said. She bit the inside of her cheek. "Aren't two security guards posted just inside the ballroom?"

"Yeah, right. That wouldn't be embarrassing at all," Dana said, her tone dripping with sarcasm. "I figured I'd come up with a solution eventually."

"Not unless you managed to suddenly sprout wings," Summer tried to swallow the snicker that was creeping up her throat, but it came out as a snort, which made her start laughing again.

"It's not funny," Dana wailed. But then she, too, began to giggle. "Stop it."

Summer's laughter proved contagious and soon they were both in stitches.

"We don't have time for this," Dana said, fighting to assume a serious expression. "We have a million things to do before tonight."

Summer wiped tears from her eyes and carefully laid the blue velvet box on the floor. "Here, take my hand," she said, pressing her lips together in an effort to choke back another chuckle.

Dana reached out her free hand and clasped Summer's.

"Okay," Summer said. "I'll pull on three. One, two, threeeee."

The attempt was an utter failure. Dana slipped onto one side, making it appear as though Summer was dragging her across the floor like a rag doll.

"Come on. Let's try again," Summer said. "But this time, give me both hands."

Forgetting her other hand was filled with pearls, Dana turned it over and reached for Summer. Beads rolled across the floor in all directions, sending both women into a new fit of laughter.

"What the heck is going on in here?" Robert asked.

The women turned to see Robert, Justin and Maxwell, standing at the foyer entrance, bewildered expressions on their faces.

"We could hear you guys all the way down the hall," Justin chimed in.

Maxwell sniffed. "It sounds more like you're preparing to open a lunatic asylum than an art exhibit. And look there." He waved his hand at the floor. "Beads are all over the floor. We better get them cleaned up before someone slips and falls."

"Good call," Summer said, still trying to catch her breath. "Dana, want to help me pick up these beads?"

"That sounds like a job for an intern," Dana replied, still giggling. She looked over her shoulder at the trio of men. "Help," she said. "I've fallen and I can't get up."

"Wait, is that what happened?" Justin asked. "You fell on those beads?" He moved toward her, his concern obvious. "Are you okay?"

"I'm okay, and I didn't fall," Dana said. "But I really can't get up without some help."

Robert and Justin each took hold of an arm and lifted Dana to her feet with ease.

"You guys are on your own with those damn beads," Dana said. "Nothing else needs to be done right now, so Summer and I are heading to the spa to get our hair done for the reception. I had your costumes delivered to your rooms, so get dressed and we'll meet you back down here between six and six-thirty."

"Wait," Justin said. "Summer – I've barely seen you for the last couple of days. I've got like thirty-five or forty things to tell you about. Can you hang back? You can catch up with Dana in like, nine minutes – tops, I promise."

Summer mentally translated his message.

35: Change of plans; 40: I've done something you need to know about; 9: I need to talk to you in private

Keeping her expression neutral, she nodded at her brother. Then she rolled her eyes and smiled at Dana. "It's a twin thing. You go on ahead and I'll be there in a couple of minutes."

"No way, Jose," Dana countered. She looped her arm through Summer's. "I'm not letting you out of my sight. You've been AWOL all day long and I'm going to need your help getting into my costume."

"Okay. You're the boss." Summer kept smiling, even though her curiosity was killing her. "You know, my brother is one of those guys who has timed how long it takes him to get ready. Since he can do it in between eleven and sixteen minutes, he figures everyone should be able to do that. I've tried to tell him that girls need about thirty-five minutes just to do their make-up, and around sixty more to do everything else, but he just doesn't get it." She turned to Justin, watching the minute changes in his expression as he translated:

11: Don't worry, I've got this; 16: Trust me; 35: Change of Plans; 60: Danger, get ready to run.

"We'll start catching up one minute after the reception ends. I promise," she said.

1: I love you.

Summer stooped down to pick up the blue box and handed it to Robert, trying not to touch him or look into his eyes in the process. "This little beauty is from Mrs. Burton. Sorry it took me so long to get back here, but she's quite a talker."

Robert smiled his sexy, nerdy smile and took it from her without even checking the contents.

"Come on, let's go," Dana said, pulling her into the corridor.

Summer glanced over her shoulder. "By the way, she didn't even ask for a receipt."

"That's because I already gave her one," Robert replied.

"Without having possession of the necklace? That was a risky move."

"Not really. The necklace had already been appraised, and I trusted the both of you to get it to me."

She returned his smile, hiding the fact that his words cut through her like a knife. *"God, I wish I was worthy of your trust. Maybe one day..."*

As Dana and Summer walked arm in arm to the spa, Summer pretended to listen to Dana's lighthearted chatter, but her thoughts were focused on one thing. *"If I want to live, I've got to figure out how to keep Gordo from getting his hands on the painting without breaking the terms of our deal. And I have to get Justin to safety. And I've got come up with those plans while I'm getting my hair done and helping to host a costume party. No problem. No problem at all."*

Chapter Thirty-Eight

"Your costume looks a lot more comfortable than mine," Summer said, inspecting the high waist of Dana's red velvet gown.

Dana sat on a chair in the parlor of Summer's suite, dislodging the foam rubber toe separators the pedicurist had used to protect the polish while it dried.

"Yeah, but yours will look a lot better," Dana said, giving Summer's low-cut, royal-blue satin costume an envious glance. "That's going to look amazing on you."

"Here," Summer said, "let me help you with your shoes."

She knelt down and helped Dana squeeze her swollen feet into a pair of black pumps and then steadied her as she stepped into a long, crinoline slip. Just as she finished tying the slip's apron strings into a bow at Dana's back, Dana gasped.

"Did I tie it too tight?" Summer asked.

"No, it's just that Junior is extra active this afternoon. Here – feel." She took hold of Summer's hand and placed it against her belly.

The baby obliged by kicking the moment Summer's hand touched Dana. It was the first time Summer had ever felt the movement of an unborn baby and her eyes widened with surprise and delight at the unusual sensation.

"Hey, baby girl," Summer cooed, reluctantly drawing her hand away. "You know, you're going to give her an identity crisis if you keep calling her *Junior*. Have you thought of a girl's name, yet?"

"Not yet. I'm waiting for inspiration."

"Inspiration?"

"Yeah." Dana shifted her gaze to her bulging belly and gave it a gentle pat. "Your brother says that when the right name pops into my head, I'll just *know* it's the one."

"I don't know that I'd take baby-naming advice from someone named Justin Tyme." Summer spread the burgundy costume open on the floor. "Here, if you step into your gown, we won't mess up your fancy hairdo."

"Okay," Dana chirped. "But I feel like a whale, so I'll need your help to keep my balance."

As the two women struggled to get Dana into her costume, Summer's mind raced. Most of her plan was in place, but she still had a few details to work out. *"I'll tell Justin about Gus Murphy's hidden loot during the reception and then later tonight, we can sneak up to Gus's old quarters to retrieve it. Hopefully, there's enough cash to give Justin a fresh start somewhere far away."*

"Thank goodness you're here," Dana said, sighing with relief as the dress passed over her baby bump. "Normally, Emma would help me, but these days, that would be like the blind leading the blind. She's going to have enough trouble getting into her own costume."

"Emma?" Summer asked, giving Dana her full attention. "Robert's sister Emma?"

Dana groaned. "Don't tell me I forgot to tell you that she's coming – momnesia strikes again."

Summer furrowed her eyebrows, confused. "I thought she couldn't travel because of her pregnancy. Isn't she about to give birth any day now?"

"She's eight months," Dana said as she slid her arms into the costume's puffy sleeves. "She wasn't planning to come, but after I told her all about Justin – and about you and Robert – well, I don't think anything could have kept her away. She and her husband, Ole, are flying down on his corporate jet this afternoon."

"That's great." Summer gulped, hoping Dana wouldn't notice her lack of enthusiasm. "Robert will love seeing her. But I hope you didn't exaggerate. I mean, Robert and I are just friends – and you and Justin barely know one another, either." She pressed her lips together. Things were getting out of hand. *"It's one thing for me and Justin to disappear while we're little more than acquaintances. But Emma is Dana's best friend and Robert's only living relative. Meeting her would take things to the next level."*

Dana raised her eyes to meet Summer's. "Are you worried Justin and I are moving too fast? If you are, I'd understand."

Summer looked down, pretending to fuss with the dress. "No, I..."

"I mean," Dana interrupted, "I know the odds are stacked against our relationship working out, but Jesus, he just *gets* me. And I can't remember ever enjoying a man's company so much – or laughing so often." She giggled. "Like when we were talking about baby names. He told me he wants to have a son one day, just so he can name him Hammer."

"Hammer Tyme? That sounds like something he'd do." Summer rolled her eyes and then turned her attention to the zipper on Dana's costume. *"Damn it, Justin,"* she silently reprimanded her brother. *"Did you have to be so charming? She'll be hurt when you up and disappear tomorrow."*

Fortunately, the long zipper slid up without a hitch. The high-necked bodice fit perfectly and thanks to the crinoline slip, the bottom portion of the dress was full enough to conceal Dana's protruding belly.

Summer decided to change the subject. "Wow, Dana, you look great!" She picked up a bottle of water and took a drink. "But don't look until I put your head thingy on." She twisted the cap back onto her bottle and reached for Dana's headpiece – a ring of matching red velvet with gold beading trim and ribbon streamers.

The stylist at the spa had used a foam rubber doughnut to create a puffy bun in Dana's short hair, and the hairpiece ringed the bun like a crown.

"Oh my goodness," Summer said, clasping her hands together. "You look gorgeous. Go take a look."

After thoroughly inspecting herself in the bedchamber's full-length mirror, Dana returned to the parlor, grinning. "Okay – now it's your turn!"

Summer's stylist had chosen to put spiral curls in most of her thick, shoulder-length blonde hair. The curls were held back from her face with two narrow, platted braids, crisscrossed over her head and decorated with small, white silk flowers. While Dana was checking out her costume in the next room, she had donned the front lacing corset, ruffled pantaloons, and a hooped crinoline slip.

"I think I can get my dress on without messing up my curls," Summer said, already lifting the royal blue gown over her head. "But I'm definitely going to need help with the zipper." A ring of white silk roses encircled the low neckline of the costume and continued around her shoulders, concealing the cap sleeves of the gown.

"Okay, but you're going to have to lift the front of your hoop skirt, so the back part will go down. That's the only way I'll be able to get close enough to zip you up," Dana said.

Summer chuckled, fumbling with her skirt. "Thank God we don't have to dress like this every day."

"I think I'd have to start a new fashion," Dana said as she tugged at Summer's zipper. "Victorian sweatpants." Once the zipper got past Summer's waist, it closed easily. "Okay, you're all set."

Summer dropped her skirt back into place and turned to face Dana. "What do you think?"

Dana's eyes grew wide. "Holy cow. I think I just figured out why Victorian women wore this stuff. Your boobies look like they're floating on pillows and your waist looks like it's twelve inches around."

Summer smirked. "Yeah, right. Let me see." She turned toward the narrow hallway that separated the parlor from the bedchamber.

"Okay, while you're admiring yourself, I'll stop at the bathroom. Then we need to get down to the ballroom to make sure everything is set before the clients start to arrive."

Dana moved through the door without difficulty, but Summer had to lift one side of her hoopskirt up to make it through. "Either I need a smaller hoop or this place needs wider doors."

She was still mumbling about the impractical outfit when she reached the mirror and dropped her skirt into place. Unexpected tears sprang to her light brown eyes when she saw the reflection of a fairy princess. She had always claimed that she hated dressing up, but now she realized she'd been lying to herself.

She remembered being five years old and watching her foster mother dress her *real* daughter up as Cinderella for Halloween. The woman had told her the state didn't waste taxpayers' money on costumes for foster kids, so she could either go trick-or-treating dressed as a bum or put a pillow case over her head and go as a ghost.

"Cinderella," she whispered. "God, how I wanted to be Cinderella – to have a fairy godmother."

"I don't think the costume comes with a fairy godmother," Dana said, walking up behind her. "But Robert's eyes are going to pop out of his head when he sees you in that getup."

Summer blinked away her tears along with the long-buried memory. "You're pretty sneaky for a whale," she teased. "Now, come on, let's see if I can fit through the door to the hallway."

Chapter Thirty-Nine

When they stepped out of the elevator on the first floor, Summer felt an overwhelming connection to Margaret Plant and the Victorian Era. "This hotel was built to accommodate women dressed like us," she said. "Outfits like ours are the reason they built the Promenade Corridor so wide – so two women could pass one another without having to lift their skirts."

"That makes sense," Dana replied absently. She craned her neck to look down the hall toward the Starlight Ballroom. "Damn – I think some of the clients are already here. They're an hour early." She picked up her pace.

"Maybe they couldn't figure out how to sit down in their costumes, either."

Both women automatically scanned the foyer floor for loose beads before stepping through the towering, double doorway entrance to the Starlight Ballroom. Summer watched Dana as her gaze swept around the room, taking in each of the display cases and paintings. She nodded with satisfaction, but then frowned when she spied a couple in the middle of the room, talking with Robert.

"That's Miles Prescot and his latest conquest – or maybe wife number seven – or eight – it's hard to keep his women straight," Dana said. "He's one of our richest clients, but he's a disgusting human being." She wrinkled her nose as though smelling bad fish. "I hate kissing his ass, but we have to because it appears he'll be the bidder to beat when we offer the Tissot at the auction."

"His date is beautiful," Summer said. "She looks like a runway model." The dark-haired woman kept her eyes down, focusing on her shoes. *"She reminds me of the prostitutes Gordo kept locked up in the house with me while I was his prisoner. They said they tried to concentrate on something beautiful to keep their minds off the ugly reality of their lives. I wonder..."*

"Yeah." Dana smiled at Summer, her eyes dancing with mischief. "One of Mr. Prescot's goals is to always be accompanied by the most beautiful woman in the room. I can hardly wait to see his face when he gets a load of you and learns that you're with *Robert*."

"Maybe I should keep my distance," Summer said, suddenly nervous. "I mean, I wouldn't want to offend a valuable client."

"Are you kidding?" Dana asked. "If I had a little more time, I'd sell tickets to watch this. Last year, when Robert's girlfriend, Lisa, turned out to be a hustler, Miles Prescot rubbed his nose in it without mercy – and I know he's done the same thing to lots of other men."

"But I don't want to hurt Robert's chance to sell the Tissot for the best price possible."

"You really don't understand the way arrogant pricks like him think, do you?" Dana shook her head and looked back across the room. "When he realizes he's lost the *I have the prettiest date* contest, he'll break the bank, if that's what it takes to make damn certain he wins the top art prize." She smirked. "By the end of the show tomorrow, he'll be bragging that owning *Bride On Stairs* is the only thing that was important to him."

"Wait a minute," Summer said, recalling Violet's near-drowning while working in Cape Cod. "That name sounds familiar. Is Miles Prescot, by any chance, related to a *Kingsley* Prescot?"

"Yep," Dana said. "The very same. Lucky for Miles, his dad up and died before investigators could gather enough evidence to charge him with bank fraud, so he inherited the family fortune."

"Rich womanizer with no scruples. Sounds like the apple didn't fall far from the tree." Summer shook her head. *"Why do the bad guys always seem to win?"*

"Maybe he didn't fall *far*, but Miles must have fallen really *hard*, or landed on a rock or something, because Kingsley Prescot was *way* better looking."

When several more clients entered the ballroom, Dana donned a professional demeanor. "Time to mingle. Try to keep everybody's attention focused on the displays. Remember, the objective is to sell the art." Then she frowned. "Dammit – I forgot – we need to check-in with Bobby – I mean, *Robert*, first. I told him about the whole bead-necklace-breaking thing and he decided he wants us to wear some of the Victorian jewelry tonight." She gave Summer an impish grin. "Which means, I get to see the looks on Robert's and Miles Prescot's faces when they get their first glimpse of you." She looped arms with Summer. "Come on, Cinderella, your prince is waiting."

As the two women crossed the room, Summer saw Justin, dressed in a black Victorian tux with long tails, a white vest, and a white bow tie, step out from behind a burgundy curtain in the corner of the room. She knew his red toolbox was stashed behind the curtain and that, although it looked exactly like a standard chest-of-drawers model on casters, it had been modified. A secret compartment with hooks for hanging had been added to the back of the toolbox and the framed forgery of Tissot's *Bride On Stairs* was hidden there.

After the reception, Justin and one of Gordo's lackeys planned to trip the security camera feed to show a loop of video that Justin had previously recorded and installed. For fifteen minutes, the guards would believe they were watching the displays, while Justin and his accomplice turned off the alarm and switched the two paintings. Tomorrow, Gordo's flunky would wheel the toolbox to the loading dock during the chaos created by the hotel fire and load it onto a truck that Gordo would arrange to have waiting there.

"But if my plan works, they won't get away with it," Summer mused. *"As long as Alex Washington and his friends manage to put out all of Gordo's fires before they get started, there will be no chaos. And before Gordo gets his hands on the toolbox, I'll tip off the police. Justin will be long gone by then, so he'll be safe, and if I'm lucky, the cops will take Gordo into custody before he catches on to what happened."*

Summer pressed her lips together trying not to think about how many times luck had *not* been on her side. *"And because technically, we will have fulfilled the terms of the deal we made with The Broker, he won't go after Justin and me either."* She glanced up, hoping Margaret Plant's spirit could hear her thoughts. *"Margaret, if you and Andy and Violet can do anything to help things go my way, I'd be forever grateful."*

Summer pointed her thumb at Justin. "I'll join you guys in a minute, Dana, but first, I need to talk to my brother."

Dana smiled and waved to Justin, who swiped a Derby hat off his head and gave her a low bow, in character with his costume. "Sorry, Summer, but family time has to wait." She giggled as she pulled Summer across the room. "Get it? *Family time* with the *Tyme family?*"

"Oh God," Summer moaned. "I'm afraid my brother's dumb sense of humor is rubbing off on you already."

"Like I said, we're a match made in Heaven."

Just then, Robert turned and saw them approaching. Like Justin, Robert wore a black Victorian tuxedo, his jacket cut short in the front with long coattails, and a white vest. But instead of a bow tie, he wore a silk ascot, the same blue color as his eyes. For once, Summer was pleased to have an eidetic memory. She never wanted to forget Robert's expression as his eyes devoured her. *"Oh, what I'd give for a lifetime with him."* But she knew she couldn't stay. Even if her plan went off without a hitch, Gordo wouldn't give up until she was dead, and anyone she cared about would always be in danger.

"Hello there, Dana," a woman called.

Dana stopped short, still holding Summer's arm. "Why, hello, Ms. Kuntz." She tugged Summer closer. "I don't believe you've met my amazing intern, Summer."

Summer reluctantly turned away from Robert's gaze, but then smiled when she noticed the attractive brunette's tall black hat featured steampunk-style goggles.

"Summer, Ms. Kuntz owns one of the most prestigious marketing companies in the country." She wiggled her eyebrows at Summer. "Maybe she has a position…"

"Please, call me *Carolanne*," the woman interrupted. She gave Summer a fleeting smile before returning her attention to Dana. "Now, tell me, kiddo, whose idea was it to dress up like Victorians for this shindig?"

"Mine, why?" Dana absently rested a hand on her belly. "And please don't tell me you're one of those people who hates to dress up. You look great."

"On the contrary." Carolanne slid her fingers down the side of her form-fitting black gown and gave her puffy rear bustle a pat. "I love dressing up. Besides, it's a brilliant marketing strategy."

"You really think so?" Dana asked, lifting her chin with pride.

"Yes, I do," Carolanne said. "In fact, I wouldn't be surprised if you break several sales records at the auction tomorrow."

Summer frowned. "What does dressing up have to do with art sales?"

Carolanne pointed toward the back of the ballroom, where the top prize of the art show was displayed – James Jacques Joseph Tissot's painting, *Bride On Stairs*.

The art books Gordo instructed Summer to read touted the painting as one of Tissot's finest works. As the title suggested, the subject of the painting was a Victorian bride, descending an elaborate staircase to join her betrothed and a throng of guests. Completed in 1863, it wasn't a huge painting – only about twenty-eight inches wide and forty inches tall, but experts agreed *Bride* provided an unparalleled example of the renowned artist's extraordinary ability to incorporate shading, rich colors and intricate details into every aspect of his work.

"The secret to selling art is to make it personal," Carolanne said. "Watch how people react as they stand in front of the Tissot. It's fascinating. The Victorian attire allows them to experience the painting as if they were standing among the guests at the bottom of the stairs, admiring the bride. That makes it personal. They're going to want to hold onto that feeling – to relive it every time they view the painting."

Dana grinned with obvious delight. "It's a shame we only have one of his paintings to auction."

"True," Carolanne agreed, "but everyone will to want to buy *something* to remind them of this evening." She glanced in the direction of another display, where costume-clad people were beginning to gather.

Summer bit her lip to suppress her guilt. *"If Gordo gets away with stealing the Tissot and making everyone believe it was destroyed in a fire, it would ruin everyone's memory of this evening – especially Dana's. My plan to stop him has to work."*

"You've got good instincts," Carolanne told Dana. "When you get tired of working for Robert, you should give me a call." She raised her glass of wine to acknowledge a familiar face in the growing crowd. "You'll have to excuse me, now – I just spotted young Aaron Wood. His *obscenely* wealthy father is looking for an agency to market his son's graphic art." She smiled and strutted off in the direction of a young man who, with his floppy top hat and oversized bowtie, appeared to be dressed more like the *Mad Hatter* than a true Victorian gentleman.

"I can't believe everyone is arriving so *early*," Dana cried. "This *never* happens." She took Summer's arm and started across the room again. "Come on, let's get our jewelry from Bobby. Then I need you to go tell the kitchen staff to start serving the hors d'oeuvres right now. After that, I want you to position yourself near the *Bride* to drum up as much interest as you can. And don't hesitate to use Carolanne's idea about getting people to picture themselves *in* the painting."

A half an hour later, Summer stood next to *Bride On Stairs*, immersed in a discussion with several investors about the finer points of the painting. She tried to focus her attention on the Tissot, but every time she learned someone's name, the person's matching stolen credit account information popped into her thoughts.

"I'm simply amazed by Tissot's talent," Joy DiVenuti commented. "I mean, just look at the details of the bride's dark hair. Even though she's wearing a long veil, the coiled braid on top of her head and spiral curls covering her ears seem to *shine* beneath the tulle netting."

Summer agreed, but found it impossible to keep Joy's credit data separate from the woman that she now knew to be a philanthropist and cancer survivor with a great sense of humor and positive attitude.

"Tissot put the same level of detail into the shading on the carved pillars and handrail spindles," Summer added. "He even painted a floral design on the wallpaper in the distance."

"And just look at the bride's expression," Linda Weigel said. The middle-aged blonde woman wore a yellow gown, similar to the one worn by the character Belle, in the *Beauty and the Beast*. When she smiled at her husband, a sturdy man with a short grey beard, top hat and red-vested tuxedo, wide dimples appeared on her cheeks. "Even though she's trying to smile, you can see a trace of tears in her eyes from all the excitement."

"I'm not sure she's excited," Bob Weigel teased. "You can't see her fiancé's face. Maybe he's ugly and she's trying to decide whether or not to haul ass back up the stairs."

Linda chuckled and gave Bob a light smack on his upper arm. "Stop that – you're going to spoil this romantic painting for me."

"They look like such a happy couple," Summer thought. *"I hope they pay attention to the warning email I sent and put a stop on all bank transactions before Gordo's hackers get a chance to mess with their accounts."*

"I'll bet you'd look great wearing those," Bob said, pointing to the double strand of lustrous pearls encircling the bride's neck. "Why don't we check out the jewelry display to see if we can find something similar?"

"You don't have to ask me twice," Linda said.

After they left, an equally charming couple of men stepped in to take their place.

"One thing you can say for the Victorians," one of the men said, "they sure had a sense of style. Just *look* at that dress, Andre."

"I'm *looking*, I'm *looking*," the other man replied.

Summer knew the couple were wedding dress designers and that they possessed the smallest financial portfolio of all the guests, so she turned her attention to another patron and pretended not to notice that they took several pictures of the bride's low, scooped neckline with tiers of short ruffles resembling a lace cape around her shoulders, and the wide, floral sash that separated the tight, beaded bodice from the full satin skirt.

"I swear the little flower girl in the painting is the spitting image of my niece," June Steding told Summer.

Summer tried to block the sweet widow's financial records from her mind by focusing on the golden-haired child near the bottom of the staircase. Looking angelic, yet bored, the child held a nearly empty basket of pink roses in one hand and clutched a rose stem in the other. "You must have an adorable niece," she said.

Before June could reply, Miles Prescot elbowed his way to the front of the small crowd, causing June to spill wine down the front of her dress.

Oblivious to the accident he had caused, the obnoxious man crowed, "Enjoy the painting, folks, because after tomorrow you'll never see it again – unless you're lucky enough to get an invitation to my country estate, that is."

Summer scowled but bit her tongue as she handed June a cocktail napkin to dab against the spill.

"No one stands a chance of winning against me," Miles continued.

"Thank goodness I decided to wear black and drink white wine," June joked as she gave her dress a few halfhearted swipes. "It shouldn't stain."

"Have you seen the wooden music box with the applique of a little girl on the lid?" Summer asked, guiding June away from the braggart. "I'll bet your niece would love it."

After Summer introduced June to a few other single guests, she circled the room, stopping to chat about the various displays with anyone who looked lonely. She was careful to appear knowledgeable about the art, while avoiding the use of exact quotes from the books she had memorized.

Mrs. Burton, wearing a fitted Victorian gown that matched the red color of her walker and balancing a tall, bejeweled powdered wig on her head, was pleased to find Summer wearing her cameo necklace. "Everyone who sees it on you will want to own it," she gushed. "But I won't be surprised if Robert insists on buying it for you to keep."

Summer blushed, recalling the feel of Robert's tender touch as he fastened Mrs. Burton's cameo around her neck. "I don't know about that, but I do agree this necklace is special. It's like you were saying earlier – it feels like it embodies the essence of its original owner."

"You see there? That necklace belongs with you," the elderly woman said, patting her hand against her heart. "Now, if you'll excuse me, it appears some of my friends have arrived."

Summer helped herself to a glass of red wine from the tray of a server passing by, and then watched Mrs. Burton totter over to join a trio of senior citizens who were examining the contents of a display case near the ballroom entrance. She jumped when Justin suddenly appeared at her side.

"Finally – we need to talk," he said, nodding his head toward the foyer.

"Yes, we do." Summer followed him, and after scanning the area to make sure no one was listening, lowered her voice and spoke quickly. "Let me go first, Justin. I've changed the plan in ways I can't undo, so I need you to listen and do exactly what I say. After the reception, I want you to exchange the painting, just like you're supposed to. Then come to my room. I have a line on some untraceable cash and I want you to take it and go someplace far away – someplace without casinos and preferably, someplace where Gordo would never think to look for you. Get your hands on a copy of the *Wall Street Journal* every year on our birthday. When it's safe, I'll put a coded message in the classifieds to let you know where I am."

"I'm not stupid," Justin said in a harsh whisper. "I recognize a two-hundred when I hear one."

200: forget about me – save yourself

"I'm not taking off anywhere without you," Justin continued. "Or Dana. She's my fifty-two, so don't try to eighty-six me. It's my thirty-three as much as yours. Besides, I haven't told you my forty."

52: The real deal; 86: Get rid of; 33: This is my fight; 40: I've done something you need to know about.

"But, Justin..."

"Don't *'but Justin'* me," he said, glancing over her shoulder into the ballroom. Suddenly, his expression darkened into a mask of anger. "Wait. What the hell is *he* doing talking to Dana?"

Summer turned to look and was startled to see fear on Dana's face.

"That son of a bitch," Justin said, his mouth curling into a snarl. "Stay here," he commanded. "Seventy-five, Summer. This could be a sixty."

Summer caught her breath.

75: Stay on your toes. 60: Danger. Get ready to run

Chapter Forty

Summer wanted to follow Justin, but found it impossible to move. She blinked hard, hoping her eyes had deceived her, but when she opened them, Marty Russo was still there. *"Why is that monster here? And how does Justin know him?"*

Marty was more than just another one of Gordo's goons. He had been one of the two men who had taken Edward and her into the desert. Later that horrific night, he was the one who tied her to a chair in Gordo's barn. The one who smiled when he removed her blindfold and gave her a drink of water, before leaving her alone with parts of Edward's mutilated body piled on a table next to her.

"Marty's the one Gordo will send to kill me when he discovers I've double-crossed him." Summer gulped. *"And he'll enjoy the job – take his time."*

She couldn't hear the conversation in the distance, but watched Justin take Dana in his arms and kiss her. Then he shook hands with Marty as if they were strangers. *"Please don't do anything to upset him, Justin. He's crazy. Just stick to the plan."*

Justin gave Dana another hug and patted her belly. Determined to go help her brother, Summer took a deep breath and blew it out, but before she could take a single step in Justin's direction, she heard Robert behind her.

"Speak of the devil," Robert said in a sing-song voice. "There's Summer now."

Startled, Summer forced a smile and turned to find Robert entering the foyer. There was little doubt the couple walking next to him were Emma and her husband, Ole. Emma's dark brown hair and pale blue eyes were the same colors as Robert's, and her emerald green gown was stretched tight across her baby bulge. Her husband, dressed like Robert, save his green bowtie, was a tall, Nordic-looking man with a square jaw, sandy-blond hair and hazel eyes.

"Hello, Summer," Emma said, her wide smile also like Robert's. "I've been dying to meet you. And wow – you're even prettier than Dana said you were."

Summer made a quick decision to feign ignorance of the situation brewing behind her. "Don't be fooled by the fancy dress and hairdo," she said. She brushed her hands over her royal-blue hoop-skirt and then turned her head to one side to show Emma her spiral curls, while at the same time, stealing a glance over her shoulder. She looked back just in time to see the trio split up.

Dana and Justin headed in her direction, while Marty melted back into the crowd. Summer managed to continue smiling. "I've heard so much about you, Emma. Dana, and of course, Robert, both think the *world* of you. And you must be so excited to be expecting..."

"Emma!" Dana cried as she rushed into the foyer, her arms outstretched.

Summer stepped aside to allow the two best friends to embrace – a simple act that turned comical, due to their pregnancies. After a few failed attempts, Emma, the taller of the two, laughed and stretched over Dana's belly to hug her friend around the shoulders.

While the others were distracted, Justin stepped close to Summer and whispered, "Another thirty-five to protect Dana. She's a twenty and that guy's a real twenty-one, and sixty-eight. Thirty-two?"

Summer gave her brother a slight nod to let him know she understood his message.

35: Change of plans; 20: The person is good/an innocent; 21: The person is bad/evil; 68: I can't get away; 32: Any ideas?

Summer whispered back, "Nine. Till then, twenty-five."

9: I need to talk to you in private. 25: Be careful.

Then she smiled at Robert, who was laughing along with the two pregnant women.

"Let's have a look at you," Emma said. She took a step back, still holding both of Dana's hands. "You're getting so big!"

"Look who's talking," Dana said, her eyes fixed on her friend's protruding belly.

Emma grinned. "Yep – only three weeks until we finally meet our little man." Then she frowned. "Are you feeling okay? You look stressed out."

Dana closed her eyes and took a deep breath. "I'm all right. I just had a run-in with someone, but Justin rescued me." Her eyes widened. "Oh…you haven't met Justin yet." She released one of Emma's hands and signaled for Justin to join her.

Justin stepped close and gave Emma a fleeting smile before returning his gaze to Dana. "Emma, I'm looking forward to getting to know you, but you'll have to excuse me for just a minute, first. I'm going to grab a bottle of water for Dana." He gave Dana a wink and then headed for the bar.

Emma smiled at Justin's receding back and nodded her approval. "I'm glad to see you found someone who looks out for you, but what happened? Someone must have acted like a real jerk if he managed to get under *your* skin."

"I just ran into an awful man that I had hoped I'd never see again," Dana said. "It was kind of a shock."

"Who are you talking about?" Robert interrupted. He took a step closer to Dana. "You like everybody, except…wait. Don't tell me the married bastard who got you *pregnant* is here."

Summer's antenna for trouble threatened to vibrate her brain apart. *"Marty's the father of Dana's baby? No. That can't be true."* Then she groaned. *"Of course it's true."*

Dana had said the father of her baby stayed in her apartment for a couple of days and that he had become furious when she wouldn't agree to steal from Robert. If her protective landlord hadn't come to her rescue, Dana was certain the man would have become violent. Then, because she was both embarrassed and afraid, she had told

Robert and Emma that she didn't want the father of her baby in her life because he was a married man.

Summer had no problem picturing Marty as the horrible man in Dana's story. On more than one occasion, she had witnessed his cruel treatment of the prostitutes that Gordo kept in the same house where she had been imprisoned.

"But, like any skilled sociopath, Marty can be tremendously charismatic when it suits his purpose." Summer pictured good-looking, tall, blond Marty sidling up to Dana in a crowded bar. *"Getting naive Dana to fall for him would have been almost too easy. And obviously, he'd have had no qualms about using GHB to render her unconscious – or trying to force her to steal for him."* She shuddered, as an image of Edward's mutilated body flashed through her mind. She didn't want to think about what might have happened to Dana, had her landlord not intervened. *"There's no way any of this is a coincidence."*

"Please, Robert – let it be," Dana begged. "It's over." She managed a weak smile. "I told Martin the baby belongs to Justin, who was sweet enough to play along. That means Martin's out of the picture for good."

"That's great," Robert replied. "But I still want that creep out of here."

"I shouldn't have said anything," Dana muttered. She dropped Emma's hand and stepped closer to Robert, placing her balled fists on her hips. "I'm not a kid anymore, Bobby. I don't need your protection. Besides, this evening is too important to the McNeal Foundation for you to go and spoil it with misguided macho heroics."

"It's not just about you," Robert replied, clenching his jaw. "What about all the *other* women in that ballroom? What's to stop him from doing the same thing to any one of them?"

Dana's arms dropped to her sides as her bravado melted away. "I didn't think of that." With tears pooling in her eyes, she turned to Emma. "What should I do?"

"Bobby's right, Dana," Emma said, keeping her voice low. "The guy's a sleazy, self-centered, lying cheater, who's already proved that he doesn't care if his actions hurt an innocent woman."

Sensing her twin's return, Summer tilted her head and watched him twist open the cap on a bottle of water and hand it to Dana. She mumbled her thanks and took a sip.

Justin glanced around the tense little group and then met Summer's eyes. He casually crossed his arms while holding up nine fingers and then held up three fingers on one hand.

93: Do you understand what's happening?

Summer shrugged. *"Maybe Marty didn't give up when Dana's landlord chased him off after all. Maybe he shared his plan to make a big score with Gordo."*

"I don't plan to make a scene," Robert continued. "Please. Point Martin out to me. I just want to make sure he isn't crashing the reception."

"You guys stay here," Justin said. "I'll go introduce Robert to Martin." He gave Dana a crooked grin. "Don't worry, pumpkin belly – the two of us will keep each other in check and we'll be back here before you even have time to miss us."

"I'm going, too." Summer insisted.

"Going where?" Maxwell asked, as he entered the foyer wearing a white Victorian tux with a hot pink ascot, along with matching gloves and a white top hat with a pink ribbon around the brim. Next to him, their arms linked, stood a short, muscular man dressed in a modern-day pilot's uniform. Gesturing with his free hand as if he were an orchestra leader, Maxwell continued. "And why in the world are all of you out here instead of in there, promoting the art?" He gave the pilot a coy smile. "That's what always happens, Charlie. The Production Manager leaves for fifteen minutes and everything goes to hell in a handbasket."

"Yeah, right," Dana grumbled. "More like an hour and fifteen minutes."

Robert shook his head without responding and strode to the ballroom entrance. "Come on, Justin. Let's go."

"That's better," Maxwell called, completely misunderstanding the situation. "Back to work, my pets!"

Justin stepped to Robert's side and Summer, Dana, Emma, and Ole fell in behind the pair, resembling a colorful string of ducks as they moved in single file across the crowded ballroom.

Marty Russo wasn't difficult to locate. His fedora and striped gangster costume didn't fit into the Victorian Era motif. He had cornered one of the pretty young servers near the back of the ballroom, next to a display of cut crystal glassware. When the girl saw the group approaching, she smiled at them as though they were the Cavalry coming to her rescue. The moment Marty turned enough to create an opening, she scooted away.

Justin and Summer exchanged worried glances. They were the only ones who had noticed that Marty patted his concealed shoulder holster as they advanced toward him – a rattlesnake's warning.

"I suppose this angry mob means that little sex kitten told you she's upset with me," Marty said, with no attempt to disguise the sneer in his voice. "But there's really no need for you to rally around to protect her honor. I mean, I might have enjoyed spending another weekend thrashing around in her bed if she weren't knocked up, but..." He raised his open palms and smirked at Justin. "She's all yours, buddy."

The look on Justin's face told Summer that he believed Gordo's thug was lying about having a relationship with Dana. She put her hand on her brother's shoulder and felt his muscles tighten and then relax. Flexing his muscles was a technique Justin used to remain calm, but it didn't always work.

"Twenty-nine," she whispered.

29: Don't take the bait.

Justin gave her a half-hearted smile and quietly rattled off a quick series of numbers. "Eleven, seventeen, forty, fifty."

11: Don't worry; I've got this; 17: I have a plan; 40: I've done something you need to know about; 50: Never let a mark get under your skin.

It took Summer a moment to realize that Justin was referring to Marty when he said *fifty*. Although their future was bleak, she had to hide a smile. Her brother had figured out that she was planning a double-cross and he was on her side. *"The bastards might win, but we won't go down easy."*

"This event is for invited guests only," Robert said. He articulated every syllable as if honing each one to a sharp point. "So, I'm going to have to ask you to leave."

Marty grinned again, clearly enjoying himself. "Sorry to spoil your big moment there, Baron Von Sour Grapes, but I'm the guest of a woman who's here representing a *broker*. So you and your posse of pussies should probably run along now and do whatever it is that you're supposed to be doing. After all, if this evening gets spoiled, I'm sure it would kill each and every one of you." He gave Summer a pointed stare before picking up his drink.

Gooseflesh rose on Summer's arms as the meaning of Marty's threat became clear: If she and Justin didn't perform their assignments exactly as they had been instructed, he would kill everyone they cared about. *"Wait – what else did he say?"*

Summer replayed Marty's words in her mind:

"I'm the guest of a woman who's here representing a broker."

"Oh my God." Summer frantically searched the faces in the crowd. *"I think Marty just made a mistake. He let it slip that there's player on the board that we don't know about. Someone who's here representing The Broker. That could ruin everything."*

Chapter Forty-One

Attempting to run a double con was similar to becoming a double agent. To have any shot at pulling it off, Summer knew she would have to lure Marty's accomplice – the other agent, so to speak – out of hiding.

"I'm sorry, sir," she said, stepping to Robert's side. "But I'm afraid we can't take you at your word. I'm sure you understand, what with all the deceptive people in the world. We're going to have to meet your date and see her invitation."

Marty glared with contempt. "Don't screw with me, blondie." He slammed his rocks glass on the top of the display case, drawing gasps from Emma and Dana. But once Summer donned her poker face, not even someone as threatening as Marty could put a chink in it...at least, not with so many witnesses around.

"She's absolutely right," Robert agreed. "If you're here as someone's guest, please ask her to come over here to clear up this little misunderstanding."

Marty muttered an expletive under his breath. "You want to meet her? Fine." He raised his arm and whistled across the room as if he were hailing a cab. The action brought instantaneous glares of disapproval and a few muttered insults from wealthy onlookers, but Summer and the rest of her group just stared in the direction Marty had indicated.

A tall, auburn-haired woman, dressed in a white mermaid style dress and holding a feathered mask over her face, glanced in their direction, and then turned away. When he whistled a second time, she shook her head. But when he held up a fist, she set down a glass of wine and walked toward them in a straight line, ignoring everyone on either side of her, as if she were a model strutting down a runway.

When she reached their table, she stopped directly in front of Marty. It struck Summer that the woman's model demeanor had given a false impression. Up close, she exhibited the attitude of a dog who had been summoned to the feet of its cruel master.

"Show these losers our invitation," Marty commanded.

The woman fumbled with one hand, attempting to release the clasp on her beaded clutch without lowering her mask.

"You might as well put it down," Emma said, gently edging her way to the front of the group. "I already recognized you."

The woman bowed her head and ignored Emma, acting as if opening her purse required her full attention.

Robert grunted as though he'd been kicked. "Lisa? Is that you?"

"Lisa?" Dana echoed.

When Marty's mouth dropped open, Summer realized that he hadn't been aware of Lisa's connection to Robert until that moment. *"What an idiot,"* she thought. *"The sadist couldn't resist taunting Dana, even though he's supposed to be keeping a low profile."* While everyone else's eyes were riveted on Lisa, she glanced at her twin to confirm that he had noticed the same thing. Much to her surprise, Justin stood with closed eyes, massaging his mouth with the fingers of his left hand. She nudged him with her elbow.

Justin opened his eyes, but for the first time in her life, Summer couldn't read his expression. He dropped his hand and leaned close to her ear. "That's Alissa," he whispered in a monotone, as if unable to comprehend her presence.

Summer's mind whirled. *"Lisa's the gold-digger who broke Robert's heart. Alissa was the woman Justin tried to help in Vegas by counting cards in the mob's casino. How can they be the same person? And why is she here with Marty?"*

Without uttering a single word, Lisa/Alissa dropped her mask on the table and, keeping her eyes averted, withdrew the invitation from her clutch.

Marty snatched it from her and tossed it onto the table. "Let's go, baby," he said, grabbing Lisa's upper arm. As he turned, he eyed Summer with raised eyebrows, making it clear that he expected her to fix whatever issues his arrogant blunder had caused.

"Wait just one damn minute," Robert sputtered. "What are you doing here, Lisa?"

Summer was too flustered to salvage the situation, but fortunately Emma intervened.

"Isn't it obvious?" Emma crossed her arms over her enormous belly and narrowed her eyes. "Once you figured out she was only after your money, she moved on and seduced some other unsuspecting art dealer."

"Is that true?" Robert asked.

"A leopard can't change its spots," Dana said.

Lisa licked her lips as the color drained from her already pale face, but didn't respond. Marty tightened his grip and jerked her arm, snapping her out of her trance.

"Don't say nothin', baby," he said, pulling her toward him. "Nobody died and made him king. He wanted to see our invitation and we showed it to him, so he can damn well kiss my ass." Marty curled his lips into a sneer. "Let's go."

Summer watched Lisa grab her purse and mask, stealing one last glance at the group before Marty dragged her away. *"She might have done everything they say she did, but I know that look. She's not here because she wants to be."*

"Well, of all the nerve," Emma said, staring after Lisa.

"Let it go," Ole said, wrapping an arm around his wife. "Getting all worked up isn't good for the baby."

Robert rubbed a fist in his open palm as if grinding out his temper. "Ole's right. We're all better off without her and I, for one, don't care to hear any more of her lies."

"Those two deserve one another," Dana said. She laid a hand on her protruding belly and bit her lip as she watched the couple disappear into the crowd.

Robert nodded. "Okay, then. It's done." He took a deep breath and blew it out. "Now, like Maxwell said, this is a big night for the McNeal Foundation and we've got work to do." He glanced at his watch and then scanned the room. "Dana, what happened to all the servers? You know the rule. Well-fed buyers with drinks in their hands tend to loosen their purse strings."

"That's strange," Dana said. "They're supposed to serve for another hour. I'll go find the manager."

"That's my girl," Justin said, bending down to give her a quick kiss. "You go set them straight. And tell them to bring out some more of those little spinach pastry things."

"We know you guys have to work the crowd," Ole said. "So don't worry about us. I think we're going to find a quiet table where we can sit and enjoy looking at all the costumes. Emma shouldn't be on her feet this long, anyway."

"That's right," Emma agreed. She gave Summer a nod and then smiled at her brother. "We'll have plenty of time to visit after the reception's over." She waved and then allowed Ole to guide her toward a small group of tables in the middle of the room.

"I'm sorry you got sucked into that mess, you two," Robert said. "It had nothing to do with you."

"If it involves Dana, it involves me," Justin said. "But don't worry. Karma has a way of balancing things out and those two slime balls have a whole shitload of it coming their way."

"Yeah, maybe," Robert agreed. He tugged one of Summer's curls. "You okay?"

"I'm fine," she assured him. "By the way, Mrs. Burton was hoping to talk to you tonight. You should be able to find her by looking for the tallest powdered wig in the ballroom."

He lifted her hand and kissed it. "Thanks. You're one in a million, Summer."

She didn't want to think about how much his opinion of her was going to change over the course of the next few days, so Summer turned to Justin the moment Robert left. "Ninety-three?"

93: Do you understand what's going on?

Justin shrugged. "Seventy-nine. I'm such a dumb ass. Twenty-seven, but one-hundred. Seventeen, so nine.

79: I got played; 27: I'm sorry; 100: Payback is a bitch; 17: I have a plan; 9: We need to talk in private.

"Agreed," Summer said, glancing around the crowded room. "Come on. We should be able to slip outside to compare our seventeens and get back before anyone misses us."

They started for the door, but before they reached it, Dana rushed up to them. "What am I going to do?" she wailed. "The reception is going to turn into a disaster and it's all my fault!"

"Slow down, pumpkin," Justin soothed. "What's the problem?"

Summer poked Justin in the ribs and nodded toward the door, frustrated by the interruption. He held up his forefinger in reply – the universal sign for *wait a minute*. Summer glared at him. Since when did Justin put someone else's needs before hers?

"Sure, take your time," she silently chided her brother. *"After all, Dana's concerns about the party are way more important than discussing plans to save our lives."*

"When everybody started arriving an hour early," Dana continued, "I told the event planner to go on and start serving, but I forgot the arrangements were for a three-hour reception. They served for three hours and stopped. I offered to pay for another hour, but the kitchen is closed and all the food we ordered is gone, so there's nothing they can do." She sniffed, looking as though she might burst into tears. "Usually people arrive late to these things and they leave early, but not tonight. I didn't realize wearing costumes would turn a normal reception into a full-blown party. Robert is going to be furious with me."

"What's the big deal?" Justin asked. "Can't they just drink for the last hour?"

"It doesn't work that way," Dana said. "The food and drinks are a package deal, measured in hours."

"Okay." Justin ran a hand through his blond hair. "Why don't we order pizza for everybody? I already ordered some Domino's for the security guys. I'll just call and order more."

Dana laughed. "Not a chance. For one thing, these people don't eat pizza. They eat quiche and bruschetta and truffles and oysters and..."

"They've been eating all that hoity-toity crap for three hours," Justin said. "Trust me, your biggest issue will be avoiding the stampede when we start serving Domino's."

"I wouldn't dare serve something so hot and messy around the display cases." Dana subconsciously licked her lips. "Even though I sure could go for a slice of thin crust Hawaiian right about now."

"Why don't we move the party into the Lobby Lounge and open a tab? That way Maxwell and I can button up the gallery for the night, and you guys can keep hawking the art until the bar closes."

Dana frowned. "Even if I agreed to your plan, where could we buy enough pizza to feed a crowd this size?"

"Trust me." Justin grinned. "I know a guy."

"I think you better know a *lot* of guys," Dana said, smiling for the first time since rejoining them.

"Justin," Summer said, trying to keep her irritation out of her tone. "Don't forget, I need your help with that thing. Why don't you give Dana your guy's number and let *her* place the order?"

"I think it would be better if I handle it myself," Justin said. "I know the guy, so he'll believe me when I say I need to order thirteen more pizzas...or maybe I should get thirty-five, since these people been starved for pizza for so long. What do you think? Maybe split the difference and get twenty-five?"

13: Follow my lead; 35: Change of plans; 25: Be careful.

"What the hell is he up to?" Summer frowned. *"And since when does he take the lead?"*

"It's too noisy in there, so I'll go outside to place the order," Justin told Dana. "Why don't you go tell Robert what we're up to?"

"He's going to think we're crazy," she replied, a smile lighting her face. "But a pizza party actually sounds like fun."

Summer bit her tongue until she and Justin got outside. "I thought we were going to discuss both of our plans and then decide which one was the best."

"We will, but first I'm going to call Anthony to order the 'za."

"Fine. You do that." Summer crossed her arms to make sure her twin caught her sarcasm. "It's not like we have something *important* to discuss or anything."

Justin ignored her and punched out a number on his cell phone. "Good evening to you, too, Domino's," he joked. "Listen, I need to place a huge order, so you should probably go get Anthony." He covered the mouthpiece while he waited for the manager to come to the phone. "This is a good thing for everyone, Summer. Dana will make her boss happy, it's the perfect excuse to clear the room so that I can switch the paintings, and all those rich people will *finally* get a decent meal." He gave her a crooked smile. "And best of all, that asshole, Marty, is going to..."

He dropped his hand from the mouthpiece. "Hey, Anthony, this is Justin Tyme. I'm the guy who placed an order for ten large pizzas to be delivered to the Belleview Biltmore at ten o'clock, remember?" He turned his back on his sister. "Yeah, well, it looks like I need to quadruple my order. Yep, that's right, forty large pizzas – delivered to the same place – as soon as you can get here. Mix up the toppings, but make sure to include a few of those thin crust Hawaiian ones...and better send a couple gluten-free ones for good measure." He listened, nodding occasionally. "Sound's good, Anthony. I won't hold you to a thirty-minute delivery, but please hurry. They tell me this crowd could get ugly if they don't get fed pretty soon."

Summer continued to fume as her twin took his time, joking with the manager and thanking him profusely before hanging up. *"Finally.* Now tell me, when did you find out that monster, Marty, fathered Dana's baby?"

Chapter Forty-Two

"What are you talking about?" Justin shook his head in confusion. "Marty's not the father of Dana's baby. But unless he's a bigger idiot than I think he is, he knows I'm not either. After all, he just gave me her name a week ago, along with the names of all the other marks."

"Wait," Summer screwed up her face, confused. "Back up. How do *you* know Marty?"

Justin rubbed his wrists, as if the name evoked a bad memory. "He was the goon who was holding me prisoner in Gordo's barn. And the reason I decided to escape." He shook his head. "I was pretty sure he wasn't going to let me go, even if you did everything you were supposed to do for Gordo."

Summer closed her eyes, her stomach threatening to lurch as she pictured her brother tied to a chair in that horrible barn. She recalled the taunting, mechanically altered voice on the phone. Marty's sick idea of a joke. "You didn't tell me because you knew I'd been tied up in that same barn."

"Yeah, but I didn't know how bad it had been for you until you told me about Edward. But none of that matters now. Neither of us are prisoners anymore and once we get ourselves out of this mess, we'll never have to see either one of those pricks again. So, what gave you the crazy idea that bastard was...you know."

"Marty *is* the father of her baby." Summer crossed her arms. "Didn't you wonder why Dana was so afraid of him?"

"I figured he was just being an asshole." Justin frowned. "Besides, Dana said the father is some married guy. No one's ever been stupid enough to marry Marty. And Dana would *never* date a guy like that. *Never.*"

"They didn't *date*, exactly." Summer bit her lip. "Dana met him in a bar. She doesn't remember leaving with him, but she thinks she must have gotten drunk and invited him home, because they were naked in her bed when she woke up."

Justin's lips moved, but no words came out.

"I'm almost positive that's not what really happened," Summer quickly added. "I think Marty dosed her with Rohypnol and raped her. Anyway, he...he stayed with her for a couple of days and tried to force her to steal from the Foundation's account. When she refused, he got mean. Fortunately, her landlord kicked him out before he got too rough. A few weeks later, she discovered she was pregnant and made up the married guy cover story."

Justin balled his fists and closed his eyes, his fury obvious as he processed the unsettling information.

"Wow, he must care about Dana more than I thought." Summer bit her lip again. *"Maybe I shouldn't have told him what happened."*

She watched as Justin flexed his muscles a few times and then took a deep breath and blew it out. When he finally opened his brown eyes, he wore the emotionless expression he used whenever he played poker.

"Okay," he said, his voice flat and cold. "Marty will get his – I'll make sure of it. But for now, we need to focus." He rolled his head in a slow circle as if to clear his thoughts.

Summer nodded. "There's no way this is all a coincidence...Robert's old girlfriend showing up here with Marty Russo – Gordo's enforcer? Her using two names?"

"Yeah. I knew something wasn't right the second I saw Alissa in there. After all, she's the reason I got into trouble with the mob to start with."

"But the time line doesn't make sense. You only met her a couple weeks ago. Robert broke up with *Lisa* well over a *year* ago."

"Follow the breadcrumbs, Summer." Justin ran a hand through his hair. "Robert breaks up with Alissa – who used to call herself

Lisa. She goes to Vegas. Maybe hoping to hook up with some other rich dude. I don't know. Anyway, somehow she crosses paths with either Gordo or Marty and tells them about a rich art broker who deserves whatever is coming to him because he gave her the boot. Obviously, she tells them about Dana, too. They figure she's the weakest link between them and Robert's money." Justin's eyes flashed with hatred. "So Gordo sics Marty on sweet, little Dana."

"And when that plan fails..."

"Gordo decides to pull you into this mess. He figures it gives him a two-fer. He gets Robert's money *and* he gets to make you do his bidding one more time. All he had to do was set a trap for your stupid brother."

Summer searched her mind, looking for memories to refute Justin's hypothesis, but found none. "You're not stupid, but I think you're probably right about the rest of it. You were dragged into this freak show because Gordo wanted me back in his stable." Summer shifted her gaze to the floor, unable to look at her brother. "Tell me exactly how you met Alissa."

"Well, I was just about to go into one of the little casinos a few blocks off the strip when all of a sudden this black car pulled up and some big guy shoved Alissa out." Justin rubbed his jaw. "Thinking back, I bet the guy was Marty. Anyway, I helped her up off the sidewalk and bought her a drink to calm her down. She told me a sob story about owing a bad guy a gambling debt. Ten-thousand dollars. Supposedly, he was forcing her to turn tricks until she paid it back with interest. She said she just wanted to go home to Indiana and forget all about Vegas. I believed her. I said I could probably pay off her debt in one night by counting cards. She seemed so happy." He shook his head. "Anyhow, we agreed the big casinos on the strip were less likely to notice someone on a winning streak, so we headed there. Alissa suggested the *Lady Luck*. It sounded good to me and – well, you know the rest."

Summer's heart sank. "During the year that Gordo held me prisoner, he must have found out that you spend a lot of time in Vegas. And you've always been a sucker for a damsel in distress." Tears welled in her eyes. *"Nothing ever changes. The monsters always hold the winning hand. And this time, the biggest monster wants me under his thumb...or dead."*

Justin laid a hand on her shoulder and gave her a gentle squeeze. "I'd hug you if you weren't wearing a dress designed to keep men three feet away from you."

Summer looked up in time to see his crooked smile – the one that reminded her they possessed a great deal of experience in escaping from bad situations.

"One." He winked at her. "Now, come on – eighteen and twenty-six because fifty-five and one-hundred. Seventeen, but you'll need to seventy-five, okay? Just thirteen."

Summer gave him a closed-lip smile. She knew he was using their twin codes to force her to think about what he was telling her.

1: *I love you;* 18: *Keep your chin up;* 26: *Keep it together;* 55: *They just messed with the wrong twins;* 100: *Payback is a bitch;* 17: *I have a plan;* 75: *Stay on your toes;* and 13: *Follow my lead.*

"So what's your seventeen?"

"It starts when the pizza arrives. Once we clear the ballroom, I'll convince Maxwell to take a break with his pilot friend. That shouldn't be too hard to do. Next, I'll need you to distract the guy in the security office for a couple minutes, while I disable the alarms and switch their camera feed to the recording I installed. That'll give Marty and me about twenty minutes to switch the paintings, just like we planned."

"Are you going to be okay working with Marty?"

"Don't worry." Justin narrowed his eyes. "I won't kill him. I've got something better in mind. I'll tell you about it later. For now, I just need you to distract the security guy for a couple minutes and then disappear for about a half hour. Stay out of sight and then meet me outside by the pool. If anyone notices we were missing, we'll tell them we took a walk around the grounds to get a little fresh air." Justin checked his watch. "Come on, let's go show our faces around the ballroom and then I'll go meet Anthony in the lobby."

∽

Justin's plan to lure the guests from the Starlight Ballroom worked like a charm. The Domino's manager, Anthony Hinckley, along with two of his employees, stood in the foyer of the ballroom with stacks of pizzas in their arms, while Justin carried an open pie through the room.

"The reception is moving down the hall to the Lobby Lounge," he announced, while allowing the delicious scent to waft through the air. "Open bar and free pizza." When he found Dana, he presented the Hawaiian pizza to her. "Lead the way, my lady," he said, giving her an exaggerated bow.

Dana eyed the pizza hungrily. "Oh, Justin, you remembered to order my favorite kind."

"Of course, I did." He kissed her cheek. "Now, off with you!"

The Domino's staff and party guests followed Dana down the Promenade Corridor as though she were the Pied Piper. Robert jogged ahead to open the bar tab, while Justin and Summer swept the room to make sure everyone left – except Marty, who they discreetly concealed behind the curtain next to Justin's special tool box. Once the ballroom doors were closed and security guards were posted there, the twins went into action. Summer grabbed one of the pizzas and took it to the security office in the basement, while Justin stopped to talk to Maxwell and then circled back around to the employees' entrance to the ballroom.

At exactly ten-fifteen, Summer tapped on the security office door. When the middle-aged guard appeared, she smiled. "I didn't want you to be left out," she said, holding out the Domino's box.

"Wow, that's really nice of you," he said. He reached for the pizza while taking a step back toward his chair and glancing over his shoulder to keep an eye on the security monitors.

Summer dropped the box to the ground.

"Oh, no!" she cried. She made a show of turning to the side and trying to stoop down to pick up the pizza, intentionally causing the hoop skirt of her costume to fly up in the back. The action simultaneously offered the man a beautiful view of her ample breasts peeking over her corset in the front, and a glimpse of her ruffled pantaloons in the back. As she hoped, it was a sight no red-blooded heterosexual man could resist.

"I'm so sorry," she told the gawking security guard. "I don't have a clue how women were supposed to function in dresses like this!" Summer pushed the hoop down in the back a little harder than necessary, so that it threatened to flip up in the opposite direction. "Perhaps you'd better help me before I lose all respectability."

"Excuse me ma'am?"

Summer gave him a well-practiced, embarrassed smile and pointed at the pizza. "I'm afraid you're going to have to pick it up yourself."

The man checked the security monitors and then smiled at her. "No problem."

As he stooped to pick up the box, Summer bent over again more carefully, pressing a hand against the cameo necklace, which seemed to tingle against her throat. "Does everything look all right down there?"

The man looked at the ruffled petticoat peeking out from the bottom of her dress and then up at her, his face filled with confusion.

"The pizza," she clarified with a radiant smile. "Is it okay? At least it landed upright." She noticed a quick flash of static cross the monitors and then the Ballroom appeared exactly as it had before: the art exhibits in perfect order, with no people in sight.

"I'm sure it's fine," the man said, retrieving the box from the floor.

"Okay, then, I guess I better let you get back to work," Summer said.

The security guard automatically scanned the monitors before replying. "I guess so. Thanks again for your thoughtfulness."

"My pleasure," Summer said. She started to curtsey but stopped after making only a slight dip. "Maybe I shouldn't press my luck."

"Maybe not," the man agreed. He waited for her to step outside, then bid her a good night and closed the door.

Summer congratulated herself with a quick fist pump and then carefully mounted the servants' staircase to the second floor. From there, she took the elevator to her suite on the fourth floor. She was yawning before she reached her suite. "I know, Margaret, I know," she said as she turned the antique key in her lock. "But it has to be a quick visit. I have to meet Justin at the pool in a half an hour."

The cameo necklace tingled once again as she lifted the back of her hoop skirt and flopped backward onto her bed. The clouds descended the moment she closed her eyes.

Chapter Forty-Three

Summer relaxed into the fluffy clouds. She no longer feared the journey into the spirit realm, but so much had happened, it felt like an eternity had passed since her last visit. She reflected on the events of the day.

Just this morning, she woke up in Robert's hotel suite, terrified from having witnessed Andy's memory of his own murder. Afraid that she would face the same fate as Andy – stuck in the spirit realm until she earned her redemption – and soothed by Robert's kisses, she had decided to stop Gordo – even at the risk of being killed for double crossing him.

"I wonder if Andy already knows that I met Alex?" Summer mused. Meeting an elderly man who had played a significant role in Andy's memories seemed like a coincidence at the time, but now she wasn't sure. *"I wonder if the spirits conspired to make that encounter happen?"* She smiled when the mist began to dissipate.

The first thing that came into view was the small parlor table in her hotel suite. Margaret Plant occupied her usual seat, but the Victorian spirit appeared a few decades younger than she usually did. She wore a blue-green dress with a deep, v-shaped neckline and huge, puffy sleeves, cuffed with wide rings of white lace just below her elbow. The same white lace covered the tight bodice, showing off her ample bosom and narrow waist. A thick braid of deep brown hair was coiled on top of her head, held in place by two gold hairpins in the shape of butterflies.

"Wow, Margaret – you were real stunner when you were younger," Summer thought, unable to take her eyes from the spirit. *"Why don't you appear like this all the time?"*

Margaret's demure smile told Summer that she had read her thoughts, but she didn't respond. Instead, she spoke to the empty chair on her right. "Try again, Winnie," she coaxed. "Just envision that you and I are enjoying a nice chat together, just as we did the last time I wore this dress."

Summer frowned at the chair, wondering who Margaret saw there and trying not to be disappointed by Andy and Violet's absence.

Margaret shook her head and sighed. "Perhaps we should try again later. Summer's visit will be short, so it would be unwise to waste it teaching you to how to make yourself visible." As she turned to face Summer, a teapot materialized in her hand and three teacups, nestled in saucers, appeared on the table. "It seems your plans are progressing marvelously," she said as she filled the teacups.

"I'm glad it *seems* that way," Summer said, wishing Margaret was pouring strong coffee instead of tea. "In truth, I have no idea if any of my plans are going to work. And Justin refuses to leave town, so I don't know if I'll be able to save his life, let alone mine. In fact, my ingenious plan might actually have put even *more* people in danger."

As she listened, Margaret scooped three teaspoons of sugar into her tea and stirred it thoughtfully.

"I prefer only a *whisper* of sugar in *my* tea."

Margaret smiled as she and Summer turned toward the empty chair, where the voice had come from.

"Winnie, you never could stand to be left out of a conversation." Margaret pushed the sugar bowl closer to the third cup.

As Summer stared open mouthed, the semi-transparent image of a young woman appeared. She wore a pink dress, similar in design to the one Margaret was wearing, but her thin body didn't fill it out nearly as well. She had mousy-brown hair, a long, hooked nose, and her gray eyes were set a bit too close together. Yet her perfect posture, together with the elegant dress, a cameo necklace, and an *enormous* gemstone brooch in the shape of a peacock, offset her physical imperfections, giving the woman an aristocratic appearance.

Summer's necklace tingled. She covered it with her hand, surprised to realize the two cameo and diamond-studded pendants were identical, other than the fact that the woman's pendant hung from a thin ribbon, while hers was suspended from a chain of white gold.

Margaret noticed Summer's reaction and held an open palm in the thin woman's direction. "Summer, this is Mrs. Winnifred Pew. She purchased the cameo you're wearing while staying at the Belleview Hotel during its inaugural winter season – 1897."

"My husband, Newton, insisted on buying it for me," Winnie cooed, fondling her necklace. "He said the carving was the spitting image of my profile."

Summer blinked back her surprise and smiled, trying not to think about Winnie's long nose and praying that she couldn't read her mind the way Margaret could.

Margaret coughed and picked up her teacup. Summer was certain she was trying not to laugh, but Winnie didn't seem to notice.

"Thank God – apparently not every spirit can wander through my brain whenever they please," Summer mused.

Winnie extended her thin arms and flexed her long fingers. "It's simply grand to call on friends for tea after all this time."

Summer drummed her fingertips on the table, trying to figure out what this woman and her necklace had to do with the dangerous situation unfolding in the Starlight Ballroom. *"Obviously, she can't read my thoughts or she would get to the point."*

"Yes, that's all well and good," Margaret agreed. "But right now, we have important business to discuss, remember?"

"Yes, I remember," Winnie replied. She spooned a tiny bit of sugar into her tea, stirred it, and then took a sip. "But first, I want to explain how I came to be here." She lifted her narrow chin, clasped her hands in her lap, and turned her attention to Summer. "You see, I had *planned* to wear my precious cameo to heaven. But when I died, a thief, disguised as a traveling preacher, tricked my *true* mourners into closing their eyes, while he pretended to pray over my body. No one noticed he stole my necklace, even though I was ranting like a mad woman the whole time."

Margaret slowly shook her head back and forth in a show of empathy.

"When the scoundrel dropped the cameo into his pocket and closed the lid on my coffin, I was too furious to take the lighted path," Winnie continued. "I stayed with my necklace, still hoping to reveal his despicable actions. Unfortunately, the wretched man sold my necklace the very next day and I've been attached to it like a genie in a bottle ever since – going only where the cameo went and seeing only what the person wearing it saw." Winnie smiled. "Now, I don't mean to imply that my existence has been all misery and onions. In fact, I've seen a good number of interesting happenings over the years. Why, I even witnessed..."

Margaret cleared her throat.

"You're quite right," Winnie said. "I'm getting carried away. It's just so exciting for me to be able to talk to someone after all this time. Why, when Gloria opened my jewelry box and I discovered we were at the Belleview, I felt faint with relief. For the first time since my death, I was able to observe my surroundings from my *own* perspective. And I could continue doing so, even *after* she closed the jewelry box."

"As I explained to Winnie, that happened because she's been here before," Margaret said, "and..."

Summer rolled her eyes. "And spirits can go any place they went while they were alive – I already know how all of that works."

Margaret arched her eyebrows in silent reproach at both Winnie's tendency to ramble and Summer's impatience, but said nothing.

If Winnie noticed Margaret's rebuke, she ignored it. "As I was saying, I was excited to be out, and intrigued by the situation you described to that negro man in the restaurant. When you prepared to leave, I thought I'd be forced back into the jewelry box. When that didn't happen, I was a bit confounded, still uncertain how my situation had suddenly changed after all these years. I thought perhaps the negro had magic, so I followed him – that is, until I realized that someone was wearing my cameo."

Summer resisted the urge to explain that the term *negro* was no longer acceptable. "You could tell when I put the necklace on?" she asked.

Winnie nodded. "Yes. And what a delight to find that you were attending a costume ball! It reminded me of..." She glanced at Margaret, who shook her head. "Ah, yes. Perhaps I'd best save those ruminations for later." She took a sip of tea as if to collect her thoughts. "When Margaret noticed me at the party, she took me aside and explained what was happening. Afterward, I told her about following the negro around. She believes it would be helpful for you to know how *he* spent the afternoon."

For the second time, Summer cringed at the Winnie's use of the crude racial reference. "That *African-American* man's name is Alexander Washington and he is a war hero – one the Tuskegee Airmen."

"A war hero," Winnie repeated. "Well, I suppose *that* explains how he came to be sitting in the cafe of this magnificent hotel, being served by a white woman – and why he appears to have the run of the place."

Summer's jaw dropped.

"Winnie," Margaret clucked, "I know that you've been trapped in a jewelry box for most of the last century, but Lee surrendered to Grant long before you died. Things changed a great deal during our lifetime and they were bound to keep changing – especially once educated men *proved* that a person's intelligence isn't connected to the color of his skin. In fact, a man of mixed race currently serves as *President* of the Republic and he stayed as an honored guest at the Belleview shortly before his election to office."

"Don't be preposterous." Winnie shook her head with disbelief.

Margaret gave her friend a tender smile. "Don't worry. You'll have plenty of time to catch up on all of that, as long as we work together with Summer. A scoundrel far worse than the one who stole your necklace is going to try to burn this hotel down. And if he succeeds, you'll most likely be forced back into your cameo."

Margaret paused a moment to let her words sink in and then continued. "Now, because the Belleview will be closing for renovation soon, very little effort is being put forth to keep the building in top form. And it's tripled in size since you wintered here, so that means there are countless places where the ruffian could start fires."

"The Belleview has tripled in size?" Winnie asked. "But it was already so enormous..."

"Oh, for the love of God, Winnie," Margaret snapped. "Will you please just tell Summer what Alexander Washington accomplished this afternoon?"

Chapter Forty-Four

Winnie sniffed and lifted her long nose into the air. "Well, I never..."

"You never what?" Margaret shot back. "Never get to the point?"

Summer didn't dare waste valuable time watching the two strong-headed spirits bicker. "Please, Winnie," she said, resting her open palm against her heart in what she hoped was a non-judgmental expression of concern. "The men we're trying to stop are truly evil. In addition to the hotel being at risk, several *lives* are in danger."

"Hmph," Margaret muttered, as she morphed into the middle-aged woman Summer was accustomed to seeing. "I suppose if one dresses like a young girl, one acts like a young girl."

Winnie ignored Margaret and picked up her teacup, pretending the altercation had not occurred. After taking a long sip, she carefully settled her cup back into its saucer. "As I was saying...at first, I believed the negro... *Washington*, had magic, so I followed him. You see, when I was a girl, one of our livery hands had magic. I once saw him waving a chicken bone over a lame horse and..."

"So you followed Washington, *and*?" Margaret interrupted, her frustration evident.

Winnie slowly blinked her eyes and let out a breathy sigh. "Well, it's no wonder I became distracted. After all, Washington was marching right down the middle of the Promenade Corridor, bold as brass – and the people we passed along the way were wearing the most *peculiar* clothing I've ever seen."

When Winnie's eyes pleaded for empathy, Summer followed Margaret's lead and faked an understanding nod.

Oblivious, Winnie continued her narrative. "I didn't come to my senses until we entered a magnificent, round solarium, with walls of glass, save one. The chandelier that hung from the towering domed ceiling was so unusual...why, I felt I'd been transported into a Jules Verne novel."

Summer, afraid that a verbal response might sidetrack Winnie again, said nothing. *"She must be referring to the new lobby."* She thought about how the lobby's modern construction must have appeared to the Victorian woman. The books Gordo had given her said it had been built in the 1990s, during the brief period when the hotel was under Japanese ownership. Incorporating the principles of feng shui, the round lobby was designed to serve as a portal, transporting hotel guests back and forth between the modern elements of the hotel, like the spa, and its historic sections. The concept failed spectacularly. Most locals despised the modern space from the start and could hardly wait for it to be demolished as a part of the upcoming renovation.

"For a moment," Winnie continued, "I didn't know where I was. But then I recalled Margaret's passion for the Orient and deduced she must have had the magnificent solarium built sometime after my last visit to the hotel."

Margaret rubbed her chin. "I did love the Orient, but that space was built *long* after *my* demise. What happened next, Winnie?"

Thankfully, the flighty woman hadn't lost her train of thought again. "Washington walked right up to the counter and asked the clerk if a *Sharon Delahanty* was available to meet with him."

Summer wasn't surprised to learn that Alex was acquainted with the Belleview Biltmore's assistant manager, resident historian, and part-time docent. During the hotel tour that she and Dana took shortly after checking into the hotel, Sharon had mentioned that a few old soldiers still visited the Belleview Biltmore to reminisce about the time they had spent there during World War II.

"Apparently, the woman worked in an office located right behind the counter." Winnie puckered her face as though she'd tasted something sour. "When she appeared in the doorway, Mrs. *Delahanty* was wearing *men's pants.* And Washington behaved as though they were *close acquaintances.* He even addressed her by her *familiar name.*" Winnie sniffed at the memory. "I was appalled until it became apparent that he was a *holy* man."

"How did you come to *that* conclusion?" Margaret asked.

"Because he told Mrs. Delahanty that one of his friends is a friar who's willing to come pray at the hotel."

Margaret raised her eyebrows. "A friar?"

Winnie nodded. "Yes. Washington told Mrs. Delahanty the friar was willing to pray all night if that's what it took to keep those wretched men from burning the hotel down."

Margaret shook her head, bewildered. "I don't see how a holy man...Winnie, dear, do you think you could let Summer watch your memory of that meeting, like we discussed?"

Winnie clung to her cameo necklace as if it were a security blanket. "I'm not sure, but I'll try. You said all I have to do is *think* about being there, correct?"

"Yes," Margaret coaxed. "Close your eyes. That's right. Now, pretend Summer is standing at your side as you watch Alexander Washington. He called on Sharon Delahanty. Can you see her? Don't worry. You'll recall every detail, as long as you keep your eyes closed and don't talk."

Winnie shuddered as the mist dropped over the table.

Margaret's voice grew faint. "You said Mrs. Delahanty was happy to see him, remember?"

Summer took deep breaths, hoping to avoid the queasy stomach that sometimes accompanied moving from one memory to another.

It didn't work.

The fog parted, dropping Summer into the scene so abruptly that she barely kept a scream from escaping her throat.

Winnie gasped, drawing Summer's attention to the memory, despite a wave of nausea that made her feel as though she'd just dismounted from a Tilt-A-Whirl. She surmised the reason for Winnie's reaction was that Sharon had come out from behind the registration desk to give Alex a warm embrace.

"It's so good to see you, Alex," Sharon said. She took a step back and smiled at the old man. Then she noticed his serious expression. "Is something wrong?"

"I'm afraid so," Alex said. "I need your help, but I'm afraid you're going to think I've lost my marbles."

"I don't think there's much chance of that. I've known you for years, and your mind is as sharp as a razor." She took the old soldier by his hand. "Now tell me. What's wrong?"

Alex glanced around the large, open lobby. "Not here. Can you take a break to sit on the veranda with me?"

Sharon glanced over her shoulder at the reception desk. "Lauren, I'm going to take my lunch break. If anyone calls, tell them I'll be back in half an hour."

She took Alex by the arm and led him through a door to a quiet veranda, next to the entrance to the spa. They sat in wide white rocking chairs, shaded by a giant oak tree. Once settled, Alex didn't mince words.

"Sharon, we might pretend otherwise, but we both know this old hotel is home to a lot of ghosts."

"Now, Alex..."

"Just hear me out, Sharon." Alex rubbed his hand over his short, nubby gray hair. "They're here, including an old friend of mine – Lieutenant Andrew Turner. I met a young lady today who has the power to talk to some of them. And I know she's telling the truth, because she knew things about me and my friend that she just couldn't have known otherwise."

"Alex, a lot of people pretend to..."

"You've got to believe me, Sharon. This girl isn't some kind of con artist – she's the real McCoy."

Summer gulped, feeling the blush rush up her cheeks. *"Thank God you believe that about me."*

"She's a spiritual medium?" Sharon asked.

"No – I get the feeling that this is her first experience with ghosts. But that's not the point." Alex chewed on the inside of his cheek for a moment, trying to put his thoughts in order. "She's in a hell of a pickle, this girl – and so are we. She tells me there's going to be a robbery at that fancy art show tomorrow, and to cover it up, somebody's going to set fire to the hotel."

Sharon's eyes grew wide. "Why are you telling this to me instead of the police?"

Alex frowned. "If the police get involved, she and her brother will be killed. We have to figure out a way to stop them ourselves."

"Stop them? You want us to stop thieves and murderers?" Sharon shook her head with disbelief. "I hate to be the one to break it to you, but you're not the young, strong fighter pilot you once were, and I'm just the curator of a historic hotel. No superpowers here."

"We don't have to fight anyone. We just have to stop them from burning the place down." Alex rubbed his head again. "And I have a plan that just might work."

"I still think we should go to the police, but tell me your plan."

"We should put together a scavenger hunt for the employees." He grinned at her bewildered expression. "Yes, you heard me. But not a normal scavenger hunt – a sort of safety-practice scavenger hunt. I have a friend – a fire marshal and he said he'd help out – said he'd stay all night if necessary."

"There's that term again," Winnie muttered. "What's a scavenger..."

As the words left Winnie's mouth, Summer dropped backward through the veil of clouds, flailing and grabbing for anything that could stop her fall.

"Winnie!" Margaret's voice sounded far away as Summer continued to plummet through the inky nothingness, as though dropped from an airplane without a parachute.

"Concentrate, Winnie! Both of you! Think about having tea with me."

Summer fought her panic. Closing her eyes tight, she replayed the moments just before she joined Winnie in the lobby of the Belleview Biltmore. In slow motion, she visualized grains of sugar falling from Winnie's spoon into her tea. She shifted her gaze and watched Margaret's spirit shift from a version of her young self to one that was older – wiser. Summer felt the chair under her bottom and reached out to touch the table. To her astonishment, it was there. She opened her eyes, still reeling from the fall.

"Good girl," Margaret cooed. "You're all right now, darlin'."

Summer felt a sense of déjà vu as Margaret turned to the empty chair and spoke to Winnie.

"I warned you not to talk," Margaret chastised her friend. "It breaks your concentration – and poor Summer had to pay the price for your lapse."

"I'm sorry." Winnie's voice was filled with remorse. "But I didn't understand what they were talking about."

"You don't know what a scavenger hunt is?" Summer asked, hoping conversation would stop the room from spinning.

"At first, I thought *scavenger* was just another word for *criminal*." The faint shadow of Winnie's form appeared in her chair. "But if that were true, Washington's plan made no sense."

"A scavenger hunt is a game," Margaret said.

Summer glanced at Margaret, impressed that she knew the term, given that scavenger hunts didn't become popular until the early 1930s.

"They've held several of them in the hotel over the years," Margaret explained, reminding Summer that she could read her thoughts.

Margaret turned to Winnie. "It's similar to the game *Hide the Flag,* but instead of sending your guests to search for one flag, they must search for a whole list of items."

While Margaret discussed scavenger hunts with Winnie, Summer replayed the memory of Alex and Sharon in her mind, as well as the conversation she and Margaret had with Winnie prior to that misadventure. Then she smacked the heel of her hand against her forehead.

"Winnie," Summer said, trying not to laugh. "Did Alex happen to mention the friar's name to Sharon – to Mrs. Delahanty?"

Winnie nodded. "Yes, I believe he did. As I recall, he referred to the man as Friar Marshall."

Margaret groaned. "I believe you misunderstood him, Winnie. Is it possible that Washington referred to his friend, the *fire marshal,* who could *stay* – not *pray* – all night if necessary?"

Winnie screwed up her face, her doubt evident. "Why would anyone put a marshal in charge of fires?"

Having had so much practice concealing her true emotions over the years, Summer's voice carried no hint of mockery. "A fire marshal's job is to *prevent* fires. He inspects buildings and looks for dangerous situations that might cause a fire to break out, and he makes sure the sprinkler systems are in proper working order."

"Ah, I see." Winnie fiddled with the handle of her teacup. "That would make more sense."

Margaret nodded in solemn agreement. "Do you want to try to show Summer the rest of your memory or would you prefer to simply tell her about Washington's plan?"

Summer shifted uneasily, hoping Winnie would choose the latter option.

"I don't think I'm ready to try sharing my memories again just yet." Winnie turned her head and daintily cleared her throat behind her hand.

"So then," Summer prompted, "Tell me what Alex and Sharon decided to do."

"They discussed the matter at some length," Winnie began. "But eventually decided to call the staff together to announce the scavenger hunt. The workers are to search the hotel, looking for potential fire hazards, and if they find one, they are to report it, using the odd box contraptions they carry in their pockets."

"Two-way radios," Summer explained. "They transmit voices using a specific broadcast frequency." Observing Winnie's blank stare, Summer bit her lip. "Never mind how they work. They're called walkie-talkies."

"Yes," Winnie replied, all smiles now. "That's what they called them – *walking talkies*. The staff is to walk about and talk into them if they spot a danger. They are to wait for the friar – I mean, the *fire marshal* to arrive before continuing their search. I suppose Washington's friend is going to remove the various dangers."

"But how do they know where to search?" Margaret mused.

"Mrs. Delahanty *lied*," Winnie replied, widening her eyes as if sharing a juicy piece of gossip. "She told the workers to search closets, the attic, the basement, guest rooms, the kitchen – everywhere – like an Easter egg hunt. She said she has a *list* of their locations, but she absolutely does *not*." Winnie paused for effect. "The worker to spot the greatest number of dangers is to be awarded two day's pay. They were *most* enthusiastic about *that*."

"Good idea to tell them there's a list," Summer thought. *"Otherwise, there'd be nothing to stop cheaters from first setting up fire hazards, and then reporting their so-called discoveries."*

Summer caught her breath when Andy and Violet suddenly materialized. Violet sat in the remaining chair and Andy stood behind her with his hand resting on her shoulder.

"We've been organizing all the spirits we could reach," Andy said, as calmly as though he'd been with them all along. "They're going to try to help the staff as much as possible, but I warned them to be subtle. It wouldn't do at all if the staff was scared away from an area by too much paranormal activity. Those who are able will move objects to make hidden fire traps more obvious. Others will try to steer workers away from sections of the hotel that contain no danger. Meanwhile, Violet and I will follow Gus's men, tripping sprinklers to make sure every fire they try to start is eliminated."

"You mean Gordo's men, right?" Summer asked.

Andy pressed his lips into a thin line and nodded, but Summer was sure that in his mind, Andy was still battling Gus Murphy and his followers.

"Did you know Alexander Washington would be here today?" Summer asked, unable to control her curiosity.

Andy rubbed the bottom of his nose with his forefinger. "Alexander carries one of my old dog tags in his pocket. He's done that ever since I died. It's kept us connected through the years. I thought you could use another ally, so last night I visited his dreams – suggested that someone might need his help at the hotel today. It was pure coincidence that you showed up at the restaurant when you did." He gave her a cocky half-smile. "But I might have encouraged him to start talking about himself to that waitress."

"I want to help with the scavenger hunt, too," Winnie said, unable to conceal her excitement.

Summer felt her cameo tingle and turned to the woman, wishing she wasn't such a bumbler. *"Winnie's more likely foul up the scavenger hunt than aid the cause. But she means well, so..."* She sighed. "Winnie, I'm going to approach Robert about buying your necklace. That way you can stay right beside me – my closest ally until this is over."

Winnie sat straighter in her chair and lifted her chin with pride as she cast a superior glance around the table. "I think you've made a wise decision, my dear. I've always been quite loyal to those wearing my necklace."

"As if you had a choice. The only time you got released from your jewelry box was when your necklace was being worn."

Margaret and Violet both smiled.

Summer stared into Violet's sparkling, powder-blue eyes. *"I sure hope no one else learns to read my thoughts."*

Violet smiled in response. "Together we might all earn redemption tomorrow. By the way, has Margaret already explained the concept of *becoming* to you?"

Summer shook her head.

"I'll do that later," Margaret said. "Right now, it's time for Summer to wake up."

The mist dropped over the scene before Summer could protest.

Chapter Forty-Five

Summer woke in her hotel bed, still in her costume, the back of her hoop skirt flipped up behind her. She glanced at the clock and noted she'd been asleep for twenty-five minutes. After a visit in the spirit realm, she always felt as refreshed as though she'd slept for hours, but now her thoughts churned with frustration over unanswered questions. *"Damn it, Violet – thanks for giving me one more thing to wonder about."*

She rose and made quick work of freshening up, thankfully noting her banana curls were still intact. After peeking into the hall to make sure the coast was clear, she made a beeline for the elevator and pressed the call button.

Seconds felt like hours as Summer waited for the doors to open, silently praying she wouldn't run into anyone she knew enroute to meeting Justin by the pool. To her relief, the only people on the elevator were two maids.

The Hispanic women smiled in unison at the sight of Summer's Victorian costume.

"You look beautiful," said the older of the two.

The younger maid gave a brief nod of agreement as she stepped out of the elevator, pulling the older woman along by the elbow. "Come on, Martha. You search the closets down there and I'll go this way."

Summer cocked her head. *"I'll bet they're looking for fire hazards."*

Realizing her companion had been overheard, the older woman gave Summer an apologetic smile. "She misplaced her cell phone. We're trying to find it."

"Well, good luck with your search," Summer replied. *"And I really mean that."* She stepped into the elevator and pressed the button to the second floor, figuring she was less likely to be seen if she descended the boxed spiral stairs near the first-floor lobby, and then walked around the perimeter of the hotel to reach the pool.

She didn't count on the fact that a beautiful woman descending the famous stairs of the Belleview Biltmore in period clothing would create a photo-op for camera-wielding tourists. By the time she stepped onto the flower-lined path leading to the pool, Justin had spotted her and was trotting in her direction.

"How'd it go?" she asked when he reached her.

"We exchanged the paintings without getting caught and Marty's still alive." Justin gave his twin a wicked smile. "At least he is for *now*. Gordo might fix that after..."

"There you are!" Dana cried from the hotel veranda. She waved a hand to beckon them. "I've been looking for you guys."

"Damn," Justin said under his breath. "That was close." He flashed Dana a wide grin and returned her wave, but before heading in her direction, he whispered, "Still need to nine later, but it's all good. Forty, but sixteen. Seventy. Marty fifty-five and one-hundred."

As always, Summer didn't lose a step in translating his coded message.

9: We need to talk in private; 40: I've done something you need to know about; 16: Trust me; 70: You're going to love this; 55: These guys just messed with the wrong twins; 100: Payback is a bitch

Summer shook her head. One-hundred was *always* one of Justin's favorite codes. "Can't you tell me *now*?" she pleaded, keeping her voice low.

"Nope," Justin said, striding toward Dana. "Maybe next time, you'll be where you're supposed to be when you're supposed to be there."

Summer scowled. "I was only a couple minutes late."

"Close only counts in horseshoes and hand grenades."

"Two, Justin," Summer hissed, matching him step for step. "Two, two, two!"

2: I hate you

Justin grinned at her irritation. "Later – sixteen, seventy." He climbed the steps to the veranda and gave Dana a quick kiss.

16: Trust me; 70: You're going to love this

"What about 1670?" Dana asked.

"Trivia," Justin replied without missing a beat. "I was telling Summer that mail started being delivered on a regular basis around 1670."

"Wait." Dana crossed her arms over her belly. "Let me get this straight. While the rest of us are working our butts off to generate competition for tomorrow's auction, you guys are out here discussing *trivia*? Seriously?"

"Geez, pumpkin belly," Justin cocked his head to the side. "You're awfully worked up. Just how long have you been looking for me?"

Summer held her breath. *"If she's been looking for us this whole time, we're screwed."*

"Only a few minutes," Dana admitted.

"Thought so." He lifted one of her petite hands, kissed it, and then tucked it inside his own. "We just stepped out for a quick breath of fresh air, but we're good now, right Summer?" He glanced over his shoulder at his sister and grimaced to emphasize they'd just had *another* close call.

"Totally." Summer forced her most radiant smile. "Come on. Let's get back inside and start twisting more arms."

"I'm sorry if I was acting like a big old grouch," Dana said. "It's just that this is the first time I've ever been trusted to play a key role in the McNeal Foundation's signature fundraising event and I keep messing up – first with my *momnesia,* and then Martin had to go and show up here – of all places. And now I just can't stop worrying about..." She looked as though she might cry, but instead, she shook her head. "Never mind. Let's get back to work."

"Hey, now." Justin lifted her chin and smiled down at her. "You're being too hard on yourself. I don't think many people could have pulled off a Victorian costume reception for a bunch of rich artsy farts, but you did – and you did it while you're growing a *baby*. I think that's pretty freaking *amazing*."

"My brother's right," Summer agreed. "The reception is a giant success and I'm sure tomorrow's auction will be incredible as well. You should be proud of yourself, Dana."

"Proud?" Dana pulled her hand back and covered her eyes. "How can I be proud of anything ever again, now that everybody knows I let a disgusting, violent psycho get me pregnant?"

Margaret Plant's philosophy flashed through Summer's mind. "Dana, a wise friend of mine always says, 'It's never about what happened, it's about what happens *next*.' In other words, it doesn't matter how your baby came to be, it's what happens *after* she's born that matters."

Dana dropped her hands to her belly, tears welling in her eyes. "And what if Junior inherits her father's evil traits?"

"She won't," Justin said. He kissed Dana's forehead. "If there is one thing I'm *absolutely* certain of, it's that kids aren't genetically programmed to be like their parents. Your baby's DNA won't affect her character. I mean, I guess it's natural to worry, but babies aren't born evil and violence is *not* a genetic trait."

"That's easy for *you* to say," Dana quipped.

Justin gave Summer a pointed stare over the top of the sullen woman's bowed head and mouthed the number *thirty-two*, his expression imploring her to come to his aid.

32: Any ideas?

Summer bit her lip as she translated and then gave her brother a slight nod. "Dana, he might be an irritating ass, but in this particular instance, my brother knows what he's talking about. You see, he and I..." Her voice faltered. She swallowed the lump in her throat and started again. "Justin and I tell everyone...we always say our parents deserted us..." She glanced at Justin for approval before continuing.

Justin squeezed his eyes shut and nodded.

"He's afraid the truth might change how Dana feels about him." Summer understood his concern. The facts about their childhood had ruined more than one of her *own* budding relationships.

Summer took a deep breath, realizing that Dana had turned her head and was watching her with a mix of concern and curiosity. "The truth is, our mother was always a violent woman," she began. "When things didn't go her way – and that happened pretty often, she'd explode. When we were five years old, she killed our father. She died in a prison brawl a few months later."

Dana's eyes widened and she stiffened as she shifted her gaze from Summer to Justin.

"Dana," Summer said, coaxing her to pay attention. "My point is that, even though Justin and I went through a lot of horrific stuff growing up, we always knew violence wasn't hereditary. It's an option. Whenever something bad happens, you can choose to get violent or you can choose to deal with it another way. Justin and I choose to be nonviolent, no matter what."

Justin placed one hand on each of Dana's shoulders and took a step away so that he could look into her eyes. "If two messed up little kids with no parents could figure that out, then it'll be a no-brainer for your baby. A kid raised with your love is going to turn out great. Hell, she'll probably even *shit* sunshine and rainbows."

Dana giggled as Justin pulled her into a close embrace and rained little kisses in her hair.

Watching this intimate moment, Summer realized why her brother had refused to leave town. He was in love. Head over heels, last-a-lifetime love. She cringed. *"My plan to get Gordo and Marty arrested with the stolen Tissot better work. Otherwise, they'll come after these two and..."* She felt limp, imagining the terrifying possibilities.

A chill ran down Summer's shoulder as goose bumps rose the length of her arm.

"Well, then," Margaret whispered into her ear. "We'd best not fail."

"Thanks, Margaret." Summer closed her eyes, thankful for the spirit's presence. *"I keep forgetting that I'm not alone anymore."* She took a deep breath and plastered on a smile. "Okay, guys, I'm beginning to feel like a third wheel," she teased. "You can stay out here if you want to, but I'm heading back into the reception."

Chapter Forty-Six

When all but a few slices of the pizza had been devoured and the bartender announced, "Last call for alcohol," satisfied guests began to leisurely drift toward the exits of the Lobby Lounge. Summer smothered a yawn and glanced at the grandfather clock that stood next to the stairs. It was quarter past midnight.

"This has been fun," Gloria Burton said. "But I'm ready to put my feet up and take this powdered wig off."

"Are you staying at the hotel for the night?" Summer asked.

"You bet I am. It's the only way I could be sure I'd make it to the auction. It starts in less than twelve hours, you know."

Summer flinched. Unless every aspect of her plan worked perfectly, both she and the historic hotel were in serious trouble. *Jesus. So many things can go wrong. This might well be the last twelve hours of my life.*" She swallowed her fear and maintained a cheerful expression, hoping Ms. Burton wouldn't notice the change in her demeanor.

As she opened her mouth to bid the old woman a good night, the cameo necklace tingled. *"Is that your way of telling her goodbye, Winnie?"* Summer fondled the edges of the valuable pendant. "Oh, Ms. Burton, I forgot to tell you that, uh, my research indicates your cameo was purchased by Newton Pew as a gift for his wife, Winnie, in 1897."

"My goodness. That's amazing! *Winnie*, you say?" Ms. Burton closed her eyes for a long moment. Then she smiled and reopened them. "Yes.

That name sounds just right." She gave Summer an approving nod. "You'll take good care of Winnie's cameo, won't you dear?"

"I promise." Summer gulped, knowing she might not be alive to keep that vow.

As Gloria Burton shuffled off, rolling her trusty walker down the Promenade Corridor, Summer scanned the room. *"I still have time to check one thing off my bucket list – to spend a night with a man I love. Well, maybe it's too soon to call it love, but it's as close as I'll ever get."*

She licked her lips when she spied Robert on the far side of the room. The obnoxious real estate mogul, Miles Prescot, had him cornered. *"I'll bet Robert would appreciate being rescued right about now."*

As she made her way across the still-crowed room, Justin stepped into her path. Summer instantly felt guilty that she longed to spend her last hours on earth making love to Robert, a man she'd only known a week, instead of spending that time reviewing and honing tomorrow's plan with her twin.

"Hey, Summer," Justin said. "Forty-three – tell Robert that Emma and Ole said they'd see him in the morning, okay? Emma's beat, so they're calling it a night."

43: I need a favor

Summer started to protest, but stopped when she realized that Justin's request gave her a perfect excuse to approach Robert. Then she noticed Justin's worried expression. "Six?"

6: Are you okay?

"Yeah, but I've got to go. I don't want to leave Dana alone right now." He glanced over his shoulder toward the boxed-spiral staircase. "She's terrified that Marty will find out that he's the father of her baby and worm his way back into her life, but fifty-four."

Summer's instinct for trouble went on high alert as she translated.

54: I've got it under control

She glanced around and lowered her voice. "Twenty-four, Justin. I mean it. Just thirty-four.

24: Don't do anything stupid; 34: Stick to the plan

Justin smirked. "Twenty-eight. Remember what I told you by the pool? Seventy.

28: It's too late for that; 70: You're going to love this

Summer's eyes widened as she cupped her hand around Justin's upper arm. "Nine, right now!"

9: I need to talk to you in private

Justin shook his head, refusing to move. "I've got to go, remember?" He gave her a wink. "But don't worry, nineteen."

19: The plan is working great

"Damn it, Justin, sixty-five. And as for Dana, fifty, remember?

65: You're being too reckless; 50: Never let a mark get under your skin.

Summer regretting referring to Dana as a mark even before she saw her brother flush with anger.

"Sixty-nine, Summer. Four," Justin snapped in a low, growling voice. "Besides, seventy-two. Can't you just sixteen for once?"

69: Screw you; 4: Mind your own business; 72: It's already done; 16: trust me

Summer knew her brother hadn't been this angry with her for a long time. A similar dispute had driven them apart four years earlier. And even though she'd been right that time – the woman he'd fallen for had been an undercover detective who ruined the con they were running and almost got them arrested – she regretted the falling out. Plus, things hadn't worked out well for either of them since they'd parted ways.

"I'm sorry, Justin," Summer said. "But forty-six."

46: I'm worried about you

"Thirty-nine, Goddamn it." Justin yanked his arm away. "I'm out of here. Dana's waiting."

39: Leave me alone!

Summer flinched at the sting of his rebuke, but made no further attempt to stop him.

Justin turned for the stairs, then paused on the bottom step long enough to call over his shoulder. "Forty-nine, Summer. And one. No matter how pissed I get – *one*." Then he climbed the stairs two at a time, the long coattails of his costume flapping behind him.

49: Take care of yourself; 1: I love you

Summer watched until her brother disappeared, seething with anger and worry. *"Margaret, I'd sure appreciate anything you and the others can do to help protect my dumb-ass brother. He must not un-derstand how dangerous Gordo and Marty really are. Otherwise, he wouldn't be acting like such a love-sick idiot."* She took a deep breath and blew it out.

"But didn't you *both* choose love tonight?" Margaret's soft voice whispered in her ear.

Summer bit her lip. *"Yeah, I guess that's true."* Her negative feelings evaporated with the realization. *"And I'm glad both of us got a taste of love, even if it can't last much longer."* The grandfather clock chimed twelve-thirty, interrupting her musings. *"I'll explain everything to Justin in the morning. I'm sure I can make him understand that he has no choice. He needs to get as far away from here as possible. And if Alex's scavenger hunt worked, I just might be able to pull off the double-con and disappear without Robert finding out that I was involved."*

Summer tugged her bodice down to reveal a bit more cleavage. *"But I'll worry about all of that tomorrow. Tonight is mine."*

She donned an alluring smile and set her course for Robert.

Chapter Forty-Seven

"Here comes that pretty filly again," Miles Prescot quipped when he noticed Summer approaching. He held his hand out, opening their tight circle to make room for her at his side.

Robert turned and smiled at her, a mixture of joy and relief in his eyes.

"Poor Robert. Looks like you've just about had your fill of that pompous jerk."

If Miles Prescot wasn't such a wealthy client, Summer might have spoken out loud, but instead, she bit her tongue. She offered him a smile, but her indulgence of his sexual overtures stopped there. Ignoring the man's obvious invitation to stand next to him, she squeezed her hoop-skirted costume between Robert and the gorgeous woman who had accompanied Prescot to this event. She glanced at the fingers of the woman's left hand to determine if the tall, slender brunette was his latest wife or just an escort. *"No ring. Lucky you!"*

Prescot didn't appear to register Summer's lack of interest. "You know, a girl with your obvious assets..." To stress his vulgar point, he rolled his forefinger in a circle, pointing at her breasts. "Deserves to run in the *winners'* circle."

His suggestion made Summer's flesh crawl. She continued to smile, but wrapped her fingers around Robert's upper arm. Robert covered her hand with his own, sending a clear signal that she was *his* date.

Prescot raised his eyebrows and smirked as he lifted his drink in a salute to Robert. "Congrats. It looks like the filly's chosen the dark horse in this race – at least for *now.*"

In the uncomfortable seconds that followed, Summer fought the urge to say, *"I don't appreciate being compared to a horse – especially by a nasty jackass."* She cast a rueful glance at the delicate garland of white silk roses that encircled the low neckline of her royal blue ball gown. *"Probably reminds the creep of the Kentucky Derby."*

The beauty at Prescot's side pretended not to notice the insulting flirtation. Instead, she formed her lips into a pretty pout and raised her empty glass. "Miles, I want more wine, but zee bartender, he has stopped servink."

Summer was intrigued by the woman's Russian accent. *"Mail order?"* she wondered.

"Perhaps der es a bottle of Dom Perignon in our suite. Yes?"

Like a dog rediscovering a favorite toy, Miles reached out and scooped the brunette into the curve of his arm. "Sure, baby." He slid his hand down and squeezed her butt. "You can *bathe* in the stuff if you want to." He winked at Summer. "Would you like to join us? We're in the Honeymoon Suite – it's really something to see."

Summer felt the bile rise at the back of her throat. *"Not even if you were the last man on earth and coated in chocolate."*

Before she could choke out a reply, Robert intervened. "I think you already have your hands full with Natalia, don't you, Miles?"

"I'm *kidding,*" he said with a cheesy grin. "I kid. It's one of my many charms. I'm a kidder." He kissed Natalia on her cheek. "Isn't that right, baby?"

"Jes," the brunette agreed. "Miles – he es a verdy funny man. I like dat. Verdy much."

"Impressive that she can say that with a straight face," Summer thought.

"Well, then, you two have a nice evening," Robert said. "And good luck at the auction tomorrow."

"I have all the luck I need in my wallet," Prescot said. He turned and sauntered toward the corridor, with Natalia at his side.

Summer watched him exit, hoping he would trip and fall on his face. *"God, I hate the thought of that clown owning a painting as precious as* Bride on Stairs. *I almost regret having to call the police to tell them Gordo stole it. I hope the police have to hold it as evidence for a long, long time."*

When they were gone, Summer pretended to shudder. "I feel like I need a shower every time I get near that snake. You should have told him you're staying in the *Presidential* Suite."

"And risk bruising his fragile self-esteem? Not a chance," Robert said. "Just think if it this way. The more we inflate his ego, the more he'll spend to acquire *Bride on Stairs*. And the higher the sales price, the bigger our commission – and the more the McNeal Foundation can support the arts."

"But doesn't it bother you to know that he's going to be responsible for that fantastic painting? I mean, he'd probably be just as happy displaying a picture of a matador on black velvet, as long as he was able to brag about how much he paid for it."

"I know." Robert took off his glasses and rubbed the lenses with a cocktail napkin. "Maybe I'll be able to convince him to loan the painting to a gallery. I could offer to put a plaque by it saying he owns it and how much he paid for it."

"That's really tacky, but it just might work," Summer said, gazing into his clear blue eyes.

Her heart skipped a beat as she recalled the passion they'd shared that morning. Maxwell had interrupted them to announce the Tissot painting had arrived several hours earlier than expected. And every moment since then had been packed with preparations for the costume reception, followed by hosting responsibilities and of course, helping distract security so Justin and Marty could replace the real Tissot with a fake.

Now there were only eleven hours left before the auction was scheduled to begin.

"I'll either be on the run or dead by the time the auction is over," Summer mused. The thought of never seeing Robert again made her heart ache. *"But I'll be damned if I'm going to waste these last precious hours feeling sorry for myself."*

Robert paid the bar tab and bid goodnight to a few lingering guests. Then he escorted Summer down the elegant Promenade Corridor toward the elevator. As they walked arm in arm down the arched walkway, the golden light of the chandeliers and their Victorian costumes enhanced the hotel's historic ambiance.

"I wish I could travel through time," Robert mused. "It would be cool to see this place when it first opened. Who knows? Maybe Tissot stayed here. He was in the United States right around that time, you know."

"I haven't seen his spirit hanging around," Summer joked. "But I'll be sure to keep an eye out." The cameo tingled on her neck, reminding her that Winnie was listening. She smiled, certain the busy body spirit would love to join the conversation. She touched a hand to the necklace. "I'm afraid I've fallen in love with Gloria Burton's cameo. I don't suppose I could buy it on a lay-away plan, right?"

Robert chuckled. "Funny you should ask. Apparently, Ms. Burton has taken quite a shine to you. She asked me to pull the necklace from the auction and sell it to you outright, for whatever price you can afford, and under any terms you can manage."

Summer caught her breath, touched by the generous offer. "She's so sweet. Of course, I wouldn't *dream* of taking advantage of her that way."

"Well, why don't you wear it tomorrow?" Robert said. "It will make her happy and we can talk about the purchase price later. Maybe we can deduct payments from your salary."

"Salary?" Summer frowned. "I'm an intern. I don't get paid. And my internship is over tomorrow."

Robert feigned confusion. "Did I forget to mention that the McNeal Foundation is planning to offer you a full-time job?"

Summer's eyes widened. "What? I mean...thanks, but I...a job?"

"Don't look so surprised," Robert said. "You've earned this opportunity. I'm going to need more help after Dana has her baby, and I can't imagine anyone I'd rather work with."

Stunned, Summer gulped. "*Oh, Robert. You have no idea how much I wish that could happen. This is the first time I've ever wished I could become the person I'm pretending to be.*" She bit her lip. "*But it's just not possible.*"

"I know – you have a lot of questions. I'll put you in touch with personnel after the auction, okay? And don't worry. I'm sure you'll be more than satisfied with our offer." He pushed the button for the elevator. The doors opened immediately. "After you, my lady."

Like a real Victorian gentleman, Robert held Summer's hand aloft, guiding her as she gracefully swished her hooped skirt through the doors and turned, pirouette style, to face the front. Chuckling at the way her dress filled most of the compartment, he stepped in and pressed the button for the fourth floor.

Meanwhile, Summer's thoughts raced. *"I know I can't stay, but God – how can I leave? What will he think if I just disappear?"* She closed her eyes and took a deep breath. *"Stop! Don't think about that now. You have less than eleven hours left. Enjoy them."*

"Are you tired?" Robert asked.

"It's been a long day, but no...I'm actually kind of keyed-up." Summer smiled as she fluttered her eyelashes. "Perhaps der es a bottle of Dom Perignon in your suite. Yes?"

Chapter Forty-Eight

Robert laughed, but when their eyes met, his expression sobered. "You're amazing, Summer. Clients raved about you all night – said you were more knowledgeable than art dealers with decades more experience." He lifted her hand to his lips and gave it a gentle kiss. "And you were, by far, the most beautiful belle at the ball. I felt unbelievably flattered when you took my arm."

"You're too kind, sir." Summer's subdued tone didn't reflect the light, snappy come-back she had intended.

They eyed one another, neither speaking as the lift continued to rise. When the doors opened, Robert stepped into the fourth-floor elevator lobby and bowed slightly as he offered Summer his arm. She felt a guilty rush of pleasure when she wrapped her hand around his upper arm and felt his bicep tighten. With each step down the corridor, she felt more self-conscious. By the time they reached Robert's suite, she felt like a teenager planning to lose her virginity after Senior Prom.

Summer eyed the blue cravat knotted around Robert's neck, and blushed at the thought of taking it off and opening his shirt to reveal his naked chest. *"You're being ridiculous,"* she chided. *"What's wrong with you?"*

Outside the door to his suite, Robert fished the antique key from the pocket of his long-tailed, Victorian coat. "You know, it's kind of late." He cleared his throat. "I'd hate to…I mean, I think…maybe we should call it a night."

"What the hell? You had no problem asking me to come to your room late last night." Embarrassed, Summer dropped her gaze to the floor. *"Maybe he senses this weird vibe I'm giving off."*

"Hey...hey, there." Robert said as he lifted her chin. "It's not that I don't want...I mean, the more I get to know you...I don't know – I think we might have a real shot at something extraordinary here." He lowered his voice. "That's why, well – maybe we should wait. I mean, I want our first time together to be really special – memorable. Okay?"

Summer nodded, still trying to sort out her conflicted emotions.

He removed her hand from his arm, lifted it to his mouth and kissed it. Then he slipped his key into the lock. "Let me grab the box for your necklace real quick, and then I'll walk you to your room."

Summer attempted to smile to hide her disappointment, but couldn't help dwelling on the word *memorable*. She wanted to explain about her memory – that she would never forget a single second of their time together for the rest of her life, but given her situation, the concept of time struck her as even more ironic than the concept of memory.

While waiting alone in the hallway, Summer glanced at the hooped skirt of her ball gown, triggering a completely different kind of memory. *"Wait a minute. We're wearing Victorian clothing in a historic hotel. Why does that feel like it's important?"* Her mind sorted through information she'd read on the subject of costumes until it came across the article she had been searching for:

Embodied Cognition or *Enclothed Cognition* is a phenomenon that involves the symbolic meaning of clothes and the physical experience of wearing them. When we put on a piece of clothing, we adopt some of the characteristics associated with it, even if we are unaware of the phenomenon. Clothing affects how others perceive us and how we perceive ourselves, actually altering our psychological state. We associate certain clothing with specific behaviors – what the clothing represents – and our brains adjust our thinking processes accordingly.

"Of course!" Summer rolled her eyes. *"It's the reason Dave used to dress like a priest when we were running our Camp Sucker con. Women automatically trusted him in that garb. And now, since Robert and I have been dressed like this all day, we're starting to act like a proper Victorian couple."*

When Robert reappeared, the blue velvet box clasped in his hand, Summer smiled. *"I'll be damned if I'm going to spend the rest of the night alone because of some stupid clothing phenomenon."*

She walked slowly, her arm resting on Robert's, as he escorted her to her room. *"Think, Summer. Find a solution to the problem."* They stopped at her door and he waited while she unhooked a tiny beaded chatelaine bag from the sash at her waist, opened it, and removed her room key. As she fit the key into the lock, an idea clicked into place. *"If the costume is the problem, the costume has to go."*

Summer shot a glance at Robert over her shoulder. "You'll have to come in for a minute. Dana's not here to unzip my dress, and I don't want to sleep in this thing." She swept into the room and held the door open for him, an expectant look on her face.

Robert hesitated, but then stepped inside. "I guess this is where a lady-in-waiting would come in handy." He chuckled.

The cameo tingled as Summer closed the door, reminding her that Winnie Pew's spirit could see and hear everything the person wearing the necklace did. *"Sorry, Winnie, but the next few hours are private."* She gave Robert a demure smile. "First things first," she said. She unfastened the pendant, took the jewelry box from his hand and dropped the cameo inside. *"Good night, Winnie."* Summer closed the lid with a click and placed the blue velvet box on the parlor table.

Then Summer lifted the back of her dress to access the bow that held the multi-tiered hooped slip part of the costume in place. She untied the ribbon and let the lacy slip fall into a neat stack, with each hoop nesting inside the last. Next, she lifted the sides of her silky gown and did another pirouette, this time, stopping with her back to Robert. She pulled her blonde banana curls aside and waited.

Robert leaned over and kissed the back of her neck before grasping the pull tab at the top of the zipper. Slowly, he tugged the tab, opening the ball gown all the way down to her hips. The sensation of being undressed gave Summer an erotic thrill, but she stayed focused.

The instant Robert removed his hand from the zipper, she spun back around, and before he had time to object, she slipped the ball gown off her shoulders. The silky dress slid down Summer's body like a rush of royal-blue water, pooling at her feet.

Robert dropped his gaze to the floor, but Summer made no move to cover herself. She watched as Robert's eyes darted between her black, spiked-heels and an empty spot on the floor several times. It was obvious that, despite the tempting situation, he was still trying to behave like a Victorian gentleman.

"I don't know about you, Robert, but..." She leaned forward, inched her ruffled pantaloons down to her ankles, and then kicked them off. She knew he wouldn't be able to resist checking to see what items of clothing she was still wearing. "I think this moment right here – well, it feels pretty damn special to me."

Robert lifted his eyes and stared at the tight, white corset that barely concealed her nipples, as well as her silky white thong that was decidedly *not* Victorian attire.

She smiled and bit her lower lip while fiddling with the bow of the pink ribbon that crisscrossed the front of her corset, holding it closed. "And I have absolutely no doubt that this could become a *very* memorable night." She crooked her forefinger at Robert.

Robert shook his head, as a smile turned up one side of his mouth. He reached over the crumpled dress, lifted her into his arms, and carried her down the hall to the bedroom. But halfway to the bed, he stopped short and carefully lowered Summer to her feet.

Summer's first thought was that somehow Gordo had discovered she was plotting against him and had broken into her room. Terrified, she turned to look, but no one was there. The unexpected rush of adrenaline made it difficult to reason, so it took a moment for Summer to understand Robert's hesitation.

Then she noticed the hotel staff had folded back the comforter on only one side of the bed. The crisp, white sheets were clearly intended to welcome a single occupant.

"Oh, no – it's the gentleman thing again," Summer thought. *"This thing has got to go."* She pulled the long-tailed coat off Robert's shoulders and let it fall to the floor. Then she pushed his suspenders down. As she reached up to untie his scarf, he pulled her into a tight embrace and crushed his lips against hers. *"Welcome back to the twenty-first century,"* she thought, returning his passionate kiss.

Summer wasn't sure which of them made the first move to the bed, but suddenly, they were falling backward, their bodies tangled together. Resisting the urge to rip it off, she straddled Robert and unbuttoned his shirt, while he ran his fingers over her skin and teased the tops of her breasts.

Once his bare chest was uncovered, Summer imitated Robert's actions, running her fingers over every inch of his exposed skin. After she made a few unsuccessful attempts to bend his arms at odd angles in order to free them from his shirt sleeves, Robert laughed and rolled her onto her back.

He stood and, without taking his eyes off her body, tossed his glasses onto the nightstand and pulled off his puffy-sleeved shirt. When he sat on the side of the bed to remove his shoes and socks, Summer curled her body around his, enjoying the fact that her touch made him moan. He stood for a second time – this time, to drop his pants to the floor.

Summer's body refused to lie still as she watched him, craving the weight of his body on hers. Her hands slid over her corset to her hips and thighs and then back up, stopping momentarily to squeeze her breasts as Robert ogled her.

With his erection poking at his black, silk boxers, demanding to be unsheathed, Robert climbed back into the bed next to her. He slid one hand up her thigh to cup her mound while, at the same time, using his teeth to pull at the bow on her corset. When her breasts slipped out over the top of the tight laces, he abandoned the effort and lowered his mouth onto her nipple.

Summer was unable to muffle a squeal of delight. She arched her back, moaning with pleasure, her hands tangled in his mop of thick, mahogany brown hair.

When Robert stroked the wet silk of her thong underwear, Summer rolled her hips in circles, her moist core begging for more attention. He acquiesced by sliding a finger beneath her thong to gently stroke her clitoris.

Summer's head whipped back and forth as she moaned, certain she couldn't stand the tension one more second. When he slid his finger inside of her, she bucked against it, wanting...needing more. He slid her panties down her legs and then paused for a moment, as if deciding whether to stop and unbuckle the ankle straps of her shoes. Instead, he slid her thong over the black heels and tossed them aside. Then he reinserted his finger and began to lick Summer's warm, wet center in all the right places.

Summer bent her knees and pressed her heels into the mattress, raising her lower body up, nearly out of her mind with desire. "Please," she cried. "*Please.*"

Robert pushed a second finger into her core and began wiggling them deep inside of her, while still nibbling at the swollen bead of her clitoris.

Summer cried out, as stars exploded behind her closed eyelids. Her body jerked, and her muscles tensed as though wave after wave of electricity pulsed through her. Robert lifted his head to watch the results of his actions, a smile revealing that he was pleased with his efforts.

When Summer finally relaxed, Robert began working his way up her body, kissing her corseted torso and then taking her breast into his mouth.

"*Jesus Christ,*" she thought. "*If I've been having orgasms all these years, what the hell was that?*" She blew out a breath, still reeling from the force of her climax. "Come here," she whispered, tugging at his arms.

When they kissed, Summer felt her passion instantly reignite. She had an overwhelming desire to feel Robert inside of her. Right now. When she reached for his penis, he shifted to the side and pushed his boxers down, unceremoniously kicking them to the floor.

Robert rolled onto his back as Summer's fingers encircled his manhood. She slowly moved her hand up and down, enjoying the fact that it was his turn to moan. She repositioned herself and heard him suck in a sharp breath when she took him into her mouth and began to lick the tip and sensitive vein on the underside of his penis with her tongue. With her hand still wrapped around him, she opened her lips and gulped his shaft until it touched the back of her throat. Then she pulled back, using her tongue to tease him as she withdrew. She continued sliding him in and out of her mouth until she began to taste drops of salty pre-ejaculate fluid. Then she pulled back and shifted her position so she could straddle him.

"No. We shouldn't," Robert said, his face contorted with misery. He cupped the cheeks of her butt, keeping her from sliding down onto his penis. "My protection is back in my room."

"That's not a problem," Summer murmured, acutely aware that this was the first time she'd ever said that to a man.

Her mind attempted to list the potential hazards of having unprotected sex, but she quashed all such thoughts. *"If I get killed later today, it won't matter, and if by some miracle I escape and go into hiding, well then, at least I'll have this memory to hold onto."*

Robert didn't make any further protests as she rotated in small circles, inching him into her warm, welcoming body. She continued to rock on top of him until she had enveloped his full length.

"Jesus Christ," he hissed between clenched teeth. "You feel amazing."

Summer splayed her hands against Robert's chest to brace herself as she lifted up a few inches and then slowly dropped back down. She enjoyed watching the subtle changes in his facial expressions and the sensation of being in control, but after repeating the motion more than two dozen times, she had to pause for a rest.

In one swift motion, Robert flipped her onto her back. He slipped out in the process, but it only took him a moment to bury himself inside of her again. He lay on top of Summer, his forearms looped over her curled-up legs, the weight of his body pressing down on her shins, stretching her legs wide apart.

Being partially immobilized beneath Robert amplified the erotic sensations Summer experienced as he pounded himself into her core. She clawed at his back, losing control as she climbed toward another frenzied peak. She arched her back and pushed up to meet his every thrust.

"Oh, shit," Robert muttered. He tried to pull out, but she crossed her legs over his back, holding him in place. "I can't last any longer," he cried. "I've got to..."

"No – stay with me," she insisted.

It was the first time – and she knew it would most likely be the last time – that she felt a man explode inside of her. The hot sperm shot into her as he drove in a few more thrusts and then collapsed onto her chest.

"Jesus Christ," he moaned. "That was incredible."

"Mmmm, yes it was," Summer said, still enjoying the sexual afterglow and wishing it could last. She squirmed at the odd sensation of sperm trickling down the crack of her butt, forming a wet spot beneath her.

Robert rolled to Summer's side and curled his arm under his head, using it as an extra pillow. He watched her as she stretched out her legs and rolled her ankles. "I never did that before," he said.

When Summer shot him a quizzical look, he laughed. "Let me re-phrase that. I mean, I've never had sex without *protection* before. Are you okay? I mean, I don't have any diseases or anything – I promise... but are you on the pill or something?"

"Yeah, I am," she lied, while silently praying, *"Please, God – don't let me get pregnant. Even if Gordo doesn't catch me, I can't go on the run with a baby."*

Robert nodded, visibly more relaxed.

"And for the record," Summer added, "I've never done it without protection, either. But it felt right – you know – special."

Robert grinned at her. "And *memorable.*" He reached over and pulled one of the tiny silk roses from her tousled hair. "But I'm afraid we really messed-up your fancy hairdo."

"Damn," Summer teased. "If I would have known *that* was going to happen, I never would have..."

When their eyes met, they both fell silent.

Robert traced the outline of her face with the silk rose. "You know, I think I finally understand the people who claim they knew instantly when they met *the one.*"

"Give me a break. You didn't even *notice* me when we first met," Summer teased, even though her heart ached to tell him she felt the same way. "At least not until I dumped a cup of hot coffee on your lap."

Robert laughed. "Who knows? That might be a fun story to tell our grandkids one day." He covered his mouth to conceal a yawn. "Sorry. It's been a demanding day and I think it's starting to catch up with me."

Summer slid closer to Robert, hoping to fire up his passion for a second round. *"I don't want to waste this precious night."* She traced wide circles on his skin with her fingers, allowing each circle to travel a little further down his abdomen than the last.

Robert groaned and caught her hand in his own. "Come here," he said, pulling her into an embrace. "Give me a few minutes to rest than then we'll go again...slower next time." Robert yawned again. "Just a few minutes, okay?"

Despite her determination to stay awake, Summer felt the exhaustion of the long day overtake her. She pulled the comforter over them both and rested her head against Robert's shoulder, smothering a yawn of her own. Her eyes drifted closed as she melted into him, content and at peace. *"I could stay right here with you forever."*

She pressed her lips together, trying to stay in the moment. Trying not to remember that forever didn't belong to them. Trying not to mourn for everything she and Robert might have shared – the life they could have had, if only things were different. If only she had never crossed paths with Gordo or Marty.

A few moments later, they were both fast asleep. The fog dropped over Summer, transporting her to the spirit realm.

She heard the voice of Andy Turner. "Now you know how we feel," he said.

Chapter Forty-Nine

When the fog began to clear, Summer found herself at the familiar parlor table. Margaret busied herself pouring cups of tea. Across from her, Violet dabbed at the corners of her eyes, while Andy, his eyes aglow, chewed on his lower lip.

Summer recognized the mood instantly – it was the mix of excitement and concern among team members on the night before a con takes place – with a couple of notable differences. No one was talking. Or looking at her, for that matter.

"What's wrong with everybody?" Summer wondered. *"Wait a minute..."* A sense of mortification and dread crept up her spine. *"I fell asleep wearing nothing but a corset and high-heeled shoes."*

She braced herself, looked down, and exhaled with relief. She was clothed in the gray silk blouse and black slacks she'd been wearing before the costume reception.

"Thank God for small favors," she thought. *"It would have been awkward to carry on a conversation with my boobs hanging out like a milk-maid in a porno film."*

The pot jiggled in Margaret's hand and she spilled hot tea on the table next to the fourth cup. Summer glanced up, surprised to see that the Victorian spirit was trying not to laugh. *"Dear God, she read my thoughts."* Summer cringed and shifted her gaze to Violet, who had demonstrated the same mind-reading ability on previous occasions.

If Violet heard Summer's thoughts, she hadn't found them funny. They all watched in silence, as Margaret waved a hand over the mess, making it disappear, and then slid a filled teacup to each of them. Andy frowned at his cup and with another wave of her hand, Margaret turned his drink into a beer.

"Andy's right," Violet announced.

Summer jumped at the sound of her voice. Like most young women of the WWII Era, Violet styled her thick blonde hair with two huge victory rolls pinned in opposite directions on top of her head, drawing attention to her cornflower-blue eyes. The rest of her shoulder-length hair fell in soft curls against the collar of her fitted, pink blouse.

Summer cocked her head. "Right about what?"

"He said you know how it feels to have evil come into your life and threaten all that you hold dear," Violet said. "But of course, you're luckier than I was."

"Lucky?" asked Summer, incredulous. *"If I stay, I'll be killed and maybe Robert and Justin will be killed as well. If I run, I'll be alone for the rest of my life, always looking over my shoulder. You call that lucky?"*

"I didn't say you are *lucky*," Violet countered. "I said you are luck-ier than *I* was. You have the opportunity to save Robert's life. Do you have any idea what I would have been willing to sacrifice to have had that chance?" She glanced at Andy as the fog dropped over the scene. "When he died, I lost everything."

Summer drifted in the fog, contemplating how it must have felt for Violet to learn of Andy's murder after the fact, and then be told she had to go into hiding. When the veranda of the tea house at the Japanese Gardens appeared at the edge of the clouds, Summer peered at it, waiting for the mist to part. Instead, short clips from Violet's memories began to emerge just beyond the clouds, as if they were silent movies.

In the first scene, Violet sat curled up in a rattan chair – her arms wrapped around her knees – her face buried. An elderly Japanese woman approached, wearing baggy tan clothing and a pointy straw conical hat, held in place by a ribbon chin strap. Her pants were cuffed well above her ankles, showing her white, split-toed tabi socks and zori slippers – the woven straw-soled predecessor of the flip-flop. She carried a small, cast iron teapot and two cups, all painted with images of colorful dragons.

Suddenly, Violet's voice filled the air, as if the mist had been wired for surround sound. "For days, I just bawled and bawled. But then Mr. Hawakawa's mother, Asuka, helped me realize that I wasn't the *only* person who had suffered a loss or been forced into hiding at the closed garden attraction. She told me that each Japanese person was permitted to take only one small suitcase of personal belongings with them to the internment camps. The rest of their possessions were sold right out from under them – their businesses, homes, furniture – everything. And the personal treasures they left behind, like photographs, were thrown out with the garbage."

As the first video clip disappeared, a second emerged. In this scene, Violet and several Japanese people gathered in the tea house to share a meal.

"Mr. Alvord wanted to sponsor all of his Japanese employees, but he was only granted permission to sponsor four of them – Mr. Hawakawa and his wife, Chiyoko, his mother, Asuka, and his brother, Motoki. The others, along with their families, were rounded up and loaded into a truck headed for an internment camp in Colorado. Fortunately, Mr. Alvord didn't give up *that* easily. He greased the truck driver's palm and *voila,* the driver allowed his captives to escape while he was eating his lunch on the side of the road near the Japanese Gardens."

Summer glanced around the full table, surprised to see four young children among the crowd. *"The government imprisoned American citizens? Even little children?"*

"Sadly, yes," Violet said in answer to Summer's unspoken questions. "After the attack on Pearl Harbor, people were outraged, and they felt incredibly vulnerable. They needed someone to blame, and they needed to believe they could do something, *anything,* to keep their families safe. If German citizens had been as easy to pick out of a crowd as the Japanese, folks probably would have gone after them, too."

Each time a memory faded, another came into focus – vignettes of Japanese people working inside a potting shed, tending a chicken coop and preparing food in the kitchen of the closed restaurant.

"In addition to Mr. Hawakawa's family and me, eleven people took refuge at the Japanese Gardens. We worked in shifts so that no more than four people would be seen outside at once…and we kept the children hidden at all times," Violet said. "Supplies were strictly rationed, but Mr. Alvord and my parents brought whatever food they could spare, including rice, flour, pork and canned milk for the children."

Summer smiled at the sight of Violet collecting eggs, disguised as a Japanese farmer, her hair tucked out of sight beneath a conical hat.

"My upbringing at The Rosery sure came in handy. We kept the flower gardens in decent shape, raised chickens and grew vegetables. Daddy built a small vegetable and flower stand near the road, and on Sundays, Mr. Hawakawa and his wife traded our surplus produce and flowers for ration coupons." Violet giggled. "Of course, the town folk didn't realize there were so many of us working the fields. They were amazed that Mr. Hawakawa and his three workers were able to raise enough produce and flowers to fill the stand every week. They often commented that the Japanese were *incredible* gardeners."

The next video clip showed how the group turned the once popular tea room into their living quarters. The windows were painted black to keep light from seeping out, and all but a few of the round dining tables had been pushed into one corner of the room and stacked, one turned upside down on top of another. Next to the tables, rows of chairs draped with tablecloths were used to provide a bit of privacy between sleeping areas. Straw mats on the floor served as beds. Across the room, the group gathered around the remaining tables for meals and to listen to the radio.

"We'd all been put through the wringer and felt like prisoners of war," Violet said. "But at least I knew my sentence would come to an end as soon as the soldiers left, taking Gus Murphy and his gang with him. I'd be able to return to The Rosery, where my soft bed and loving parents were waiting for me. But what about everyone else? I wracked my brain trying to think of how I could help them, but it was Asuka who came up with the answer. She believed they would suffer less persecution if they conquered the language barrier, so I began teaching them English and in the process, learned to speak Japanese."

All at once, the video clips changed, depicting life outside of the Japanese Gardens.

"A few months after the soldiers left the Belleview Biltmore, Daddy figured it was safe for me to come home. We never knew that Gus and the those other bad-news characters disappeared during the evacuation of the hotel. I took a job as an instructor at the War Bride School at MacDill Air Field. My job was to teach Japanese wives how to speak English, cook American dishes, and dress properly – to wear dresses instead of kimonos and walk in high-heeled shoes."

Images of celebrations began to light up the edge of the mist. "When the war ended, I tried not to be jealous of the girls who welcomed their soldiers back home. I attended their weddings and took gifts to welcome their babies. I went back to work with my parents on the farm and helped my sisters take care of their growing families."

"I know how hard it can be to watch everyone else get all the things you want," Summer empathized. *"It's kind of the story of my life."*

"I waited patiently for time to heal the hole in my heart, as everyone said it would," Violet continued. "But it didn't happen. After the war, Mr. Powell and his associates bought the Belleview Biltmore. They managed to erase most traces of the war years, save a few, intentional reminders – like a coat of black paint on one of the interior windows. The restored hotel was filled with light and music and happiness again, but it would never be the same for me."

"What happened to Mr. Hawakawa and the others?"

"The Japanese Gardens reopened after the war, but unfortunately, the local folks' resentment of Japanese people didn't end when the bullets stopped flying. I suppose traditional Japanese buildings, clothing and food brought back too many bad memories. A few years later, the attraction closed for good and Mr. Hawakawa moved his family to California, where gardeners were welcome, regardless of race. When they tore everything down and built houses on the property, most people forgot the Japanese Gardens ever existed."

"How sad." Summer thought about the bright red bridge and the gilded pagoda, wishing it had survived.

"Everything changes. My sisters, Daisy and Iris, talked their husbands into moving their families to New York, where there were plenty of good paying jobs, while I stayed with Mother and Daddy, trying to keep The Rosery afloat."

"You never fell in love again?" Summer wondered.

"Love can't flourish in a heart shattered by guilt," Violet said. "If I hadn't insisted that Andy return the two chandeliers he'd helped Gus to steal, then he wouldn't have been killed and…"

There was a pause as a vignette of the Belleview Biltmore appeared. "Everyone says that dwelling on *what might have been* is a waste of time, but it made me feel better to drop violets down the elevator shaft where Andy died. I wanted him to know I would *always* love him. Sometimes, if I listened carefully, I could hear him say that he loved me, too. Of course, at the *time*, I thought I *imagined* hearing his voice."

Summer smiled, recalling the first time she heard Andy and Margaret talking in the elevator. *"It totally freaked me out."*

The clouds grew dense, obscuring any additional images.

"When my parents died, I sold the farm," Violet said. "The new owner plowed it under to make room for more houses, so the only thing that remains of The Rosery is the name of the road. Meanwhile, weeks became months and then years, and before I knew it, several decades passed by. It became increasingly difficult to remember Andy's voice…his touch…his kiss. Near the end, all I had left of him were a few faded photographs. I grew old, still comforted in the knowledge that one day, I would join Andy in heaven. But even *that* didn't work out like I thought it would."

The fog melted away and a moment later, Summer returned to her seat at the parlor table.

"I knew Violet would go straight to Heaven," Andy said. "So, when she was dying, I visited her and explained that I needed to earn my redemption before I could join her."

"But I'd waited to be with Andy long enough," Violet said, taking control of the discussion. "I stepped off the lighted path, determined to remain with him until we could cross over together."

"It was wonderful to see her again," Andy said, "But the more time we spent together in the spirit realm, the more we realized that we didn't want to cross over. We ached to step back in time – to live the life that was stolen from us. We wanted to take long walks – build a home, have a family of our own – grow old together."

"And, besides – how could we ever be sure that Andy had earned his redemption?" Violet asked, shaking her head slowly. "We decided to remain in the spirit realm, rather than take the chance that we'd be separated."

"But then you arrived," Andy said. "Your situation was so similar to mine, I knew I had to teach you that redemption is worth whatever price you pay, no matter the cost. And when you decided to do the right thing, even if it costs you your life, I knew you would be saved from the limbo I've endured all these years."

"And because Andy helped save your soul, God decided to answer our prayers," Violet murmured.

Summer picked up her teacup, trying not to let emotion-laden thoughts creep into her mind, but it was no use. *"Great. You two cross over into Heaven together. And I take your place, stuck in the spirit realm, trying to earn redemption for all the other bad stuff I've done during my life?"*

"The fate of one soul is never linked to the fate of another," Margaret said. "Still, it's interesting how serendipity comes into play at times."

Andy smiled and took Violet's hand. "When Emma arrived, we understood that we had been granted the opportunity to live again."

"Wait just a minute," Summer said, alarm bells going off in her head. "What's any of this got to do with Robert's sister and her baby?"

"They are talking about *Becoming*," Margaret said. "Let me explain."

Chapter Fifty

Summer shot an uneasy glance at Violet and Andy, who were gazing at one another as if mesmerized. She crossed her arms, leaned back in her chair and returned her attention to Margaret. *"Okay, explain."*

"To the living, life and death are black and white," Margaret began. "Even if they can't agree on the details, everyone acknowledges that life begins at one point and ends at another. But what happens next? Millions have devoted their lives to the task of unraveling that mystery, but the answer continues to elude us all."

"Then how do Violet and Andy know the lighted path leads to Heaven – or Hell?" Summer asked.

"They *believe* it does, as do I," Margaret said. "But faith is not the same thing as fact. In truth, we in the spirit realm don't know that much more about the next steps in the eternal journey than the living. However, we are certain about three things." Margaret raised her forefinger. "First, we know a bright light appears the moment death comes calling. Second..." She raised another finger. "Immediately after spirits separate from their earthly bodies, most travel into that light without a moment's hesitation." She raised a third finger. "And finally, we know that no spirit can be forced to take the lighted path against its will."

"What's the light got to do with Emma and her baby?" Summer wondered.

If Margaret read Summer's thought, she chose to ignore it. "You already know that some spirits elect to leave the lighted path and remain in the spirit realm. Or, as in the case of Gus Murphy, a part of a spirit can break off and remain here as a ghost, while the rest of his spirit travels into the light. You've also learned that a spirit can choose to attach itself to a specific object, as Winnie Pew did with her cameo pendant."

Summer sighed at the unnecessary refresher course. *"Eidetic memory, remember?"*

"A spirit can travel anywhere he went while he was alive," Andy interrupted. "But a ghost like Gus can't do that because he only retained a tiny portion of his memories. Ghosts usually haunt the place where they died, but not Gus. He scares folks away from his money and..."

Margaret coughed. "Andy, I believe it would be best if you allow me to relay this information."

Andy gave Margaret a quick nod of submission and picked up his beer.

"Now, where was I?" Margaret curled her fingers into a loose fist to cover her mouth and daintily cleared her throat. "Ah yes...links between the spirit realm and the world of the living."

Summer uncrossed, and then re-crossed her arms, worrying her lower lip to keep from peppering Margaret with questions.

Margaret frowned at Summer's impatience before continuing. "When a spirit has experienced a similar trauma to one a living person has experienced, they can form a bond – as we have done with you. It's called *Connecting.* The bond of a connection is quite fragile, yet it allows us to share thoughts and memories while your body sleeps, in the hope that learning lessons from our past can help you resolve issues in your own life."

"Or in my case," Andy cut in, "to keep you from repeating my mistakes. And after *Becoming*, I'll help guide..."

"After becoming *what?*" Summer asked. She felt the knot tighten in the pit of her stomach.

"*Please*, Andrew," Margaret snapped. "Allow me to explain this in my own way."

Violet laid her hand on Andy's arm, silencing any protest he might have considered making.

"As I was saying..." Margaret returned her attention to Summer, her voice taking on the tone of a schoolmarm. "There are several types of links between the world of the living and the spirit realm. Some links occur frequently, while others are quite rare. For instance, when a living person is near death, the curtain between our realms thins, allowing the living to converse with a multitude of spirits. Countless people have witnessed dying individuals who smile or mumble incoherently – perhaps they even tap their toes to music no one in the living world can hear. We spirits call this form of communication *Tweening*."

Summer stopped fidgeting, her interest momentarily piqued.

"Another link," Margaret said, "occurs when a person donates a part of his body to another person. This process is called *Gifting*. Because a part of the donor is still *technically* alive, the spirit of the donor can remain in the world of the living, as a guest of its host."

Summer cocked her head, unable to keep one question from surfacing. *"Like demonic possession?"*

When Violet and Margaret chuckled, Summer's nostrils flared with annoyance at the way both women had learned to read her thoughts.

"No, no...*Gifting* is not possession," Margaret assured Summer. "For one thing, it can only take place if the donor's spirit is *welcomed* by the spirit of the recipient. Also, the donor's spirit doesn't alter or dominate the host spirit. It simply shares the experience of life, sometimes offering advice or providing additional knowledge. Whether the living person is aware of the donor spirit's presence or not, it comes and goes as it pleases – a welcome houseguest of sorts."

Summer squeezed her arms over her ribs, barely controlling her impatience. *"Come on, Margaret, get to the point. What has any of this got to do with Robert's sister?"*

Margaret pressed her lips together and poured a fresh cup of tea. "The biggest problem with young people is they've not yet mastered the skill of *listening* for more than a few minutes without *interrupting*. She huffed and gave both Andy and Summer a stern look. Then she scooped three teaspoons of sugar into her cup and stirred.

Andy gave a nod to indicate he accepted the reprimand.

"Sorry," Summer said, trying not to smile at the absurd notion that Margaret thought Andy, born in the late 1920s, was still a young man.

After Margaret's spoon was nestled in her saucer and she'd taken a sip of the steaming hot brew, she picked up where she had left off. "I wanted to explain a few of these phenomena so that you'd understand that *Becoming* is simply *one* of the options available to spirits when specific conditions are met."

"Okay, I get it. Lots of options. Now, what the heck is Becoming?" Summer leaned forward, put her elbow on the table, and propped her head against her fist.

"I won't pretend to understand how, or when, a spirit joins a pregnant woman, any more than I know what happens at the other end of the lighted path," Margaret said. "I do, however, know that it usually takes a brief period of time for a newborn baby to develop into a fully realized spirit. I also know that there are exceptions."

Summer was all ears now – as if she were a naive teenager, listening to Margaret explain about the birds and the bees.

"One of those exceptions is when *Becoming* takes place," Margaret said. "*Gifting* is when a spirit *shares* a living body with another spirit. *Becoming* is when two spirits agree to merge into a single entity."

Summer's stomach did a flip. *"Here we go again – if a spirit takes over a person, it's called possession."*

Margaret shook her head. "The living are always quick to describe any spirit activity they don't understand as possession, but no. *Possession* is what happens when a *ghost* attempts to *forcefully* take control of a living person's spirit. Ghosts are often confused with demons. They can usually be extricated – excised, if you will, but that phenomenon isn't relevant to the issue at hand."

Summer forced images from *The Exorcist* and *Rosemary's Baby* from her thoughts and refocused her attention on Margaret's explanation.

"After two spirits merge, they continue to grow together, producing a single spirit at birth." Margaret took a sip of her tea to give Summer a chance to absorb the concept.

"So the baby becomes a mix of the two spirits, the same way its looks are a mix of both parents?"

"Exactly," Margaret agreed. "And just like one parent's physical characteristics might be more dominant than the other, the more developed spirit will usually become more dominant...especially when the *Becoming* takes place late in the pregnancy."

"What difference does it make when the...when *it* happens?" Summer asked.

"A spirit that lived a full life has undergone wide range of experiences and developed certain skills, while an unborn spirit has acquired none of these things. If the *Becoming* happens early in a pregnancy, the merged spirit continues to develop. By the time it's born, it might forget all of the skills and memories of its previous life, or it might forget the memory of how a skill was acquired, yet still possess the ability. For instance, a young child might know how to play a violin from the moment it is introduced to the instrument. No one knows how the child achieved this accomplishment – not even the child itself. The memory of learning to play the violin was lost in the merging of spirits, yet the ability to play is retained."

Summer recalled that, at the age of five, Mozart was already entertaining European royalty by performing music he had composed. "Was Mozart..."

"Perhaps." Margaret shrugged. "I don't know if *all* child prodigies are the result of merged spirits, but many of them are. The later in the pregnancy the merging takes place, the more memories the fully realized spirit is likely to possess. Some might even remember important moments from their former lives."

"Okay, so..."

"I plan on *Becoming* with Emma's son," Andy blurted, unable to contain his excitement any longer. "And Violet is *Becoming* with Dana's daughter." He grinned. "We can't live the exact lives we had, but we will have a second chance to be alive – to be together. To live out our dreams."

"Wait...you plan to merge with Emma's and Dana's babies?" Summer's eyes grew wide. "But what if they don't want any part of this?"

Margaret nodded. "You're a good friend to worry about that, but both women have already agreed to the *Becoming*."

"I connected with Dana earlier tonight," Violet said. "I explained that it was possible for my spirit to join with that of her baby. Also, I promised that if she allowed our spirits to unite, I would do everything I could to bring joy into her life. When I explained that I could overpower any violent characteristics her baby might have inherited from its father, she was quite relieved."

"And I visited Emma," Andy said. "It turns out that she's always wanted to have an adventurous son with a good heart and the determination to overcome obstacles to achieve his dreams. She was worried that since both she and Ole had been born into wealth and prominence, their son might not possess those qualities. I promised I would endeavor to be the son she desires."

Summer's mouth went dry as she tried to comprehend these new developments. For the first time, her eidetic memory failed to produce any helpful information.

Andy took a swig of his beer. "The one bad thing is, we won't be around to help you tomorrow."

Summer jerked her head up. "Why not?"

"Once the *Becoming* is complete," Violet said, "our spirits will no longer exist in this realm." She gave Summer a tender smile.

"Why can't you wait for a couple of days?" Summer asked, trying to ignore the feeling that she was being abandoned for the umpteenth time in her life.

"Becoming has to take place while the pregnant woman is asleep, so that her spirit can watch over the process," Margaret explained. "And since both women plan to leave the Belleview Biltmore after the auction tomorrow, time is short. If Violet and Andy wish to take advantage of this rare opportunity, they must act tonight."

"Even if we stayed, we probably couldn't do anything more to help you," Andy added. "But don't worry. All of the spirits at the hotel know about the potential danger. If a fire starts, I'm sure they'll alert the staff."

Summer nodded, her head spinning.

"So, I guess this is goodbye," Violet said. "Thank you both for your kindness and understanding. I'm sure we'll all meet again in

Heaven one of these days." She blew a kiss across the table, first to Summer and then to Margaret.

"Have a good life, darlin'," Margaret said, as Violet began to fade from sight.

"I simply couldn't be any more proud of you, Summer," Andy said. "Now, I know you're scared, but fly straight into the battle tomorrow. As long as you remember the redemption of your soul is at stake, nothing can sway you from your target. And if you do the right thing, your future will turn out just swell, no matter what happens." Then he turned to Margaret, the impish grin of a daring young soldier lighting his face. "Thank you for everything, Margaret. I don't know how I'd have managed in this realm without you."

Margaret nodded and dabbed her eyes. "You go on now, and take care of that sweet girl."

"I will," he said. "I'd better go catch up with her now. We have some things to talk about before..." He disappeared without finishing his thought.

"Don't fret, Summer," Margaret soothed, raising her teacup as if a toast. "I'm still here. By the way, you've never asked how it is that you and I managed to establish such a strong connection."

Summer eyed the Victorian woman, suddenly curious.

"Despite what you may think," Margaret said, "I possess *far* more experience in dealing with vile men and carrying out nefarious escapades than you do." She winked at Summer. "And I'll be at your side, no matter what happens next."

"Wait," Summer pleaded as the fog dropped over the scene, engulfing her. *"Don't leave me hanging. I want to hear more about this sordid past of yours."*

Chapter Fifty-One

Summer floated in the clouds for what felt like a long time. At first, she amused herself by imagining the types of messy situations a Victorian woman might describe as *nefarious escapades*. Next, she replayed various moments from her encounters with the spirits, as if watching film clips from a favorite movie. Then, when she couldn't distract herself any longer, she thought about what might happen after the auction. Normally, she was proud of her ability to control her mind – to keep her emotions locked a vault within her subconscious. But now, her worst-case scenarios flowed unabated – as though the heavy door of the vault had been flung wide open, allowing all of her fears to run amok.

"Stop it!" she told herself. *"Even if things go horribly wrong, Margaret says life is an eternal journey. I'll still exist, even if I'm no longer among the living. And if I die, I'll need to step off the lighted path. I wonder how long I'll have to hang out in the spirit realm to earn redemption for all the crap I've pulled?"* She thought about Violet and Andy choosing to start their lives over and wondered if she might like to do the same thing one day. *"No,"* she decided at last. *"I don't want to die, but I have no desire to start over, either. Living one life is quite enough even if I would have liked it to last a lot longer."*

She felt a pleasant tickle against her neck and realized she was no longer in the spirit realm. *"What's that?"* Summer shifted her head toward the pleasant sensation, trying to identify it, and yawned.

"Good morning, sleepy head."

Teetering on the brink between sleep and consciousness, she caught a whiff of Robert's scrumptious, masculine scent. A smile parted her lips as his kisses began to drift down to her breasts. "I'll only give you a couple of hours to stop that," she murmured. She rolled onto her side and slid her leg over his thigh.

He jerked when he felt the spiked heel of her shoe brush against his skin. "God, you must think I'm some sort of cretin – not even waiting long enough for you to get undressed last night." Robert sat up, unbuckled the strap from around one of her ankles, slipped her shoe off and began rubbing Summer's foot.

"I think I'm going to have another orgasm," she said, her voice still thick with sleep.

He chuckled and reached for her other foot, repeating the process. Then he began working his way up her legs, kissing and massaging the inside of her calves, the backs of her knees, her inner thighs.

Summer lay as still as she could manage, enjoying every second, memorizing each touch...each kiss.

When he reached the top of her thigh, Robert stopped and straddled her body. Balanced on his knees to keep most of his weight off her, he reached down and untied the pink bow at the top of her corset. Then he unwrapped the ribbon from the hooks, slowly crisscrossing back and forth the length of her abdomen until the corset fell open.

"Whoa," Robert said, his voice almost reverent.

He bent down and kissed Summer's belly, sending shivers through her as soft and rough sensations simultaneously flooded her senses – the combination of the softest lips she had ever felt and the scratch of whisker stubble.

Summer started to moan. With Robert straddling her, she felt like a sleek motorcycle, engine purring, Robert revving her throttle.

"Two can play this game," she thought, sliding her hand up his thigh in search of *his* throttle.

"Not yet," Robert whispered. "Lay back and let me explore every gorgeous inch of you."

Summer hesitated. She didn't like being examined, even though she knew most of her flaws weren't visible – they had to do with her character. But she trusted Robert and more than that – she wanted him to remember her after she was gone. She closed her eyes and focused on the feel of his touch.

"He has callouses – does he play racquet sports or do they come from working out...maybe golf?" Her heart was heavy with the knowledge she wouldn't have the days and months – the years it would take to learn everything about Robert that she wanted to know. She considered attaching her spirit to something he treasured, but immediately rejected the idea. She didn't want to be around when he met someone new.

The odd mix of pleasure, excitement and melancholy disappeared the moment her cell phone rang.

Robert groaned and flopped onto his back. "Not again," he protested.

"I could let it go to voicemail," Summer said, already reaching for the ringing phone. She knew her precious time alone with Robert had come to an end. "But if I did, they'd probably send a search party."

"Yeah, I know. Better answer it."

Dana's loud, cheerful voice clashed with the intimate ambiance. *"If you only knew what you were interrupting,"* Summer thought. She held the phone between them, so Robert could hear. It would be easier if she didn't have to repeat everything the bubbly woman had to say.

"Where are you guys?" Dana demanded. "I thought you'd beat us down here, for sure. We've got coffee and a tray full of amazing Danish pastries. Are you on your way?"

To her surprise, Robert answered. "Take it down a notch, Dana. We just woke up."

"What do you mean, you 'just woke up'?" Dana sounded so incredulous Summer couldn't help but giggle. "Don't you remember what *day* this is? Or that Emma's here? Jiminy crickets, Bobby! I never thought I'd see the day when you..."

"Put a cork in it, kiddo." Robert gave Summer a sad shake of his head. "We'll be there in a few minutes." He mouthed the words

"Hang up." Then he sat up and swung his legs over the side of the bed.

Summer ended the call without a word and dropped the phone back onto the nightstand. Then she pulled the sheet over her naked body.

"I promise to make this up to you," Robert said. He got to his feet and began collecting his clothes. "It might take twenty years, but I promise."

Summer couldn't think of an appropriate response, so she switched topics. "Dana's pretty keyed up, but I'll bet her level of concern is nothing compared to Maxwell's. He's probably having kittens by now."

"That's okay. He's not happy unless he's running around warning everybody that the sky is falling." He held up the pants of his Victorian costume and frowned.

Summer admired his naked body, but forced herself to stay in the moment. "I'm pretty sure Dana is going to want me to return all of the costumes to the shop this morning. Why don't you just leave yours here? You can put on one of the hotel robes for the dash down the hall to your room."

"Great idea," Robert said, tossing his pants on the bed.

He pulled on his boxer shorts while Summer got out of bed and retrieved two thick, white robes from her closet. She slipped into one of the robes and handed the other to Robert, aware that he was still watching her.

"You know," he said, "I've always admired fine art, but I swear, I've never seen anything that can compare to you."

"Oh, yeah, I'm sure," she replied, running a hand through her tangled hair. "Mona Lisa's got nothing on my bed head."

Robert pulled her close. "Eventually, you're going to realize just how exquisite you are." He gave her a tender kiss and then stepped away. "I can only hope you'll still want me after you figure that out."

He picked up his glasses, socks and shoes, grabbed his room key and walked to the door. With his hand on the knob, he turned and smiled. "In the meantime, what would you think about staying here at the Belleview Biltmore an extra couple of days after the auction? Just you and me?"

"You mean, no interruptions?" Summer teased. "I'd love nothing more." It was the truth, even if it was a fantasy. "But until the auction's over, let's just focus on doing our jobs, okay?" She smiled. *"You'll be a lot safer if Gordo doesn't find out that I care about you."*

Chapter Fifty-Two

By the time Summer had gotten dressed, collected everyone's costumes and returned them to the shop, it was almost noon. She took a few minutes to hide her *go bag* – a small backpack containing her ID and other essential possessions outside, where she could retrieve it in a hurry. Then she rushed to the Starlight Ballroom to begin greeting guests. To her surprise and relief, none had arrived yet.

"Don't worry, this is normal," Dana assured her. "No one wants to be early... it makes them look too eager. They want everyone to believe they could care less about winning the auction."

"Besides," Emma chimed in, "the heavy-hitters know we'll start with the less expensive items. Most of those guys won't bother to bid on anything until we're about halfway through the auction."

"Oh, that's right," Summer said, recovering from her initial surprise that Emma would be so familiar with the operation. "You've probably attended the McNeal Foundation auctions lots of times."

"Every single year of my life," Emma said. "Our parents thought it was important for us to understand the workings of the Foundation. After we lost them, our aunt continued the tradition. I was thinking about using my pregnancy as an excuse to skip this year, but..." Emma gave Summer a coy smile. "I changed my mind at the last minute."

Summer recalled Dana saying that Emma wanted to meet the twins who had turned the heads of both her best friend and her brother. She blushed and changed the subject. "Well, I must say, neither of you two ladies look any worse for wear after last night's party."

"When you don't drink alcohol, the morning after is a lot easier," Emma said.

"Yeah," Dana agreed. "And it was wonderful to sleep in Justin's arms. But I still had crazy dreams about my baby."

Summer tried to conceal her curiosity. "Really?"

"Me, too!" Emma blurted at the same time, her eyes wide with excitement. "I dreamed I was sitting next to my grown-up son in an open cockpit airplane. It was so thrilling – he zoomed all over the sky, spelling out his name."

"Wait – you didn't tell me you had decided on a name," Dana said. "What is it?"

"That's the crazy part... we *hadn't* decided on a name. I think this was a premonition. He wrote the name *Andrew* in the sky, and I woke up positive that if we choose that name, our beautiful son will grow up filled with joy and have the courage to chase his dreams."

Summer sucked in a sharp breath. *"Oh my God. Andy really is in there!"* She resisted the urge to touch Emma's baby bulge.

"I *love* that name," Dana said, nodding her head with approval. "Andrew *what?*"

"We're still wrestling with that one," Emma said. "Now, tell me about *your* dream."

"Shoot... you're probably going to think I made up my dream, just to top yours," Dana said, wrinkling her brow.

"No, I won't... I promise," Emma replied. She drew a cross over her heart with her forefinger. *"Please,* tell me."

"Okay," Dana conceded. She puffed out her cheeks and let out an exaggerated sigh. "I dreamed about a sparkling angel with a wreath of little purple violets in her blonde hair." Dana ran her tongue between her lips to moisten them. "She was beautiful, but then, all of a sudden, Martin appeared out of thin air, looking super-scary. He carried a gun in one hand and a big ol' knife in the other. First, he tried to cozy up to the angel – you know, like he was trying to tempt her to be like him."

Summer nodded. *"Sounds like something Marty's spawn would do."*

"But the angel refused," Dana continued. "Martin got mad and threatened her with the knife, but she just smiled and pulled him into her arms. And then poof! He disappeared. When she opened her arms, a bouquet of violets fell at her feet. She picked them up and handed them to me. They were the most beautiful flowers I've ever seen."

"Oh, my. What do you suppose it means?" Emma asked.

"I think it was God answering my prayers," Dana said. "He was telling me that I don't have to worry about my baby taking after her horrible father anymore because he's given her the soul of an angel – you know, a good-hearted child who can turn violence into violets."

Emma clapped her hands together. "That's amazing! You should name her Violet."

"I'm way ahead of you," Dana said, grinning at her friends. "Her name is going to be Violet Angelica."

"Way to go, Violet," Summer thought. She gave Dana a light pat on her big belly. "I think that's a *perfect* name for your daughter."

Their conversation was cut short by the arrival of several art collectors and a few brokers. The trio gave one another knowing looks and split apart to personally welcome as many of the guests as possible.

After escorting Joy DiVenuti to a prominent location in the theater, Summer noticed Sharon Delahanty and Alexander Washington hovering near the entrance. Sharon smiled when their eyes met but Alex, with his hands shoved into the pockets of his pants, looked worried.

Summer continued to shake hands and greet wealthy art patrons as she made her way to the assistant hotel manager and the elderly Tuskegee Airman.

"How did the scavenger hunt turn out?" Summer asked. She was nervous, even though everything was going according to plan so far.

"How the heck did you know about that?" Alex asked. A crooked grin appeared on his weathered face. "Never mind – I should have guessed that Lieutenant Turner would keep you informed." He winked at Sharon. "He's one of those ghosts you don't believe in."

"I never said I didn't believe..." Sharon noticed the twinkle in the old man's eyes and pressed her lips together. "This is no time to try to get my goat, Alex." She turned her attention to Summer. "My crew found several suspicious fire hazards, but we still have a couple of serious concerns."

Alex nodded and pulled one of his hands out of his pocket to rub his chin. "Something's just not right. I feel it in my gut."

"I'm afraid I agree with Alex," Sharon said. "And so does the fire marshal. The hazards the workers found would have *accelerated* a fire quite a bit – but they wouldn't have *triggered* one."

"And that's not the only bad news," Alex said.

"That's right," Sharon said. "One of my girls came to me complaining about the guy I hired to set up the fire safety scavenger hunt. Of course, I didn't really hire anyone, but I played along and asked her what the problem was. She said that it wasn't fair that the guy was setting up new fire hazards in places they'd already checked." Sharon raised her eyebrows to emphasize the seriousness of her information. "The girl said he was in the basement, near a staircase where she had *already* found a fire hazard. After he left, she checked and found a *second* pile of oily rags stuffed under the steps."

"Oh, no," Summer groaned. "There's no telling how many hazards Marty might have reset."

"That's worrisome, all right." Alex folded his arms across his chest. "But I'm more troubled that we don't know how the thug plans to start the fire in the first place."

"As long as I set off the fire alarm *before* the fire starts, I think it will be okay," Summer said. "They'll be forced to make their move during the initial chaos...before the police and fire fighters arrive."

"Maybe they won't see the need to start a fire," Alex agreed.

Sharon wrung her hands. "I know my staff should continue to search the hotel, but I'm afraid of what those hoodlums might do if they're caught in the act of setting a fire."

"You're right to worry," Summer agreed. "Those guys are the worst of the worst." She paused, forcing back nightmarish memories of the night they murdered Edward. "Stop the contest right away. And you can warn your staff to expect an alarm, too. Maybe you can tell them you're conducting a second contest... to see how quickly and effectively they can clear the hotel during a fire drill. The moment the auctioneer starts accepting bids for *Bride on Stairs*, I'll sneak out and pull the alarm."

"Let me worry about that," Alex said. "They might be watching you, but no one will notice a skinny old man."

Summer nodded. "You're right. It would be less suspicious if I stay in the ballroom until the alarm goes off. Plus, I'll be able to start moving people outside."

"How will setting off a fake fire alarm stop the theft?" Sharon asked.

"Because I know how they plan to escape with the art," Summer replied. "I'll call the police to report the theft. They won't get very far, and hopefully, everyone here at the hotel will be out of danger when they're arrested."

"And catching those crooks will finally allow Lieutenant Turner to rest in peace?" Alex asked.

Summer caught her breath, remembering that Andy was already gone. She nodded her head, opting not to divulge the details of his *Becoming*.

With the plan in place, the trio went their separate ways – Sharon headed for her office to announce a staff meeting, Alex went to get a cup of coffee and find a chair near a fire alarm, and Summer resumed seating wealthy clients, starting with Mrs. Burton.

The elderly woman's face lit with delight when she noticed the cameo around Summer's neck. "It warms my heart to know that you'll be wearing Winnie's lovely pendant for decades to come," she said, lifting one hand from her walker to take Summer's hand. "I know you'll take wonderful care of it."

Summer touched the necklace, experiencing an unexpected wave of emotion. *"I'll have to turn it in at the front desk before I make my escape."* She slipped on her poker face and smiled. "I loved...I mean, I *love* wearing it."

After seating Mrs. Burton with her friends and stashing her walker out of the way, Summer turned and gasped. Gordo and Marty were sitting side by side, no more than ten feet away. Marty raised two fingers in the shape of a V under his eyes and then pointed at her to emphasize the fact they were watching her every move. Summer steadied her weak knees for a moment and then started for the door, pausing only long enough to scan the vicinity for Lisa. She was nowhere in sight.

The woman's absence gave Summer a flicker of hope. She knew all too well how it felt to be coerced into doing terrible things. *"I'm almost positive it wasn't her idea to hurt Robert or Justin. I hope she can break free and make a fresh start somewhere, once Gordo and Marty are cooling their heels in prison."*

Dana waved at her from a high-top table in the foyer, where she and Emma were drinking orange juice.

"Are you guys okay?" Summer asked.

"Swollen feet and aching backs, but we're fine," Dana replied. "Just taking a quick break."

"Why don't you go on inside and take a seat?" Summer asked. "I can finish up out here."

Emma rubbed her lower back. "Thanks, Summer. That sounds great. The auction will be starting in a few minutes anyway."

Dana hesitated. "Are you sure?"

"Come on, Dana," Emma said, tugging on the petite woman's arm. "Hurry up before she changes her mind." She gave Summer a friendly wink.

As the two pregnant friends waddled toward the ballroom entrance, Summer remembered that she hadn't yet given Justin the tiny recorder or brought him up to speed on her plan. "Hey," she called after them. "Have you seen my brother?"

"Not since breakfast," Dana said. "You might check with Maxwell." She waved her hand in the direction of the flamboyant exhibit manager. "He might *look* calm, but he's been running everyone *else* ragged all morning."

Summer nodded. "Will do. I'll see you later." She watched the two women disappear into the ballroom, momentarily consumed with thoughts about the blended spirits of the babies they were carrying.

She shook her head. *"There will be plenty of time to think about Violet and Andy later. Right now, you need to stay focused."*

Maxwell, decked out in a navy-blue suit with thin, fluorescent-green pinstripes and a matching fluorescent-green tie, placed both palms on his cheeks when he saw her approach. "You look gorgeous, darling," he said, drawing a circle in the air with his forefinger. "Give us a little twirl."

Summer turned in a circle, showing off her form-fitting, little black dress.

"*Marvelous*," he said with a nod of approval. "I wish I could wear tighter fashions." He pinched his non-existent love handles. "But I'm too easily tempted by buttered croissants and caramel lattes."

Summer knew he was fishing for a compliment and supplied one. "Are you kidding? You look *amazing*, Maxwell." She smiled, hoping to bolster the sincerity of the compliment and then asked, "By the way, have you seen my brother around?"

"Let's see," Maxwell said, already becoming distracted by a few straggling guests. "I hired a couple of hunks to carry art pieces to the podium when they're called up for auction, and I put Justin in charge of showing them the ropes. But that shouldn't have taken more than a few minutes, so if you see him, please tell him to stop lollygagging and come find me. I have a *hundred* more tasks lined up for him."

Summer edged her way down the wall to the back of the ballroom and slipped behind a curtain, where Justin had stored the specially modified toolbox on wheels. She resisted the urge to grin at the thought of Gordo and Marty serving time for stealing *Bride on Stairs*, Tissot's masterpiece that was now hidden in a secret compartment of the toolbox.

"Don't get cocky – focus." She lifted the hem of her dress and fished around in a tiny pocket, sewn into the lining. She removed the miniature recorder, opened the top drawer of the toolbox and dropped the sliver of black plastic into a corner.

She thought about the damning evidence the recorder held – a file in her own voice, listing every detail of the bank account information she had stolen from Robert's computer. *"Who knows? It's so small, maybe the police won't find it. After all, they'll only be searching for the painting."* Her optimism lasted just a few seconds. *"As soon as Gordo is in custody, he'll start trying to make a deal. He'll probably try to convince the police that the scam was all my idea and use the recording as evidence."* Her brief flicker of hope died as she closed the drawer.

Summer was about to make a discreet exit when her twin popped behind the curtain. "I thought I'd find you back here," Justin said. "Is the file stowed away safe and sound?"

Summer gave him a nod and pointed to the drawer containing the recorder.

"I hate that Gordo is going to hack all these people's bank accounts," Justin said. "Can't we do something to stop him?"

"I already did," Summer replied. "I wrote an email to all of the clients on the list, warning them that their accounts have been hacked. The timer is set to send the email close to the end of the auction, so their real purchases won't be affected, but they should be able to freeze their accounts before Gordo can get at them."

Justin frowned. "That's cool, but what about the deal you made with The Broker?"

"I learned a lot about contracts working for that law firm in Seattle." Summer smiled. "Our agreement with The Broker says I have to steal the banking information from Robert and turn all of it over to Gordo. I did that. The agreement *doesn't* say I can't tell everyone their accounts have been compromised."

"That's perfect." Justin grinned. "I didn't know how to stop that bastard from stealing everybody's money, but *you* did. And *you* didn't know how to protect the painting, but *I* did. Which means that Gordo and his asshole sidekick are about to figure out that messing with the Tyme twins was a piss-poor idea."

Summer's stomach did a flip. "Oh, no, Justin. Don't tell me you took the painting out of the toolbox."

Justin's face lit up with the pride of a child watching someone open a homemade Christmas present. "Nope," he said. "The painting Marty and I put in there last night is still right where we hid it. That's why Gordo can't accuse us of not holding up our end of the deal. I was supposed to help Marty switch the paintings and I did exactly that."

Summer narrowed her eyes. "Go on…"

"Well, remember the day the painting was delivered? It got here early – before the security system was fully operational or the extra security guards arrived. When Maxwell left me alone to start the installation while he went to find Robert, it was the perfect opportunity to make the switch. So, I did." Justin chuckled. "I was going to tell Marty that we didn't need to risk making the switch after the reception, but after I found out what he did to Dana… well, I decided not to mention it."

Summer's heart sank. "You mean you and Marty…"

Justin laughed again. "Yep – that asshole helped me stash the *fake* painting in the toolbox and put the *real* painting back on display. Wouldn't you love to see the looks their idiot faces when they discover they stole a forgery?"

Summer closed her eyes. *"Christ, Justin, you have no idea what you've done!"*

Chapter Fifty-Three

Summer could have concealed her anguish from most people, but not her brother. She turned and pretended to peek out of the curtain, struggling to compose herself. *"My only chance to get out of this mess alive was to get Gordo and Marty sent to prison for stealing the Tissot. That chance is gone now."* She bit her tongue, fighting back a surge of hysteria.

Margaret's voice whispered in her ear. "I'll be at your side, no matter what happens."

Summer felt a shiver run down her spine, followed by a remarkable sense of calm acceptance. *"Thanks, Margaret. I guess we only need to focus on saving the others."* She squared her shoulders and turned back to her brother, managing to smile. "So that's my surprise? Your forty we never got the chance to discuss?"

40: I've done something you need to know about.

Justin nodded. "See? I *told* you that you were going to love it. And best of all, since there was no theft... well, not really, anyway – Robert and Dana will never have to know anything about this whole ball of crap. In fact, Gordo and Lisa might actually have done us a *favor*. Without them, we might never have *met* Robert and Dana."

"So, you're sure that what you feel for Dana is the real thing?" Summer cocked her head, watching her twin.

Justin's brown eyes glowed with love in a way Summer hadn't seen since he was twelve years old and found a puppy. Summer had liked the cute mutt, but from the instant he picked it up, Justin *loved* it. He spent every free moment with it, even smuggling the dog into his bed at night. For two, glorious weeks, they had managed to keep the pup hidden. Then, while the twins were at school, their foster parents discovered the dog in the back yard shed and took it to the pound. Losing his puppy broke Justin's heart. Since then, Summer knew that, except for her, he hadn't allowed himself to get attached to anything or anyone.

"It wouldn't be fair to get involved with Dana unless you're positive that you're ready to settle down, Justin," Summer warned. "Are you sure you're prepared to raise another man's child – *Marty's* child?"

"I can't explain it..." Justin rubbed his chin. "But there's not a single doubt in my mind about any of it. Somehow, I just *know* she's the one for me. And her child will be *mine*, not Marty's."

"Okay, then," Summer said, wrapping an arm around his shoulders. "You have my blessing. And I know you're going to give little Violet a better life than the two of us ever dreamed possible." She blinked back tears, knowing she'd couldn't be a part of his new family. *"The Broker might not come after us, but Gordo will, the second he realizes he got duped. I'll need to draw him as far away from here as I can, and hope to God that killing me will satisfy his thirst for revenge."*

"Don't you feel the same way about Robert?" Justin asked. "I thought I saw sparks..."

"Let's talk about our love lives later," Summer said, pulling away from her twin. "Right now, I need you to listen carefully. When the auctioneer starts accepting bids on the Tissot, I'm going to trip the alarm so that Gordo will think the hotel is on fire," she lied. "When you hear the alarm, you get Dana and everybody outside and make sure they stay with the crowd, okay?"

"All right, but where will you be?" Justin narrowed his eyes with suspicion.

"Don't worry about me. Once the alarm goes off, I figure Marty and Gordo will want to get out of here fast – before the fire department shows up. If you're already outside with the crowd, they'll grab the toolbox and take it out through the loading dock to their truck. I plan to stay hidden in the hotel until I'm sure they're gone – you know, to make sure they don't decide they need a hostage or anything."

"Sixty-six. What aren't you telling me?"

66: I don't believe you.

"Sixteen," Summer pressed her lips together, knowing she'd miss using their secret language. "I'm just worried Gordo will do something to put the people we care about in danger, that's all," she said. "Nineteen, as long as you twenty-four."

16: Trust me; 19: The plan is working great; 24: Don't do anything stupid.

"Okay," he agreed. "I'll get everyone outside and keep them together. Just twenty-five, okay? One."

25: Be careful; 1: I love you

"One back at you." Summer took a last look at her brother and then stepped out from behind the curtain. *"More than you'll ever know."* Her mind whirled as she made her way to a long rectangular table that had been set up near the exit to accommodate accounting staff. She took a seat at the end of the table, where it would be easy to slip away, then closed her eyes and rubbed her temples, feigning a headache. *"Okay, Margaret – since my plan to get Gordo arrested for grand theft is in the crapper, I figure I'll wait until the auction gets going, then duck upstairs, grab Gus's money and see how far I can get away from here before Gordo catches up with me."*

"I'm sorry it turned out this way, darlin'." Margaret's voice came from the empty chair next to Summer.

Summer glanced at the accountants, who were busy with their final preparations. Nothing indicated they had heard the spirit's voice. She closed her eyes again. *"I'm scared, Margaret."*

"Don't be," Margaret cooed. "No one ever wants to depart this world, but at least you'll leave with the certainty that it's just another small step on the path of your eternal journey."

Before she could respond, the lights in the Starlight Ballroom were dimmed and then raised three times, signaling everyone to take their seats. Excited chatter filled the air as Summer rose and headed for the foyer to resume ushering wealthy clients to their seats. She felt the knot tighten in her stomach when she noticed that Marty wasn't in his seat next to Gordo.

"Where the hell is he?" Her thoughts flew to the various fire-accelerants the staff found hidden throughout the hotel. *"If he decided to set the fire early, why would Gordo still be in his seat?"* Then, with an audible sigh, she saw the horrible man emerge from the men's restroom, located in the foyer of the Ballroom. *"I guess even demons have to pee,"* she thought.

They spotted one another in the same instant. Summer turned around and pretended to study the auction schedule, hoping he would walk by without acknowledging her. Unfortunately, he stopped right behind her and leaned over, bringing his lips to her ear.

"That's alright, baby," he whispered, making Summer's flesh crawl. "I don't mind if you turn your back on me. I prefer the view of your ass anyway." He gave her butt a rough squeeze and chuckled.

It was a nasty, humorless laugh.

Summer flinched, but said nothing. She understood Marty's intention was to remind her what lay in store, if she were to step out of line – rape, torture and death. She held her breath, watching him saunter back into the ballroom. *"He doesn't suspect a double cross yet. Otherwise, he wouldn't have walked away."* She shuddered and resolved to accomplish two things. *"I've got to lead him as far away from here as possible and then make sure he doesn't take me alive."*

Robert's voice attracted her attention. From behind a podium on the stage, he welcomed the guests and reminded everyone that the proceeds of the auction would help the McNeal Foundation provide tuition assistance to underprivileged art students and support a host of equally deserving projects. Then he rapped the gavel and turned the stage over to the professional auctioneer.

Summer sighed. It was no use thinking about the life she might have had with Robert, but neither did she want to dwell on what would happen a few hours from now. She was proud of the fact that her hard work had contributed to making the auction a success, so she decided to watch a few minutes of the sale before making her escape.

The auctioneer began with the cut-glass collection and jewelry, moving from the less expensive items to the more exquisite pieces, some of which were worth nearly half-a-million dollars. Summer was about to sneak away, when her cameo pendant began to tingle.

"Sorry, Winnie," she murmured. "But the plan has changed. I've got to get out of here."

The pendant thumped against her throat. *"What the heck are you trying to tell me?"* she wondered.

Chapter Fifty-Four

"Margaret," Summer silently pleaded, *"Please tell Winnie I have to leave and I can't take her with me because..."* She couldn't finish the thought. It was still too hard to process the truth – she would be on the run until she was dead.

Margaret's voice was as clear as if she was speaking directly into Summer's ear. "I know Winnie's not the shiniest mirror in the parlor, but I'm certain she understands what's at stake today and wouldn't be trying to get your attention just to prattle on about some nonsense. If she's trying to communicate, you should listen."

"And just how do you propose I do that? I can't exactly run up to my room for a quick nap, you know."

"Don't be impertinent," Margaret said. "Find a quiet place and I'll help form a connection."

The tingle of the cameo against her skin grew stronger by the second as Summer stood and walked to the foyer on wobbly legs, forcing herself to smile each time a guest caught her eye. Near the exit, Maxwell was flirting with a young man – teasing him about his scruffy beard.

"Damn it," Summer hissed under her breath. *"Maxwell will never let me leave without undergoing an interrogation."* She darted into the ladies' room before either of the two men noticed her.

The small bathroom was adorned with Victorian décor – wallpaper with pastel stripes, floral paintings in gilded frames, narrow walnut doors on the stalls and ivory sinks with gold fixtures. To the left of the entrance sat a short chaise, upholstered with burgundy velvet. Summer slid down onto the couch, listening carefully – hoping the stalls were empty.

"Now what?" she mumbled. She closed her eyes and yawned before realizing she was doing so. "I can't..."

She drifted into the clouds, her protest still on her lips.

"Are you sure she can hear me?" Winnie asked.

"Yes," Margaret replied. "We may only have a moment, though. What's troubling you, Winnie?"

Summer strained her eyes, but was unable to see the two Victorian spirits in the mist.

"Well," Winnie began, "it happened while I was having a visit with Maisie Plant – Morton's second wife. Are the two of you acquainted?"

"That's not important," Margaret snapped. "Go on with your story."

"Well, Maisie was telling me about a set of pearls she lost. She was hoping they might be here, since there's so much Victorian jewelry in the auction. Poor dear hasn't had any luck though, I'm afraid."

Margaret groaned. "What in the *world* do Maisie's pearls have to do with Summer?"

"Nothing and *everything*," Winnie shot back. "You see, it's not what we were *talking* about it's where we were *standing* whilst we were chatting... near the grand fireplace in the foyer of the ballroom, across from the water closets."

"Don't play games, Winnie," Margaret said. "Tell us what you know."

"I'm trying to do that very thing," Winnie complained. "From our position in front of the fireplace, I spied that wretched man who caused the dreadful scene at the costume gala last evening."

Summer feared she might bite a hole in her tongue, but she managed to remain silent. *"What's the big deal? I know he's here."* She felt a shiver remembering Marty's threat and wondered how long it would take him to catch her.

"Yes," Winnie said. "But when I saw him, he was wearing a *disguise.*"

"You must be mistaken," Margaret replied. "That particular man is currently seated in the ballroom and he's not wearing a disguise."

"Not *anymore*, he's not," Winnie persisted. "I know it sounds most peculiar, but I'm absolutely *certain* he was dressed as a *scullery servant*. He pushed a cleaning cart into the gentlemen's water closet, and shortly thereafter, he emerged dressed as a *gentleman*. That's awfully suspect behavior, don't you agree?"

Before Winnie could elaborate, the door to the restroom opened. Summer fell through the clouds as if she had concrete blocks tied to her feet. She muffled a scream as she bolted awake.

"I'm sorry," a middle-aged woman said as she passed by. "I didn't mean to startle you."

"It's okay," Summer managed to say. "I was just – resting my eyes."

The woman offered her a polite smile as she pushed open a stall door and stepped inside.

Summer had several more questions for Winnie, so she closed her eyes and waited for the fog to engulf her. Nothing happened. By the time she heard the toilet flush, Summer knew there was no point in continuing to try to reestablish the connection to the spirit realm.

"Why would Marty have been dressed as a janitor?" she puzzled. *"Why was he pushing a cart? And why risk changing his clothes in a bathroom that's right next door to the auction? Unless..."* Her blood felt icy in her veins. *"That's where he plans to ignite the fire."*

Summer jumped to her feet, fighting a growing sense of panic. *"What was Marty thinking? If the fire starts that close to the ballroom, lots of people could be injured."* She closed her eyes and balled her fists, hating everything about him.

"Are you sure you're all right, honey?" The woman asked as she stepped to the sink and turned on the tap.

Summer wanted to shout and wave her arms – to tell the thoughtful woman that she was in danger and needed to leave the hotel immediately, but she couldn't afford to start a panic. "Thanks for asking, but other than being really tired, I'm fine," she lied.

Summer opened the door and stepped out of the bathroom, just in time to spot Alex coming around the corner. *"Thank God."* She waved at the elderly Tuskegee Airman, hoping to signal him without drawing unwanted attention from Maxwell and his new friend.

Alex shuffled over to her and spoke just above a whisper. "I thought we was supposed to pretend we didn't know one another until this whole hullabaloo was over with." He cocked his head, trying to analyze her expression. "I wanted to see how close they're getting to auctioning off that *Bride on Stairs*... but it can wait. You look like you just walked barefooted through a big ole' patch of sand spurs. What's wrong?"

"I think I know where Marty's going to start the fire," Summer said. She bit her lip.

Alex nodded and rubbed his chin. "Better fill me in, so we can figure out how to spoil the bastard's plan."

Summer pointed at the door to the men's restroom. "Winnie – another spirit – saw him take a cleaning cart in there. He left without it."

Alex narrowed his eyes. "Best let me take a look."

Summer's eyes filled with tears. "I should be the one to do it. My great plan to save the hotel, my brother, and myself just blew up in my face anyway."

"That's what plans do best," the old soldier replied, giving her a wink.

"Yeah, right." She smiled, despite the circumstances. "I think you better go pull the fire alarm while I try to dismantle whatever Marty rigged up to start the fire."

"Slow down and take a breath, Missy," Alex said. He gave her hand a gentle squeeze. "We don't even know for sure that your friend saw what she thinks she saw. And besides, that there's a *men's* room."

"I'm not going to let you go in there alone." Summer reached for the doorknob.

"Yes, *ma'am!*" He gave her a mock salute.

"Is there a problem?" Maxwell called. He took a step in their direction, but was clearly reluctant to leave the bearded young man.

"Just handling a complaint about a running toilet," Summer called back. "No big deal. This gentleman volunteered to help me. If we can't fix it real quick, we'll send for a maintenance guy."

Maxwell stepped back and wrinkled his nose. "Okay, but be careful. Don't spoil your pretty dress or anything."

As she opened the door, Summer took a deep breath and blew it out, hoping to calm her nerves. *"Maybe it's nothing. Winnie could be mistaken about any number of things."* She took two steps into the room and froze, staring at a large janitor's trolley. *"Or she could be one-hundred percent right about everything."*

Alex stepped around her and eyed the cart, looking for an obvious ignition source. The top shelf of the trolley held a few screw drivers, a bolt cutter, some light bulbs, and a pile of toilet paper rolls. On one side of the cart, a mop stood in a bucket of dirty water. On the opposite side, a canvas laundry bag was stuffed with linens that smelled suspiciously of something akin to lighter fluid. A canvas curtain hid the contents of the lower shelf.

Alex glanced at Summer. "I think it's time for you to skedaddle, young lady."

Summer shook her head. "No dice. Pull back the curtain, Alex. We need to know what we're dealing with."

It was as if time moved in slow motion as Summer watched the thin fingers of Alex's age-spotted hand lift the edge of the canvas, revealing the horror below. Aside from television, Summer hadn't seen a bomb before, but there was no mistaking what it was. A cell phone was partially buried in the middle of eight large bricks of explosives. Several wires led from the phone to various points on the explosives – some were twisted around visible metal pins, while other connections were buried in the putty. Summer took an involuntary step backward.

"Dear God. Marty wasn't planning to start a fire to create a distraction. He means to blow this place up and keep the fire burning until there's absolutely nothing left." She glanced at the door. *"And he planted the bomb in here so that the initial blast would kill most of the people in the ballroom... including me."*

Alex carefully folded the canvas back over the top of the cart. Then he reached for the bomb.

"Wait," Summer cried. "Do you know what you're doing?"

Alex pulled back his hand and rubbed it through his short, gray hair. "It's been a long while since I've seen a bomb, and back in my day, they didn't look like this, but I expect the basic principles are the same."

"How can they even be *remotely* the same?" Summer argued. "They didn't even *have* cell phones in your day."

"Nope," Alex agreed. "When we dropped bombs on a target, they hurtled down from the sky with such speed that the impact created all the sparks we needed to make 'em go boom." He paused to study the bomb. "In place of speed and impact, I figure the fella who made this one is counting on that phone to generate an electric current strong enough to trigger the ignition."

"So, do you know which wires we need to cut to keep that from working?"

"Nope. I don't know much of anything about how to defuse a bomb." He rolled his shoulders, obviously pondering the problem.

"Then hold the door open. I'll try to push the cart outside before it goes off."

"I'm afraid that won't work." He pointed to the wheels, which she now noticed were laying at odd angles on the floor. Marty had used the bolt cutter to cut through both axles, crippling the trolley.

Alex shuffled around to the bucket and pulled back on a handle to wring water from the mop. "Mops and buckets, I know about," he said. Then he leaned the mop against the wall and reached in for the bomb.

"Hold on, Alex. Shouldn't we get out of here and call the bomb squad?"

"Nope – not yet." Alex grunted as he lifted the bomb from its resting place. His voice was eerily calm – as if he was in a trance. "That fella, Marty – he could ring that phone before they can get here." He bent down and gently lowered the bomb into the dirty water.

Summer watched, barely breathing. "Will water stop a bomb from exploding?"

"Nope," Alex replied as he stood and rubbed his lower back. "But it sure as heck stopped my cell phone from working, one time when I accidentally dropped it in the toilet." He grinned as Summer's expression shifted from fright, to surprise, to understanding. A ruined phone couldn't receive a call or generate an electric pulse.

"Now, let's move," he said. "I'll head back down the hall to pull the fire alarm and I'll have Sharon alert the bomb squad. You make use of the chaos to get yourself as far away from here as you can."

Summer threw her arms around Alex's neck. "How can I ever thank you?"

"You already have. You helped redeem the soul of an old friend, and you made me feel useful again." He gently pushed her away and opened the door to peek out. "The coast is clear. Now go on – scoot."

Summer paused to remove the cameo. *"Thanks for everything, Winnie."* She handed the pendant to Alex. "This doesn't belong to me. Please return it to Robert – the guy who's in charge of the auction." Then she dashed out.

"Did you fix the running toilet?" Maxwell asked.

Only then did Summer realize they had only been in the bathroom a few minutes. She glanced over her shoulder and saw Alex moving one of the high-top tables in front of the bathroom door.

"No...there's water everywhere. I'm going to run and get someone from maintenance. Meanwhile, tell everyone the bathroom is out of order. Summer raced down the hall to the elevator, stepped inside and pushed the button for the fourth floor. From there, she planned to take the servants' stairs to the room on the fifth floor that had been Gus Murphy's quarters during WWII. Beneath a floorboard where his bunk once stood, she knew she would find enough money to fund her escape.

Just as the doors were sliding closed, an arm shot through the opening, causing them to reopen. Summer's heart sank as Marty stepped in, a gun leveled at her heart. Gordo followed right behind.

Chapter Fifty-Five

"Not feeling quite so smart now, are ya' blondie?" Marty pushed in close to Summer and teased the gun across her cheek.

Summer flattened herself against the back wall, praying that someone else would get on the elevator – a distraction to give her time to think. "You can't do this," she cried, sickened by the wobble in her voice. "I held up my end of the deal we made with The Broker and…"

"Bullshit," Marty hissed. "You think that memory of yours makes you so much smarter than everybody else, but I didn't get this far by believing whatever some bitch told me. To wrangle an invitation to this party, I had to set up my own account with the McNeal Foundation. I decided to use an alias, figuring it would be a good way to make sure you were giving me valid banking information…you know, if my numbers were right, probably so were the rest of them."

Summer felt the handrail of the elevator cab digging into her back, but she didn't move. "I did exactly what I was supposed to do," she insisted. "The banking information is on a recorder in the top drawer of the toolbox."

Gordo nodded at Marty, who immediately backhanded her across the face. She would have crumpled if Marty hadn't pushed her back against the wall. Summer cringed more from the excited glint in the monster's eyes than the pain itself. He slid his free hand up her thigh as his boss continued talking.

Summer squeezed her knees together as a horrible thought crossed her mind. *"Please, God, no matter what happens, don't ever let this despicable excuse for a human being learn that he fathered Dana's baby."*

"I guess your timing was a bit off with that anonymous email you sent," Gordo said, recapturing her attention. "You know – the one that warned me and all the other investors that our accounts have been hacked. By tomorrow, those files won't be worth the price of a cup of coffee and you know it."

Summer groaned, realizing her mistake. She had been tired when she set up the email. *"I set the timer using Central Standard time, rather than Eastern, so the email went out an hour earlier than it was supposed to."* She wanted to point out the fact that sending the email didn't violate their deal, but knew better. That argument might have worked with the impartial Broker, but not Gordo.

"I can make it up to you," she said, her eyes begging Marty to believe her. "I've got money stashed up on the fifth floor. Lots of it. That's where I was going. I was on my way to get it – to protect it from the fire."

"Bullshit," Marty scowled. He pulled back his meaty hand from her thigh to give her another slap.

"Wait," Gordo said. "Think about it. It might be true. Why else would she be going to the top floor of a hotel that she knew we were about to blow up?"

Summer still had the presence of mind to act surprised at Gordo's slip of the tongue. "Blow up? You said you were starting a fire...a distraction. What about my brother...all those people..."

Gordo smiled. "You got me, toots. You and your dumb-ass brother were never going to make it out of this deal alive."

"The Broker will kill you..."

"The Broker won't do shit," Gordo said. "I'll tell him it was an accident...we must have used too big of a charge and you died along with a lot of other people in the fire. Who's to know any different?"

"But maybe you won't die in the fire after all," Marty said. He licked the side of her face. "I could take you with us. Of course, by the time I've treated you to a few of my *special thrills*, you might wish you *were* dead."

He pulled her body against his, making sure she felt his erection. Summer recoiled, sickened by the realization that even the *thought* of torturing her had excited him.

Just as the doors opened onto the fourth floor, the fire alarm sounded.

"What the f..." Marty muttered.

"Someone must have spotted the bomb," Gordo reasoned. "I told you the bathroom was a stupid place to leave it."

"You said to make sure the auction was hit with the full blast," Marty countered. "Where else could I put it?"

"There's no time to argue," Gordo barked. "You run your ass downstairs and load up the toolbox. We need to get the truck off the property before the bomb squad gets here and seals up the exits."

"By myself?" Marty asked, belligerent. "We shouldn't split up. Besides, I'm looking forward to teaching Toots here what happens to double-crossing whores."

Gordo growled. "Don't be stupid. For one thing, she needs to die in the fire to keep The Broker from coming after us. And for another thing, that e-mail she sent cost me a lot of money. Seems only fair that she pay me back with her cash-stash." He held out his hand. "Gimmie your extra gun."

Marty didn't try to hide his disappointment, but neither did he dare disobey Gordo. He released Summer and reached around his back to pull a second revolver from the waistband of his trousers.

Gordo trained the gun on Summer, waving the barrel to indicate that she should get off the elevator. "Move quick or I swear to God I'll drag you out by the hair."

Summer did as she was told, still wracking her brain, trying to come up with a plan.

"This should only take a couple of minutes," Gordo said. "So as soon as you climb into the truck, detonate the bomb. No one knows who I am, so I'll join the rest of the survivors outside and meet up with you back at the house later."

She watched with relief as the doors to the elevator closed, carrying Marty back down to the first floor. *"At least it's one against one, now,"* she thought. *"One with a gun, but still..."*

"I'm here, too," Margaret said.

"Margaret!" Summer was certain the spirit could do little to help her, but it was comforting to know she wouldn't die alone.

"So, where's the cash?" Gordo asked.

"The elevator doesn't go to the fifth floor," Summer said. "That's where the money is hidden. We have to use the servant's staircase."

Gordo narrowed his eyes. "You better not be lying." He aimed the gun at her head. "If you hand over the money, I promise to make it quick. Screw with me and I'll shoot out your kneecaps and leave you to burn in the fire."

Summer gulped. "The access to the stairs is right there." She wanted to run, but knew Gordo meant what he said, and she preferred a quick death. *"Sorry I couldn't do a better job of protecting your hotel, Margaret."*

"Don't be daft, Summer," Margaret said. "You've done amazingly well and I'm proud of you."

A single tear trickled down Summer's jaw. *"What does it feel like to die?"*

"I honestly can't tell you that," Margaret said. "Spirits are able remember every single moment of their lives except for the one when they cross over. For me, it was similar to falling asleep. I closed my eyes in one world and my dreams carried me into another one."

"That doesn't sound too bad," Summer thought, as she reached the top of the stairs. The walk to Gus Murphy's quarters at the end of the hall felt like her death march. She decided to distract herself. *"Tell me, Margaret – if Alex's plan to stop the explosion by ruining the phone doesn't work, can you spirits warn everybody to get out before it goes off?"*

"It's doubtful," Margaret replied. "Spirits can connect with the living when they are close to death, and form connections with some people as they sleep. On very rare occasions, we can converse with an individual through thought, as you and I manage to do. But normally, spirits have very little influence over the actions of people who are wide awake in the living world. Ghosts, on the other hand..."

"Maybe my twin brother could hear you the same way I do. Could you try that?" There was no answer. *"Where did you go, Margaret?"* She trudged the last few yards, wishing with all her might that Margaret would come back.

Summer opened the door to the room at the end of the corridor. "It's in here, hidden under the floorboards."

"Get it," Gordo said.

"I need something to pry up the floorboards," Summer explained. "A little pocketknife is sewn into the hem of my dress." She touched the side of her skirt. "It should do the trick."

Gordo gave her a half-smile. "You always were resourceful. You know, it's a goddamn shame things have to end this way. We could have made a great team if you weren't such a friggin' liar."

In spite of the deadly situation, Summer scoffed and crossed her arms. "Team? Who are you trying to kid? I made an honest mistake taking your money during that con in Vegas and you knew it. But instead of letting me pay you back with interest, you killed my partners and made me your slave. And even after I earned you a *lot* more money than I took, you wouldn't let me go. You know damn well that I'd *still* be a captive in your whore house if I hadn't worked out a deal with The Broker to bargain for my freedom...and even then, I struck a deal where you wouldn't get hurt as long as you left me alone."

Gordo snickered, amused by her tirade. "Get on your knees before you take out the knife. Move slow and easy."

Summer balled her fists. She wasn't finished. "And you call me a liar? It was *you* who hired Lisa to set Justin up – to make The Broker believe my brother owed you a debt so you could drag me into a second deal. And even if we *hadn't* done anything to skirt around the terms of the deal, you were going to kill us with your bomb...along with a lot of innocent people. How could you do such a horrible thing?"

Gordo raised his eyebrows and smirked – an expression so smug that Summer finally understood. Her knees buckled and she sank to the floor. "You planned to kill everyone right from the start. If all those rich people died in a fire at a historic hotel, there would be chaos. You'd be able to wipe out their bank accounts before their beneficiaries knew what was happening. Killing me and everyone I care about was just a *bonus*."

"Good for you," Gordo mocked. "You figured it out. That email you sent might cause me a few headaches, but all in all, everything is working out just fine... well, for me, anyway. We're going to blame the explosion on terrorists, so..."

All at once, the air was filled with an evil presence. It felt as if an ominous demon had been released from the depths of hell into the room.

"I summoned Gus Murphy," Margaret said, knowing only Summer could hear her. "The living can often feel the presence of ghosts, and this one is *extremely* protective of his money."

"This horrible feeling is coming from Gus's ghost?" Summer reveled in the terror that filled Gordo's wide eyes.

"What the..." Gordo stammered. "Is this one of your tricks? Did you release some kind of hallucinogen?" He covered his mouth and nose with his arm and aimed the gun at Summer's head. "You bitch. I guess I'll have to do without your extra cash."

Summer managed to squeeze her eyes shut and picture Robert's kind smile before she heard the gun fire. Her eyes rolled back in her head and everything went black.

Chapter Fifty-Six

"*Margaret was right,*" Summer thought, her eyes still closed. "*I don't remember dying.*"

The evil ambiance that permeated the room only a moment before, had evaporated. She took a deep breath and blew it out, allowing her whole body to relax. "*Wait. Why am I still breathing? How can I feel my cheek throbbing against the floor?*"

She opened her eyes and found herself face to face with Gordo. The vacant look in his eyes left no doubt that he was dead, even before she noticed the red hole in the middle of his forehead or the blood pooling on the floor around him. Repulsed, she sat up and scooted away from his body until her back was pressed against the wall. Rubbing her sore jaw, she fought to clear the cobwebs from her memory.

"*Marty must have sneaked back up here and killed him,*" she decided. "*But why? And where is he? Why didn't he kill me, too?*"

Gordo still clutched the gun in his outstretched hand. For a split second, she thought about taking it, but dismissed the idea. "*Marty's probably trying to set me up for the murder.*"

She heard sirens in the distance. "*Maybe the bomb went off and the hotel's on fire. Did he leave me here to burn alive? Maybe he's coming back – maybe he plans to take me someplace private, where he can take his time killing me. Or maybe someone else is working with Marty...Lisa?*"

Summer looked around the room, almost numb with terror. "*One thing is for sure – whatever Marty's planning, it's going to be bad for me. I better get out of here while I can.*" She glanced at the floorboards, trying to decide whether to take an extra few minutes to retrieve Gus's hidden loot. When she heard what sounded like someone stepping on a squeaky floorboard, she decided against it.

Ignoring her queasy stomach and aching head, Summer steeled herself and got to her feet. She shot a glance at the open door. *"If someone's out there in the hall, I'm toast."*

"The window," Margaret said.

The window was partially open. *"I forgot that you can move things."* Adrenaline pumping, Summer wasted no time shoving the paned window the rest of the way up. *"Margaret, did you see what happened to Gordo?"*

"No," Margaret replied. "I saw him fall at the same moment you fainted. Serendipity, I say. Now go. I'm needed elsewhere."

Feeling totally exposed in the bright sunshine, Summer climbed out onto the fire escape. In the distance, she saw a wide variety of flashing lights, but no trace of fire or debris from an explosion. *"No problem – I just have to stay out of sight while climbing down five stories of a white hotel on a rusty, rickety fire escape, while wearing a black cocktail dress and heels."*

Despite several slips, scratches, banged-up knees, and close calls, she managed to make it to the ground in one piece and incredibly, without being spotted. *"Maybe my luck is changing."*

She flattened her body against the hotel to get her bearings. Gus's quarters were at the end of the East Wing, which actually faced north, but it had been built at the east end of the existing hotel structure and the name stuck.

"I could probably cut across the golf course, but I can't leave without my go bag – especially since I don't have Gus Murphy's money."

That morning, she had stashed a small bag of essential supplies beneath the veranda of the Lobby Lounge, figuring it would be convenient to pick it up from there after setting off the fire alarm. But of course, things hadn't gone according to plan, and now that entire area was a hive of law enforcement activity.

"So much for good luck. Even if I conned a few people out of some cash, I wouldn't get far without my passport. There's no easy way out.

I'll have to blend into the crowd and retrieve the bag when no one's looking."

When she peeked around the corner of the hotel, she spotted Sharon Delahanty, arms crossed, back rigid, watching the activity from a distance. She resembled a steadfast general, determined to remain vigilant, despite being temporarily ousted from her command of the troops.

Summer rubbed her palms together in an attempt to wipe off the rust stains while trying to decide how to subtly attract Sharon's attention. Unfortunately, the woman spotted her before she came up with a plan.

"Summer!" she called.

Summer raised her finger to her lips, hoping Marty and his accomplice – or accomplices – weren't within hearing range.

Sharon frowned and walked over to Summer. Before speaking, she glanced over her shoulder, to where the hotel workers and guests were gathered on the lawn, as if checking to make sure they hadn't followed her. "Why are you still here? Alex said you had to run...that some awful men are after you."

"I'll tell you, but come around the corner first. We'll be a little less conspicuous there."

After they had stepped out of sight, Summer began. "Alex is right. I do have to run. But I've got to get something first." She paused, wondering if Sharon knew how close they had all come to death. "Say – it looks like Alex's crazy idea to stop the bomb from exploding actually *worked*."

Sharon smiled. "Yes, it did. The bomb squad went on and removed the wires and everything, but they said it was pretty smart of him to figure out that water would render the phone useless as a trigger. Thank goodness those crooks didn't use one of those newfangled *waterproof* phones, but then again, they obviously didn't know what they were doing. They could have started their fire with *way* less of that explosive putty stuff. The police said that if that bomb would have gone off, it would have done a great deal of damage to the hotel – *including* the Starlight Ballroom. I hate to think how many people might have gotten hurt."

Summer decided not to inform her that Gordo's intent was to kill as many people as possible. "Please tell Alex I'm super-proud of him."

Sharon smiled at the mention of her friend. "I'm sure he knows. As soon as the police are finished searching the hotel for any more explosives, I expect the old goat will take up residence in the Lobby Lounge to tell the story repeatedly. Heck, I won't be surprised if he offers to sign autographs." She giggled at the thought.

"Oh, shit. If the police are searching the hotel, it won't be long before they find Gordo's body. I'd better get out of here ASAP." Summer cupped the woman's forearm to emphasize the seriousness of her situation. "I need your help, Sharon. I stashed a black bag under the veranda, right behind the pink hibiscus bush. My passport is in it. Can you get it for me without telling anyone what you're up to? And bring it back here on the double?"

Sharon nodded. "I can sure try."

Summer watched as the assistant hotel manager made her way across the courtyard and moved around the edge of the crowd toward the veranda. With relief, she noticed Robert standing near a group of armed security guards. He was directing them to form a circle around the various pieces of art that he had obviously insisted on bringing outside, to keep them out of harm's way.

A short distance away, she spotted the others. Justin had one arm linked around Dana, but their attention seemed focused on Emma and Ole. Emma appeared to be in distress. Ole wrapped his arms around her. Summer couldn't tell if he was trying to comfort her or keep her from falling – or both things at once. He said something to Justin, who then took off at a run.

"What's wrong with Emma? Is it the baby? Is it Andy? Did he change his mind about merging with the other spirit?" Without making a conscious decision to do so, she edged closer. She was only forty feet from her friends when she felt the muzzle of a gun press into the small of her back.

"Thought you'd manage to pull a fast one, didn't you?" Marty growled. "Come on now – back up, nice and easy – around the corner where you were hiding before. I've got an automatic Sig Sauer ready to cut your spine in half if you get cute."

He took a step back and she had no choice but to follow the sadistic creep.

"You think you're so smart. When my bomb didn't go off, I knew you were up to something. I decided to park the truck in the lot and circle back around – let the boss know there was a kink in the plan and see what he wanted me to do. And what do you know? I was just in time to get a great view of you climbing down the fire escape in that sexy little dress of yours." He chuckled. "I thought about taking you out and watching you fall, but I have to admit, I was enjoying the show too much to end it that quick. Now, tell me – how'd you manage to give Gordo the slip?"

Every fiber of Summer's body told her to run to the ring of armed guards for protection, but she resisted that nearly overwhelming urge. *"If I try to escape, Marty'll start shooting and there's no telling how many innocent people he might hit."* She shuddered with revulsion as they took another step backward. "You know damn well I didn't get away. You shot Gordo...well, you or Lisa did."

Marty yanked her arm so hard, she winced as he spun her around to face him. "Bullshit! Gordo's been shot? Where is he?"

Summer registered the shock on the beast's face and knew in an instant that he didn't have anything to do with what had happened. "We were on the fifth floor. He's dead. I didn't see. Someone shot him. I thought..."

Marty looked up at the windows of the hotel, as if searching for his boss. Summer knew he wasn't smart enough to formulate plans on his own. Gordo had conditioned him to follow orders in exchange for rewards. Clearly, he was lost without his mentor. Her mind raced, trying to decide if she could use this to her advantage.

Emma's cries suddenly pierced the air. "It's my baby – it's Andrew! He's coming!"

Her howl of pain seemed to bring Marty out of his stupor. Summer caught her breath as his expression changed, morphing from confusion to one of morbid curiosity and pleasure. He cocked his head and smiled when Emma cried out a second time.

Summer's eyes widened as the danger of the escalating situation became clear. *"He's not just a sadist, he's insane. And the one person who could control him is dead."*

While Ole busied himself helping his wife lay down in the grass, Marty raised his pistol and played it over the crowd. "Gordo said he'd pay me a bounty for every one of these rich pecker-heads I disposed of today. He was gonna double it, if I could make their deaths look accidental. That wasn't as much fun, but it was kind of interesting to see what would happen...you know, see how many I could kill at once." He shifted his gaze to her and snarled. "If it weren't for you screwing everything up, I'd have already earned enough bounties to buy that red Jaguar I've had my eye on. But maybe I can still have some fun." He turned back to the crowd in the distance and fingered the trigger of the gruesome looking pistol, as if itching to begin shooting. "This baby holds thirty-two rounds and I have a couple of extra clips in my pockets."

"If you didn't kill Gordo," Summer said, hoping to distract him. "That means whoever did, is still on the loose. Maybe someone isn't happy about you and Gordo trying to pull off a job in their territory. They might be searching for you right now – aiming to kill you, too."

Marty glared at her. "Any stupid son of a bitch who tries to take me out is gonna damn well wish he hadn't."

"I know you're a great shot," she back-peddled. "But look at what you'd be up against – an armed private security force, local police, the bomb squad, the FBI – heck, they've probably got snipers positioned on the roof, hiding behind the gables. *No one* could win against those odds." She tried to sound conspiratorial. "On the *other* hand, you have the Tissot painting in your truck. If you took off right now, you could sell it and keep all the money for yourself...maybe even take over Gordo's operation."

Marty grunted, thinking the matter over. Summer took advantage of his momentary loss of focus to steal a glance over her shoulder. She saw Justin, helping two paramedics push a gurney across the lawn toward Emma. Robert had joined the small group surrounding his sister. Summer wanted to cry out – to warn them that they were still in grave danger, but she knew better.

"I think you're right about one thing," Marty said. "I need to get that painting out of here before this shit storm gets any worse." He smiled at Summer and gently wrapped a lock of her blonde hair around his finger. "And *you're* coming with me. And you're going to behave like a *good* little girl."

He continued to twist her hair around his finger as he crooked his elbow, pulling her close, until his face was inches from hers. "Because, if you give me any grief, I'm going to begin shooting people – starting with your two preggo friends and your brother." He held her close for several seconds without speaking, his hot breath reeking of sour wine. "So, do we have an understanding?"

"Yes," Summer squeaked. She held back a whimper, fearing that if he realized how much pain he was inflicting, he'd rip the lock of hair from her head for the fun of it.

"Good girl." Marty turned for the parking lot, dragging her along by her hair as if walking a reluctant dog. "Gordo had everything figured out," he said. "We were supposed to drive the truck to Miami and meet up with a guy who owns a fishing boat there. He owes Gordo, so he agreed to take us to Cuba, no questions asked. We were gonna fence the painting there." He glanced at her and chuckled. "You know, the boat ride to Cuba's supposed to take about fifteen hours. I was worried I was gonna get bored, but not anymore. I'm sure you'll be able to keep me entertained."

"I don't have my passport," Summer said, desperate for an excuse to return to the hotel.

He laughed as he unlocked the passenger door and untangled his finger from her hair. "No problem, Toots. I don't expect you to survive much more than twelve hours of the trip, anyway. Of course, you could surprise me and break a record."

Chapter Fifty-Seven

Summer's stomach lurched as the meaning of Marty's words sank in. Desperate with the realization this might be her last chance to escape, she grabbed the doorframe with both hands, trying to resist being shoved into the truck. *"Please, God – someone – anyone – don't let this happen to me."*

Without a moment's hesitation, Marty hit the knuckles of her closest hand with the butt of his gun. "Get in and put your hands on the dash," he growled. "And if you want to keep those digits, you won't try anything else."

Terrified beyond rational thought, Summer whimpered and tucked her injured hand into her armpit. Then she did as she was told. Marty strode around the front of the truck, his eyes never leaving hers. Still watching her, he opened the driver's side door and laid his gun on the seat while he shrugged off his suitcoat. He draped the coat over the center console, picked up his revolver, and climbed behind the wheel.

"Safety first," he said, reaching for his seatbelt. He clicked it closed with one hand while holding the gun on her with the other. "Now it's your turn – fasten your seatbelt," he said. "I don't want you to get any cute ideas about jumping out. And remember..." He gave her one of his most charming smiles – as if butter wouldn't melt in his mouth. "If I have to shoot you, I won't aim to kill you – I'll just make you wish I had."

When she fumbled for her seatbelt with her still-painful hand, Summer noticed *all* of her fingernails had taken on a blueish hue.

Her mind automatically searched for information related to the situation and a moment later, presented an article from a medical magazine she had read.

Shock can occur as the result of serious emotional distress, or in response to experiencing or witnessing a terrifying or traumatic event. The most observable symptoms of emotionally induced shock include: denial, confusion or hallucinations, dizziness, lightheadedness, fainting, and bluish lips and fingernails. Initial treatment principles include: Monitor blood pressure, heart rate and breathing, keep patient warm and hydrated, and provide reassurance of safety. Seek medical help for severe symptoms, or if symptoms persist more than thirty minutes.

Summer felt her heart racing, but doubted she'd be lucky enough to faint. Marty continued to taunt her as he drove to the side exit of the hotel.

"I sure hope your body is as tough as your talk. If so, you might be able to help me break one of my records. Did you know that the saying 'death by a thousand cuts' comes from executioners in China? Sometimes they made more than three times that many cuts before their prisoner died, but they never managed to keep anyone alive for more than three days or so. My personal record is only fifteen-hundred and twenty-seven cuts. But I made the ritual last for nine sweet days, so..."

Summer closed her eyes and did her best to tune out Marty's unnerving chatter. *"Margaret, are you here?"* she pleaded.

There was no answer. She hadn't felt this hopeless since the night she spent in Gordo's barn, tied to a chair, with parts of Edwards's dismembered body piled on a table beside her. She recalled the sound of Edward's screams as Marty tortured him to death. *"Marty enjoyed making Edward scream. He knew no one could hear him out there in the desert. Just like he knows that no one will hear my screams on the way to Cuba."*

"Then you best not go to Cuba with him," Margaret said.

Summer didn't try to stop the tears of relief from running down her cheeks. *"I thought you were gone."*

"I'm sorry, darlin'," Margaret's voice sounded like a warm hug. "But I was *Tweening* with Andy. He heard all the commotion and felt as helpless as...well, as helpless a *baby*, I suppose. For everyone's sake, I had to intervene and calm his disposition."

"Please tell me he's all right," Summer begged. *"And Emma, too."*

"Yes, they'll both be fine," Margaret replied. "I managed to convince Andy that the presence of his spirit wouldn't improve matters, and further attempts to return to the spirit realm might cost him the chance to share a life with Violet."

"Could Andy have done that... returned to the spirit realm?" Summer asked, grateful for the distraction.

"Not without harming the other half of the merged spirit – it would always feel as though it were missing a part of its soul. Once Andy understood that, he settled down. Unfortunately, the ordeal sent poor Emma into labor a few weeks early, so there is still reason for concern. If the two spirits fail to completely merge before the birth, they will live as two separate entities, fighting for control of one body – a condition often diagnosed as a mental malady of one sort or another. And I've never heard of two spirits *Becoming* less than twenty-four hours before a baby is born. Even if the merge is successful, Andy will probably retain several memories from his former life...and perhaps even from the time he spent in the spirit realm. Ah, well. No use crying over spilt milk – what is done is done and what will be, will be."

"What will be, will be," Summer repeated. *"I hope everything works out. Those two have done so much for others, they deserve to have a wonderful life together."* She sniffed. *"And maybe I deserve whatever Marty has in store for me because of all the terrible things I've done."*

Margaret sighed. "Nonsense. Only folks with good hearts and a conscience believe they deserve punishment. You may have made your share of mistakes, but the concept of paying for wrongdoing never occurs to *true* evil-doers – at least, not until they stand before the lighted path."

"Thanks, Margaret. Listen – can you stay with me till the end? I don't want to die alone."

"I'll stay with you for as long as I can, but I can't go anywhere I didn't travel while I was alive."

"Have you been to Cuba?" Summer opened her eyes, suddenly aware that Marty was making a U-turn. She was surprised to see they were still in Belleair – turning around at the gated entrance to Belleview Island.

"Every one of these goddamn streets either dead-ends or circles back around to the main road," Marty grumbled.

Summer reclosed her eyes. *"Pretty soon, he'll realize there's only one way in and out of this neighborhood. You're right, Margaret. I can't let this maniac take me to Miami, but I can't risk jumping out this close to the hotel, either – I'd be putting Justin and the others right back in danger. Do you have any ideas?"*

Before the spirit had a chance to respond, Marty broke their connection. "Looks like the only way to drive a truck out of this place is to go over the bridge by the guard house."

He pulled over to the side of the road and turned to her, the charming smile back on his face. It was the innocent expression of an aging blond surfer boy – the one that had made it possible for him to seduce naive women like Dana, who believed bad guys always *looked* like bad guys.

"Okay, sweetheart, I'm sure they'll have a roadblock set up there, so I'm going to need your cooperation to get us out of here."

"Cooperation?" Summer stared at Marty. It was an absurd request. She tried to figure out if she could she use it to her advantage, but shock was numbing her senses, making it difficult to think clearly. *"The roadblock might provide my last opportunity to escape without endangering anyone that I care about."*

Marty smiled at her dazed expression. "Yeah, I know. You're feeling grumpy. You don't want to go on this trip with me, and you'd probably rather not help me right now. But you're going to, anyway."

She pulled her gaze away and looked out the front window, hoping the police might have already noticed the truck. Unfortunately, Marty had stopped before the sharp curve in the road that led to the exit.

He rubbed the cold barrel of his gun up her neck and bumped it lightly against her chin. "Come on, Summer," he said, "Look at me. I need you to pay attention."

She turned back to face him, wishing he would just kill her and get it over with.

"This truck is painted with a catering company logo," Marty explained. "The guards will probably let us pass, but just in case they ask, we were hired to cater the auction, and now we're headed for another gig. We're both dressed in black, so they should buy that story."

Summer glanced at her lap. *"How fast can I unhook my seatbelt and push open the passenger door?"*

Marty gently lifted her chin with his gun barrel a second time. "Don't go thinkin' about getting cute." He tucked his revolver under a sleeve of his suitcoat on the console. "I'm going to leave my Sig right here, where I can reach it real quick. Play along and nobody gets hurt. Give me trouble and I'll have no choice but to kill all those cops manning the blockade. I don't *want* to do that, but I *will*. It's up to you. Think about it – you don't want to die with something like *that* on your conscience, do you?"

Chapter Fifty-Eight

Summer's thoughts were jumbled, and she felt dizzy as she considered her options. *"Edward and Dave died because of my Camp Sucker scheme. Justin almost got killed because Gordo wanted me back in his stable...and it was also my fault that he almost got blown to bits, along with Robert, Dana, Emma, Ole, and...Jesus...so many other people."* She shook her head. *"I can't be responsible for any more deaths."*

She shifted her gaze to the coat on the console, where Marty's gun was hidden. *"If I could move things with my mind the way Margaret does, I'd throw that horrible thing out the window – make it more of a fair fight. If only..."* She sighed with resignation. "Please – don't kill anyone else," she mumbled. "I'll behave."

"Good girl. Now, open the glove compartment," Marty instructed. "There's a box of tissues in there. Wipe those tears. And smooth your hair, for God's sake. You look like hell. And pull your skirt down to cover your knees. We don't want anyone to notice the scratches you got from climbing down that fire escape."

With robotic motions, Summer did as she was told. Even without looking, she felt Marty watching her every move.

"To tell the truth, I'm a little disappointed in you, Summer. I didn't expect you to give up so easily. I was sort of looking *forward* to killing those guards." Marty grinned.

Appalled, Summer watched the psychopath from the corner of her eyes, as he adjusted the rearview mirror to show his reflection and then ran his thick fingers through his hair, smoothing it into a neat wave. The amused expression in his blue eyes made her cringe.

"But don't you worry about letting me down," he said. "I'm sure you'll get your second wind once we're on the boat. I mean, people *always* fight to stay alive, right?" He smirked as he adjusted the mirror back to its original position. "Of course, some fight *harder* than others. And looks can be deceiving, too. I've seen some really big guys give up and die on me pretty quick, while some women lasted *way* longer than I expected them to. Hell, one little girl was still begging to live even after I flayed the skin from her feet and burned off three of her fingers with a blowtorch. That was *impressive.* I regretted having to slice her throat, but Gordo called and told me I had to get back to work, so..."

His deranged laughter sent chills up Summer's spine. She cowered against the passenger's side door and reached for the handle.

"But Gordo won't interrupt me ever again, now will he?" He laughed again, his eyes glowing with anticipation. "We'll have the whole trip to Cuba to learn what you're made of. I'm interested to see how long you'll fight...and to see if that memory of yours will have any effect on the game."

"Game?" Summer couldn't stand it any longer. She slid one hand to the seatbelt lock and rested the other on the door handle. *"On three, I'll press the seatbelt button, jerk the door open and run,"* she told herself. *"Either I'll get away or he'll kill me – either option is better than what he's got planned."*

Unfortunately, Marty noticed what she was doing. He chuckled. "Ever hear of child safety locks, Summer? That door won't open until I unlock it. Wouldn't want you to fall out and get hurt or anything."

Summer slumped in her seat, defeated.

"Come on now, don't be like that," Marty said as he put the truck into gear. "Sit up and look pretty."

When the truck came around the sharp turn that led to the exit, Summer saw that Marty was right about the blockade. The gated access to the hotel and surrounding neighborhood consisted of a small bridge, with a single lane entrance on one side of a guardhouse, and an exit lane on the other. Two police cars were parked behind the barrier arm of the entrance side of the gate, effectively blocking it. A few yards down the road, an officer directed all approaching traffic to turn around before reaching the bridge. The barrier arm for the exit lane was also down. One uniformed policeman directed exiting cars to stop and roll down a window, while four additional men, armed with rifles and wearing vests stamped with the letters FBI, looked through the car's windows. A few additional officers clustered in the driveway of the East Gate Cottage – a private residence, located directly behind the guardhouse.

Marty eased to a stop behind two cars and a van. "Don't forget." He gave Summer a wink. "These guys are depending on you to save their lives."

They both watched intently as the first officer spoke to the elderly driver of the first car in the line. Summer guessed the driver told the officer they lived in the neighborhood, because he turned to confer with the man in the guardhouse. Apparently satisfied, he nodded at the guard, who raised the barrier arm and let the car pass.

While the police officer waved the next car up, the security guard dropped the barrier arm back into place. This time, the cop walked around to the back of the car to check the license plate and asked the driver to open his trunk. One of the FBI agents aimed his gun as the trunk popped open, but a moment later, he shouted, "Clear," and slammed it closed. Again, the car was waved through.

The next vehicle was a cargo van. After a few questions, the officer directed the driver to circle around to the right and park in the wide driveway of the East Gate Cottage. When he saw that their truck was next in line, he directed Marty to the same area, rather than having him pull up to the gate. Summer had driven enough trucks to understand that the officer's intention was to provide Marty with a wider turning radius.

"Isn't this exciting?" Marty asked as he turned right and squeezed into the driveway, next to the van.

One of the FBI agents made an open fist and raised it up, signaling Marty to shift the truck into park. Once Marty did so, the officer made a twisting motion with his fist, instructing him to turn off the engine. Marty complied once again. Then the officer rolled his fore-finger in a circle – the universal signal to roll down the window.

"Don't cha' just love charades?" Marty asked, faking a yawn. "You know, these guys really should be wearing helmets. Those vests won't help at all if I decide to blow their heads off." He smiled at her before pushing the window button. "It's up to you, Summer. Convince them we're just innocent bystanders and they all get to go home and bang their wives tonight. Play games and they all die."

His demeanor shifted slightly when the vested officers opened the back door of the cargo van and allowed a German Shepherd to jump in. "Damn it...the mutt's probably a bomb sniffer. My explosives were packed in a suitcase, so hopefully, there's no residue back there, but...well, the dog might complicate things."

Summer held her breath as the officers finished checking the van and directed it to back out of the drive. By the way Marty was resting his hand on the key, she could tell he was trying to determine if he should allow the search, or start the truck and attempt to run the guard gate.

"Sorry to inconvenience you folks today," one of the FBI agents said as he approached the window. "There was some trouble at the hotel a little while ago, so we're doing routine checks of all vehicles leaving the property."

The brown-haired agent appeared to be in his late thirties and his friendly, nonchalant manner had a calming effect on Marty. He took his hand off the key, but left it hanging in the ignition, where he could reach it at a moment's notice. Summer let out her breath.

"I understand," Marty said, using an equally pleasant tone. "Guess you can't be too careful."

"Can you tell me what business brought you here today?" the agent asked.

"Sure – we work for a special event planner – *Piccadilly Parties*, like it says on the truck. We were just finishing up a job when the fire alarm went off. We left our equipment and went outside like everybody else. I knew we had a second gig today, so I called our boss to check in. After I told him what happened, he said we should get back to the shop and reload for the next job – said we could come back tomorrow to pick up the rest of our stuff."

"All right," the agent said. "We'll try to get you out of here in a jiffy. Is the back of the truck locked?"

Marty shook his head. "No – but there's nothing in it but a toolbox. Like I said...most of our stuff is still inside the hotel."

The truck rocked slightly as the back doors opened and the large dog jumped in. Marty continued to chat with the agent, but Summer saw him slide his hand closer to the console, where his gun was hidden.

"I'd rather die than sit here and allow these men to be murdered." Summer forced a smile. "You guys obviously don't know our boss. If we don't get out of here pretty soon, we'll be in big trouble. Can't we go *now*?"

"Don't worry, Miss – we should be done in just a minute."

Marty gave her an approving smile and moved his hand back to rest on his thigh. An instant later, the German Shepherd reappeared, trotted over to his handler and sat at his feet. The handler gave the animal a treat, which the dog wolfed down.

"Uh-oh," Summer thought. *"Bomb-sniffing canines are trained to sit whenever they smell explosives residue in the search area."*

She wasn't surprised to see the friendly FBI agent's expression turn serious, as a second agent appeared at her window.

"I'm going to need you to step out of the truck," the first agent said, opening Marty's door.

A third agent moved closer, his rifle at the ready.

Marty pretended to be confused as he slowly unfastened his seatbelt. "Sure, officer...no problem."

"I can't," Summer said, too frantic to care about her own safety. She wiggled her door handle. "Baby locks."

Marty glared at her as he inched his hand toward his gun. "I'm sure they just meant for *me* to get out. You be quiet and sit tight."

The agent scanned the interior of the door for a moment and then pushed the lock release button. "Both of you need to get out."

Summer released her seatbelt as the agent on the passenger's side of the truck opened her door.

"Get out," the first agent repeated. "Move nice and slow."

Summer screamed, "He's got a gun!" just as Marty's hand shot under the coat on the console with the speed of a striking snake.

The agent yanked her through the open door and threw her to the ground. She landed hard, chest first. "Stay down," he barked.

His order was unnecessary. Summer felt so weak, she couldn't even lift her head.

From her place in the dirt next to the driveway, she heard Marty in the distance, cussing and screaming – first in anger, and then in pain. His shrieks, together with the snarls of a dog and the sounds of men shouting to one another, seemed to fill the air for a long time. She heard Marty scream a host of obscenities and the dog's snarls turned to yelps, which were followed by a short burst of gunfire, and then silence.

Even when one of the FBI agents placed two fingers against her neck, Summer remained on the ground with her eyes squeezed shut, unable to stop shivering. She heard the squawk of a radio.

"Hey, boss. It's Sullivan. The perp is down. He tried to run. We attempted a K-9 capture, but when he got Thunder in a chokehold, Brady was forced to take him out. The K-9's all right and no other officers were harmed during the confrontation. The female appears to be in shock. She has some minor abrasions, but no serious injuries, as far as I can tell."

Summer relaxed, allowing the fluffy mist to overtake her.

Chapter Fifty-Nine

"I'm alive and Marty isn't." Summer basked in that incredible fact as she floated into the familiar mist, but troubling questions immediately began to surface. *"Why didn't Marty shoot everyone like he planned? Why didn't he kill me – or at least shoot out my knees? That agent couldn't have pulled me out of the truck fast enough to stop him, and Marty could have fired dozens of bullets within a few seconds."*

"Yes, that blackguard might have committed a great deal of harm, had you not conceived a plan to stop him," Margaret agreed, as the mist parted.

"Me?" Summer drifted into a white, wicker rocking chair on the front porch of the East Gate Cottage, pain-free, but still confused. *"What* plan?"

Margaret, attired in a black skirt and white blouse, smiled at her from an identical rocking chair. When she reached out her hand, a silver teapot materialized in her grasp and two rosebud-adorned cups and saucers appeared on the wicker table between the two chairs.

"I told you once before, that you and I both faced tremendous obstacles in our youth. To improve our circumstances, we were forced to keep company with unsavory companions and, on occasion, deal with outright brutes and ruffians. Since we were no match for such men physically, we developed sharp minds to *outwit* those who tried to control us...or do us in, for that matter." Margaret poured steaming tea into the cups.

Summer tried to clear her thoughts. "But I *didn't* outsmart Marty. I thought he was going to *shoot* me."

The corners of Margaret's mouth twitched slightly as she pushed a cup of tea across the table. "But you *did* outwit him darlin' girl. Don't you remember? You told me to move his gun. It was a brilliant idea to use my levitation abilities, if I do say so myself."

Summer frowned. "I have an eidetic memory, Margaret. I'd remember if I said that."

Margaret stirred a heaping teaspoon of sugar into her cup. "You *thought* it and I can read your *thoughts*, so it's the same thing. Don't you recall? You wished you could move things the way *I* do. You wanted me to throw his gun out the window."

"You threw Marty's gun out the window?" Summer asked, still trying to make sense of Margaret's explanation.

"No – the windows of the conveyance were closed. But while that horrid braggard was jabbering on about all the abominations he had so *proudly* committed, I managed to slide the gun out of its hiding place and stow it behind his seat."

Summer's mouth dropped open. "You hid Marty's gun from him?"

"Yes." The Victorian spirit smiled. "When he discovered it had gone missing, his confused expression was *most* entertaining." She scooped two more helpings of sugar into her cup and stirred.

"What happened after that? My memory is...it's *fuzzy*." Summer shook her head, attempting to rid herself of the unfamiliar sensation.

"Without a weapon, he simply behaved like the coward that he was," Margaret replied. "He made a grab for you, but he was too late. One of the deputies had already pulled you to safety."

"So, did Marty try to fight his way out? Try to overpower one of the agents and take his gun?"

"No – Marty attempted to run away." Margaret sipped her tea. "He didn't get far, though. One of the deputies released a rather enormous dog in pursuit. That evil-hearted wretch wailed like a small child under the dog's assault, but his cries garnered him absolutely no sympathy. I found his bawling quite satisfying, actually – a small retribution of sorts for those poor, innocent souls he boasted about having slaughtered." She paused and moved her fingers to form the sign of the cross. "May they finally rest in peace."

"But I heard the dog yelping – like it was hurt."

"Yes," Margaret said knitting her eyebrows together. "Unfortunately, the cad realized the deputies were holding their fire because they didn't want to risk harming their fine animal. Marty must have been quite strong, because he picked the dog up off the ground and attempted to hold it close to his body. I supposed he hoped to use it as a shield to further his escape."

"And that's when the agents shot him?" Summer asked, still trying to reconcile the sounds she heard with Margaret's explanation.

"Not at that moment. The dog was a match for the criminal's strength. It wriggled around to face him and continued to attack. I believe the miscreant wrapped his arm around the dog's neck in an attempt to stop it from biting, without anticipating the animal's natural response to such grave danger."

Summer squinted her eyes, trying to visualize the scene.

Margaret chuckled. "The dog relieved itself upon the rotten bastard."

Summer couldn't suppress a snicker. "No wonder he started cussing a blue streak."

"Yes," Margaret continued. "And I'm afraid that's when he made yet another unwise decision – to take revenge on the poor dog for the perceived offense, rather than continuing to use it as a shield." She shook her head. "He attempted to choke the life out of the animal, however, the moment it yelped with pain, the dog's master stepped forward and shot Marty dead." She lifted her cup to her lips and took a sip. "I normally abhor violence, but I must admit that I found this *particular* death to be a just conclusion to this nasty business."

Summer nodded, picturing Marty's dead body, soaked in dog urine. *"Do spirits feel humiliation?"* The satisfying image was almost instantly replaced by a more frightening one. She glanced nervously around the lawn. "Did Marty cross over into the light or is his spirit still here?"

Margaret's eyes sparkled as she straightened her shoulders. "Yes, he's gone. A host of like-minded spirits here at the Belleview gathered, to make sure he understood the spirit realm would be...well, a most *undesirable* place for him to remain."

"How did you do that?" Summer asked, breathing a sigh of relief.

"I told you that we spirits can appear as we looked at any point throughout our lives. I don't think I mentioned that we can also appear as our bodies look any time after our *deaths*. Some spirits even find entertainment in determining which of us can appear the *most* gruesome." A thin smile of satisfaction crossed her lips. "When Marty spied a large gathering of rotting corpses, he flew into the light so fast, you'd have thought that dog was still chasing him." She started to lift her cup but paused a moment. "He died without repenting his evil deeds, so I'd be willing to bet that he's already been banished to the fires of hell."

"Thanks, Margaret. You saved my life." Summer sighed. "Unfortunately, when the police investigate, they're bound to find that recorder, hidden in the tool box in the back of the truck. The file with all the client's banking information is recorded in my voice. That means that, even if they *don't* hold me responsible for Marty's bomb – which they most likely *will* do – I'll still be sent to prison."

"Yes, I'm sorry I couldn't hide that device for you, but I'm afraid distracting *these* guards would prove much more difficult than tricking a dullard like Marty." Margaret clucked. "But let's not spoil the victories of today with worries that belong to tomorrow."

Summer nodded and raised her cup to toast Margaret's wisdom. "Truer words were never spoken." She took a sip of tea, grimaced, and returned the cup to its saucer. *"I still don't like tea."*

Margaret chuckled and waved her hand, turning the tea into a tall glass of beer. "No matter what happens, you must remember that when your situation was at its most dire, you revealed what was in your heart. You wanted to throw that gun out of the *window*, not use it to take revenge on that wretched man. And you were willing to sacrifice your life to save the lives of others – to save my beloved hotel. You've earned your redemption, darlin' girl."

Summer bit her lip. *"Unless I was the one who shot Gordo and my mind managed to block out the memory."*

Their conversation ended when someone tapped Summer on the shoulder. "Miss Tyme – can you hear me? Miss Tyme?" It was the gruff voice of FBI Agent Sullivan.

When she turned to look at him, Summer fell through the clouds and woke with a start. The light hurt her eyes and her head throbbed.

"Everything's gonna be all right now, Miss Tyme," Agent Sullivan soothed. The muscular man knelt at her side, squinting, trying to peer into her eyes. "Your pupils don't appear to be dilated. Can you sit up?"

He helped her sit and then wrapped a warm, wool blanket around her shoulders. Summer shivered, despite the mild afternoon temperature. "Is he...is he..." her voice cracked.

"Dead?" Agent Sullivan asked. "Yeah. You don't have to worry about that psychopath hurting you ever again. Now, here – try to drink some of this." He held a plastic bottle to her lips. "You've been through a lot and this will help."

She breathed out a sigh of relief and then took a tentative sip from the bottle. She pulled back, grimacing. "What *is* that?"

"Oh, sorry...it's bottled tea. I don't like the taste of it, either, but it's the only drink the security guard had in his cooler." He held the bottle out to her. "Try to drink some more. You need hydration."

Summer took the bottle and, ignoring the unpleasant taste, drank a few thirsty gulps. *"Margaret – if I didn't know better, I'd swear you had something to do with this."*

"That's good," Agent Sullivan said. "As soon as you're ready, I'll take you back to the hotel. My boss wants to have a doc check you over in the medical triage tent before she takes your statement."

Summer had to admit the tea was making her feel better. She wrinkled her nose and took another swig. "I think I can get up now," she said.

When he helped her to her feet, Summer decided that Agent Sullivan could easily be mistaken for an offensive lineman on a pro football team. He wrapped his thick arm around her back for support as he escorted her to a black SUV, parked a few yards away. When they reached the car, Summer turned to survey the macabre scene behind them.

If not for the FBI agents milling around, the white truck, with its pink *Piccadilly Parties* logo, wouldn't look at all out of place parked in the driveway of the white, two-story, East Gate Cottage. Yet, less than an hour ago, Marty had held her prisoner inside that truck, forcing her to listen as he described the gruesome details of his plan to torture her to death.

Summer shifted her gaze to the side yard of the elegant Victorian home and was comforted by the sight of two FBI agents, standing guard over Marty's blanket-covered body. As she turned away, Summer noticed the German Shepherd and his handler in the front yard of the cottage, playing a game of tug-o-war with a knotted rope, behaving as though Thunder's life and death skirmish had already been forgotten.

She felt a few cobwebs clear from her consciousness. "Wait a minute," she said, rubbing her sore jaw. "Why did you guys set up a medical triage tent at the hotel? Did some people get hurt? Is my brother safe? Have you heard anything about the condition of a pregnant woman named Emma? What about an old man named Alex? He helped sound the alarm and..."

The agent held his palms up in protest. "You'll have to ask my boss most of those questions, but I can tell you that it's not unusual for us to set up a triage unit when a situation develops in the midst of a crowd. You know, in case anyone's high blood pressure acts up because of all the excitement and what not."

He opened the car's rear passenger door for her.

Summer took a deep breath and exhaled. "How about the hotel – the Belleview Biltmore – is it okay, too?"

"As far as I know. Once the hotel was cleared, everybody was allowed to go back inside to resume their activities, while we continued searching the grounds for the perpetrator." He gave her a crooked half-smile. "You know, my team and I thought we drew the short straw when we got assigned to search exiting vehicles." He winked at Summer. "But we're not whining anymore – not after taking down that miserable dirt-bag and saving the life of his hostage. I guess the good guys *do* get lucky every now and then."

Summer looked away to hide her confusion as she slid into the seat. *"Why is he referring to me as a hostage rather than a suspect?*

Does the FBI know about Gordo's murder? Do they think Marty killed him? Do they know Gordo forced me to work for him? Will any of that make a difference in my trial?"

Chapter Sixty

Miles Prescot was the last person Summer expected to run into when she reached the hotel. She hadn't laid eyes on him since the costumed reception, during which the pretentious art collector had bragged ad nauseum about how he would be the new owner of the Tissot painting, *Bride on Stairs*. Apparently, Prescot had been waiting for his car to arrive when he saw Summer step from the black SUV and was too self-absorbed to notice the discombobulated state of her appearance. She shrugged off the blanket and smoothed her dress.

"Don't think for a minute that I don't know this auction was rigged from the start!" he shouted. "Allowing buyers to remain anonymous stinks of conspiracy. You're probably protecting his identity because you know he's a drug lord...or a terrorist, maybe."

Before Summer had time to think of a reply to these outrageous accusations, Agent Sullivan stepped in. "I'm going to have to ask you to move away from the lady, sir," he said, towering over the angry multi-millionaire. "And I suggest you don't make me ask twice."

"Back off, asshole!" Prescot bellowed. "Don't you know who I *am*?"

"No," replied Sullivan. "But I do know that you're resisting a directive from the FBI." He flashed his badge.

Momentarily speechless, Prescot gaped as the agent took Summer by the elbow and guided her toward the large triage tent, set up next to the hotel's entrance. A red cross on each wall of the white tent clearly identified it as a temporary medical facility.

The news that Prescot had lost the bid for *Bride on Stairs* gave Summer a little more spring in her step. *"He didn't deserve to own such a treasure. He just wanted to see how many people he could make grovel at his feet for a chance to view it."* She hoped the new owner, whoever he was, would loan it to a museum, where the public could admire the masterpiece.

Prescot, ignoring Summer's obvious need for medical attention, shouted after her. "The FBI, huh? Big surprise! I knew this operation was corrupt! I'm frickin' thrilled I didn't buy that crappy painting. I'd be willing to bet it's not even worth the five-million that anonymous, drug dealing terrorist paid for it!"

Agent Sullivan turned to give the loudmouth a hard stare and Prescot flinched. Thankfully, the arrival of the wealthy man's limo ended the testosterone-inflamed confrontation. Prescot dove inside his car, cursing the driver for keeping him waiting. Only then did the statuesque Natalia rise from the concrete bench at the entrance and glide over to the car. Without looking right or left, she allowed the limo driver to take her elbow and help her into the back seat, next to Prescot.

"Which prison cell would be worse," Summer wondered, *"hers or mine?"*

"I thought we agreed not to spoil the victories of today with worries that belong to tomorrow," Margaret said.

"Hey, Margaret, I didn't know you were still with me, but you're right. For today, it's enough to know that I'm alive, Marty and Gordo aren't, and that ass didn't win the bid for the Tissot."

But it was impossible for Summer to maintain that bright outlook. She had already begun to dread the moment when everyone learned the truth about her and Justin. She knew Robert and Dana wouldn't want anything to do with the Tyme twins once the FBI revealed their respective roles in Gordo's scheme.

Sullivan held open the flap of the triage tent for Summer and she trudged in with a heavy heart, keeping her eyes on the grass.

"Summer!" Justin cried. As he ran forward to embrace his twin, she could tell he'd been crying. He lifted her off her feet and swung her around in a circle. "I was so worried about you! Forget *nine* lives – this kitty has at least *forty-five* of them!"

Despite her muddled thinking, Summer had translated the coded message even before Justin set her back on the ground.

9: I need to talk to you in private; 45: Play dumb – they're fishing for evidence

"Are you sure I don't have more lives than that?" Summer asked, tears welling in her eyes. "Because I feel like I've burned through at least *ninety* of them today."

90: Do you know where I was and/or who I was with?

Justin jerked his head in a quick nod before they shared a bear hug.

"Yeah," Justin whispered. "That's why it's so *damn* good to see you."

"We've *all* been out of our minds with worry." Robert's voice came from behind Summer.

Summer released Justin and spun around, noticing for the first time that the tent was occupied by several other people. Emma lay on one gurney and Dana and Ole were sitting at either end of a second one. Apparently, the four of them had been sitting together until the moment she arrived.

Summer longed to fall into Robert's arms, but she couldn't move. *"Will holding him now make our separation harder to take later?"*

"Does it matter?" Margaret asked.

A doctor intervened at that moment, eliminating further conjecture. "I need to ask everyone who isn't in need of medical care to please exit immediately," he said. "I promise to let you back in as soon as possible."

"Come on, folks," Agent Sullivan said, continuing to hold the tent flap open. "You heard the doctor."

Justin gave Summer another hug and whispered, "Nobody's mentioned Gordo, so he probably made a clean break. Remember – *forty-five*." Before disappearing through the opening, he gave her a boyish grin and held up his forefinger.

1: I love you.

Summer gave him a smile, but her thoughts were racing in another direction. *"Surely the FBI found Gordo's body while they were clearing the hotel. Are they keeping his murder a secret? For what purpose?"*

She smiled as Dana and Ole shuffled past, squeezing her hand and offering welcome words of relief and thanks. Then Robert stood transfixed, inches away, his sky blue eyes burning into hers. He cupped her cheek in his palm and gave her lips a gentle kiss.

"I won't be far," he said, letting his hand drop. "I know you didn't do what they're insinuating you've done. I've called an attorney to represent you and Justin. Don't say *anything* to *anyone* until he gets here."

Summer's light brown eyes glittered with tears once again. *"I'd do anything for the chance to become the person you believe I am."*

"This way, sir," Agent Sullivan prompted.

After Robert exited, the agent dropped the tent flap, but his silhouette against the fabric made it clear that he was still standing guard.

"Sorry I can only offer you a limited amount of privacy," the rugged-looking doctor said. He handed Emma a set of noise-cancelling music headphones and then pulled a cord, dropping a sheet-style curtain between the two gurneys.

The doctor's mouth turned up in a half-smile, drawing attention to a rash of small, roundish scars on one side of his face. *"Shrapnel, chicken pox or acne?"* Summer mused. *"Probably shrapnel. He looks like a combat vet."*

"Oh, man!" Emma complained. "You're no fun at all." A moment later she called out, "At least you have good taste in music... I *love* Bach."

"I'm Doctor Garcia. I specialize in emergency medicine. Have a seat." He patted the second gurney. "I understand you've had a rough afternoon, Summer."

Summer chose not to respond to the doctor's rhetorical question. She ambled over to the gurney and removed her shoes, comforted by the fact that the sheet still held imprints from where her brother and friends had been sitting only moments before. She sat on one side of the hard mattress, feeling exposed in her cocktail dress, with her bare feet dangling a foot above the grass. "Emma – are you doing all right over there?" she called.

"I'm fine," Emma called back, confirming Summer's suspicion that she had removed the headphones.

Ignoring their conversation, Dr. Garcia picked up Summer's wrist and took her pulse.

"Andrew just decided to make the day even more interesting than it already was," Emma continued. "For a while there, I thought I was going to give birth in the middle of the lawn with a crowd of strangers watching."

"So, you're not in labor, then?" Summer asked. She flinched when the cold metal of the doctor's stethoscope touched her bare back.

"Oh, I'm definitely in labor, all right." Emma groaned as a contraction hit, as if to prove the point. "Whew. That one got my attention. But, as I was saying… my contractions slowed down after the initial onset, so I insisted on staying for the rest of the auction. Afterward, we learned that *you* had gone missing and I wanted to wait here with everyone else until you were found. But I must say, it's a good thing the FBI didn't take any longer to rescue you than they did. If my contractions got much closer together, Ole might have suffered a total meltdown."

"Ole's freaking out? I thought Dana said *nothing* could ruffle his feathers."

"Yeah, right. That stoic demeanor of his flew out the window with my first contraction. The moment you walked in, Ole grabbed his cell phone and called for an ambulance. They should be here any minute to take me to the hospital. I'm ready to go, but isn't it weird to think that sometime tonight, I'm going to become a *mommy*? Ow, ow, owww…" Emma groaned again.

"Not as weird as the fact that I know the spirit who is about to become your son."

"Summer, I can't tell you how glad I am that you're okay." Emma paused. "She *is* okay, isn't she, Doctor Garcia?"

"So far, so good, but if you could be quiet, put on those headphones, and allow me to complete my examination, I'd appreciate it," he teased.

Emma giggled. "Okay. I'll be good and listen to Bach for *real* this time."

"Seriously now, Summer," the Dr. said, "how are you feeling…any dizziness?"

"Not anymore," Summer replied. "I feel fine except for being sore from falling on my face twice today."

The sound of a buzzing phone came from the doctor's white coat pocket. Without a word, he fished out a smartphone, entered the passcode and then handed it to Summer.

Summer cocked her head, questioning his actions, but automatically accepted the offered phone. Then her eyes grew wide. A text message was displayed the screen.

S – Terms of the deal I brokered were clear. G violated those terms, so was subject to penalty outlined at onset. You are hereby released from that agreement. Am proposing a new deal with immediate legal benefits for you and your brother in exchange for handling a task for me. To accept, respond immediately. Details will follow. – The B

The doctor waited for Summer to absorb The Broker's message and respond.

The promise of "immediate legal benefits" was too alluring to resist, regardless of the terms. Summer typed:

Deal accepted. – S

Still stunned, she handed the phone to the doctor, who silently slipped it back into his coat pocket.

"What ties do you have to The Broker?" she wondered, watching Dr. Garcia. *"How did he arrange for you to staff this particular triage tent?"*

Summer didn't have long to ponder these new developments before a woman whipped open the tent flap and marched inside. The newcomer, who wore an FBI vest, addressed the doctor in a perfunctory manner. "Is Miss Tyme medically fit to answer a few questions before we transport her to headquarters?"

The woman possessed an average build, but everything else about her suggested she was comprised entirely of sharp corners. Her mannerisms, short, spiky brown hair, pointy chin and sour expression combined to project a hard image – as though life had robbed her of any warmth or empathy she might once have possessed. She narrowed her steely-gray eyes and scanned Summer from head to dangling feet.

The doctor frowned. "She needs medical treatment and observation."

Even the woman's flared nostrils formed small, sharp triangles. "All right, then. You treat her while I ask her some questions."

"She's *dehydrated* and in *shock*," Dr. Garcia clarified. "Her pulse is racing. I'm about to start an IV, and I don't want you or anyone else to upset her."

Summer doubted any of that was true, but she had an uneasy feeling about this woman and wasn't about to contradict the doctor.

Dr. Garcia stopped at the end of the gurney. "Excuse me, but I need to fetch some supplies from that cabinet and you're in my way." The agent frowned and took a step back. He retrieved an IV kit and then positioned himself directly between the agent and Summer before setting to work.

The agent scowled at the doctor and shuffled to the end of the bed, so that she could see Summer's face. "Miss Tyme, I'm FBI Hostage Rescue Team Leader Carla Phillips, and I think you're a *lot* stronger than the doc seems to think you are." She smiled at Summer. "You wouldn't mind if I asked you a few questions while he looks after you, now, would you?"

"Doctor, I'm still *really* dizzy," Summer said, rubbing her forehead. She hoped he wouldn't point out that she had told him she felt fine just a few minutes earlier.

Dr. Garcia nodded. "That doesn't surprise me. Normally, I would already have started you on oxygen, but we're short-staffed today, so I'm manning this tent on my own." He twisted open a valve on a green tank of oxygen and helped fit a mask over Summer's nose and mouth. "This should help. Take slow, deep breaths." He turned a crank to raise the end of the gurney where Agent Phillips was standing, obscuring her view once again, and then helped Summer scoot back against the raised section before spreading a blanket over her.

Summer stretched her aching body and closed her eyes. *"I may not be dizzy, but this bed still feels pretty damn good."* She barely flinched when the doctor inserted the IV needle.

Agent Phillips snorted. "Give me a break. She looked perfectly fine until she found out who I was." The woman stepped to the far side of the gurney. "Miss Tyme, it's been a long day for all of us, so I'm going to tell you the truth."

Summer felt one side of the mattress sink and knew the agent had taken a seat on the edge of the gurney. Even with her eyes closed, she knew Agent Phillips was watching her – looking for tells – hoping Summer would crack. *"Forty-five. Play dumb – they're fishing for evidence."*

"We know you and your brother are up to your armpits in this mess. You weren't Martin Russo's hostage, were you? You were working with him – maybe his girlfriend. The three of you planned to steal some art, but then things got out of hand. It's just a matter of time before we gather enough evidence to prove what happened. Why don't you confess so we can all call it a day? If you cooperate, we might get the judge to grant you and your brother some leniency."

Summer kept her eyes closed. *"Leniency? I'm pretty sure that isn't what The Broker had in mind when he offered me legal benefits, so fish away, sister. The only thing you're going to learn is that the water around here is way over your head."*

Just then, the flap to the tent opened. Peeking through the fringe of her eyelashes, Summer could make out Agent Sullivan's bulky outline in the doorway. "I'm sorry to disturb you, ma'am," Sullivan said. "But the ambulance is here to pick up the pregnant lady."

Chapter Sixty-One

Dr. Garcia quickly ushered Agent Phillips out of the tent to give Emma a modicum of privacy. Ole raced to his wife's bedside ahead of the EMTs and bent to give her a tender kiss.

"Go away!" Emma moaned. "I want the doctor!"

Ole stepped aside, looking so forlorn that Dr. Garcia chuckled. "Don't worry, son. When women are in the throes of hard labor, they tend not to appreciate affectionate gestures from their husbands. But never fear – she still loves you, and very soon you will have the happy family you've been dreaming about. Why don't you go stand next to Summer while we transfer your wife to the ambulance gurney?" Then he turned his attention to Emma – comforting her, while at the same time, discussing her status with the EMTs.

Summer and Ole watched in helpless horror as Emma convulsed with pain. The contractions were coming less than three minutes apart now, so Dr. Garcia and the EMTs had to work quickly to move Emma.

No babies for me, Summer decided. *Never in a million years would I put myself through that.*

Remarkably, once Emma was settled onto the new gurney and had breathed through a hard contraction, she giggled at the expressions on Summer and Ole's faces. "Don't worry, Ole – everything's going to be okay." She looked up at the EMT who was pushing the gurney toward the entrance. "My husband didn't want me to fly down here so close to my due date, and it's killing him not to say, 'I told you so.'"

Her joke managed to shake Ole out of his stupor. He leapt to Emma's side and took her hand just as another contraction hit. Ole grimaced as Emma squeezed his knuckles together, but he didn't pull away.

The EMTs stopped until the pain passed, but moments later, they were gone and Agent Phillips was back. Summer thought about closing her eyes again, but knew the Agent wasn't buying her act.

"Now, where were we?" Phillips began. "I believe you were deciding whether you wanted to confess or take your chances with a jury. I have to say, if I were in your shoes, I'd confess. I mean, the evidence against you is stacking up so high, you might not even be able to find a lawyer who'd be willing to represent you."

"Bullshit. If you guys had any tangible evidence, you'd lock me to this gurney and tell me what you have. You can't con a con artist." Summer took a deep breath and resumed her silent mantra. *"Forty-five: Play dumb – they're fishing for evidence."*

"Excuse me, ma'am," Agent Sullivan interrupted from the doorway.

"Not again!" Phillips shouted. "What is it *this* time, Sullivan?"

"It's the Department of Homeland Security – they claim they're taking over..."

An attractive blonde woman used her forearm to move Sullivan out of her way and stepped into the tent. Several DHS agents, Agent Sullivan, and Robert McNeal followed her inside. Summer caught a glimpse of her brother, standing with Dana just outside, but she knew that not even Justin could help her now.

Summer shifted her gaze to her lap and blinked back tears. This was the moment she had been dreading for days. Robert was about to learn the truth about her. *"They probably searched the toolbox and found the recorder – maybe they even found the forged painting. Now Agent Phillips will be convinced beyond a shadow of doubt that I was Marty's partner. And when they find Gordo..."*

The blonde woman walked straight over to the gurney. "Are you okay, Summer?"

Summer glanced up at the woman and then did a double-take. *"Whoa – maybe I really am in shock,"* she thought. *"Or I'm hallucinating."* Her brain could find no other logical explanation for why

Denise Matthews –the criminal investigation department supervisor at the law firm in Seattle where Summer worked – would be here – in Florida – in an FBI triage tent – wearing a DHS uniform.

Summer nodded, too confused to speak. She wanted to hug her boss, but Denise displayed no sign of the familiar camaraderie they normally shared. *"That must be it. I'm in shock and hallucinating."*

"I've already debriefed your brother," Denise said. "He feels terrible that you were put in harm's way. He asked me to tell you that your next *thirty-five* steak dinners are on him. He said he'd even spring for the Heinz *Fifty-Seven* sauce."

Summer's eyes widened. *"What the hell?"*

35: Change of plans; 57: Keep quiet and let me do the talking

"Now I'm positive this is a hallucination. Justin and I never share our secret code with anyone. But I guess I'll go along." Summer gave Denise a discreet nod to let her know she understood the message. "Tell my brother I plan to hold him to that deal."

"I will. You get some rest now. We'll talk later." Denise turned on her heel and addressed Agent Phillips with an air of authority. "I believe you were leading the FBI's operation here, correct?"

Other than their gender and approximate age, the two women had absolutely nothing in common. Denise, tall and well-toned, didn't try to disguise her curves and her blonde hair hung in loose curls around her shoulders.

Summer watched as the two women squared-off. *"This should be interesting. If this imaginary Denise is anything like my real boss, she won't depend on her good looks to get her way. She's super intelligent and can kick ass when she needs to.*

Agent Phillips glared at Denise. Before responding, she balled her fists and placed them on her hips. The bend of her elbows formed two new triangles, adding to Phillip's sharp-edged appearance. "I'm HRT Leader Phillips and I *am* in charge of this FBI operation. Who in the hell are you?"

Denise pointed to a badge clipped to her vest and then held out her hand. "I'm Senior Field Agent Denise Matthews, with the Counterterrorism Unit of the DHS. We appreciate all the FBI has done to contain this situation, but we can take it from here."

Summer watched with amusement as Phillips wrestled with the decision to ignore the hand Denise had proffered or accept her handshake. Denise had once explained how common norms of civil behavior often compelled adversaries to ease their unmitigated resistance – the first step toward submission.

"Counterterrorism?" Phillips sneered. She dropped one fist to her side and unfolded the other to shake Denise's hand. "Since when does the DHS get involved in cases of domestic armed robbery?"

"We don't," Denise said. "*This*, however, is a case of domestic *terrorism*. Martin Russo has been on our Watch List for a while now."

"Terrorist, my ass," Phillips argued. "This was a robbery gone bad, pure and simple. Martin Russo has a criminal record, you know – assault and battery *and* theft. Plus, he has ties to organized crime. He's a known associate of Gordon Adolphus, who, according to his housekeeper, *also* happens to be conveniently unavailable to answer questions at this time. Domestic organized crime comes under the jurisdiction of the FBI, not the DHS."

Summer sucked in a breath at the mention of Gordo's name. *"How is it possible that no one's found his body yet?"*

"I'm told Martin Russo left evidence of his true motive at the scene," Denise said. "Didn't your agents find a note that read: *Death to America?*"

"Oh, come on," Phillips wailed. "You can't be serious. Russo? A religious zealot? What terrorist faction was he supposedly working for? And what kind of idiot jihadist would leave his declaration note inside of a *Bible*, for God's sake? And it wasn't even *his* Bible... it was stolen from one of the hotel rooms! Plus, the imbecile left his manifesto – if you can call it that – on top of a cart that, had the bomb exploded properly, would have been blown to smithereens."

Summer had to bite her tongue to keep from laughing. It was a comfort to think that Marty would be remembered, not for his monstrous deeds as a sadistic enforcer for the mob, but for his sheer stupidity.

"I agree that Russo wasn't a devout member of ISIL, but so what?" Denise countered. "The vast majority of lone terrorists aren't affiliated with organized groups. Most are just miserable, unbalanced individuals who are attracted to a violent cause. And there's no support for the claim that there's a connection to organized crime, or that this was a run-of-the-mill robbery attempt. For one thing, mobsters aren't known for operating so far out of their own territory, and even if this was an exception, thieves don't try to blow up everything worth stealing."

Phillips had no response. Her shoulders sagged, momentarily defeated. "What about the twins? It's pretty obvious those two were working with Russo, right?"

Denise glanced at Summer, but quickly returned her attention to Phillips. "Trust me. Nothing about this situation is as simple as it appears. The Tyme siblings are an integral part of this situation, but not in the way you're suggesting."

"Don't tell me – they were working for you this whole time, but neither of them bothered to mention it," Phillips said, her voice dry with sarcasm.

"Not exactly," Denise said. "Justin became involved when a woman approached him in Las Vegas a few months ago. The distraught woman alleged that she was being forced to help Russo raise funds to carry out an act of terrorism on American soil. In an effort to save the woman's life, Justin – a professional gambler, among other things – gave her a portion of his earnings in marked bills and then notified the DHS. Unfortunately, he couldn't provide any details, so there wasn't much we could do, other than add Martin Russo's name to our Watch List and follow the money."

Summer glanced around the tent. Everyone, including Robert, was listening to Denise's fabrication with the rapt attention of children sharing ghost stories around a campfire. *"Imaginary Denise is really good at this."*

"Without our knowledge," Denise continued, "Justin continued to investigate, hoping to save the woman from Russo by getting him arrested. Justin infiltrated Russo's circle and pretended to support his plans. He learned that Russo's objective was to kill influential Americans in an act of terrorism, but he still didn't know the specific details. When he learned the plot had something to do with the McNeal Foundation's Annual Art Auction, he contacted his twin sister, a recent graduate of the School of the Art Institute of Chicago, hoping she could help him learn more about the event."

"Whoops – that was a mistake, imaginary Denise. If the FBI does a background check, they'll find out I never attended SAIC." Still, when Phillips shot her a suspicious glance, Summer did her best to look as though Denise was speaking the gospel truth.

"Twins often possess a sixth-sense that tells them when their sibling is in trouble," Denise continued. "Summer suspected Justin hadn't told her the whole truth, so she decided to fly to Florida to see if she could help. Their amateur sleuthing was dangerous and ill-advised, but not illegal. Some would call what they did brave and admirable..."

Everyone turned when the flap of the tent opened once more. An FBI agent stood in the entrance, holding a large, clear evidence bag. Alex Washington and Sharon Delahanty were right behind him. Agent Sullivan walked over and quietly conferred with the other agent.

Summer closed her eyes, suppressing a groan. *"They've got my go-bag. No matter how good she is, Denise won't to be able to sell the FBI on the story that an innocent art student just happens to possess a professional lock pick set, electronics scramblers, and a bundle of credit cards that don't have her name on them."*

Agent Phillips perked up. "What is it, Sullivan?"

Sullivan took the bag and waved Sharon and Alex into the tent. "Vasquez says he saw these two trying to hide a backpack under the porch of the hotel. He figured it probably has something to do with our investigation, so he tagged it as evidence."

Phillips gave Denise a smirk. "Let's check this out and *then* decide who should be leading this investigation." She smiled as she took hold of a stainless steel medical cart and rolled it over the grass to the center of the tent. "Sullivan, bring the bag over here – them, too."

"Wait – this feels way too real to be a hallucination." Summer pinched her arm and winced at the pain. *"Holy shit, this is really happening!"* She looked at Denise anew. *"Exactly who the hell have I been working for in Seattle?"* Memories from the last three years

took on a different light as they flashed through Summer's mind – Denise's frequent business trips – the confidential research her firm had performed for various governmental entities – the new message from The Broker – Denise's timely appearance… *"Jesus, I was so focused on hiding my past that it never dawned on me that other people might not be who they claimed to be, either."*

Chapter Sixty-Two

Phillip's voice brought Summer back to the scene unfolding in front of her. The woman crossed her arms, and eyed Sharon and Alex with suspicion. "So, you want to explain what you were up to?"

"I'm the assistant manager here at the Belleview Biltmore," Sharon said. Her voice was shaky, but clear enough to be heard. "And Alex, here, is an American hero twice over – first as a Tuskegee Airman, and just a while ago, as the man who stopped that horrible bomb from going off."

Phillips narrowed her eyes. "So why would a hotel manager and a war hero try to hide a mysterious backpack from the FBI?"

"It's my fault," Sharon said. "I found the bag and assumed one of our guests misplaced it during the excitement earlier today. I carried it inside, planning to see if I could figure out who it belonged to. But before I had a chance to look for ID, I ran into Alex. He was worried I'd get in trouble for moving potential evidence, so he suggested I put it back where I found it." She wrung her hands together. "I'm sorry. Are we in trouble?"

Alex wrapped an arm around her shoulders. "We really didn't mean to do nothin' wrong."

Phillips frowned and waved her hand in the general direction of Summer's bed. "Wait over there while we check out your story."

"Why, hi there, Summer," Alex said, smiling as he approached. "Are you doing alright, angel?"

"No talking," Phillips barked.

"Alrighty," Alex said. He rubbed his chin. "But just to be clear, you *do* know that this here is the young lady that helped me disarm that bomb, right? She's every bit as much of a hero as me... more so, even. She sent me to set off the fire alarm and tell Sharon to get everyone outside, while she headed off to call the police. The nut who planted the bomb must have caught her and taken her hostage before she could get to the phone."

Phillips glared at the old man. "Thank you for your input. Now, *please* be quiet." She turned to Sullivan. "Put on some gloves and dump the bag on this table."

Sullivan cast an apologetic glance at Alex as he donned a pair of gloves. Then he removed the back pack from the evidence bag and turned it upside down.

Summer held her breath as her passport fell onto the table – but not her tools. The only other items in the bag were eighty-nine dollars in cash and a few photographs. Sullivan spread out the photos. "These show Martin Russo at a costume party, together with an unknown woman... perhaps an accomplice."

"See there," Alex said, "I *told* you she was trying to help. Summer, you hid that bag in case the bomb went off, didn't you? You were hoping to let the FBI know who..."

"I said, be quiet!" Phillips yelled. "We're *trying* to conduct an *investigation* here." Then she waved a dismissive hand. "You two are free to go. Sullivan, get them out of here."

Agent Sullivan cast a disapproving glance at his supervisor. "This way, please," he said as he stepped between Sharon and Alex, and gently took them both by their elbows. "Watch your step on the grass, ma'am. And Sir, I'm sure I speak for *everyone* here when we *thank* you for your service to our country *and* for disarming that bomb today. Men as brave as you don't come along every day and should be treated with *respect*."

"Why, thank you, young man." Alex straightened his shoulders and shot a smug glance at Agent Phillips.

Phillips quickly returned her attention to the photographs, as if noticing them for the first time.

As her two friends left the tent, Summer smiled, certain that she was the only one who had noticed the pockets of Alex's baggy pants bulged – stuffed, no doubt, with the damning evidence he had removed from her go bag.

"Maybe the reason Miss Tyme had pictures of Russo was because she was *infatuated* with him," Phillips argued. "Maybe she was *jealous* of this other woman in the pictures."

Once Sharon and Alex were gone, Sullivan turned and faced Phillips. "I'm sorry, ma'am," he said, shaking his head. "But I was part of the team that took Russo down, and that's just not the way it was. Miss Tyme was not in that truck of her own free will. She was scared to death."

"*Sure* she was scared," Phillips continued. "She knew she was about to be *arrested*."

"I respectfully disagree," Sullivan said. "If that were the case, she wouldn't have risked her life to warn us that he had a gun."

Before Agent Phillips could protest, Denise stepped in. "Thank you, Agent Sullivan. I look forward to reading your report." Then she turned to his supervisor. "HRT Leader Phillips, please direct your team to stand down with the thanks of the DHS for a job well done. We'll take over the investigation from here."

Phillips gave Denise a curt nod to accept defeat. "My gut tells me you're dead wrong and my report is going to reflect that. If this investigation goes south, you can be *damn* sure that it's going to be *your* ass in a sling, not mine."

Without waiting for a reply, Phillips stormed out of the tent, with Sullivan trailing behind.

Denise addressed Robert next. "Mr. McNeal, I'm sure you're anxious to get back to work, so I won't keep you. I certainly hope this nasty business won't have any lasting negative effects on the good works of your great Foundation."

"Thank you," Robert said. He pushed up his glasses. "Actually, it appears we broke our sales record this year. It seems everyone wanted to have an interesting story to tell about how they made an acquisition, just a few yards from where a bomb was set to explode." He grinned. "I'm pretty sure most of them will say they had a hand in uncovering the plot." He stole a glance at Summer. "Listen, I have a trusted employee wrapping up the auction – Maxwell Bennett. So, would it be okay if I hung out with Summer for a while?"

Denise shook her head. "I'm afraid not. I need to debrief her and her brother. And besides, I believe your sister is expecting you at the hospital, isn't she?"

"Can I at least give her a hug?"

Denise frowned. Over Robert's shoulder, Summer's hands were pressed together in mock prayer. She mouthed the word, "Please?"

"Okay, fine," Denise said. "But make it quick. And absolutely *no* discussion of today's events."

Robert sat on the edge of the gurney and took Summer's hand. "Hey, I have something that belongs to you." He reached into his shirt pocket and pulled out Winnie's cameo pendant.

"Oh, wow," she murmured. "Thank you, Robert – I didn't think I'd ever see this again."

Robert fastened the pendant around her neck and then kissed behind her ear. "I didn't think I'd ever see *you* again. What were you thinking, trying to stop a terrorist on your own?"

"We can't talk about that," Summer whispered. "Just hold me, okay?"

"Okay," Robert replied, wrapping her in his arms. "But only for the rest of my life."

Chapter Sixty-Three

After Denise sent Robert on his way, she put her team to work gathering evidence, taking witness statements, and clearing the crime scene, while Dr. Garcia removed Summer's IV and helped her to her feet.

"Thanks for everything, Doc. It's always a pleasure working with you," Denise said, holding open the tent flap. "Come on, Summer – snap to. Justin's waiting for us in your room. Once you get a quick shower, we'll head over to Clearwater Beach for dinner and a few beers.

"And some confessions?" Summer asked as she walked out into the late afternoon sunshine. "I mean, come on... the DHS? It appears we've both been keeping quite a few secrets." She bumped Denise with her hip. "I'll tell you mine, if you tell me yours."

Denise chuckled. "I know a lot more about you than you think I do, but I *would* like to hear more about how you figured out what Gordo and his pal, Russo were up to."

"Would you believe me if I told you I had a spirit guide... or two... or four?"

"It wouldn't be the strangest thing I've ever heard. Also, I want to talk to you and Justin about your futures."

"Sure. After all, it's thanks to you that I still have one – a future, I mean."

～

By the time Denise drove over the Memorial Causeway Bridge, the sun was sinking below the horizon, painting the sky in brilliant hues of orange and red. While she was getting cleaned up, Summer had told Denise that some of the Belleview Biltmore's long-dead guests still occupied the hotel, and that they, along with Alex and Sharon, had helped save their home. She suspected her boss didn't believe her. Twice, Denise had asked if Summer was *certain* she felt all right.

Immediately beyond the bridge, Denise turned down a narrow road and then pulled into the crushed oyster-shell parking lot of Frenchy's Saltwater Café, adjacent to Clearwater Beach. She took a backpack from her trunk and led the way inside. Colorful picnic tables filled the large, L-shaped outdoor eating area, and island music filled the air. A robust, middle-aged man leaned against the entrance to the interior restaurant, chatting with a white-haired man, who was seated at a pass-through bar immediately to the right of the doorway.

"Hi, Raymond," Denise called.

"Hey, there, beautiful," he replied. "Long time, no see."

"It's been a while," she agreed. "Can my friends and I get a corner table in the back?"

At the sound of her voice, the white-haired man turned around. His tanned face, partially covered with a close-cropped, white beard and moustache, broke into a wide grin. "Well, look what the cat dragged in."

"Hi, Mike – shouldn't you be in Canada?" Denise walked over and hugged both men, while Summer and Justin exchanged confused shoulder shrugs.

"Headed there next week, want to come along? Sell some ice cream?" Mike asked.

"Maybe," Denise said. "I love working on the ice cream boat. Let's talk about it some more after my business dinner."

In unison, the two men shifted their gazes to Justin and Summer.

"Business, huh?" Raymond returned his attention to Denise. "Don't worry, we've your back."

Once they were seated in a corner booth, close enough to the noisy bar to drown-out their conversation, but far enough away that they didn't have to yell at one another, Denise smiled at the approach of a familiar server.

"Hey, where've you been hiding out lately?" the thin, cheerful woman asked, sliding her glasses up on the bridge of her nose. She poised a pen over her order pad. "I haven't seen you for *ages.*"

"Hi, KK," Denise replied. "Yeah, it's been way too long. Listen, I'm going to order for the table." Without looking at a menu, she ordered a fish pretzel appetizer, three cups of she-crab soup, and grilled grouper sandwiches for everybody. "And I'll take a beer – how about you guys?"

"That's the only thing you ordered that I've ever heard of," Justin quipped.

"Trust." Denise smiled. "This is the first step, but over time, you'll learn to trust me."

The moment KK left the table, Summer folded her arms. "I'm not sure about that. For the last three years, I trusted that you were a legal researcher. Why didn't you ever tell me you're with the DHS?"

"Because I'm not – at least not usually. I'm a fixer. Today, my cover was a special agent with the DHS."

"Whoa," Justin said, keeping his voice low. He craned his neck to take a look around. "You're an imposter? Does that mean the FBI will be after us as soon as they find out?"

"If the FBI checks, they'll discover that I'm a consultant with the DHS, working on a special task force, investigating American suspects named on their Watch List."

"You hacked the DHS?" Summer's eyes were wide.

"Not me, personally." Denise shifted her gaze over Summer's shoulder. "Here's KK with our beer and appetizer."

Justin sighed with relief when he saw the fish pretzel was simply a large, hot, salted pretzel in the shape of a fish, dangling from a black, oversized ornament hanger. "No glass for me," he said, taking his cold beer from KK's outstretched hand. "I'm a bottle-baby."

KK chuckled as she walked away, smitten by Justin's charm, despite having been exposed to more than her share of good-looking blond men on Clearwater Beach over the years.

"It all makes sense now," Summer said. "You're The Broker."

"No, but I do work for him." Denise tore a piece of pretzel from the fish's tail and dipped it into a ramekin of melted cheese. "This would probably work better if you just let me talk. I'll start by answering the one question that's been bothering you all day, Summer."

"Who killed Gordo?" Summer asked, her tone flat. In her gut, she already knew the answer.

Denise nodded, washing down the pretzel with a swig of beer. "Yep. It was me. I'm one of the people TB hires to enforce the terms of his deals." She paused. "By the way, you should know that TB is *very* selective about the deals he agrees to broker. His deals *never* favor guys like Gordo. But he's passionate about art, and in this instance, he thought there might be an opportunity for us to do something good..."

"*Good*?" Summer felt her stomach flip. It was all she could do to keep her voice down to a hiss. "If he wanted to do *good*, he would have called the police as soon as he found out what Gordo had planned. He wouldn't have allowed Gordo to..." She crossed her arms, fighting the sudden urge to slap Denise. "How long have you been involved in this deal? I mean, when I asked for time off work, did you already know that Gordo and Marty – the same monsters who killed my partners – were holding my brother captive – tied up in a barn? Did you know that Gordo held a gun to my head and would have murdered me if you'd been a second too late? Did you know that Marty planned to put me on a boat and..." she bit her lower lip, unable to finish the thought.

Denise listened to Summer's hushed rant without showing emotion.

"I thought you were my friend," Summer finished, angry tears welling in her eyes. "But you're just a lying..."

"Woman who saved both of our lives," Justin interrupted. "One, Summer, but twenty-six. Thirty-one, so fifty-eight. Besides, I think, maybe twenty."

Summer gulped as she translated:

1: I love you; 26: Keep it together; 31: What's done is done; 58: Let's hear this person out before deciding what to do; 20: The person next to you is good/an innocent.

"Fine," Summer said. "Talk."

"I *am* your friend, Summer," Denise began. "And I respect the hell out of you – both of you." She nodded at Justin. "I mean, the whole world has been throwing lemons at your heads since you were little kids and somehow, you two always managed to squeeze them into lemonade. TB saw it, too. He was unbelievably impressed with you when you reached out to him three years ago."

"Wait," Summer said. "Is that how I got the job in Seattle? Is he..."

"I won't tell you who he is, but yes, the law firm is one of his assets," Denise said. "TB believed hiring you would be mutually beneficial, and he was right." She smiled. "I wasn't sure you'd keep to the straight and narrow, but after tracking you for a while and putting a few temptations in your path, you won me over, too."

Summer cocked her head. "How have you been tracking me?"

"Great dental plan at the firm, don't you agree?" Denise tapped her jaw. "For our protection and theirs, we have our dentist plant a tracker in the mouths of our most valuable employees. Remember that crown you needed shortly after you came to work for us?"

Summer's tongue automatically searched for the foreign object, but felt nothing. "Can you hear everything I say?"

"No." Denise smiled. "It's just a GPS. And before you ask, no, we don't track you all the time – just when we think we need to. Today that tracker helped save your life. The deal you and Gordo made with TB didn't require you to go to the fifth floor, so when I saw you had gone up there, I decided to follow you."

"I *hate* the idea of being tracked without my consent," Summer said. "But I guess I have to admit, it's kind of hard to be too mad about it this very second."

"Yeah, my timing was pretty good, if I do say so myself," Denise said. She paused as the waitress served their cups of soup.

"I don't know what happened to the fish," Justin said to KK, shaking his head at the small bite of pretzel, dangling precariously from the hook. "We were just talking, and it disappeared. Maybe a hungry dog snuck in here or something."

"Maybe," KK said. She gave him a friendly smile. "Those things do tend to disappear. Better keep an eye on your soup." She tucked her empty tray under her arm and turned her attention to other customers, clamoring for her attention.

Without missing a beat, Denise resumed her story. "Just as I got to the door, Gordo started confessing about how his deal with TB was made under false pretenses – that they had used Lisa to set Justin up. That, by itself, would have been enough to violate the terms of the deal. But then the asshole proceeded to tell you all about how he was going to trick TB into believing that your murder was an accident. I was about to pop the jerk, when suddenly you fainted and he went nuts and started shooting in the air." She took a swig of her beer. "I don't know what he thought he saw, but it petrified him. He thought you were dead – began raving like a crazy man – something about how a boogey man killed you, and how it wasn't going to get him. He even pissed his pants. Nuts, huh? Anyway, when he turned to run, I took him out."

Summer tried to keep her jaw from hanging open while she digested the conflicting information about the woman she *thought* she knew. *"My boss –the woman I've been working with for three years, just admitted she murdered Gordo. And obviously, this wasn't her first kill. Or even her second. But then again, Gordo was about to execute me. And I kind of like that he was almost scared to death by a ghost... and that both Gordo and Marty died in pools of urine. Still... Denise? A fixer? An assassin? Does she expect me to go back to Seattle and just forget all of this happened?"*

Chapter Sixty-Four

"Hey, Summer – are you okay?" Justin asked. "If you ask me, fifty-three."

53: I believe everything will be all right

Summer shook her head to regain her focus. "So, let me get this straight – you killed Gordo because he violated the terms of his deal with The Broker, and then you just left me there to handle the mess when I came to." Anger rose, filling her mouth with a sour taste. "And because Marty wasn't a part of the deal, you were – what – just fine with letting him kill me?"

"No." Denise set down her spoon, a wounded expression playing across her face. "I checked you to make sure you were okay and then I raced down the stairs to catch Marty. Unfortunately, he was already gone, so I decided I'd catch up with him later. I went back upstairs to look after you and hide Gordo's body, but you had disappeared."

Summer recalled the squeak of the floorboards just before she climbed out the window and shimmied down the fire escape. "So, you would have stopped Marty from kidnapping me?"

"Of course," Denise confirmed. "I would have explained everything to you right then, if you had just stayed put."

"Geez, Summer," Justin interjected, "What's wrong with you? When you woke up on the floor next to the dead body of the creep who'd been about to kill you, I can't believe you didn't figure out that your boss was secretly a ninja warrior, working for a clandestine underworld figure with a sense of justice...or that she had flown down to

419

Florida as his enforcer, but she really had *your* best interest at heart."

"Point taken," Denise said. "I should have confided in you right after I saw that ruckus at the costume party. It made me suspicious that Gordo's deal with TB wasn't on the up and up, so I should have acted right then. The reason I decided to keep quiet was because the two of you were *also* acting fishy."

"Point taken," Justin echoed.

"Wait," Summer said. "Does this mean that Gordo's body is still upstairs in the hotel? Why didn't the FBI find him?"

"The FBI wasn't looking for dead bodies. They were sniffing out bombs. Plus, they only glossed over the fifth floor because it's unoccupied. That would be an unlikely place for a terrorist to plant explosives. And since the hotel's getting ready to close for renovation, there are huge piles of crap in most of the rooms on the fifth floor. It was easy to move some of it – to hide him in plain sight, so to speak." Denise took a big spoonful of soup. "You should eat, Summer. Your body needs nutrition."

"It's good soup," Justin said. "Wonder why it's called *she*-crab instead of *he*-crab."

"Female crabs have roe – crab eggs – inside of their bodies," Summer said. "That makes for a more flavorful soup."

"And she's back!" Justin said, a grin splitting his face.

Summer punched her brother on the arm.

"I'll never stop being amazed by your memory," Denise said. "But it's a double-edged sword. It's the reason we kept you in the dark about the research you do for us."

"Because you were worried I'd rat you out if I found out what you were really doing... you and The Broker?"

"No," Denise said. "We were worried that if the wrong people found out about your memory, they'd come after you – either to pull everything you already know out of your head, or to use you the way Gordo did."

Summer took a spoonful of soup, letting the truth of the matter sink in.

"I won't tell you who TB is, or discuss the full extent of our mission,"

Denise said. "But I will tell you that we are one of several small agencies that operate in the shadows, and report to the highest levels within our government. The knowledge we gain by dealing covertly with the underworld is distributed to various law enforcement agencies in due course, and done so in a manner that can't be traced back to us. We usually operate independently, but as you saw today, we can call on the DHS and other known agencies whenever we need back-up. And we're self-funded – mostly by the deals TB makes with criminals."

"That TB guy must charge a high fee for his deals, to be able to afford a fixer, and be willing to take a chance on getting charged with murder," Justin reasoned.

Denise smiled. "Most deals don't require so much oversight – or clean-up. But that's none of your concern. As I said earlier, I brought you here to discuss your futures."

"I don't think I can go back to doing legal research for you in Seattle," Summer said.

"That's fine," Denise replied. "The jobs we want to offer you are in Chicago. We want you both to move there. We're in the process of negotiating with the McNeal Foundation to set up and fund a new division within their organization – Art Authentication and Security. The outcome of those negotiations depends on the decisions you two make."

"I'm game," Justin said. "Dana lives in Chicago. How much does it pay?"

"Jesus, Justin," Summer said. "I swear, you have the impulse control of a moth near a flame." She turned to Denise. "If *new division* is code for setting up a *money laundering* scheme at the McNeal Foundation, we want no part of it."

Denise frowned. "Justin, the jobs pay well. And, Summer, when I told you that we work with bad people to do good things, I meant it. Both sections of the new division would be all about doing *good* things." She raised one finger at a time each time she stressed a word. "One section would help *recover* or *retain* art while we do *research* to authenticate ownership, and then *return* the piece to its *rightful* owners."

"You're using r's as a memory device," Justin observed.

"Yep. Most of us mortals don't have your memories," she said, smiling at Justin.

"Exactly what would my job be?" he asked.

"You would lead the *second* section of the division. Again, she raised a finger with each emphasized word. Its purpose would be to *research, report* and *resolve* security *risks* at various art installations around the world and then *reimagine* designs and install *revolutionary* security systems."

"Sounds great," Justin said. "I like to travel and I *love* dissecting security systems. Plus, it would be fun to be one of the *good* guys for a change." He glanced between Summer and Denise. "I know you wouldn't waste my sister's smarts working for me, so I figure she's going to lead the first section you mentioned, right?"

Summer's necklace tingled. *"Winnie, I can't tell if you're worried or excited. Maybe you're both – like me."*

"That's right." Denise turned her attention to Summer. "A small part of your job would involve hacking, but most of it would consist of doing research. For instance, your first assignment would be to transfer Gordo's assets to the company."

"You want me to steal Gordo's assets?" Summer asked.

"I suppose that's one way of looking at it," Denise cocked her head and lowered her voice. "Here's another. If Gordo's murder was discovered, there would be an investigation that might lead to you and your brother. It might even create friction between gangs and lead to more violence. No one wins in that scenario. On the other hand, if the DHS leaks information that Gordo was under federal investigation and that he and his assets have disappeared, everyone will assume he decided to cash out and retire on an island somewhere."

Summer bit her lower lip. "What about his body? Someone's bound to find him pretty soon."

"He's already gone – I expect the DHS arranged for him to be buried in a potter's field somewhere."

"What about Marty? No one's going to believe he was a terrorist any more than Agent Phillips did."

"Perhaps not," Denise said. "But Marty wasn't known for his

brains. It wouldn't be too hard to convince people that he went off the deep end after Gordo left him high and dry. Who knows? Maybe he decided to steal a painting and retire himself." She scraped the last of her soup from the bowl. "The truth is, neither of their disappearances will cause much of a ripple. Gordo was trying to expand his wheelhouse, but most of the mob would rather stick to money laundering, prostitution and human trafficking. Most likely, they'll appoint a more *traditional* thinker to take over Gordo's territory. We might even maneuver a promotion for Lisa. She's smart enough to know that Gordo and Marty planned to get rid of her next, so she owes us a favor or two. That could come in handy."

"What will you do with Gordo's money?" Summer asked.

"Like I said, we're a self-funded group. Gordo has about ten million in assets. Half of that will go into operating the new Art Authentication and Security Division of the McNeal Foundation, until it's able to start earning its keep. The other half was already spent to purchase *Bride on Stairs*."

Summer coughed to keep from choking on her soup. "You were the anonymous bidder that Miles Prescot was talking about?"

"Yes." Denise wiped her mouth with a napkin. "We had planned to steal the painting from Gordo and let Prescot deal with the fallout, when and if he ever discovered that he'd purchased a forgery. But we had to switch gears when we realized Justin put the *real* painting back into the auction."

Summer couldn't resist a smirk, thinking about how angry Miles Prescot had been that someone besides him won the bid for the Tissot painting. "I admit, I'm glad you stopped Prescot from getting his hands on the *Bride*," she admitted, "but what are you going to do with it?"

"Well, if you accept this job offer, I'll turn *Bride on Stairs* over to you – for a little while, anyway. Rumor has it that the owner decided to sell her at the McNeal auction because he learned that someone has stepped forward to challenge the legal ownership of the painting. *That* someone claims his late uncle lost the painting when Germany invaded Poland, and says the family wants it back. The current owner didn't want a legal battle on his hands, so he decided to sell before a lawsuit is filed."

"And you want me to find out if the claim is true?"

"That's right. This type of research work should be ideal for someone with your memory." Denise smiled. "If the guy's claims are true, the painting should go back to his family. If not, we'll loan it to a museum, where it can be appreciated by the public. Either way, it's a better outcome than if that pompous ass, Miles Prescot, had bought it – especially since he's under federal investigation for securities fraud. The painting might have disappeared into the black market if he suddenly needed to raise cash for his criminal defense fund."

Summer recalled that Kingsley Prescot – the man who once tried to rape Violet – had been under federal investigation when he died and left his fortune to his son, Miles. *"That apple really didn't fall far from the tree, did it?"*

The conversation was put on hold when KK arrived with their dinners and doled out the plates with a practiced hand. "You guys ready for another round?"

"You read my mind," Justin said, giving her a wink.

KK slid her glasses back up the bridge of her nose and returned his wink before disappearing back into the restaurant.

"Okay, it's going to take me about five minutes to eat this sandwich," Denise said, eyeing the huge filet of grouper on a bun. I need an answer by the time I'm done."

"I don't need five minutes," Justin said. "I'm in. Where do I go when I get to Chicago?"

"I guess I'm in, too," Summer said. "But I need to know what you're going to tell Robert."

"The bad guys are dead and no one else got hurt, so we're going to stick with the story that you two are innocent do-gooders who were dumb enough to try to stop a terrorist. We figure that story will go over better than if we were to say that a con artist and her gambler brother got jammed up between their *normal* life of crime and a different one. Plus, it makes it easier for you to start over. We're offering each of you a blank slate. New identities from Witness Security, without becoming a part of the WITSEC program."

She took a healthy bite from her sandwich, and as she chewed, she unzipped a pocket on her backpack and pulled out three flash drives – one blue, one pink and one black.

She handed the blue drive to Justin and the pink to Summer. "These contain the profiles for your new lives – your school records, your work histories, your bank account information, tax records – the works. Just like WITSEC, except you get to keep your names." She smiled. "You'll have no trouble memorizing this stuff, right?"

"Bank account?" Justin said. "Is there anything in it?"

Denise nodded. "There's enough to get you set-up in Chicago. Plus, each of you has a nice little nest egg in individual 401k savings portfolios, which you'll be able to transfer over to your new jobs at the McNeal Foundation. We figure Gordo owed you that much."

"Sweet," Justin said.

"I'm going to be your handler at the company – at least for now. That means I'll be giving you your assignments. Contact procedures and your job descriptions are included on those drives. You report to work in two weeks, so you need to get yourselves moved to Chicago pretty quick." Denise shot them a serious look. "Listen, I wish you both well, but don't ever forget who you *really* work for, or what's at stake... if *either* of you fall back into your old habits, we'll drop you *both* like hot potatoes."

"So, I have to be my brother's keeper for the rest of my life?" Summer flinched at the thought.

Justin, who was busy carving away his tasty sandwich, bite by bite, paused. "No worries. Summer may have three years of practice at living the straight-and-narrow under her belt, but I'm a quick study. Besides, I have incentive. I'm about to become a dad."

Summer nodded at her twin. "Yes, you are." Then she smiled at Denise. "I can't believe I finally got myself a fairy godmother."

"Humph – first time anyone's ever called me *that*," Denise said. "You know, considering the shitty hands the two of you have been dealt since birth, it's impressive that you can still believe in magic."

Denise pushed her plate to the side of the table, then reached back into her backpack and pulled out a laptop computer. She opened it, logged in, and inserted the black flash drive. "I just changed the password to *$1st$Fairy$Godmother!* This drive contains all the offshore banking information you'll need to transfer Gordo's financial assets, as well as a durable power of attorney, authorizing you to sell his material assets. And even though you probably don't need it, it also contains the access code for Gordo's account with the McNeal Foundation." She turned the computer around to face Summer. "Happy hacking."

Denise pushed her chair back and stood. "Listen, it's been a really long day, so I'm going to go visit with my friends at the bar and let them tell me all about how good I used to look wearing a stars and stripes bikini." She tossed a one-hundred-dollar bill on the table. "When you're done here, pay the tab and call a taxi to take you to Morton Plant Hospital. I expect your friends are as anxious to see you guys as they are to see that new baby. I'll touch base in a few weeks."

Summer grinned at her brother, barely able to comprehend all that had happened. *"We're alive, and no one is trying to kill either of us. We both have futures – good ones. You can make a life with Dana. And I can spend the next few days with Robert at the Belleview Biltmore to start working on our own happy ending."* She bit her lip. *"And I'm going to get to hold baby Andrew in my arms tonight. I can't wait to tell Margaret."*

"Fifty-nine, don't you think?" Justin asked.

Summer looked around at the cheerful café with the giant swordfish hanging on the wall, colorful lights strung haphazardly, people laughing and island music playing. For the first time in her life, she was delighted to know that she would remember every detail of this moment. "Yep, fifty-nine," she agreed.

59: Everything is perfect

Epilogue

"We couldn't have asked for a prettier day for a wedding," Summer quipped, as she walked up the sidewalk to the Chicago Cultural Center.

Every time Summer approached the magnificent gray stone building, nicknamed the *People's Palace*, she couldn't help but reflect upon the similarities between it and the Belleview Biltmore Hotel. Both opened in 1897 and highlighted the incredible architecture of the Victorian Era, including crystal chandeliers suspended from high arched passageways, intricately carved crown molding, gold leaf accents and shiny brass, marble and mosaic décor. Even more remarkable, both structures boasted ballroom ceilings constructed of Tiffany glass panels.

"Margaret, are you here?" Summer silently asked.

The spirit did not answer.

"It's gorgeous weather," Robert agreed. "And I'm glad you suggested they get married here at the CCC. This building would be a piece of art, even without its galleries."

She and Robert both believed that the unique scent and aura of historic buildings should be savored, so they paused in the lobby to absorb its delicious ambience. Recalling the details of the Belleview Biltmore's elegant Promenade Corridor, Summer felt a familiar twinge of loss for the hotel that was no more.

"Margaret, are you here?" she repeated. Once again, her silent question went unanswered.

"Man, I wish I could travel through time," Robert said. "Back to when this was Chicago's first public library – can you imagine what it was like back then?"

"And I wish I had a nickel for every time you've told me you'd like to time travel," Summer teased. "But I must admit, this place makes me wish I could go back in time to relive our wedding day."

"I know." Robert wrapped her in his arms. "It's a shame we can't spend our anniversaries at the Belleview Biltmore the way we planned, but I'm still glad we got married there, aren't you?"

"Absolutely. It's where we fell in love and you changed my life forever." Summer smiled. *"Along with a few spirits and the DHS."* She kissed his cheek. "Besides, you saved the most important part of the hotel for me."

Memories flickered through Summer's mind like flashbulbs firing one after another. They had married in a small ceremony on Friday, May 29, 2009 – the last wedding to take place before the Belleview Biltmore closed for renovation. They spent their wedding night in the suite where they first made love and participated in the hotel's closing festivities the following day, including a Victorian costume party on the lawn. Later, they joined the new owners and other well-wishers in the Lobby Lounge, where everyone eagerly discussed the details of the upcoming renovation and reminisced about days gone by. However, when some of the more adventurous party-goers had invited them to tag along for a tour of the closed-off fifth-floor of the hotel, Summer declined. *"I have no desire to run into Gus Murphy's ghost ever again,"* she had decided. *"He can keep his hidden loot."*

At the end of the weekend, Robert noticed how reluctant Summer was to leave their suite, even though they were continuing their honeymoon in Paris, and looking forward to a private tour of the Louvre. Assuming she was upset that they wouldn't be able to return to the hotel for at least three years, Robert secretly arranged to purchase the suite's furnishings, and hired a crew to recreate their love nest in a wing of their Chicago estate.

When they returned home, Summer had been thrilled with the surprise and immediately claimed the parlor of the suite as her personal study. A few years later, when it became evident that the grand hotel would never receive her promised renovation, Robert helped mend Summer's broken heart by purchasing a few items from the Belleview Biltmore, to be used as décor in her study – two original paned windows, a decorative mantle, and a single panel of Tiffany glass from the ballroom ceiling, which he had framed with polished wood from the hotel's original flooring.

Summer loved having a permanent connection with the hotel. She had hung Winnie's pendant in an open shadowbox, so the spirit would be able to come and go as she pleased, but for the last twenty-two years, the necklace held only memories. As soon as Winnie was certain her prized cameo was in good hands, she had decided to travel the lighted path.

Whenever Robert and her two children were away from home, Summer slept in the guest suite, relishing long, private visits with Margaret at the parlor table. Although Summer never developed a taste for hot tea, she and Margaret became fast friends. It was good to be able to discuss her life's journey with someone who understood that not everyone was born with a silver spoon in her mouth, and that women must sometimes walk a deeply shaded path to reach the sunshine. Sometimes they discussed Andy and Violet's progress in their new lives, but more often, Margaret helped Summer resolve cases involving stolen or lost art, or offered sage advice with regard to handling personal matters. Margaret delighted in the fact that Summer had named her two daughters, Belle and Ariel – not after famed Disney princesses as most people supposed, but as a nod to the name of the town surrounding the Belleview Biltmore – Belleair.

Summer enjoyed her friendship with Margaret, but she was glad Robert never learned about her past, or how close they had all come to dying at the McNeal Foundation Art Auction that year. He rarely mentioned the bomb scare, and if he did, he referred to it as "an unpleasant interruption." He usually spoke of the auction at the Belleview Biltmore as "the year I met the love of my life" or "the year my sister stole the show by giving birth to my nephew, Andy."

Summer's thoughts were interrupted by an usher, stationed at the roped-off stairs to the Rotunda. The man resembled a tuxedoed bouncer. "Are you here for the Tyme-Johannsen wedding?" he asked.

"Yes," Robert said, producing their invitation. "I understand it's to be an intimate affair. Only two hundred and fifty of the bride and groom's closest friends and relatives were invited to attend."

Ignoring Robert's attempt at humor, the usher unhooked the rope and repeated a set of well-rehearsed instructions. "Please join the other guests for cocktails in G.A.R. Hall, right behind the Rotunda on the second floor. When the cocktail hour concludes, guests will be escorted to Preston Bradley Hall on the third floor, to witness the exchange of vows, followed by a formal reception."

"I was hoping to say hello to our niece – the bride, before the ceremony," Summer said. "And maybe catch a glimpse of our two daughters in their bridesmaids' dresses. Is the bridal party sequestered nearby?"

"You won't be able to see them before the wedding," the usher said, shaking his head. "They're at Millennium Park for a photo shoot."

"Are the groomsmen with the bridal party?" Robert asked. "The groom is our nephew. We'd like to wish him good luck, too."

The usher frowned. "I thought you said the *bride* was your *niece.*"

"She is," Robert said. He jerked his thumb at Summer as though he was hitchhiking. "The bride is her brother's daughter. The groom is my sister's son."

Summer was about to launch into the anecdote about how Justin and Dana lived only a few houses away from Ole and Emma, so the groom was almost literally marrying the girl next door. But she could tell from his bored expression that the usher just wanted them to go away.

"Are the groomsmen in the park, too?" she repeated.

"No. They're in the Chicago Room," he replied, already starting to turn his attention to another couple who, like them, looked as though they were dressed to attend a prestigious wedding. "Take the stairs to the second floor. The Rotunda and Hall are straight ahead. The Chicago room will be on your right."

Robert mumbled his thanks to the man's back before taking Summer's elbow and ascending the wide, pink marble staircase. He was too busy admiring the embedded mosaics on the ornate banister to notice that two of Justin's top employees were chatting at the top of the stairs, partially blocking their path.

"Lance and Steve," Summer whispered in Robert's ear. "Regional Managers at McNeal Security Systems."

Robert gave her a wink to let her know he appreciated her unfailing ability to recall such details. "Excuse us, Lance – how's it going, Steve?"

The men took a step back, allowing Robert to guide Summer around the newel post while artfully avoiding the duo's attempts to get him to weigh in on their discussion about perceived minor security system flaws at the CCC. "Sorry, guys, but we have to scoot if we're going to have time to wish Andy luck before the ceremony."

Robert tapped on the door of the Chicago Room, and opened it a few inches. "Everybody decent in there? Your Aunt Summer is with me."

They were both surprised to find the room teeming with people.

Summer heard Andy's deep voice before she picked him out of the crowd. "Come on in, Uncle Robert! You, too, Aunt Summer. Have a glass of champagne with us."

"Whoa, dude," another man asked, "Is that your *hot* aunt or just one of your regular ones?"

Summer chuckled, recognizing Ethan's voice. He'd been one of Andy's best friends since childhood, but never one of the brightest.

"Just ignore him, Uncle Robert," Andy said. "He's been in love with Aunt Summer since *forever*."

"Hey," Ethan said, his voice light-hearted. "Let her know I'm still available."

"Yeah, it's a real shocker that no woman has snapped you up yet, E." Andy gave his friend a light punch on the arm. "Now, shut up before her husband kicks your ass."

"No worries," Robert said, his lips twisting into a tolerant half-smile. "Fortunately for me, she's into old men."

Summer chuckled. At fifty-nine and still wearing the Clark Kent style glasses she had always found sexy, Robert remained a handsome man. His hair had grayed, but remained thick, and he worked hard to stay in decent shape.

They made a striking couple. Summer's body had bounced back from her two pregnancies remarkably well. Although fifty years old, she was sometimes mistaken for an older sister of twenty-year-old Belle and eighteen-year-old Ariel.

"Sorry, man," Ethan said, his tongue obviously loosened by champagne. "But seriously – she's the coolest woman I've ever met. I mean, the books she wrote when we were kids were great. And then, when I found out that her *real* job was hunting down art thieves and shit, it was even better – it was like discovering that she was Super Girl, you know?"

"I loved your Andrew Turner books, too," Andy chimed in, obviously trying to steer the conversation away from his friend's infatuation with his aunt. "The wonder boy who could turn back time with his magic airplane. God, we spent *hours* reliving his adventures. Sometimes I felt like I really *was* Andrew Turner."

"Yeah," Ethan agreed, smiling at the memory. "You always insisted on being Captain Andrew and I was your trusty sidekick, Alex the Ace Washington. Remember the one with the fire? They flew back in time and lassoed a glacier."

"And when they flew over the fire, the glacier melted, saving Margaret Plants-A-Lot's castle and flower garden," Andy continued.

"I can't believe the two of you still remember those stories," Summer said, with a shake of her head. "Then again, you were my two biggest fans. My *only* fans, come to think of it, since no one was interested in publishing my books."

In truth, Summer hadn't ever pursued publishing her children's books. They had been Margaret Plant's idea. The night after Andy *Johannsen* was born, she and Summer discussed her concerns over the fact that Andy's *Becoming* had occurred less than twenty-four hours before he was born. She worried that Andy would retain too many memories of his former life as Andy Turner and thus, would never be comfortable growing up as Andy Johannsen.

"But we might be able to fool his memory," Margaret had said. "After all, Edgar Allan Poe once wrote, 'The boundaries which define Life from Death are at best shadowy and vague. Who is to say where one ends, and the other begins?' Perhaps the same is true when a spirit is reborn."

Margaret and Summer hoped that children's stories that contained characters and situations similar to those from Andy's past, along with obvious fantasy happenings, would provide him a plausible alternative explanation for the origin of his strange memories, thus allowing him to merge his former life with his present one.

Each time an old memory surfaced, Summer would incorporate it into a new story. For instance, when Andy developed a terrible fear of falling, she wrote a story wherein Captain Andrew fell off a cliff, but his magic plane swooped in and caught him, just in the nick of time. The story of the fire had developed from his memories of Gus Murphy's and Gordo Adolphus's attempts to burn down the Belleview Biltmore.

"What I really remember," Andy said, a wide grin spilling over his face, "is how mad Violet got when E and I trampled through her flower garden, pretending to put out the fire with a melting iceberg."

"Yeah, but she got over it," Ethan said.

"Violet *never* stayed mad at you guys for too long," Robert agreed.

"You hear all that, Margaret? Our plan worked really well. Andy believes his memories came from my books."

Even though Andy accepted that his vivid memories of flying a crop duster and a WWII bomber were the result of an active imagination, he never lost his desire to fly. He was "a natural," as his flight instructors were fond of saying, and obtained his pilot's license before he even graduated from high school. He enjoyed developing a lucrative career within his father's investment company, but his passion remained piloting airplanes. Whenever he traveled on business, the regular pilot of the company's corporate jet flew as his co-pilot, and he was always at the controls whenever he and Violet took trips to private getaways around the world. So, it was no surprise when the couple announced they planned to spend their honeymoon island-hopping throughout the Caribbean.

"Yes, things worked out quite well for Andy and Violet, didn't they?" Margaret asked.

"It's about time you showed up. I was getting worried you wouldn't make it." Summer accepted a glass of champagne, happy

to let others talk while she carried on a silent conversation with Margaret.

"I told you I wouldn't miss their wedding, as long as it was held somewhere I'd gone while I was alive," Margaret said.

"It's a good thing Violet and Dana were willing to let me help choose the venue – and that Chicago has so many wonderful, historic buildings to choose from. Have you been here long?"

"A while," Margaret said. "I needed to move a few place cards around in Preston Bradley Hall in order to open the seat next to yours."

Summer winced, knowing how many hours Dana and Violet had spent on the seating arrangement, but before she could reply, Robert interrupted her connection with the spirit.

"Andy and Violet have been practically inseparable from the time they were babies," he said, polishing off his glass of champagne. "But if we're going to get him to the altar on time today, everyone but the groomsmen should probably start clearing out of here."

Summer nodded her agreement. "Think you can handle that job?"

Robert was always good at directing others. He clapped his hands to draw everyone's attention and then asked those who weren't a part of the wedding party to stand and offer quick well-wishes on their way out. Within ten minutes, the only people in the room, other than Robert and Summer, were Andrew, Ethan, and Justin's three sons, Nicholas, Miles, and Christopher.

Summer smiled at the thought that *none* of the young men went by their formal names. Andrew had been called Andy from the moment he was born, and everyone but his mother called Ethan, simply *E*. Justin and Dana's eldest son had been born when Violet was only two years old, and their other two sons had followed in quick succession. Justin had championed silly names like Hammer, Crunch, and Party, but Dana had nixed them all. She thought she had won the battle, when Justin agreed to name their first son Nicholas Ole, their second, Miles Robert, and their third, Christopher Thomas; however, she soon discovered she was wrong on all three counts. Each of the nicknames Justin gave his sons stuck: Nick-O Tyme, Mil-R Tyme, and ChrisMas Tyme.

Summer gave E and each of her dear nephews a hug and a peck on the cheek before she and Robert stepped out of the room and went to join the other guests for cocktails in the *Grand Army of the Republic Hall*, known as the G.A.R. After claiming an open high-top table, Robert went to the bar to get them each a glass of wine, providing Summer an opportunity to continue her private conversation with Margaret.

"This establishment works quite well for gatherings," Margaret said. "But it still seems strange to hear music in a building where, in my time, only hushed voices were permitted."

"It's just as hard for me to imagine the CCC as a library," Summer silently replied. *"Modern libraries don't possess a fraction of this astounding architecture – thirty-foot high marble walls with coffered ceilings and stained-glass domes – it's a shame they don't design buildings like this anymore."*

"Yes, I think Mr. Coolidge and his partners would be extremely proud to know their architectural masterpiece has stood the test of time. I first visited here shortly after the library opened. Back then, the building housed a bookseller and I purchased several books to entertain guests during the second winter season of the Belleview."

"Do you remember which books you bought?"

"I purchased dozens, but the most popular book that year was Abraham – Bram – Stoker's new work of fiction, called *Dracula*. I had just returned from Europe, so I had the books delivered to me at the Palmer House, where I packed them with the other treasures I had purchased for the Belleview that autumn."

"The Palmer House is still around, too," Summer said. *"It was on my list of potential wedding venues."*

"It's no wonder the Palmer House is still here. An unlucky thirteen days after the original one opened, it was destroyed in the Great Chicago Fire, so they used fireproof materials when they rebuilt it. That's one of the reasons I liked staying there. But enough chit-chat. We need to discuss a serious matter."

Summer frowned, her natural distrust of joyful optimism threatening to boil to the surface. *"What's wrong? Please don't tell me that*

Violet and Andy will be denied the life together they dreamed of for so long."

"The fact that they've been dreaming of being married for so long is exactly why I'm concerned," Margaret said. "When they stand together to be wed, I fear strong memories of their former lives may emerge."

"I don't think so," Summer countered, taking care not to speak out loud. *"You were there when Andy was talking about the books. He really believes he imagined those memories. And Violet hasn't ever shown any sign of retaining her memories, other than the fact that she's always had a green thumb and, of course, she's always been drawn to Andy."*

"Their memories are buried, but they're still there, guiding their lives. I've always been able to connect with them. You might recall that I visited Andy just after his *Becoming* – during the upheaval at the Belleview – hours before he was born into his new life."

"Of course, I remember. I have an eidetic memory."

"Hmph," Margaret said.

After all these years, the Victorian spirit still had the ability to make Summer feel like an insolent child who had interrupted an important lesson.

"Sorry. Please go on."

"Well, that was the last time I appeared to Andy as my adult self, but it's not the last time I connected with him... or Violet, for that matter. Whenever I connected with either child, I took on the form of my child-self at their age. I helped them stay on course – to continue blending their spirits, learning from the past and protecting the most esteemed parts of themselves, while also allowing the other halves of themselves to flourish. For instance, Andy's love of flying comes from his former life, of course, but his *legal prowess* comes from the part of his spirit which was created by his *current* father's seed, which shares *those* passions."

"That makes sense. You know, I always wondered if Violet's memories of Rosery Farm influenced her love of plants."

"Yes, Violet's former life is the reason she became a horticulturist in this one. She also remembers her promise to Dana before her *Becoming* – to help the other half of her blended spirit reject its father's nature by turning violence into violets. She honors that pledge by helping to establish community gardens and teaching children that improving their neighborhoods will improve their lives."

Summer smiled, thinking of all the times she had heard people refer to Andy and Violet as "old souls" or comment that they were "wise beyond their years." She nodded. "So, *you help them blend their old lives with their new ones, the same way you've always helped me. So, what's wrong with Andy and Violet remembering their past lives? I mean, I remember my past life, but I chose to leave it behind and live a better one.*"

"Yes, but your choice was entirely *yours*. Their decisions could affect two *innocent* souls. It's one of the reasons I wanted to attend their nuptials."

Robert returned with two glasses of mimosa. "The bartender said they'd be calling us to Preston Bradley Hall soon." He cocked his head. "That's weird. Saying that name out loud just reminded me of Henry Bradley Plant for some reason."

"Probably because we were talking about the Belleview Biltmore earlier," Summer said, keeping a nonchalant tone in her voice. "That, along with the Victorian architecture in here, is bound to draw similarities where none truly exist."

"I suppose so," Robert said.

She smiled and tapped her glass against his. "Here's to spending lots of time in places that bring back happy memories."

"I'll drink to that," he replied.

Summer often wondered if Robert was more sensitive to the presence of spirits than he realized. He'd never forgotten his paranormal encounters at the hotel and he sometimes sensed when Margaret was in the vicinity.

"I never told Robert – or anyone else – about Andy and Violet. I guess I figured the fewer people who knew about their Becoming, the easier it would be for them to blend with their other halves into single entities. I sure hope that was the right thing to do."

"Me, too," said Margaret.

The lights dimmed and rose again three times, just as they did in theaters, letting guests know that it was time to move to the next venue.

"I guess that bartender knew what he was talking about," Summer quipped.

Ushers took up posts along the path between the wings of the iconic CCC, guiding the herd of guests to the stunning marble staircase that led to Preston Bradley Hall, and escorting those unable to climb stairs to a nearby ramp.

The Johannsen side of the family was almost comically smaller than the Tyme side. Andy was the only child of Emma and Ole Johannsen, both of whom had been orphaned in their youth. Robert and Summer's family represented his entire extended family. Violet's family, on the other hand, consisted of her three brothers, parents, maternal grandparents, twelve aunts and uncles, and more than twenty first cousins.

Additionally, because Andy and Violet had grown up only a few doors apart, most of their friends and neighbors were mutual acquaintances. And to further confuse matters, Dana and Justin both worked within divisions of the McNeal Foundation, a corporation run by Robert and Emma, so most of the employees in attendance had friends on both sides of the wedding aisle.

To alleviate seating complications, Andy and Violet had opted to seat guests at twenty-six round tables, arranged in staggered circles around the hall. The ceremony would take place on a small round stage in the middle of the room, beneath the aqua fish-scale design of the massive Tiffany dome above. Following the ceremony, a string quartette would take the stage to play throughout dinner, pausing for toasts and speeches. Afterward, a band would replace the quartette and the floor surrounding the stage would become a dance floor.

Preston Bradley Hall was so exquisitely ornate, it didn't require much additional decoration. White gauze curtains hung from each of the twenty-foot high arches that scalloped the edges of the round hall, granting the room privacy. The tables, as well as the ten chairs that surrounded each one, were covered with silky, white linen, and each chair back was tied with a wide, seafoam green bow. A sprawling arrangement of pastel flowers and candles graced the center of each table, and the round stage was covered with so many flowers, it resembled a float from the Parade of Roses. On the floor next to the stage, a musician sat at a baby grand piano softly playing love songs.

Summer smiled and pulled back the empty chair to the left of hers. *"I know you could move it yourself, Margaret, but I thought I'd save you the trouble."*

"Thank you, darlin'."

Robert stood behind Summer's chair, watching her, his head cocked with silent curiosity.

Summer winked at her husband as she moved over and slid into her seat. "I hate to waste a perfectly good spot. If this place is as haunted as the Belleview Biltmore, you never know. A wandering spirit might like to watch the wedding with us."

He cast a nervous glance at the chair and then chuckled at the silly notion.

As guests continued to file in and get settled, Summer entertained their tablemates with a heartwarming story about a recent case, handled by the McNeal Foundation. While cleaning out the basement of a home her family had occupied for three generations, a German woman discovered a painting, along with a note written by her great-grandfather. The note explained that during WWII, her great-grandfather had promised a dear Jewish friend that he would keep the painting hidden until it was safe for him to take it back. Summer's research revealed that the reason the man had never returned for the painting was that he and most of his family had perished in Auschwitz. However, one daughter had survived, immigrated to the United States, married and raised a family. So, after ninety years in a dark basement, the painting was finally going home.

Summer was still thinking about the happy ending of that case, when the soft background music concluded. The wedding prelude music began with a vocalist who joined the pianist to perform *Somewhere Over the Rainbow*. Once their brilliant rendition of the song silenced the room, Handel's classical symphony, *Water Music Suite* began to play through the surround sound system. The pastor ascended the grand staircase, crossed to the center of the room, and climbed the three steps to the stage. Andy and his groomsmen, E, Nick-O, Mil-R, and ChrisMas, filed in behind the pastor, taking their places in a semicircle on the right side of the stage. When Pachelbel's *Canon* began to play, two of Dana's brothers drew back a pair of gauze curtains, creating an entrance beneath one of the room's arches.

Dana's other two brothers escorted their grandparents to the table next to where Summer and Robert were seated, to join other members of her immediate family. Next, their father accompanied Dana and her mother to the table. It was obvious to everyone in attendance that Dana and Justin had created a happy home for themselves and their four children, and today, Dana looked as proud and radiant as any mother could.

When Beethoven's *Ode to Joy* began to play, all eyes turned toward the arched doorway to watch the bridal party make their entrance. Summer squeezed Robert's hand as Ariel, their youngest daughter, entered the room, wearing an aqua-blue, chiffon gown. Rhinestones sparkled on the halter-style, fitted bodice and a diamond-shaped rhinestone applique accented her narrow waist. Her blonde hair was pulled up into a stylish bun and she carried a small bouquet of flowers that matched the centerpieces on the tables.

When Ariel reached the stairs to the stage, ChrisMas, blushing such a bright shade of red that he really did remind Summer of Christmas time, stepped forward to offer his hand to his cousin. Summer held her breath as Ariel accepted his hand and climbed the steps. She didn't start breathing again until her daughter had taken her place on the left side of the stage.

"The hall looks like something out of a fairytale, and your daughter looks like a princess," Margaret said.

"Thanks. I agree. She's beautiful. But it makes me sad to think that she's not going to be my baby much longer. She's headed to college in a few weeks."

"Nonsense," Margaret replied. "As an intelligent woman, she knows to keep her allies close, and there's no better ally than one's own mother."

"I hope you're right about that." Summer smiled at Robert, who was busy taking photos with his phone.

The next two bridesmaids, Violet's cousins from Dana's side of the family, possessed Dana's elfin stature. When the first of the two reached the steps, Mil-R moved forward to offer her his hand, and then Nick-O followed suit, accompanying the third bridesmaid to her spot on the stage. As Violet's closest friend, Belle had the honor of serving as maid of honor.

Summer and Robert always joked that, while their beautiful girls didn't look or act like sisters, they both resembled their parents. Impulsive Ariel had Summer's blonde hair and Robert's blue eyes, while demure Belle had Summer's light brown eyes and Robert's thick, dark hair.

Always graceful, Belle appeared to float across the room to the stage. There, she was met by an uncharacteristically serious E, who escorted her across the stage and kissed her hand before returning to his place in the groomsmen's line.

Summer had to muffle a giggle when Robert stopped taking pictures to growl at E under his breath. "Don't worry," she whispered. "He has about the same chance with Belle as he does with me."

Then the first notes of Wagner's *Bridal Chorus* filled the air, mixed with the shuffling sounds of two hundred and fifty guests getting to their feet. Andy stepped to the top of the stairs to watch Violet and her father enter through the gauze curtains and make their approach.

Justin's hair had thinned a bit, and he had the body of a man who was married to an excellent cook, but time had done little to dampen his sense of humor. He jumped in front of Violet with his arms outstretched, a panicked look on his face, as if he had changed his mind about giving his little girl away. When the laughter of the guests died down, he grinned, moved to his daughter's side and offered her his arm. Violet took it and gave him a peck on the cheek before her eyes began searching for Andy.

Violet was stunning in her mermaid-style wedding gown with a lace overlay and sleeves. The lace pattern on the bodice of her dress was outlined with rhinestones and tiny pearls, as was the ruffled base of her skirt and train.

Neither Violet or Andy looked *exactly* like the spirits Summer had met twenty-two years ago, but she and Margaret had both remarked that the resemblance had grown stronger in recent years. Today, Violet's similarity to her former self was more noticeable than ever. Even the curls she wore on either side of her rhinestone tiara and long veil, reminded Summer of the victory rolls the former Violet had worn. And her bouquet of two dozen scented, long-stemmed white roses, tied together with an aqua-blue ribbon, put Summer in mind of The Rosery Flower Farm.

When they reached the stage, Justin took Violet's hand from his crooked arm and placed it into Andy's hand. Then he stepped back, allowing Andy to help her climb the stairs. While Justin took his place at the table with Dana, the young couple stood together on the stage, gazing at one another as if they were the only people in the room.

When the Bridal Chorus came to a close, the room remained silent. It was as if everyone was watching a perfect sunset and no one wanted the moment to end.

When Andy suddenly took Violet into his arms and kissed her, Summer realized she had witnessed this kiss before – in the Japanese Gardens, during WWII. *"They're just like that painting. After ninety years in the dark, they're finally going home."*

"They're feeling like they've waited an eternity for this day to come, but they're not sure why," Margaret said. The concern in her voice was palpable. "If they figure it out, they may damage the bond with the other half of their souls."

"What should we do?"

"I'm not sure there's anything we *can* do."

At that moment, the pink lights around the edge of the dome began to flicker, breaking the mesmerizing spell that had been cast over the room.

"Did you do that?" Summer asked.

"I don't think so," Margaret replied. "Perhaps God sent a few angels to help out."

Summer wrinkled her nose with doubt, but her connection with Margaret was broken before she could suggest an alternate hypothesis.

"Hey dude," E said in a voice that was meant to be a whisper, but carried throughout the silent hall. "You jumped the gun. You're supposed to say your vows before you kiss her."

A second wave of laughter rippled through the tables as the pastor stepped up and took control of the situation. "I'm pleased to see that you are both eager to get on with things, but your best man is correct…the kissing part comes after the vows. But first, let us bow our heads in silent prayer."

Robert bumped Summer's arm to get her attention and whispered. "These would have been perfect pictures, if it weren't for these weird spots."

Summer kept her head bowed as if praying while she glanced at Robert's phone. The first picture was taken the moment before the kiss – while the two were staring into one another's eyes. She took the phone from her husband's hand and began reviewing his photographs more closely.

From the moment their hands touched, two orbs floated above Violet and Andy. When they kissed, the orbs merged into an elongated figure eight, and when the lights flickered, the orbs disappeared altogether.

"Margaret, I think they know who they were, but they're happy with the new people they've become."

"I believe you're right, darlin,'" Margaret replied.

Just as the silent prayer came to an end, Summer flipped back to the photo of the merged orbs. "I think this one is my favorite," she told Robert, taking care to keep her voice low. "Look at the two circles."

"It looks like an infinity symbol," he said.

"Exactly." Summer nodded. She smiled and watched as the pair exchanged vows. "It's a sign. The whole universe agrees. Infinity is exactly how long those two should remain together."

The End

Tyme Twin Codes

TYME TWIN CODES:

1: I love you	2: I hate you
3: That was funny	4: Mind your own business
5: Back up my story	6: Are you okay?
7: I want to ditch the person we're talking about	8: I'm happy/content with the person we're talking about
9: I need to talk to you in private	10: I need your help!
11: Don't worry; I've/we've got this	12: You take the lead.
13: Follow my lead.	14: The plan is not going well
15: We need to escape	16: Trust me
17: I have a plan.	18: Keep your chin up
19. The plan is working great	20: The person next to you is good/an innocent
21: The person next to you is bad/evil	22: The person next to you is a perfect mark
23: The person next to you is a cop	24: Don't do anything stupid
25. Be careful	26: Keep it together
27: I'm sorry/my bad	28: It's too late for that
29: Don't take the bait	30: Take the lead.
31: What's done is done	32: Any ideas?
33: This is my fight .	34: Stick to the plan.
35: Change of plans	36: The person I'm with is suspicious
37: I failed to do what I was supposed to do	38: I've got to go/I'm late
39: Leave me alone!	40: I've done something you need to know about
41: You're right	42: You're wrong
43: I need a favor	44: Don't worry about me, I'm all right
45: Play dumb – I don't think they have any evidence	46: I'm worried about you
47: Don't worry about me	48: The Tyme Twins can't be stopped.
49: Take care of yourself	50: Never let a mark get under your skin.
51: This person/situation scares me	52: This is the real deal
53: I believe everything will be all right	54: I've got it under control
55: These guys just messed with the wrong twins	56: Wait till I tell you what happened while we were apart
57: Keep quiet and let me do the talking	58: Let's hear this person out before deciding what to do
59: Everything is perfect	60: Danger. Get ready to run
61: Right now	62: Later
63: Stop grandstanding	64: Stop trying to control everything
65: You're being too reckless	66: I don't believe you.
67: No time to argue	68: I can't get away
69: Screw you	70: You're going to love this
71: Play it cool till we get a chance to talk	72: It's already done/handled
73: Watch your back	74: Don't trust anyone!
75: Stay on your toes.	76: You do things your way, I'll do things my way
77: Things are looking up	78: Things are not looking good.
79: Did I/we get played?	80: Where are you?
81: Do you need my help?	82: I can handle this on my own.
83: I'll call you when I get free	84: Go to/call the police
85: We need to make a plan - quick!	86: Get rid of it
87: Quit acting so bossy	88: I need help/company
89: I need space	90: Do you know where I was/am and who I was/am with?
91: Important/key information is unknown	92: I/you don't know what's going on
93: Do you understand what's happening/going on?	94: I don't know/trust all the players
95: I do know/trust all the players	96: You're the best
97: You're the worst	98: This is wonderful!
99: This is terrible!	100: Never forget payback is a bitch.
200: forget about me – save yourself	

About the Author

Born in St. Louis, MO, BonSue Brandvik moved to Florida four decades ago. After she and her husband, John, built their home in Belleair, she became intrigued with local history, and in particular, the cause to save the historic Belleview Biltmore Hotel from demolition. Although the fight to save the hotel was lost in 2015, she is determined to maintain a record of the hotel's grandeur and its impacts on local development, by including historic details within the story lines of a four-book series, titled "Spirits of the Belleview Biltmore."

BonSue offers to speak to local groups about writing historic fiction and creating alternate realities. She also leads a local writers' critique group, and she helps the elderly record their memories for posterity. When not writing, BonSue enjoys photography, gardening, SCUBA diving and spending time with family.

Website: BonSueBrandvik.com
Email: BonSue@BonSueBrandvik.com
Facebook: www.facebook.com/BonSueBrandvik/
Twitter: @BonSueB

Additional copies/formats of these books are available on-line at Amazon, Barnes and Noble, and most other reputable book sellers.

2017 – The photo above is all that remains of the grand Belleview Biltmore following demolition (Approx. 36k of 820k square feet.) The shell of the structure was moved nearby & will be incorporated into the Belleview Inn, Belleair, FL

CPSIA information can be obtained
at www.ICGtesting.com
Printed in the USA
LVHW111752081118
596436LV00002B/277/P